KT-223-393

Virginia Woolf was born in 1882, the third of four children. Most of her early education was provided at home by her parents, enthusiastic but unaccomplished teachers.

Following the death of her father in 1904 (her mother had died in 1895), and her second serious mental breakdown, Virginia's first publication, an unsigned review, was printed in *The Guardian* and in 1905 she began a connection with *The Times Literary Supplement* which was to last almost to the end of her life. During the years leading up to the First World War, Virginia lived in Gordon Square, Bloomsbury, where she soon became an active and prominent member of the famous literary group which was subsequently known as the 'Bloomsbury Circle', including among her friends men like Lytton Strachey and Leonard Woolf, whom she agreed to marry in 1912.

In March 1915 *The Voyage Out*, Virginia Woolf's first novel, was published to enthusiastic acclaim. In 1917 Virginia and Leonard Woolf founded The Hogarth Press which was later to publish most of Virginia's major works as well as works by other contemporary literary talents.

Mrs Dalloway, Virginia Woolf's fourth novel, was published in 1925 and was immediately recognized as a major achievement. Recurring bouts of madness plagued both her childhood and married life and in March 1941 Virginia Woolf took her life. By the time of her death, she had won a foremost and enduring place in English letters.

Also by Virginia Woolf

Fiction
The Voyage Out
Night and Day
Jacob's Room
To the Lighthouse
Orlando
The Waves
The Years
Between the Acts

Short Stories
A Haunted House
Mrs Dalloway's Party (ed. Stella McNichol)

Biography
Flush
Roger Fry

Criticism and Essays
The Common Reader: First Series
The Common Reader: Second Series
A Room of One's Own
Three Guineas
The Death of the Moth
The Moment
The Captain's Death Bed
Granite and Rainbow
Contemporary Writers
Collected Essays (ed. Leonard Woolf)
Books and Portraits (ed. Mary Lyon)

Memoirs
A Writer's Diary (ed. Leonard Woolf)
Moments of Being (ed. Jeanne Schulkind)
The Diary of Virginia Woolf, Vol. 1 1915–1919 (ed. Anne Olivier Bell)
The Diary of Virginia Woolf, Vol. 2 1920–1924 (ed. Anne Olivier Bell)

Drama
Freshwater: A Comedy (ed. Lucio P. Ruotolo)

Letters
Virginia Woolf and Lytton Strachey: Letters (ed. Leonard Woolf and James Strachey)
The Flight of the Mind, The Letters of Virginia Woolf, Vol. 1 1888–1912 (ed. Nigel Nicolson)
The Question of Things Happening, Vol. 2 1912–1922 (ed. Nigel Nicolson)
A Change of Perspective, Vol. 3 1923–1928 (ed. Nigel Nicolson)
A Reflection of the Other Person, Vol. 4 1929–1931 (ed. Nigel Nicolson)

Virginia Woolf

Mrs Dalloway

A TRIAD PANTHER BOOK

GRANADA
London Toronto Sydney New York

Published by Granada Publishing Limited in 1976
Reprinted 1978, 1979, 1980, 1981

ISBN 0 586 04446 9

First published by The Hogarth Press Ltd 1925

Granada Publishing Limited
Frogmore, St Albans, Herts AL2 2NF
and
3 Upper James Street, London W1R 4BP
866 United Nations Plaza, New York, NY10017, USA
117 York Street, Sydney, NSW 2000, Australia
100 Skyway Avenue, Rexdale, Ontario, M9W 3A6, Canada
PO Box 84165, Greenside, 2034 Johannesburg, South Africa
61 Beach Road, Auckland, New Zealand

Made and printed in Great Britain by
Richard Clay (The Chaucer Press) Ltd
Bungay, Suffolk
Set in Linotype Pilgrim

Granada ®
Granada Publishing ®

MRS DALLOWAY

MRS DALLOWAY said she would buy the flowers herself.

For Lucy had her work cut out for her. The doors would be taken off their hinges; Rumpelmayer's men were coming. And then, thought Clarissa Dalloway, what a morning – fresh as if issued to children on a beach.

What a lark! What a plunge! For so it had always seemed to her when, with a little squeak of the hinges, which she could hear now, she had burst open the French windows and plunged at Bourton into the open air. How fresh, how calm, stiller than this of course, the air was in the early morning; like the flap of a wave; the kiss of a wave; chill and sharp and yet (for a girl of eighteen as she then was) solemn, feeling as she did, standing there at the open window, that something awful was about to happen; looking at the flowers, at the trees with the smoke winding off them and the rooks rising, falling; standing and looking until Peter Walsh said, 'Musing among the vegetables?' – was that it? – 'I prefer men to cauliflowers' – was that it? He must have said it at breakfast one morning when she had gone out on to the terrace – Peter Walsh. He would be back from India one of these days, June or July, she forgot which, for his letters were awfully dull; it was his sayings one remembered; his eyes, his pocket-knife, his smile, his grumpiness and, when millions of things had utterly vanished – how strange it was! – a few sayings like this about cabbages.

She stiffened a little on the kerb, waiting for Durtnall's van to pass. A charming woman, Scrope Purvis thought her (knowing her as one does know people who live next door to one in Westminster); a touch of the bird about her, of the jay, blue-green, light, vivacious, though she was over fifty, and grown very white since her illness. There she perched, never seeing him, waiting to cross, very upright.

For having lived in Westminster – how many years now? over twenty, – one feels even in the midst of the traffic, or waking at night, Clarissa was positive, a particular hush, or solemnity; an indescribable pause; a suspense (but that might be her heart, affected, they said, by influenza) before Big Ben strikes. There! Out it boomed. First a warning, musical; then the hour, irrevocable. The leaden circles dissolved in the air. Such fools we are, she thought, crossing Victoria Street. For Heaven only knows why one loves it so, how one sees it so, making it up, building it round one, tumbling it, creating it every moment afresh; but the veriest frumps, the most dejected of miseries sitting on doorsteps (drink their downfall) do the same; can't be dealt with, she felt positive, by Acts of Parliament for that very reason: they love life. In people's eyes, in the swing, tramp, and trudge; in the bellow and the uproar; the carriages, motor cars, omnibuses, vans, sandwich men shuffling and swinging; brass bands; barrel organs; in the triumph and the jingle and the strange high singing of some aeroplane overhead was what she loved; life; London; this moment of June.

For it was the middle of June. The War was over, except for some one like Mrs Foxcroft at the Embassy last night eating her heart out because that nice boy was killed and now the old Manor House must go to a cousin; or Lady Bexborough who opened a bazaar, they said, with the telegram in her hand, John, her favourite, killed; but it was over; thank Heaven – over. It was June. The King and Queen were at the Palace. And everywhere, though it was still so early, there was a beating, a stirring of galloping ponies, tapping of cricket bats; Lords, Ascot, Ranelagh and all the rest of it; wrapped in the soft mesh of the grey-blue morning air, which, as the day wore on, would unwind them, and set down on their lawns and pitches the bouncing ponies, whose forefeet just struck the ground and up they sprung, the whirling young men, and laughing girls in their transparent muslins who, even now, after dancing all night, were taking their absurd woolly dogs for a run; and even now, at this hour, discreet old dowagers were shooting out in their motor cars on errands of mystery; and the shopkeepers were fidgeting in their windows with their paste and diamonds, their lovely old sea-green brooches in eighteenth-century settings to tempt Americans (but one must economize, not buy things rashly for Elizabeth), and she, too, loving it as she did with an absurd and faithful passion, being part of it, since her people were courtiers once in the time of the Georges, she, too, was going that very night to kindle and illuminate; to give her party. But how strange, on entering the Park, the silence; the mist; the hum; the slow-swimming happy ducks; the pouched birds waddling; and who should be coming along with his back against the Government buildings, most appropriately, carrying a despatch box stamped with the Royal Arms, who but Hugh Whitbread; her old friend Hugh – the admirable Hugh!

'Good-morning to you, Clarissa!' said Hugh, rather extravagantly, for they had known each other as children. 'Where are you off to?'

'I love walking in London,' said Mrs Dalloway. 'Really, it's better than walking in the country.'

They had just come up – unfortunately – to see doctors. Other people came to see pictures; go to the opera; take their daughters out; the Whitbreads came 'to see doctors.' Times without number Clarissa had visited Evelyn Whitbread in a nursing home. Was Evelyn ill again? Evelyn was a good deal out of sorts, said Hugh, intimating by a kind of pout or swell of his very well-covered, manly, extremely handsome, perfectly upholstered body (he was almost too well dressed always, but presumably had to be, with his little job at Court) that his wife had some internal ailment, nothing serious, which, as an old friend, Clarissa Dalloway would quite understand without requiring him to specify. Ah yes, she did of course; what a nuisance; and felt very sisterly and oddly conscious at the same time of her hat. Not the right hat for the early morning, was that it? For Hugh always made her feel, as he bustled on, raising his hat rather extravagantly and assuring her that she might be a girl of eighteen, and of course he was coming to her party to-night, Evelyn absolutely insisted, only a little late he might be after the party at the Palace to which he had to take one of Jim's boys, – she always felt a little skimpy beside Hugh; schoolgirlish; but attached to him, partly from having known him always, but she did think him a good sort in his own way, though Richard was nearly driven mad by him, and as for Peter Walsh, he had never to this day forgiven her for liking him.

She could remember scene after scene at Bourton – Peter furious; Hugh not, of course, his match in any way, but still not a positive imbecile as Peter made out; not a mere barber's block. When his old mother wanted him to give up shooting or to take her to Bath he did it, without a word; he was really unselfish, and as for saying, as Peter did, that he had no heart, no brain, nothing but the manners and breeding of an English gentleman, that was only her dear Peter at his worst; and he could be intolerable; he could be impossible; but adorable to walk with on a morning like this.

(June had drawn out every leaf on the trees. The mothers of Pimlico gave suck to their young. Messages were passing from the Fleet to the Admiralty. Arlington Street and Piccadilly seemed to chafe the very air in the Park and lift its leaves hotly, brilliantly, on waves of that divine vitality which Clarissa loved. To dance, to ride, she had adored all that.)

For they might be parted for hundreds of years, she and Peter; she never wrote a letter and his were dry sticks; but suddenly it would come over her, if he were with me now what would he say? – some days, some sights bringing him back to her calmly, without the old bitterness; which perhaps was the reward of having cared for people; they came back in the middle of St James's Park on a fine morning – indeed they did. But Peter – however beautiful the day might be, and the trees and the grass, and the little girl in pink – Peter never saw a thing of all that. He would put on his spectacles, if she told him to; he would look. It was the state of the world that interested him; Wagner, Pope's poetry, people's characters eternally, and the defects of her own soul. How he scolded her! How they argued! She would marry a Prime Minister and stand at the top of a staircase; the perfect hostess he called her (she had cried over it in her bedroom), she had the makings of the perfect hostess, he said.

So she would still find herself arguing in St James's Park, still making out that she had been right – and she had too – not to marry him. For in marriage a little licence, a little independence there must be between people living together day in day out in the same house; which Richard gave her, and she him. (Where was he this morning, for instance? Some committee, she never asked what.) But with Peter everything had to be shared; everything gone into. And it was intolerable, and when it came to that scene in the little garden by the fountain, she had to break with him or they would have been destroyed, both of them ruined, she was convinced; though she had borne about her for years like an arrow sticking in her heart the grief, the anguish: and then the horror of the moment when some one told her at a concert that he had married a woman met on the boat going to India! Never should she forget all that. Cold, heartless, a prude, he called her. Never could she understand how he cared. But those Indian women did presumably – silly, pretty, flimsy nincompoops. And she wasted her pity. For he was quite happy, he assured her – perfectly happy, though he had never done a thing that they talked of; his whole life had been a failure. It made her angry still.

She had reached the Park gates. She stood for a moment, looking at the omnibuses in Piccadilly.

She would not say of any one in the world now that they were this or were that. She felt very young; at the same time unspeakably aged. She sliced like a knife through everything; at the same time was outside, looking on. She had a perpetual sense, as she watched the taxicabs, of being out, out, far out to sea and alone; she always had the feeling that it was very, very dangerous to live even one day. Not that she thought herself clever, or much out of the ordinary. How she had got through life on the few twigs of knowledge Fräulein Daniels gave them she could not think. She knew nothing; no language, no history; she scarcely read a book now, except memoirs in bed; and yet to her it was absolutely absorbing; all this; the cabs passing; and she would not say of Peter, she would not say of herself, I am this, I am that.

Her only gift was knowing people almost by instinct, she thought, walking on. If you put her in a room with some one, up went her back like a cat's; or she purred. Devonshire House, Bath House, the house with the china cockatoo, she had seen them all lit up once; and remembered Sylvia, Fred, Sally Seton – such hosts of people; and dancing all night; and the waggons plodding past to market; and driving home across the Park. She remembered once throwing a shilling into the Serpentine. But every one remembered; what she loved was this, here, now, in front of her; the fat lady in the cab. Did it matter then, she asked herself, walking towards Bond Street, did it matter that she must inevitably cease completely; all this must go on without her; did she resent it; or did it not become consoling to believe that death ended absolutely? but that somehow in the streets of London, on the ebb and flow of things, here, there, she survived, Peter survived, lived in each other, she being part, she was positive, of the trees at home; of the house there, ugly, rambling all to bits and pieces as it was; part of people she had never met; being laid out like a mist between the people she knew best, who lifted her on their branches as she had seen the trees lift the mist, but it spread ever so far, her life, herself. But what was she dreaming as she looked into Hatchards' shop window? What was she trying to recover? What image of white dawn in the country, as she read in the book spread open:

> *Fear no more the heat o' the sun*
> *Nor the furious winter's rages.*

This late age of world's experience had bred in them all, all men and women, a well of tears. Tears and sorrows; courage and endurance; a perfectly upright and stoical bearing. Think, for example, of the woman she admired most, Lady Bexborough, opening the bazaar.

There were Jorrocks' *Jaunts and Jollities*; there were

Soapy Sponge and Mrs Asquith's *Memoirs* and *Big Game Shooting in Nigeria*, all spread open. Ever so many books there were; but none that seemed exactly right to take to Evelyn Whitbread in her nursing home. Nothing that would serve to amuse her and make that indescribably dried-up little woman look, as Clarissa came in, just for a moment cordial; before they settled down for the usual interminable talk of women's ailments. How much she wanted it – that people should look pleased as she came in, Clarissa thought and turned and walked back towards Bond Street, annoyed, because it was silly to have other reasons for doing things. Much rather would she have been one of those people like Richard who did things for themselves, whereas, she thought, waiting to cross, half the time she did things not simply, not for themselves; but to make people think this or that; perfect idiocy she knew (and now the policeman held up his hand) for no one was ever for a second taken in. Oh if she could have had her life over again! she thought, stepping on to the pavement, could have looked even differently!

She would have been, in the first place, dark like Lady Bexborough, with a skin of crumpled leather and beautiful eyes. She would have been, like Lady Bexborough, slow and stately; rather large; interested in politics like a man; with a country house; very dignified, very sincere. Instead of which she had a narrow pea-stick figure; a ridiculous little face, beaked like a bird's. That she held herself well was true; and had nice hands and feet; and dressed well, considering that she spent little. But often now this body she wore (she stopped to look at a Dutch picture), this body, with all its capacities, seemed nothing – nothing at all. She had the oddest sense of being herself invisible; unseen; unknown; there being no more marrying, no more having of children now, but only this astonishing and rather solemn progress with the rest of them, up Bond Street, this being Mrs Dalloway; not even Clarissa any more; this being Mrs Richard Dalloway.

Bond Street fascinated her; Bond Street early in the morning in the season; its flags flying; its shops; no splash; no glitter; one roll of tweed in the shop where her father had bought his suits for fifty years; a few pearls; salmon on an iceblock.

'That is all,' she said, looking at the fishmonger's. 'That is all,' she repeated, pausing for a moment at the window of a glove shop where, before the War, you could buy almost perfect gloves. And her old Uncle William used to say a lady is known by her shoes and her gloves. He had turned on his bed one morning in the middle of the War. He had said, 'I have had enough.' Gloves and shoes; she had a passion for gloves; but her own daughter, her Elizabeth, cared not a straw for either of them.

Not a straw, she thought, going on up Bond Street to a shop where they kept flowers for her when she gave a party. Elizabeth really cared for her dog most of all. The whole house this morning smelt of tar. Still, better poor Grizzle than Miss Kilman; better distemper and tar and all the rest of it than sitting mewed in a stuffy bedroom with a prayer book! Better anything, she was inclined to say. But it might be only a phase, as Richard said, such as all girls go through. It might be falling in love. But why with Miss Kilman? who had been badly treated of course; one must make allowances for that, and Richard said she was very able, had a really historical mind. Anyhow they were inseparable, and Elizabeth, her own daughter, went to Communion; and how she dressed, how she treated people who came to lunch she did not care a bit, it being her experience that the religious ecstasy made people callous (so did causes); dulled their feelings, for Miss Kilman would do anything for the Russians, starve herself for the Austrians, but in private inflicted positive torture, so insensitive was she, dressed in a green mackintosh coat. Year in year out she wore that coat; she perspired; she was never in the room five minutes without making you feel her superiority, your inferiority; how poor she was; how rich you were; how she lived in a slum without a cushion or a bed or a rug or whatever it might be, all her soul rusted with that grievance sticking in it, her dismissal from school during the War – poor, embittered, unfortunate creature! For it was not her one hated but the idea of her, which undoubtedly had gathered in to itself a great deal that was not Miss Kilman; had become one of those spectres with which one battles in the night; one of those spectres who stand astride us and suck up half our life-blood, dominators and tyrants; for no doubt with another throw of the dice, had the black been uppermost and not the white, she would have loved Miss Kilman! But not in this world. No.

It rasped her, though, to have stirring about in her this brutal monster! to hear twigs cracking and feel hooves planted down in the depths of that leaf-encumbered forest, the soul; never to be content quite, or quite secure, for at any moment the brute would be stirring, this hatred, which, especially since her illness, had power to make her feel scraped, hurt in her spine; gave her physical pain, and made all pleasure in beauty, in friendship, in being well, in being loved and making her home delightful, rock, quiver, and bend as if indeed there were a monster grubbing at the roots, as if the whole panoply of content were nothing but self love! this hatred!

Nonsense, nonsense! she cried to herself, pushing through the swing doors of Mulberry's the florists.

She advanced, light, tall, very upright, to be greeted at once by button-faced Miss Pym, whose hands were always bright red, as if they had been stood in cold water with the flowers.

There were flowers: delphiniums, sweet peas, bunches of lilac; and carnations, masses of carnations. There were roses; there were irises. Ah yes — so she breathed in the earthy-garden sweet smell as she stood talking to Miss Pym who owed her help, and thought her kind, for kind she had been years ago; very kind, but she looked older, this year, turning her head from side to side among the irises and roses and nodding tufts of lilac with her eyes half closed, snuffing in, after the street uproar, the delicious scent, the exquisite coolness. And then, opening her eyes, how fresh, like frilled linen clean from a laundry laid in wicker trays, the roses looked; and dark and prim the red carnations, holding their heads up; and all the sweet peas spreading in their bowls, tinged violet, snow white, pale – as if it were the evening and girls in muslin frocks came out to pick sweet peas and roses after the superb summer's day, with its almost blue-black sky, its delphiniums, its carnations, its arum lilies, was over; and it was the moment between six and seven when every flower – roses, carnations, irises, lilac – glows; white, violet, red, deep orange; every flower seems to burn by itself, softly, purely in the misty beds; and how she loved the grey white moths spinning in and out, over the cherry pie, over the evening primroses!

And as she began to go with Miss Pym from jar to jar, choosing, nonsense, nonsense, she said to herself, more and more gently, as if this beauty, this scent, this colour, and Miss Pym liking her, trusting her, were a wave which she let flow over her and surmount that hatred, that monster, surmount it all; and it lifted her up and up when – oh! a pistol shot in the street outside!

'Dear, those motor cars,' said Miss Pym, going to the window to look, and coming back and smiling apologetically with her hands full of sweet peas, as if those motor cars, those tyres of motor cars, were all *her* fault.

The violent explosion which made Mrs Dalloway jump and Miss Pym go to the window and apologise came from a motor car which had drawn to the side of the pavement precisely opposite Mulberry's shop window. Passers-by, who, of course, stopped and stared, had just time to see a face of the very greatest importance against the dove-grey upholstery, before a male hand drew the blind and there was nothing to be seen except a square of dove grey.

Yet rumours were at once in circulation from the middle of Bond Street to Oxford Street on one side, to Atkinson's scent shop on the other, passing invisibly, inaudibly, like a cloud, swift, veil-like upon hills, falling indeed with something of a cloud's sudden sobriety and stillness upon faces which a second before had been utterly disorderly. But now mystery had brushed them with her wing; they had heard the voice of authority; the spirit of religion was abroad with her eyes bandaged tight and her lips gaping wide. But nobody knew whose face had been seen. Was it the Prince of Wales's, the Queen's, the Prime Minister's? Whose face was it? Nobody knew.

Edgar J. Watkiss, with his roll of lead piping round his arm, said audibly, humorously of course: 'The Proime Minister's kyar.'

Septimus Warren Smith, who found himself unable to pass, heard him.

Septimus Warren Smith, aged about thirty, pale-faced, beak-nosed, wearing brown shoes and a shabby overcoat, with hazel eyes which had that look of apprehension in them which makes complete strangers apprehensive too. The world has raised its whip; where will it descend?

Everything had come to a standstill. The throb of the motor engines sounded like a pulse irregularly drumming through an entire body. The sun became extraordinarily hot because the motor car had stopped outside Mulberry's shop window; old ladies on the tops of omnibuses spread their black parasols; here a green, here a red parasol opened with a little pop. Mrs Dalloway, coming to the window with her arms full of sweet peas, looked out with her little pink face pursed in inquiry. Every one looked at the motor car. Septimus looked. Boys on bicycles sprang off. Traffic accumulated. And there the motor car stood, with drawn blinds, and upon them a curious pattern like a tree, Septimus thought, and this gradual drawing together of everything to one centre before his eyes, as if some horror had come almost to the surface and was about to burst into flames, terrified him. The world wavered and quivered and threatened to burst into flames. It is I who am blocking the way, he thought. Was he not being looked at and pointed at; was he not weighted there, rooted to the pavement, for a purpose? But for what purpose?

'Let us go on, Septimus,' said his wife, a little woman, with large eyes in a sallow pointed face; an Italian girl.

But Lucrezia herself could not help looking at the motor car and the tree pattern on the blinds. Was it the Queen in there – the Queen going shopping?

The chauffeur, who had been opening something, turning

something, shutting something, got on to the box.

'Come on,' said Lucrezia.

But her husband, for they had been married four, five years now, jumped, started, and said, 'All right!' angrily, as if she had interrupted him.

People must notice; people must see. People, she thought, looking at the crowd staring at the motor car; the English people, with their children and their horses and their clothes, which she admired in a way; but they were 'people' now, because Septimus had said, 'I will kill myself'; an awful thing to say. Suppose they had heard him? She looked at the crowd. Help, help! she wanted to cry out to butchers' boys and women. Help! Only last autumn she and Septimus had stood on the Embankment wrapped in the same cloak and, Septimus reading a paper instead of talking, she had snatched it from him and laughed in the old man's face who saw them! But failure one conceals. She must take him away into some park.

'Now we will cross,' she said.

She had a right to his arm, though it was without feeling. He would give her, who was so simple, so impulsive, only twenty-four, without friends in England, who had left Italy for his sake, a piece of bone.

The motor car with its blinds drawn and an air of inscrutable reserve proceeded towards Picadilly, still gazed at, still ruffling the faces on both sides of the street with the same dark breath of veneration whether for Queen, Prince, or Prime Minister nobody knew. The face itself had been seen only once by three people for a few seconds. Even the sex was now in dispute. But there could be no doubt that greatness was seated within; greatness was passing, hidden, down Bond Street, removed only by a hand's-breadth from ordinary people who might now, for the first time and last, be within speaking distance of the majesty of England, of the enduring symbol of the state which will be known to curious antiquaries, sifting the ruins of time, when London is a grass-grown path and all those hurrying along the pavement this Wednesday morning are but bones with a few wedding rings mixed up in their dust and the gold stoppings of innumerable decayed teeth. The face in the motor car will then be known.

It is probably the Queen, thought Mrs Dalloway, coming out of Mulberry's with her flowers: the Queen. And for a second she wore a look of extreme dignity standing by the flower shop in the sunlight while the car passed at a foot's pace, with its blinds drawn. The Queen going to some hospital; the Queen opening some bazaar, thought Clarissa.

The crush was terrific for the time of day. Lords, Ascot, Hurlingham, what was it? she wondered, for the street was blocked. The British middle classes sitting sideways on the tops of omnibuses with parcels and umbrellas, yes, even furs on a day like this, were, she thought, more ridiculous, more unlike anything there has ever been than one could conceive; and the Queen herself held up; the Queen herself unable to pass. Clarissa was suspended on one side of Brook Street; Sir John Buckhurst, the old Judge, on the other, with the car between them (Sir John had laid down the law for years and liked a well-dressed woman) when the chauffeur, leaning ever so slightly, said or showed something to the policeman, who saluted and raised his arm and jerked his head and moved the omnibus to the side and the car passed through. Slowly and very silently it took its way.

Clarissa guessed; Clarissa knew of course; she had seen something white, magical, circular, in the footman's hand, a disc inscribed with a name, – the Queen's, the Prince of Wales's, the Prime Minister's? – which, by force of its own lustre, burnt its way through (Clarissa saw the car diminishing, disappearing), to blaze among candelabras, glittering stars, breasts stiff with oak leaves, Hugh Whitbread and all his colleagues, the gentlemen of England, that night in Buckingham Palace. And Clarissa, too, gave a party. She stiffened a little; so she would stand at the top of her stairs.

The car had gone, but it had left a slight ripple which flowed through glove shops and hat shops and tailors' shops on both sides of Bond Street. For thirty seconds all heads were inclined the same way – to the window. Choosing a pair of gloves – should they be to the elbow or above it, lemon or pale grey? – ladies stopped; when the sentence was finished something had happened. Something so trifling in single instances that no mathematical instrument, though capable of transmitting shocks in China, could register the vibration; yet in its fullness rather formidable and in its common appeal emotional; for in all the hat shops and tailors' shops strangers looked at each other and thought of the dead; of the flag; of Empire. In a public-house in a back street a Colonial insulted the House of Windsor, which led to words, broken beer glasses, and a general shindy, which echoed strangely across the way in the ears of girls buying white underlinen threaded with pure white ribbon for their weddings. For the surface agitation of the passing car as it sunk grazed something very profound.

Gliding across Piccadilly, the car turned down St James's Street. Tall men, men of robust physique, well-dressed men with their tail-coats and their white slips and their hair raked back, who, for reasons difficult to discriminate, were standing in the bow window of White's with their hands behind the tails of their coats, looking out, perceived instinctively that greatness was passing, and the pale light of the immortal presence fell upon them as it had fallen upon Clarissa Dalloway. As once they stood even straighter, and removed their hands, and seemed ready to attend their Sovereign, if need be, to the cannon's mouth, as their ancestors had done before them. The white busts and the little tables in the background covered with copies of the *Tatler* and bottles of soda water seemed to approve; seemed to indicate the flowing corn and the manor houses of England; and to return the frail hum of the motor wheels as the walls of a whispering gallery return a single voice expanded and made sonorous by the might of a whole cathedral. Shawled Moll Pratt with her flowers on the pavement wished the dear boy well (it was the Prince of Wales for certain) and would have tossed the price of a pot of beer – a bunch of roses – into St James's Street out of sheer light-heartedness and contempt of poverty had she not seen the constable's eye upon her, discouraging an old Irish-woman's loyalty. The sentries at St James's saluted; Queen Alexandra's policeman approved.

A small crowd, meanwhile, had gathered at the gates of Buckingham Palace. Listlessly, yet confidently, poor people all of them, they waited; looked at the Palace itself with the flag flying; at Victoria, billowing on her mound, admired her shelves of running water, her geraniums; singled out from the motor cars in the Mall first this one, then that; bestowed emotion, vainly, upon commoners out for a drive; recalled their tribute to keep it unspent while this car passed and that; and all the time let rumour accumulate in their veins and thrill the nerves in their thighs at the thought of Royalty looking at them; the Queen bowing; the Prince saluting; at the thought of the heavenly life divinely bestowed upon Kings; of the equerries and deep curtsies; of the Queen's old doll's house; of Princess Mary married to an Englishman, and the Prince – ah! the Prince! who took wonderfully, they said, after old King Edward, but was ever so much slimmer. The Prince lived at St James's; but he might come along in the morning to visit his mother.

So Sarah Bletchley said with her baby in her arms, tipping her foot up and down as though she were by her own fender in Pimlico, but keeping her eyes on the Mall, while Emily Coates ranged over the Palace windows and thought of the housemaids, the innumerable housemaids, the bedrooms, the innumerable bedrooms. Joined by an elderly gentleman with an Aberdeen terrier, by men without occupation, the crowd increased. Little Mr Bowley, who had rooms in the Albany and was sealed with wax over the deeper sources of life, but could be unsealed suddenly, inappropriately, sentimentally, by this sort of thing – poor women waiting to see the Queen go past – poor women, nice little children, orphans, widows, the War – tut-tut – actually had tears in his eyes. A breeze flaunting ever so warmly down the Mall through the thin trees, past the bronze heroes, lifted some flag flying in the British breast of Mr Bowley and he raised his hat as the car turned into the Mall and held it high as the car approached and let the poor mothers of Pimlico press close to him, and stood very upright. The car came on.

Suddenly Mrs Coates looked up into the sky. The sound

of an aeroplane bored ominously into the ears of the crowd.
There it was coming over the trees, letting out white smoke
from behind, which curled and twisted, actually writing
something! making letters in the sky! Every one looked up.

Dropping dead down, the aeroplane soared straight up,
curved in a loop, raced, sank, rose, and whatever it did,
wherever it went, out fluttered behind it a thick ruffled
bar of white smoke which curled and wreathed upon the
sky in letters. But what letters? A C was it? an E, then an
L? Only for a moment did they lie still; then they moved
and melted and were rubbed out up in the sky, and the aeroplane shot further away and again, in a fresh space of
sky, began writing a K, and E, a Y perhaps?

'Blaxo,' said Mrs Coates in a strained, awe-stricken voice,
gazing straight up, and her baby, lying stiff and white in her
arms, gazed straight up.

'Kreemo,' murmured Mrs Bletchley, like a sleep-walker.
With his hat held out perfectly still in his hand, Mr Bowley
gazed straight up. All down the Mall people were standing
and looking up into the sky. As they looked the whole
world became perfectly silent, and a flight of gulls crossed
the sky, first one gull leading, then another, and in this
extraordinary silence and peace, in this pallor, in this purity, bells struck eleven times, the sound fading up there
among the gulls.

The aeroplane turned and raced and swooped exactly
where it liked, swiftly, freely, like a skater –

'That's an E,' said Mrs Bletchley –
or a dancer –

'It's toffee,' murmured Mr Bowley –
(and the car went in at the gates and nobody looked at it),
and shutting off the smoke, away and away it rushed, and
the smoke faded and assembled itself round the broad white
shapes of the clouds.

It had gone; it was behind the clouds. There was no
sound. The clouds to which the letters E, G, or L had
attached themselves moved freely, as if destined to cross
from West to East on a mission of the greatest importance
which would never be revealed, and yet certainly so it was

– a mission of the greatest importance. Then suddenly, as a train comes out of a tunnel, the aeroplane rushed out of the clouds again, the sound boring into the ears of all people in the Mall, in the Green Park, in Piccadilly, in Regent Street, in Regent's Park, and the bar of smoke curved behind and it dropped down, and it soared up and wrote one letter after another – but what word was it writing?

Lucrezia Warren Smith, sitting by her husband's side on a seat in Regent's Park in the Broad Walk, looked up.

'Look, look, Septimus!' she cried. For Dr Holmes had told her to make her husband (who had nothing whatever seriously the matter with him but was a little out of sorts) take an interest in things outside himself.

So, thought Septimus, looking up, they are signalling to me. Not indeed in actual words; that is, he could not read the language yet; but it was plain enough, this beauty, this exquisite beauty, and tears filled his eyes as he looked at the smoke words languishing and melting in the sky and bestowing upon him, in their inexhaustible charity and laughing goodness, one shape after another of unimaginable beauty and signalling their intention to provide him, for nothing, for ever, for looking merely, with beauty, more beauty! Tears ran down his cheeks.

It was toffee; they were advertising toffee, a nursemaid told Rezia. Together they began to spell t . . . o . . . f . . .

'K . . . R . . .' said the nursemaid, and Septimus heard her say 'Kay Arr' close to his ear, deeply, softly, like a mellow organ, but with a roughness in her voice like a grasshopper's, which rasped his spine deliciously and sent running up into his brain waves of sound, which, concussing, broke. A marvellous discovery indeed – that the human voice in certain atmospheric conditions (for one must be scientific, above all scientific) can quicken trees into life! Happily Rezia put her hand down with a tremendous weight on his knee so that he was weighted down, transfixed, or the excitement of the elm trees rising and falling, rising and falling with all their leaves alight and the colour thinning and thickening from blue to the green of a hollow wave, like plumes on horses' heads, feathers on ladies', so proudly they rose and fell, so superbly, would have sent him mad. But he would not go mad. He would shut his eyes; he would see no more.

But they beckoned; leaves were alive; trees were alive. And the leaves being connected by millions of fibres with his own body, there on the seat, fanned it up and down; when the branch stretched he, too, made that statement. The sparrows fluttering, rising, and falling in jagged fountains were part of the pattern; the white and blue, barred with black branches. Sounds made harmonies with premeditation; the spaces between them were as significant as the sounds. A child cried. Rightly far away a horn sounded. All taken together meant the birth of a new religion –

'Septimus!' said Rezia. He started violently. People must notice.

'I am going to walk to the fountain and back,' she said.

For she could stand it no longer. Dr Holmes might say there was nothing the matter. Far rather would she that he were dead! She could not sit beside him when he stared so and did not see her and made everything terrible; sky and tree, children playing, dragging carts, blowing whistles, falling down; all were terrible. And he would not kill himself; and she could tell no one. 'Septimus has been working too hard' – that was all she could say to her own mother. To love makes one solitary, she thought. She could tell nobody, not even Septimus now, and looking back, she saw him sitting in his shabby overcoat alone, on the seat, hunched up, staring. And it was cowardly for a man to say he would kill himself, but Septimus had fought; he was brave; he was not Septimus now. She put on her lace collar. She put on her new hat and he never noticed; and he was happy without her. Nothing could make her happy without him! Nothing! He was selfish. So men are. For he was not ill. Dr Holmes said there was nothing the matter with him. She spread her hand before her. Look! Her wedding ring slipped – she had grown so thin. It was she who suffered – but she had nobody to tell.

Far was Italy and the white houses and the room where her sisters sat making hats, and the streets crowded every evening with people walking, laughing out loud, not half alive like people here, huddled up in Bath chairs, looking at a few ugly flowers stuck in pots!

'For you should see the Milan gardens,' she said aloud. But to whom?

There was nobody. Her words faded. So a rocket fades. Its sparks, having grazed their way into the night, surrender to it, dark descends, pours over the outlines of houses and towers; bleak hill-sides soften and fall in. But though they are gone, the night is full of them; robbed of colour, blank of windows, they exist more ponderously, give out what the frank daylight fails to transmit – the trouble and suspense of things conglomerated there in the darkness; huddled together in the darkness; reft of the relief which dawn brings when, washing the walls white and grey, spotting each window-pane, lifting the mist from the fields, showing the red-brown cows peacefully grazing, all is once more decked out to the eye; exists again. I am alone; I am alone! she cried, by the fountain in Regent's Park (staring at the Indian and his cross), as perhaps at midnight, when all boundaries are lost, the country reverts to its ancient shape, as the Romans saw it, lying cloudy, when they landed, and the hills had no names and rivers wound they knew not where – such was her darkness; when suddenly, as if a shelf were shot forth and she stood on it, she said how she was his wife, married years ago in Milan, his wife, and would never, never tell that he was mad! Turning, the shelf fell; down, down she dropped. For he was gone, she thought – gone, as he threatened, to kill himself – to throw himself under a cart! But no; there he was; still sitting alone on the seat, in his shabby overcoat, his legs crossed, staring, talking aloud.

Men must not cut down trees. There is a God. (He noted such revelations on the backs of envelopes.) Change the world. No one kills from hatred. Make it known (he wrote it down). He waited. He listened. A sparrow perched on the railing opposite chirped Septimus, Septimus, four or five times over and went on, drawing its notes out, to sing freshly and piercingly in Greek words how there is no crime and, joined by another sparrow, they sang in voices prolonged and piercing in Greek words, from trees in the meadow of life beyond a river where the dead walk, how there is no death.

There was his hand; there the dead. White things were assembling behind the railings opposite. But he dared not look. Evans was behind the railings!

'What are you saying?' said Rezia suddenly, sitting down by him.

Interrupted again! She was always interrupting.

Away from people – they must get away from people, he said (jumping up), right away over there, where there were chairs beneath a tree and the long slope of the park dipped like a length of green stuff with a ceiling cloth of blue and pink smoke high above, and there was a rampart of far, irregular houses, hazed in smoke, the traffic hummed in a circle, and on the right, dun-coloured animals stretched long necks over the Zoo palings, barking, howling. There they sat down under a tree.

'Look,' she implored him, pointing at a little troop of boys carrying cricket stumps, and one shuffled, spun round on his heel and shuffled, as if he were acting a clown at the music hall.

'Look,' she implored him, for Dr Holmes had told her to make him notice real things, go to a music hall, play cricket – that was the very game, Dr Holmes said, a nice out-of-door game, the very game for her husband.

'Look,' she repeated.

Look, the unseen bade him, the voice which now communicated with him who was the greatest of mankind, Septimus, lately taken from life to death, the Lord who had come to renew society, who lay like a coverlet, a snow blanket smitten only by the sun, for ever unwasted, suffering for ever, the scapegoat, the eternal sufferer, but he did not want it, he moaned, putting from him with a wave of his hand that eternal suffering, that eternal loneliness.

'Look,' she repeated, for he must not talk aloud to himself out of doors.

'Oh, look,' she implored him. But what was there to look

at? A few sheep. That was all.

The way to Regent's Park Tube station – coul.
tell her the way to Regent's Park Tube station – M.
Johnson wanted to know. She was only up from Edinbur,
two days ago.

'Not this way – over there!' Rezia exclaimed, waving
her aside, lest she should see Septimus.

Both seemed queer, Maisie Johnson thought. Everything
seemed very queer. In London for the first time, come to
take up a post at her uncle's in Leadenhall Street, and now
walking through Regent's Park in the morning, this couple on
the chairs gave her quite a turn: the young woman seeming foreign, the man looking queer, so that should she be
very old she would still remember and make it jangle again
among her memories how she had walked through Regent's
Park on a fine summer's morning fifty years ago. For she
was only nineteen and had got her way at last, to come to
London; and now how queer it was, this couple she had
asked the way of, and the girl started and jerked her hand,
and the man – he seemed awfully odd; quarrelling, perhaps;
parting for ever, perhaps; something was up, she knew; and
now all these people (for she returned to the Broad Walk),
the stone basins, the prim flowers, the old men and women,
invalids most of them in Bath chairs – all seemed, after
Edinburgh, so queer. And Maisie Johnson, as she joined that
gently trudging, vaguely gazing, breeze-kissed company –
squirrels perching and preening, sparrow fountains fluttering for crumbs, dogs busy with the railings, busy with each
other, while the soft warm air washed over them and lent
to the fixed unsurprised gaze with which they received life,
something whimsical and mollified – Maisie Johnson positively felt she must cry Oh! (for that young man on the
seat had given her quite a turn. Something was up, she
knew).

Horror! horror! she wanted to cry. (She had left her
people; they had warned her what would happen.)

Why hadn't she stayed at home? she cried, twisting the
knob of the iron railing.

That girl, thought Mrs Dempster (who saved crusts for

the squirrels and often ate her lunch in Regent's Park), don't know a thing yet; and really it seemed to her better to be a little stout, a little slack, a little moderate in one's expectations. Percy drank. Well, better to have a son, thought Mrs Dempster. She had had a hard time of it, and couldn't help smiling at a girl like that. You'll get married, for you're pretty enough, thought Mrs Dempster. Get married, she thought, and then you'll know. Oh, the cooks, and so on. Every man has his ways. But whether I'd have chosen quite like that if I could have known, thought Mrs Dempster, and could not help wishing to whisper a word to Maisie Johnson; to feel on the creased pouch of her worn old face the kiss of pity. For it's been a hard life, thought Mrs Dempster. What hadn't she given to it? Roses; figure; her feet too. (She drew the knobbed lumps beneath her skirt.)

Roses, she thought sardonically. All trash, m'dear. For really, what with eating, drinking, and mating, the bad days and good, life had been no mere matter of roses, and what was more, let me tell you, Carrie Dempster had no wish to change her lot with any woman's in Kentish Town! But, she implored, pity. Pity, for the loss of roses. Pity she asked of Maisie Johnson, standing by the hyacinth beds.

Ah, but that aeroplane! Hadn't Mrs Dempster always longed to see foreign parts? She had a nephew, a missionary. It soared and shot. She always went on the sea at Margate, not out o' sight of land, but she had no patience with women who were afraid of water. It swept and fell. Her stomach was in her mouth. Up again. There's a fine young feller aboard of it, Mrs Dempster wagered, and away and away it went, fast and fading, away and away the aeroplane shot: soaring over Greenwich and all the masts; over the little island of grey churches, St Paul's and the rest, till, on either side of London, fields spread out and dark brown woods where adventurous thrushes, hopping boldly, glancing quickly, snatched the snail and tapped him on a stone, once, twice, thrice.

Away and away the aeroplane shot, till it was nothing but a bright spark; an aspiration; a concentration; a symbol (so it seemed to Mr Bentley, vigorously rolling his strip of turf at Greenwich) of man's soul; of his determination, thought Mr Bentley, sweeping round the cedar tree, to get outside his body, beyond his house, by means of thought, Einstein, speculation, mathematics, the Mendelian theory – away the aeroplane shot.

Then, while a seedy-looking nondescript man carrying a leather bag stood on the steps of St Paul's Cathedral, and hesitated, for within was what balm, how great a welcome, how many tombs with banners waving over them, tokens of victories not over armies, but over, he thought, that plaguy spirit of truth seeking which leaves me at present without a situation, and more than that, the cathedral offers company, he thought, invites you to membership of a society; great men belong to it; martyrs have died for it; why not enter in, he thought, put this leather bag stuffed with pamphlets before an altar, a cross, the symbol of something which has soared beyond seeking and questing and knocking of words together and has become all spirit, disembodied, ghostly – why not enter in? he thought, and while he hesitated out flew the aeroplane over Ludgate Circus.

It was strange; it was still. Not a sound was to be heard above the traffic. Unguided it seemed; sped of its own free will. And now, curving up and up, straight up, like something mounting in ecstasy, in pure delight, out from behind poured white smoke looping, writing a T, and O, an F.

'What are they looking at?' said Clarissa Dalloway to the maid who opened the door.

The hall of the house was cool as a vault. Mrs Dalloway raised her hand to her eyes, and, as the maid shut the door to, she heard the swish of Lucy's skirts, she felt like a nun who has left the world and feels fold round her the familiar veils and the response to old devotions. The cook whistled in the kitchen. She heard the click of the typewriter. It was her life, and, bending her head over the hall table, she bowed beneath the influence, felt blessed and purified, saying to herself, as she took the pad with the telephone message on it, how moments like this are buds on the tree of life, flowers of darkness they are, she thought (as if some lovely rose had blossomed for her eyes only); not for a moment did she believe in God; but all the more, she thought, taking up the pad, one must repay in daily life to servants, yes, to dogs and canaries, above all to Richard her husband, who was the foundation of it – of the gay sounds, of the green lights, of the cook even whistling, for Mrs Walker was Irish and whistled all day long – one must pay back from this secret deposit of exquisite moments, she thought, lifting the pad, while Lucy stood by her, trying to explain how

'Mr Dalloway, ma'am –'

Clarissa read on the telephone pad, 'Lady Bruton wishes to know if Mr Dalloway will lunch with her to-day.'

'Mr Dalloway, ma'am, told me to tell you he would be lunching out.'

'Dear!' said Clarissa, and Lucy shared as she meant her to her disappointment (but not the pang); felt the concord between them; took the hint; thought how the gentry love; gilded her own future with calm; and taking Mrs Dalloway's parasol, handled it like a sacred weapon which a goddess, having acquitted herself honourably in the field of battle, sheds, and placed it in the umbrella stand.

'Fear no more,' said Clarissa. Fear no more the heat o' the sun; for the shock of Lady Bruton asking Richard to lunch without her made the moment in which she had stood shiver, as a plant on the river-bed feels the shock of a passing oar and shivers: so she rocked: so she shivered.

Millicent Bruton, whose lunch parties were said to be extraordinarily amusing, had not asked her. No vulgar jealousy could separate her from Richard. But she feared time itself, and read on Lady Bruton's face, as if it had been a dial cut in impassive stone, the dwindling of life; how year by year her share was sliced; how little the margin that remained was capable any longer of stretching, of absorbing, as in the youthful years, the colours, salts, tones of existence, so that she filled the room she entered, and felt often, as she stood hesitating one moment on the threshold of her drawing-room, an exquisite suspense, such as might stay a diver before plunging while the sea darkens and brightens beneath him, and the waves which threaten to break, but only gently split their surface, roll and conceal and encrust as they just turn over the weeds with pearl.

She put the pad on the hall table. She began to go slowly upstairs, with her hand on the banisters, as if she had left a party, where now this friend now that had flashed back her face, her voice; had shut the door and gone out and stood alone, a single figure against the appalling night, or rather, to be accurate, against the stare of this matter-of-fact June morning; soft with the glow of rose petals for some, she knew, and felt it, as she paused by the open staircase window which let in blinds flapping, dogs barking, let in, she thought, feeling herself suddenly shrivelled, aged, breast-less, the grinding, blowing, flowering of the day, out of doors, out of the window, out of her body and brain which now failed, since Lady Bruton, whose lunch parties were said to be extraordinarily amusing, had not asked her.

Like a nun withdrawing, or a child exploring a tower, she went, upstairs, paused at the window, came to the bathroom. There was the green linoleum and a tap dripping. There was an emptiness about the heart of life; an attic room. Women must put off their rich apparel. At mid-day they must disrobe. She pierced the pincushion and laid her feathered yellow hat on the bed. The sheets were clean, tight stretched in a broad white band from side to side. Narrower and narrower would her bed be. The candle was half burnt down and she had read deep in Baron Marbot's *Memoirs*. She had read late at night of the retreat from Moscow. For the House sat so long that Richard insisted, after her illness, that she must sleep undisturbed. And really she preferred to read of the retreat from Moscow. He knew it. So the room was an attic; the bed narrow; and lying there reading, for she slept badly, she could not dispel a virginity preserved through childbirth which clung to her like a sheet. Lovely in girlhood, suddenly there came a moment – for example on the river beneath the woods at Clieveden – when, through some contraction of this cold spirit, she had failed him. And then at Constantinople, and again and again. She could see what she lacked. It was not beauty; it was not mind. It was something central which permeated; something warm which broke up surfaces and rippled the cold contact of man and woman, or of women together. For *that* she could dimly perceive. She resented it, had a scruple picked up Heaven knows where, or, as she felt, sent by Nature (who is invariably wise); yet she could not resist sometimes yielding to the charm of a woman, not a girl, of a woman confessing, as to her they often did, some scrape, some folly. And whether it was pity, or their beauty, or that she was older, or some accident – like a faint scent, or a violin next door (so strange is the power of sounds at certain moments), she did undoubtedly then feel what men felt. Only for a moment; but it was enough. It was a sudden revelation, a tinge like a blush which one tried to check and then, as it spread, one yielded to its expansion, and rushed to the farthest verge and there quivered and felt the world come closer, swollen with some astonishing significance, some pressure of rapture, which split its thin skin and gushed and poured with an extraordinary alleviation over the cracks and sores. Then, for that moment, she had seen an illumination; a match burning in a crocus; an inner meaning almost expressed. But the close withdrew; the hard softened. It was over – the moment. Against such moments (with women too) there contrasted (as she laid her hat down) the bed and Baron Marbot and the candle half-burnt. Lying awake, the floor creaked; the lit house was suddenly darkened, and if she raised her head she could just hear the click of the handle released as gently as possible by Richard, who slipped upstairs in his socks and then, as often as not, dropped his hot-water bottle and swore! How she laughed!

But this question of love (she thought, putting her coat away), this falling in love with women. Take Sally Seton; her relation in the old days with Sally Seton. Had not that, after all, been love?

She sat on the floor – that was her first impression of Sally – she sat on the floor with her arms round her knees, smoking a cigarette. Where could it have been? The Mannings'? The Kinloch-Jones's? At some party (where she could not be certain), for she had a distinct recollection of saying to the man she was with, 'Who is *that*?' And he had told her, and said that Sally's parents did not get on (how that shocked her – that one's parents should quarrel!). But all that evening she could not take her eyes off Sally. It was an extraordinary beauty of the kind she most admired, dark, large-eyed, with that quality which, since she hadn't got it herself, she always envied – a sort of abandonment, as if she could say anything, do anything; a quality much commoner in foreigners than in Englishwomen. Sally always said she had French blood in her veins, an ancestor had been with Marie Antoinette, had his head cut off, left a ruby ring. Perhaps that summer she came to stay at Bourton, walking in quite unexpectedly without a penny in her pocket, one night after dinner, and upsetting poor Aunt Helena to such an extent that she never forgave her. There had been some awful quarrel at home. She literally hadn't a penny that night when she came to them – had pawned a brooch to come down. She had rushed off in a passion. They sat up till all hours of the night talking. Sally it was who made her feel, for the first time, how sheltered the life at Bourton was. She knew nothing about sex – nothing about social problems. She had once seen an old man who had dropped dead in a field – she had seen cows just after their calves were born. But Aunt Helena never liked discussion of anything (when Sally gave her William Morris, it had to be wrapped in brown paper). There they sat, hour after hour, talking in her bedroom at the top of the house, talking about life, how they were to reform the world. They meant to found a society to abolish private property, and actually had a letter written, though not sent out. The ideas were Sally's, of course – but very soon she was just as excited – read Plato in bed before breakfast; read Morris; read Shelley by the hour.

Sally's power was amazing, her gift, her personality. There was her way with flowers, for instance. At Bourton they always had stiff little vases all the way down the table. Sally went out, picked hollyhocks, dahlias – all sorts of flowers that had never been seen together – cut their heads off, and made them swim on the top of water in bowls. The effect was extraordinary – coming in to dinner in the sunset. (Of course Aunt Helena thought it wicked to treat flowers like that.) Then she forgot her sponge, and ran along the passage naked. That grim old housemaid, Ellen Atkins, went about grumbling – 'Suppose any of the gentlemen had seen?' Indeed she did shock people. She was untidy, Papa said.

The strange thing, on looking back, was the purity, the integrity, of her feeling for Sally. It was not like one's feeling for a man. It was completely disinterested, and besides, it had a quality which could only exist between women, between women just grown up. It was protective, on her side; sprang from a sense of being in league together, a presentiment of something that was bound to part them (they spoke of marriage always as a catastrophe), which led to this chivalry, this protective feeling which was much more on her side than Sally's. For in those days she was completely reckless; did the most idiotic things out of bravado; bicycled round the parapet on the terrace: smoked cigars. Absurd, she was – very absurd. But the charm was overpowering, to her at least, so that she could remember standing in her bedroom at the top of the house holding the hot-water can in her hands and saying aloud, 'She is beneath this roof. . . . She is beneath this roof!'

No, the words meant absolutely nothing to her now. She could not even get an echo of her old emotion. But she could remember going cold with excitement and doing her hair in a kind of ecstasy (now the old feeling began to come back to her, as she took out her hairpins, laid them on the dressing-table, began to do her hair), with the rooks flaunting up and down in the pink evening light, and dressing, and going downstairs, and feeling as she crossed the hall 'if it were now to die 'twere now to be most happy.' That was her feeling – Othello's feeling, and she felt it, she was convinced, as strongly as Shakespeare meant Othello to feel it, all because she was coming down to dinner in a white frock to meet Sally Seton!

She was wearing pink gauze – was that possible? She

seemed, anyhow, all light, glowing, like some bird or air ball that has flown in, attached itself for a moment to a bramble. But nothing is so strange when one is in love (and what was this except being in love?) as the complete indifference of other people. Aunt Helena just wandered off after dinner; Papa read the paper. Peter Walsh might have been there, and old Miss Cummings; Joseph Breitkopf certainly was, for he came every summer, poor old man, for weeks and weeks, and pretended to read German with her, but really played the piano and sang Brahms without any voice.

All this was only a background for Sally. She stood by the fireplace talking, in that beautiful voice which made everything she said sound like a caress, to Papa, who had begun to be attracted rather against his will (he never got over lending her one of his books and finding it soaked on the terrace), when suddenly she said, 'What a shame to sit indoors!' and they all went out on to the terrace and walked up and down. Peter Walsh and Joseph Breitkopf went on about Wagner. She and Sally fell a little behind. Then came the most exquisite moment of her whole life passing a stone urn with flowers in it. Sally stopped; picked a flower; kissed her on the lips. The whole world might have turned upside down! The others disappeared; there she was alone with Sally. And she felt that she had been given a present, wrapped up, and told just to keep it, not to look at it – a diamond, something infinitely precious, wrapped up, which, as they walked (up and down, up and down), she uncovered, or the radiance burnt through, the revelation, the religious feeling! – when old Joseph and Peter faced them :

'Star-gazing?' said Peter.

It was like running one's face against a granite wall in the darkness! It was shocking; it was horrible!

Not for herself. She felt only how Sally was being mauled already, maltreated; she felt his hostility; his jealousy; his determination to break into their companionship. All this she saw as one sees a landscape in a flash of lightning – and Sally (never had she admired her so much!) gallantly taking her way unvanquished. She laughed. She made old Joseph tell her the names of the stars, which he liked doing very seriously. She stood there : she listened. She heard the names of the stars.

'Oh this horror!' she said to herself, as if she had known all along that something would interrupt, would embitter her moment of happiness.

Yet how much she owed Peter Walsh later. Always when she thought of him she thought of their quarrels for some reason – because she wanted his good opinion so much, perhaps. She owed him words : 'sentimental', 'civilized'; they started up every day of her life as if he guarded her. A book was sentimental; an attitude to life sentimental. 'Sentimental', perhaps she was to be thinking of the past. What would he think, she wondered, when he came back?

That she had grown older? Would he say that, or would she see him thinking when he came back, that she had grown older? It was true. Since her illness she had turned almost white.

Laying her brooch on the table, she had a sudden spasm, as if, while she mused, the icy claws had had the chance to fix in her. She was not old yet. She had just broken into her fifty-second year. Months and months of it were still untouched. June, July, August! Each still remained almost whole, and, as if to catch the falling drop, Clarissa (crossing to the dressing-table) plunged into the very heart of the moment, transfixed it, there – the moment of this June morning on which was the pressure of all the other mornings, seeing the glass, the dressing-table, and all the bottles afresh, collecting the whole of her at one point (as she looked into the glass), seeing the delicate pink face of the woman who was that very night to give a party; of Clarissa Dalloway; of herself.

How many million times she had seen her face, and always with the same imperceptible contraction! She pursed her lips when she looked in the glass. It was to give her face point. That was her self – pointed; dart-like; definite. That was her self when some effort, some call on her to be her self, drew the parts together, she alone knew how different, how incompatible and composed so for the world only into one centre, one diamond, one woman who sat in her drawing-room and made a meeting-point, a radiancy no doubt in some dull lives, a refuge for the lonely to come to, perhaps; she had helped young people, who were grateful to her; had tried to be the same always, never showing a sign of all the other sides of her – faults, jealousies, vanities, suspicions, like this of Lady Bruton not asking her to lunch; which, she thought (combing her hair finally), is utterly base! Now, where was her dress?

Her evening dresses hung in the cupboard. Clarissa, plunging her hand into the softness, gently detached the green dress and carried it to the window. She had torn it. Some one had trod on the skirt. She had felt it give at the Embassy party at the top among the folds. By artificial light the green shone, but lost its colour now in the sun. She would mend it. Her maids had too much to do. She would wear it to-night. She would take her silks, her scissors, her – what was it? – her thimble, of course, down into the drawing-room, for she must also write, and see that things generally were more or less in order.

Strange, she thought, pausing on the landing, and assembling that diamond shape, that single person, strange how a mistress knows the very moment, the very temper of her house! Faint sounds rose in spirals up the well of the stairs; the swish of a mop; tapping; knocking; a loudness when the front door opened; a voice repeating a message in the basement; the chink of silver on a tray; clean silver for the party. All was for the party.

(And Lucy, coming into the drawing-room with her tray held out, put the giant candlesticks on the mantelpiece, the silver casket in the middle, turned the crystal dolphin towards the clock. They would come; they would stand; they would talk in the mincing tones which she could imitate, ladies and gentlemen. Of all, her mistress was loveliest – mistress of silver, of linen, of china, for the sun, the silver, doors off their hinges, Rumpelmayer's men, gave her a sense, as she laid the paper-knife on the inlaid table, of something achieved. Behold! Behold! she said, speaking to her old friends in the baker's shop, where she had first seen service at Caterham, prying into the glass. She was Lady Angela, attending Princess Mary, when in came Mrs Dalloway.)

'Oh, Lucy,' she said 'the silver does look nice!'

'And how,' she said, turning the crystal dolphin to stand straight, 'how did you enjoy the play last night?' 'Oh, they had to go before the end!' she said. 'They had to be back at ten!' she said. 'So they don't know what happened,' she said. 'That does seem hard luck,' she said (for her servants stayed later, if they asked her). 'That does seem rather a shame,' she said, taking the old bald-looking cushion in the middle of the sofa and putting it in Lucy's arms, and giving her a little push, and crying:

'Take it away! Give it to Mrs Walker with my compliments! Take it away!' she cried.

And Lucy stopped at the drawing-room door, holding the cushion, and said, very shyly, turning a little pink, couldn't she help to mend that dress?

But, said Mrs Dalloway, she had enough on her hands already, quite enough of her own to do without that.

'But, thank you, Lucy, oh, thank you,' said Mrs Dalloway, and thank you, thank you, she went on saying (sitting down on the sofa with her dress over her knees, her scissors, her silks), thank you, thank you, she went on saying in gratitude to her servants generally for helping her to be like this, to be what she wanted, gentle, generous-hearted. Her servants liked her. And then this dress of hers – where was the tear? and now her needle to be threaded. This was a favourite dress, one of Sally Parker's, the last almost she ever made, alas, for Sally had now retired, lived at Ealing, and if ever I have a moment, thought Clarissa (but never would she have a moment any more), I shall go and see her at Ealing. For she was a character, thought Clarissa, a real artist. She thought of little out-of-the-way things; yet her dresses were never queer. You could wear them at Hatfield; at Buckingham Palace. She had worn them at Hatfield; at Buckingham Palace.

Quiet descended on her, calm, content, as her needle, drawing the silk smoothly to its gentle pause, collected the green folds together and attached them, very lightly, to the belt. So on a summer's day waves collect, overbalance, and fall; collect and fall; and the whole world seems to be saying 'that is all' more and more ponderously, until even the heart in the body which lies in the sun on the beach says too, that is all. Fear no more, says the heart. Fear no more, says the heart, committing its burden to some sea, which sighs collectively for all sorrows, and renews, begins, collects, lets fall. And the body alone listens to the passing bee; the wave breaking, the dog barking, far away barking and barking.

'Heavens, the front-door bell!' exclaimed Clarissa, staying her needle. Roused, she listened.

'Mrs Dalloway will see me,' said the elderly man in the hall. 'Oh yes, she will see *me*,' he repeated, putting Lucy aside very benevolently, and running upstairs ever so quickly. 'Yes, yes, yes,' he muttered as he ran upstairs. 'She will see me. After five years in India, Clarissa will see me.'

'Who can – what can –' asked Mrs Dalloway (thinking it was outrageous to be interrupted at eleven o'clock on the morning of the day she was giving a party), hearing a step on the stairs. She heard a hand upon the door. She made to hide her dress, like a virgin protecting chastity, respecting privacy. Now the brass knob slipped. Now the door opened, and in came – for a single second she could not remember what he was called! so surprised she was to see him, so glad, so shy, so utterly taken aback to have Peter Walsh come to her unexpectedly in the morning! (She had not read his letter.)

'And how are you?' said Peter Walsh, positively trembling; taking both her hands; kissing both her hands. She's grown older, he thought, sitting down. I shan't tell her anything about it, he thought, for she's grown older. She's looking at me, he thought, a sudden embarrassment coming over him, though he had kissed her hands. Putting his hand into his pocket, he took out a large pocket-knife and half opened the blade.

Exactly the same, thought Clarissa; the same queer look; the same check suit; a little out of the straight his face is, a little thinner, dryer, perhaps, but he looks awfully well, and just the same.

'How heavenly it is to see you again!' she exclaimed. He had his knife out. That's so like him, she thought.

He had only reached town last night, he said; would have to go down into the country at once; and how was everything, how was everybody – Richard? Elizabeth?

'And what's all this?' he said, tilting his pen-knife towards her green dress.

He's very well dressed, thought Clarissa; yet he always criticizes *me*.

Here she is mending her dress; mending her dress as usual, he thought; here she's been sitting all the time I've been in India; mending her dress; playing about; going to parties; running to the House and back and all that, he thought, growing more and more irritated, more and more agitated, for there's nothing in the world so bad for some women as marriage, he thought; and politics; and having a Conservative husband, like the admirable Richard. So it is, so it is, he thought, shutting his knife with a snap.

'Richard's very well. Richard's at a Committee,' said Clarissa.

And she opened her scissors, and said, did he mind her just finishing what she was doing to her dress, for they had a party that night?

'Which I shan't ask you to,' she said. 'My dear Peter!' she said.

But it was delicious to hear her say that – my dear Peter! Indeed, it was all so delicious – the silver, the chairs; all so delicious!

Why wouldn't she ask him to her party? he asked.

Now of course, thought Clarissa, he's enchanting! perfectly enchanting! Now I remember how impossible it was ever to make up my mind – and why did I make up my mind – not to marry him, she wondered, that awful summer?

'But it's so extraordinary that you should have come this morning!' she cried, putting her hands, one on top of another, down on her dress.

'Do you remember,' she said, 'how the blinds used to flap

at Bourton?'

'They did,' he said; and he remembered breakfasting alone, very awkwardly, with her father; who had died; and he had not written to Clarissa. But he had never got on well with old Parry, that querulous, weak-kneed old man, Clarissa's father, Justin Parry.

'I often wish I'd got on better with your father,' he said.

'But he never liked any one who – our friends,' said Clarissa; and could have bitten her tongue for thus reminding Peter that he had wanted to marry her.

Of course I did, thought Peter; it almost broke my heart too, he thought; and was overcome with his own grief, which rose like a moon looked at from a terrace, ghastly beautiful with light from the sunken day. I was more unhappy than I've ever been since, he thought. And as if in truth he were sitting there on the terrace he edged a little towards Clarissa; put his hand out; raised it; let it fall. There above them it hung, that moon. She too seemed to be sitting with him on the terrace, in the moonlight.

'Herbert has it now,' she said. 'I never go there now,' she said.

Then, just as happens on a terrace in the moonlight, when one person begins to feel ashamed that he is already bored, and yet as the other sits silent, very quiet, sadly looking at the moon, does not like to speak, moves his foot, clears his throat, notices some iron scroll on a table leg, stirs a leaf, but says nothing – so Peter Walsh did now. For why go back like this to the past? he thought. Why make him think of it again? Why make him suffer, when she had tortured him so infernally? Why?

'Do you remember the lake?' she said, in an abrupt voice, under the pressure of an emotion which caught her heart, made the muscles of her throat stiff, and contracted her lips in a spasm as she said 'lake'. For she was a child throwing bread to the ducks, between her parents, and at the same time a grown woman coming to her parents who stood by the lake, holding her life in her arms which, as she neared them, grew larger and larger in her arms, until it became a whole life, a complete life, which she put down by them and said, 'This is what I have made of it! This!' And what had she made of it? What, indeed? sitting there sewing this morning with Peter.

She looked at Peter Walsh; her look, passing through all that time and that emotion, reached him doubtfully; settled on him tearfully; and rose and fluttered away, as a bird touches a branch and rises and flutters away. Quite simply she wiped her eyes.

'Yes,' said Peter. 'Yes, yes, yes,' he said, as if she drew up to the surface something which positively hurt him as it rose. Stop! Stop! he wanted to cry. For he was not old; his life was not over; not by any means. He was only just past fifty. Shall I tell her, he thought, or not? He would like to make a clean breast of it all. But she is too cold, he thought; sewing, with her scissors; Daisy would look ordinary beside Clarissa. And she would think me a failure, which I am in their sense, he thought; in the Dalloways' sense. Oh yes, he had no doubt about that; he was a failure, compared with all this – the inlaid table, the mounted paper-knife, the dolphin and the candlesticks, the chair-covers and the old valuable English tinted prints – he was a failure! I detest the smugness of the whole affair, he thought; Richard's doing, not Clarissa's; save that she married him. (Here Lucy came into the room, carrying silver, more silver, but charming, slender, graceful she looked, he thought, as she stooped to put it down.) And this has been going on all the time! he thought; week after week; Clarissa's life; while I – he thought; and at once everything seemed to radiate from him; journeys; rides; quarrels; adventures; bridge parties; love affairs; work; work, work! and he took out his knife quite openly – his old horn-handled knife which Clarissa could swear he had had these thirty years – and clenched his fist upon it.

What an extraordinary habit that was, Clarissa thought; always playing with a knife. Always making one feel, too, frivolous; empty-minded; a mere silly chatterbox, as he used. But I too, she thought, and, taking up her needle, summoned, like a Queen whose guards have fallen asleep and left her unprotected (she had been quite taken aback by this visit – it had upset her) so that any one can stroll in and have a look at her where she lies with the brambles curving over her, summoned to her help the things she did; the things she liked; her husband; Elizabeth; her self, in short, which Peter hardly knew now, all to come about her and beat off the enemy.

'Well, and what's happened to you?' she said. So before a battle begins, the horses paw the ground; toss their heads; the light shines on their flanks; their necks curve. So Peter Walsh and Clarissa, sitting side by side on the blue sofa, challenged each other. His powers chafed and tossed in him. He assembled from different quarters all sorts of things; praise; his career at Oxford; his marriage, which she knew nothing whatever about; how he had loved; and altogether done his job.

'Millions of things!' he exclaimed, and, urged by the assembly of powers which were now charging this way and that and giving him the feeling at once frightening and extremely exhilarating of being rushed through the air on the shoulders of people he could no longer see, he raised his hands to his forehead.

Clarissa sat very upright; drew in her breath.

'I am in love,' he said, not to her however, but to some one raised up in the dark so that you could not touch her but must lay your garland down on the grass in the dark.

'In love,' he repeated, now speaking rather dryly to Clarissa Dalloway; 'in love with a girl in India.' He had deposited his garland. Clarissa could make what she would of it.

'In love!' she said. That he at his age should be sucked under in his little bow-tie by that monster! And there's no flesh on his neck; his hands are red; and he's six months older than I am! her eye flashed back to her; but in her heart she felt, all the same; he is in love. He has that, she felt; he is in love.

But the indomitable egotism which for ever rides down the hosts opposed to it, the river which says on, on, on; even though, it admits, there may be no goal for us whatever, still on, on; this indomitable egotism charged her cheeks with colour; made her look very young; very pink; very bright-eyed as she sat with her dress upon her knee, and her needle held to the end of green silk, trembling a little. He was in love! Not with her. With some younger woman, of course.

'And who is she?' she asked.

Now this statue must be brought from its height and set down between them.

'A married woman, unfortunately,' he said; 'the wife of a Major in the Indian Army.'

And with a curious ironical sweetness he smiled as he placed her in this ridiculous way before Clarissa.

(All the same, he is in love, thought Clarissa.)

'She has,' he continued, very reasonably, 'two small children; a boy and a girl; and I have come over to see my lawyers about the divorce.'

There they are! he thought. Do what you like with them, Clarissa! There they are! And second by second it seemed to him that the wife of the Major in the Indian Army (his Daisy) and her two small children became more and more lovely as Clarissa looked at them; as if he had set light to a grey pellet on a plate and there had risen up a lovely tree in the brisk sea-salted air of their intimacy (for in some ways no one understood him, felt with him, as Clarissa did) – their exquisite intimacy.

She flattered him; she fooled him, thought Clarissa; shaping the woman, the wife of the Major in the Indian Army, with three strokes of a knife. What a waste! What a folly! All his life long Peter had been fooled like that; first getting sent down from Oxford; next marrying the girl on the boat going out to India; now the wife of a Major – thank Heaven she had refused to marry him! Still, he was in love; her old friend, her dear Peter, he was in love.

'But what are you going to do?' she asked him. Oh, the lawyers and solicitors, Messrs Hooper and Grateley of Lincoln's Inn, they were going to do it, he said. And he actually pared his nails with his pocket-knife.

For Heaven's sake, leave your knife alone! she cried to herself in irrepressible irritation; it was his silly unconventionality, his weakness; his lack of the ghost of a notion what any one else was feeling that annoyed her, had always annoyed her; and now at his age, how silly!

I know all that, Peter thought; I know what I'm up against, he thought, running his finger along the blade of his knife, Clarissa and Dalloway and all the rest of them; but I'll show Clarissa – and then to his utter surprise, suddenly thrown by those uncontrollable forces, thrown through the air, he burst into tears; wept; wept without the least shame, sitting on the sofa, the tears running down his cheeks.

And Clarissa had leant forward, taken his hand, drawn him to her, kissed him, – actually had felt his face on hers before she could down the brandishing of silver-flashing plumes like pampas grass in a tropic gale in her breast, which, subsiding, left her holding his hand, patting his knee, and feeling as she sat back extraordinarily at her ease with him and light-hearted, all in a clap it came over her, If I had married him, this gaiety would have been mine all day!

It was all over for her. The sheet was stretched and the bed narrow. She had gone up into the tower alone and left them blackberrying in the sun. The door had shut, and there among the dust of fallen plaster and the litter of birds' nests how distant the view had looked, and the sounds came thin and chill (once on Leith Hill, she remembered), and Richard, Richard! she cried, as a sleeper in the night starts and stretches a hand in the dark for help. Lunching with Lady Bruton, it came back to her. He has left me; I am alone for ever, she thought, folding her hands upon her knee.

Peter Walsh had got up and crossed to the window and stood with his back to her, flicking a bandanna handkerchief from side to side. Masterly and dry and desolate he looked, his thin shoulder-blades lifting his coat slightly; blowing his nose violently. Take me with you, Clarissa thought impulsively, as if he were starting directly upon some great voyage; and then, next moment, it was as if the five acts of a play that had been very exciting and moving were now over and she had lived a lifetime in them and had run away, had lived with Peter, and it was now over.

Now it was time to move, and, as a woman gathers her things together, her cloak, her gloves, her opera-glasses, and gets up to go out of the theatre into the street, she rose from the sofa and went to Peter.

And it was awfully strange, he thought, how she still had the power, as she came tinkling, rustling, still had the power, as she came across the room, to make the moon, which he detested, rise at Bourton on the terrace in the summer sky.

'Tell me,' he said, seizing her by the shoulders. 'Are you happy, Clarissa? Does Richard –'

The door opened.

'Here is my Elizabeth,' said Clarissa, emotionally, histrionically, perhaps.

'How d'y do?' said Elizabeth coming forward.

The sound of Big Ben striking the half-hour struck out between them with extraordinary vigour, as if a young man, strong, indifferent, inconsiderate, were swinging dumb-bells this way and that.

'Hullo, Elizabeth!' cried Peter, stuffing his handkerchief into his pocket, going quickly to her, saying 'Good-bye, Clarissa' without looking at her, leaving the room quickly, and running downstairs and opening the hall door.

'Peter! Peter!' cried Clarissa, following him out on to the landing. 'My party! Remember my party tonight!' she cried, having to raise her voice against the roar of the open air, and, overwhelmed by the traffic and the sound of all the clocks striking, her voice crying 'Remember my party to-night!' sounded frail and thin and very far away as Peter Walsh shut the door.

Remember my party, remember my party, said Peter Walsh as he stepped down the street, speaking to himself rhythmically, in time with the flow of the sound, the direct downright sound of Big Ben striking the half-hour. (The leaden circles dissolved in the air.) Oh these parties? he thought; Clarissa's parties. Why does she give these parties? he thought. Not that he blamed her or this effigy of a man in a tail-coat with a carnation in his button-hole coming towards him. Only one person in the world could be as he was, in love. And there he was, this fortunate man, himself, reflected in the plate-glass window of a motor-car manufacturer in Victoria Street. All India lay behind him; plains, mountains; epidemics of cholera; a district twice as big as Ireland; decisions he had come to alone – he, Peter Walsh; who was now really for the first time in his life in love. Clarissa had grown hard, he thought; and a trifle sentimental into the bargain, he suspected, looking at the great motor cars capable of doing – how many miles on how many gallons? For he had a turn for mechanics; had invented a plough in his district, had ordered wheel-barrows from England, but the coolies wouldn't use them, all of which Clarissa knew nothing whatever about.

The way she said 'Here is my Elizabeth!' – that annoyed him. Why not 'Here's Elizabeth' simply? It was insincere. And Elizabeth didn't like it either. (Still the last tremors of the great booming voice shook the air round him; the half-hour; still early; only half-past eleven still.) For he understood young people; he liked them. There was always something cold in Clarissa, he thought. She had always, even as a girl, a sort of timidity, which in middle age becomes conventionality, and then it's all up, it's all up, he thought, looking rather drearily into the glassy depths, and wondering whether by calling at that hour he had annoyed her; overcome with shame suddenly at having been a fool; wept; been emotional; told her everything, as usual, as usual.

As a cloud crosses the sun, silence falls on London; and falls on the mind. Effort ceases. Time flaps on the mast. There we stop; there we stand. Rigid, the skeleton of habit alone upholds the human frame. Where there is nothing, Peter Walsh said to himself; feeling hollowed out, utterly empty within. Clarissa refused me, he thought. He stood there thinking, Clarissa refused me.

Ah, said St Margaret's, like a hostess who comes into her drawing-room on the very stroke of the hour and finds her guests there already. I am not late. No, it is precisely half-past eleven, she says. Yet, though she is perfectly right, her voice, being the voice of the hostess, is reluctant to inflict its individuality. Some grief for the past holds it back; some concern for the present. It is half-past eleven, she says, and the sound of St Margaret's glides into the recesses of the heart and buries itself in ring after ring of sound, like something alive which wants to confide itself, to disperse itself, to be, with a tremor of delight, at rest – like Clarissa herself, thought Peter Walsh, coming downstairs on the stroke of the hour in white. It is Clarissa herself, he thought, with a deep emotion, and an extraordinarily clear, yet puzzling, recollection of her, as if this bell had come into the room years ago, where they sat at some moment of great intimacy, and had gone from one to the other and had left, like a bee with honey, laden with the moment. But what room? What moment? And why had he been so profoundly happy when the clock was striking? Then, as the sound of St Margaret's languished, he thought, she has been ill, and the sound expressed languor and suffering. It was her heart, he remembered; and the sudden loudness of the final stroke tolled for death that surprised in the midst of life, Clarissa falling where she stood, in her drawing-room. No! No! he cried. She is not dead! I am not old, he cried, and marched up Whitehall, as if there rolled down to him, vigorous, unending, his future.

He was not old, or set, or dried in the least. As for caring what they said of him – the Dalloways, the Whitbreads, and their set, he cared not a straw – not a straw (though it was true he would have, some time or other, to see whether Richard couldn't help him to some job). Striding, staring, he glared at the statue of the Duke of Cambridge. He had been sent down from Oxford – true. He had been a Socialist, in some sense a failure – true. Still the future of civilization lies, he thought, in the hands of young men like that; of young men such as he was, thirty years ago; with their love of abstract principles; getting books sent out to them all the way from London to a peak in the Himalayas; reading science; reading philosophy. The future lies in the hands of young men like that, he thought.

A patter like the patter of leaves in a wood came from behind, and with it a rustling, regular thudding sound, which as it overtook him drummed his thoughts, strict in step, up Whitehall, without his doing. Boys in uniform, carrying guns, marched with their eyes ahead of them, marched, their arms stiff, and on their faces an expression like the letters of a legend written round the base of a statue praising duty, gratitude, fidelity, love of England.

It is, thought Peter Walsh, beginning to keep step with them, a very fine training. But they did not look robust. They were weedy for the most part, boys of sixteen, who might, to-morrow, stand behind bowls of rice, cakes of soap on counters. Now they wore on them unmixed with sensual pleasure or daily preoccupations the solemnity of the wreath which they had fetched from Finsbury Pavement to the empty tomb. They had taken their vow. The traffic respected it; vans were stopped.

I can't keep up with them, Peter Walsh thought, as they marched up Whitehall, and sure enough, on they marched, past him, past every one, in their steady way, as if one will worked legs and arms uniformly, and life, with its varieties, its irreticences, had been laid under a pavement of monuments and wreaths and drugged into a stiff yet staring corpse by discipline. One had to respect it; one might laugh; but one had to respect it, he thought. There they go, thought Peter Walsh, pausing at the edge of the pavement; and all the exalted statues, Nelson, Gordon, Havelock, the black, the spectacular images of great soldiers stood looking ahead of them, as if they too had made the same renunciation (Peter Walsh felt he, too, had made it the great renunciation), trampled under the same temptations, and achieved at length a marble stare. But the stare Peter Walsh did not want for himself in the least; though he could respect it in others. He could respect it in boys. They don't know the troubles of the flesh yet, he thought, as the marching boys disappeared in the direction of the Strand – all that I've been through, he thought, crossing the road, and standing under Gordon's statue, Gordon whom as a boy he had worshipped; Gordon standing lonely with one leg raised and his arms crossed, – poor Gordon, he thought.

And just because nobody yet knew he was in London, except Clarissa, and the earth, after the voyage, still seemed an island to him, the strangeness of standing alone, alive, unknown, at half-past eleven in Trafalgar Square overcame him. What is it? Where am I? And why, after all, does one do it? he thought, the divorce seeming all moonshine. And down his mind went flat as a marsh, and three great emotions bowled over him; understanding; a vast philanthropy; and finally, as if the result of the others, an irrepressible, exquisite delight; as if inside his brain, by another hand, strings were pulled, shutters moved, and he, having nothing to do with it, yet stood at the opening of endless avenues down which if he chose he might wander. He had not felt so young for years.

He had escaped! was utterly free – as happens in the downfall of habit when the mind, like an unguarded flame, bows and bends and seems about to blow from its holding. I haven't felt so young for years! thought Peter, escaping (only of course for an hour or so) from being precisely what he was, and feeling like a child who runs out of doors, and sees, as he runs, his old nurse waving at the wrong window. But she's extraordinarily attractive, he thought, as, walking across Trafalgar Square in the direction of the Haymarket, came a young woman who, as she passed Gordon's statue, seemed, Peter Walsh thought (susceptible as he was), to shed veil after veil, until she became the very woman he had always had in mind; young, but stately; merry, but discreet; black, but enchanting.

Straightening himself and stealthily fingering his pocket-knife he started after her to follow this woman, this excitement, which seemed even with its back turned to shed on him a light which connected them, which singled him out, as if the random uproar of the traffic had whispered through hallowed hands his name, not Peter, but his private name which he called himself in his own thought. 'You,' she said, only 'you', saying it with her white gloves and her shoulders. Then the thin long cloak which the wind stirred as she walked past Dent's shop in Cockspur Street blew out with an enveloping kindness, a mournful tenderness, as of arms that would open and take the tired –

But she's not married; she's young; quite young, thought Peter, the red carnation he had seen her wear as she came across Trafalgar Square burning again in his eyes and making her lips red. But she waited at the kerbstone. There was a dignity about her. She was not worldly, like Clarissa; not rich, like Clarissa. Was she, he wondered as she moved, respectable? Witty, with a lizard's flickering tongue, he thought (for one must invent, must allow oneself a little diversion), a cool waiting wit, a darting wit; not noisy.

She moved; she crossed; he followed her. To embarrass her was the last thing he wished. Still if she stopped he would say 'Come and have an ice,' he would say, and she would answer, perfectly simply, 'Oh yes.'

But other people got between them in the street, obstructing him, blotting her out. He pursued; she changed. There was colour in her cheeks; mockery in her eyes; he was an adventurer, reckless, he thought, swift, daring, indeed (landed as he was last night from India) a romantic buccaneer, careless of all these damned proprieties, yellow dressing-gowns, pipes, fishing-rods, in the shop windows; and respectability and evening parties and spruce old men wearing white slips beneath their waistcoats. He was a buccaneer. On and on she went, across Piccadilly, and up Regent Street, ahead of him, her cloak, her gloves, her shoulders combining with the fringes and the laces and the feather boas in the windows to make the spirit of finery and whimsy which dwindled out of the shops on to the pavement, as the light of a lamp goes wavering at night over hedges in the darkness.

Laughing and delightful, she had crossed Oxford Street and Great Portland Street and turned down one of the little streets, and now, and now, the great moment was approaching, for now she slackened, opened her bag, and with one look in his direction, but not at him, one look that bade farewell, summed up the whole situation and dismissed it triumphantly, for ever, had fitted her key, opened the door, and gone! Clarissa's voice saying, Remember my party, Remember my party, sang in his ears. The house was one of those flat red houses with hanging flower-baskets of vague impropriety. It was over.

Well, I've had my fun; I've had it, he thought, looking up

49

at the swinging baskets of pale geraniums. And it was smashed to atoms – his fun, for it was half made up, as he knew very well; invented, this escapade with the girl; made up, as one makes up the better part of life, he thought – making oneself up; making her up; creating an exquisite amusement, and something more. But odd it was, and quite true; all this one could never share – it smashed to atoms.

He turned; went up the street, thinking to find somewhere to sit, till it was time for Lincoln's Inn – for Messrs Hooper and Grateley. Where should he go? No matter. Up the street, then, towards Regent's Park. His boots on the pavement struck out 'no matter'; for it was early, still very early.

It was a splendid morning too. Like the pulse of a perfect heart, life struck straight through the streets. There was no fumbling – no hesitation. Sweeping and swerving, accurately, punctually, noiselessly, there, precisely at the right instant, the motor car stopped at the door. The girl, silk-stockinged, feathered, evanescent, but not to him particularly attractive (for he had had his fling), alighted. Admirable butlers, tawny chow dogs, halls laid in black and white lozenges with white blinds blowing, Peter saw through the opened door and approved of. A splendid achievement in its own way, after all, London; the season; civilization. Coming as he did from a respectable Anglo-Indian family which for at least three generations had administered the affairs of a continent (it's strange, he thought, what a sentiment I have about that, disliking India, and empire, and army as he did), there were moments when civilization, even of this sort, seemed dear to him as a personal possession; moments of pride in England; in butlers; chow dogs; girls in their security. Ridiculous enough, still there it is, he thought. And the doctors and men of business and capable women all going about their business, punctual, alert, robust, seemed to him wholly admirable, good fellows, to whom one would entrust one's life, companions in the art of living, who would see one through. What with one thing and another, the show was really very tolerable; and he would sit down in the shade and smoke.

There was Regent's Park. Yes. As a child he had walked in Regent's Park – odd, he thought, how the thought of childhood keeps coming back to me – the result of seeing Clarissa, perhaps; for women live much more in the past than we do, he thought. They attach themselves to places; and their fathers – a woman's always proud of her father. Bourton was a nice place, a very nice place, but I could never get on with the old man, he thought. There was quite a scene one night – an argument about something or other, what, he could not remember. Politics presumably.

Yes, he remembered Regent's Park; the long straight walk; the little house where one bought air-balls to the left; an absurd statue with an inscription somewhere or other. He looked for an empty seat. He did not want to be bothered (feeling a little drowsy as he did) by people asking him the time. An elderly grey nurse, with a baby asleep in its perambulator – that was the best he could do for himself; sit down at the far end of the seat by that nurse.

She's a queer-looking girl, he thought, suddenly remembering Elizabeth as she came into the room and stood by her mother. Grown big; quite grown-up, not exactly pretty; handsome rather; and she can't be more than eighteen. Probably she doesn't get on with Clarissa. 'There's my Elizabeth' – that sort of thing – why not 'Here's Elizabeth' simply? – trying to make out, like most mothers, that things are what they're not. She trusts to her charm too much, he thought. She overdoes it.

The rich benignant cigar smoke eddied coolly down his throat; he puffed it out again in rings which breasted the air bravely for a moment; blue, circular – I shall try and get a word alone with Elizabeth to-night, he thought – then began to wobble into hour-glass shapes and taper away; odd shapes they take, he thought. Suddenly he closed his eyes, raised his hand with an effort, and threw away the heavy end of his cigar. A great brush swept smooth across his mind, sweeping across it moving branches, children's voices, the shuffle of feet, and people passing, and humming traffic, rising and falling traffic. Down, down he sank into the plumes and feathers of sleep, sank, and was muffled over.

The grey nurse resumed her knitting as Peter Walsh, on the hot seat beside her, began snoring. In her grey dress, moving her hands indefatigably yet quietly, she seemed like the champion of the rights of sleepers, like one of those spectral presences which rise in twilight in woods made of sky and branches. The solitary traveller, haunter of lanes, disturber of ferns, and devastator of great hemlock plants, looking up suddenly, sees the giant figure at the end of the ride.

By conviction an atheist perhaps, he is taken by surprise with moments of extraordinary exaltation. Nothing exists outside us except a state of mind, he thinks; a desire for solace, for relief, for something outside these miserable pigmies, these feeble, these ugly, these craven men and women. But if he can conceive of her, then in some sort she exists, he thinks, and advancing down the path with his eyes upon sky and branches he rapidly endows them with womanhood; sees with amazement how grave they become; how majestically, as the breeze stirs them, they dispense with a dark flutter of the leaves, charity, comprehension, absolution, and then, flinging themselves suddenly aloft, confound the piety of their aspect with a wild carouse.

Such are the visions which proffer great cornucopias full of fruit to the solitary traveller, or murmur in his ear like sirens lolloping away on the green sea waves, or are dashed in his face like bunches of roses, or rise to the surface like pale faces which fishermen flounder through floods to embrace.

Such are the visions which ceaselessly float up, pace beside, put their faces in front of, the actual thing; often overpowering the solitary traveller and taking away from him the sense of the earth, the wish to return, and giving him for substitute a general peace, as if (so he thinks as he advances down the forest ride) all this fever of living were simplicity itself; and myriads of things merged in one thing; and this figure, made of sky and branches as it is, had risen from the troubled sea (he is elderly, past fifty now) as a shape might be sucked up out of the waves to shower down from her magnificent hands, compassion, comprehension, absolution. So, he thinks, may I never go back to the lamp-light; to the sitting-room; never finish my book; never knock out my pipe; never ring for Mrs Turner to clear away; rather let me walk straight on to this great figure, who will, with a toss of her head, mount me on her streamers and let me blow to nothingness with the rest.

Such are the visions. The solitary traveller is soon beyond the wood; and there, coming to the door with shaded eyes, possibly to look for his return, with hands raised, with white apron blowing, is an elderly woman who seems (so powerful is this infirmity) to seek, over the desert, a lost son; to search for a rider destroyed; to be the figure of the mother whose sons have been killed in the battles of the world. So, as the solitary traveller advances down the village street where the women stand knitting and the men dig in the garden, the evening seems ominous; the figures still; as if some august fate, known to them, awaited without fear, were about to sweep them into complete annihilation.

Indoors among ordinary things, the cupboard, the table, the window-sill with its geraniums, suddenly the outline of the landlady, bending to remove the cloth, becomes soft with light, an adorable emblem which only the recollection of cold human contacts forbids us to embrace. She takes the marmalade; she shuts it in the cupboard.

'There is nothing more to-night, sir?'

But to whom does the solitary traveller make reply?

So the elderly nurse knitted over the sleeping baby in Regent's Park. So Peter Walsh snored. He woke with extreme suddenness, saying to himself, 'The death of the soul.'

'Lord, Lord!' he said to himself out loud, stretching and opening his eyes. 'The death of the soul.' The words attached themselves to some scene, to some room, to some past he had been dreaming of. It became clearer; the scene, the room, the past he had been dreaming of.

It was at Bourton that summer, early in the 'nineties, when he was so passionately in love with Clarissa. There were a great many people there, laughing and talking, sitting round a table after tea, and the room was bathed in

yellow light and full of cigarette smoke. They were talking
about a man who had married his housemaid, one of the
neighbouring squires, he had forgotten his name. He had
married his housemaid, and she had been brought to Bourton to call – an awful visit it had been. She was absurdly
overdressed, 'like a cockatoo,' Clarissa had said, imitating
her, and she never stopped talking. On and on she went, on
and on. Clarissa imitated her. Then somebody said – Sally
Seton it was – did it make any real difference to one's feelings to know that before they'd married she had had a
baby? (In those days, in mixed company, it was a bold
thing to say.) He could see Clarissa now, turning bright
pink; somehow contracting; and saying, 'Oh, I shall never
be able to speak to her again!' Whereupon the whole party
sitting round the tea-table seemed to wobble. It was very
uncomfortable.

He hadn't blamed her for minding the fact, since in those
days a girl brought up as she was knew nothing, but it was
her manner that annoyed him; timid; hard; arrogant; prud-
ish. 'The death of the soul.' He had said that instinctively,
ticketing the moment as he used to do – the death of her
soul.

Every one wobbled; every one seemed to bow, as she
spoke, and then to stand up different. He could see Sally
Seton, like a child who has been in mischief, leaning forward, rather flushed, wanting to talk, but afraid, and Clarissa did frighten people. (She was Clarissa's greatest friend,
always about the place, an attractive creature, handsome,
dark, with the reputation in those days of great daring, and
he used to give her cigars, which she smoked in her bedroom, and she had either been engaged to somebody or
quarrelled with her family, and old Parry disliked them both
equally, which was a great bond.) Then Clarissa, still with
an air of being offended with them all, got up, made some
excuse, and went off, alone. As she opened the door, in
came that great shaggy dog which ran after sheep. She flung
herself upon him, went into raptures. It was as if she said to
Peter – it was all aimed at him, he knew – 'I know you
thought me absurd about that woman just now; but see

how extraordinarily sympathetic I am; see how I love my Rob!'

They had always this queer power of communicating without words. She knew directly he criticized her. Then she would do something quite obvious to defend herself, like this fuss with the dog – but it never took him in, he always saw through Clarissa. Not that he said anything, of course; just sat looking glum. It was the way their quarrels often began.

She shut the door. At once he became extremely depressed. It all seemed useless – going on being in love; going on quarrelling; going on making it up, and he wandered off alone, among the outhouses, stables, looking at the horses. (The place was quite a humble one; the Parrys were never very well off; but there were always grooms and stable-boys about – Clarissa loved riding – and an old coachman – what was his name? – an old nurse, old Moody, old Goody, some such name they called her, whom one was taken to visit in a little room with lots of photographs, lots of bird-cages.)

It was an awful evening! He grew more and more gloomy, not about that only; about everything. And he couldn't see her; couldn't explain to her; couldn't have it out. There were always people about – she'd go on as if nothing had happened. That was the devilish part of her – this coldness, this woodenness, something very profound in her, which he had felt again this morning talking to her; an impenetrability. Yet Heaven knows he loved her. She had some queer power of fiddling on one's nerves, turning one's nerves to fiddle-strings, yes.

He had gone into dinner rather late, from some idiotic idea of making himself felt, and had sat down by old Miss Parry – Aunt Helena – Mr Parry's sister, who was supposed to preside. There she sat in her white Cashmere shawl, with her head against the window – a formidable old lady, but kind to him, for he had found her some rare flower, and she was a great botanist, marching off in thick boots with a black tin collecting box slung between her shoulders. He sat down beside her, and couldn't speak. Everything seemed to race past him; he just sat there, eating. And then half-way through dinner he made himself look across at Clarissa for the first time. She was talking to a young man on her right. He had a sudden revelation. 'She will marry that man,' he said to himself. He didn't even know his name.

For of course it was that afternoon, that very afternoon, that Dalloway had come over; and Clarissa called him 'Wickham'; that was the beginning of it all. Somebody had brought him over; and Clarissa got his name wrong. She introduced him to everybody as Wickham. At last he said 'My name is Dalloway!' – that was his first view of Richard – a fair young man, rather awkward, sitting on a deck-chair, and blurting out 'My name is Dalloway!' Sally got hold of it; always after that she called him 'My name is Dalloway!'

He was a prey to revelations at that time. This one – that she would marry Dalloway – was blinding – overwhelming at the moment. There was a sort of – how could he put it? – a sort of ease in her manner to him; something maternal; something gentle. They were talking about politics. All through dinner he tried to hear what they were saying.

Afterwards he could remember standing by old Miss Parry's chair in the drawing-room. Clarissa came up, with her perfect manners, like a real hostess, and wanted to introduce him to some one – spoke as if they had never met before, which enraged him. Yet even then he admired her for it. He admired her courage; her social instinct; he admired her power of carrying things through. 'The perfect hostess,' he said to her, whereupon she winced all over. But he meant her to feel it. He would have done anything to hurt her, after seeing her with Dalloway. So she left him. And he had a feeling that they were all gathered together in a conspiracy against him – laughing and talking – behind his back. There he stood by Miss Parry's chair as though he had been cut out of wood, talking about wild flowers. Never, never had he suffered so infernally! He must have forgotten even to pretend to listen; at last he woke up; he saw Miss Parry looking rather disturbed, rather indignant, with her prominent eyes fixed. He almost cried out that he couldn't attend because he was in Hell! People began going out of the room. He heard them talking about fetching cloaks; about its being cold on the water, and so on. They were going boating on the lake by moonlight – one of Sally's mad ideas. He could hear her describing the moon. And they all went out. He was left quite alone.

'Don't you want to go with them?' said Aunt Helena – poor old lady! – she had guessed. And he turned round and there was Clarissa again. She had come back to fetch him. He was overcome by her generosity – her goodness.

'Come along,' she said. 'They're waiting.'

He had never felt so happy in the whole of his life! Without a word they made it up. They walked down to the lake. He had twenty minutes of perfect happiness. Her voice, her laugh, her dress (something floating, white, crimson), her spirit, her adventurousness; she made them all disembark and explore the island; she startled a hen; she laughed; she sang. And all the time, he knew perfectly well, Dalloway was falling in love with her; she was falling in love with Dalloway; but it didn't seem to matter. Nothing mattered. They sat on the ground and talked – he and Clarissa. They went in and out of each other's minds without any effort. And then in a second it was over. He said to himself as they were getting into the boat, 'She will marry that man,' dully, without any resentment; but it was an obvious thing. Dalloway would marry Clarissa.

Dalloway rowed them in. He said nothing. But somehow as they watched him start, jumping on to his bicycle to ride twenty miles through the woods, wobbling off down the drive, waving his hand and disappearing, he obviously did feel, instinctively, tremendously, strongly, all that; the night; the romance; Clarissa. He deserved to have her.

For himself, he was absurd. His demands upon Clarissa (he could see it now) were absurd. He asked impossible things. He made terrible scenes. She would have accepted him still, perhaps, if he had been less absurd. Sally thought so. She wrote him all that summer long letters; how they had talked of him; how she had praised him, how Clarissa burst into tears! It was an extraordinary summer – all letters, scenes, telegrams – arriving at Bourton early in the morning, hanging about till the servants were up; appalling *tête-à-têtes* with old Mr Parry at breakfast; Aunt Helena formidable but kind; Sally sweeping him off for talks in the vegetable garden; Clarissa in bed with headaches.

The final scene, the terrible scene which he believed had mattered more than anything in the whole of his life (it might be an exaggeration – but still, so it did seem now), happened at three o'clock in the afternoon of a very hot day. It was a trifle that led up to it – Sally at lunch saying something about Dalloway, and calling him 'My name is Dalloway'; whereupon Clarissa suddenly stiffened, coloured, in a way she had, and rapped out sharply, 'We've had enough of that feeble joke.' That was all; but for him it was as if she had said, 'I'm only amusing myself with you; I've an understanding with Richard Dalloway.' So he took it. He had not slept for nights. 'It's got to be finished one way or the other,' he said to himself. He sent a note to her by Sally asking her to meet him by the fountain at three. 'Something very important has happened,' he scribbled at the end of it.

The fountain was in the middle of a little shrubbery, far from the house, with shrubs and trees all round it. There she came, even before the time, and they stood with the fountain between them, the spout (it was broken) dribbling water incessantly. How sights fix themselves upon the mind! For example, the vivid green moss.

She did not move. 'Tell me the truth, tell me the truth,' he kept on saying. He felt as if his forehead would burst. She seemed contracted, petrified. She did not move. 'Tell me the truth,' he repeated, when suddenly that old man Breit-kopf popped his head in carrying *The Times*; stared at them; gaped; and went away. They neither of them moved. 'Tell me the truth,' he repeated. He felt that he was grinding against something physically hard; she was unyielding. She was like iron, like flint, rigid up the backbone. And when she said, 'It's no use. It's no use. This is the end' – after he had spoken for hours, it seemed, with the tears running down his cheeks – it was as if she had hit him in the face. She turned, she left him, she went away.

'Clarissa!' he cried. 'Clarissa!' But she never came back.

It was over. He went away that night. He never saw her again.

It was awful, he cried, awful, awful!

Still, the sun was hot. Still, one got over things. Still, life had a way of adding day to day. Still, he thought, yawning and beginning to take notice – Regent's Park had changed very little since he was a boy, except for the squirrels – still, presumably there were compensations – when little Elise Mitchell, who had been picking up pebbles to add to the pebble collection which she and her brother were making on the nursery mantelpiece, plumped her handful down on the nurse's knee and scudded off again full tilt into a lady's legs. Peter Walsh laughed out.

But Lucrezia Warren Smith was saying to herself, It's wicked; why should I suffer? she was asking, as she walked down the broad path. No; I can't stand it any longer, she was saying, having left Septimus, who wasn't Septimus any longer, to say hard, cruel, wicked things, to talk to himself, to talk to a dead man, on the seat over there; when the child ran full tilt into her, fell flat, and burst out crying.

That was comforting rather. She stood her upright, dusted her frock, kissed her.

But for herself she had done nothing wrong; she had loved Septimus; she had been happy; she had had a beautiful home, and there her sisters lived still, making hats. Why should *she* suffer?

The child ran straight back to its nurse, and Rezia saw her scolded, comforted, taken up by the nurse who put down her knitting, and the kind-looking man gave her his watch to blow open to comfort her – but why should *she* be exposed? Why not left in Milan? Why tortured? Why?

Slightly waved by tears, the broad path, the nurse, the man in grey, the perambulator, rose and fell before her eyes. To be rocked by this malignant torturer was her lot. But why? She was like a bird sheltering under the thin hollow of a leaf, who blinks at the sun when the leaf moves; starts at the crack of a dry twig. She was exposed; she was surrounded by the enormous trees, vast clouds of an indifferent world, exposed; tortured; and why should she suffer? Why?

She frowned; she stamped her foot. She must go back again to Septimus since it was almost time for them to be going to Sir William Bradshaw. She must go back and tell him, go back to him sitting there on the green chair under the tree, talking to himself, or to that dead man Evans, whom she had only seen once for a moment in the shop. He had seemed a nice quiet man; a great friend of Septimus's, and he had been killed in the War. But such things happen to every one. Every one has friends who were killed in the War. Every one gives up something when they marry. She had given up her home. She had come to live here, in this awful city. But Septimus let himself think about horrible things, as she could too, if she tried. He had grown stranger and stranger. He said people were talking behind the bedroom walls. Mrs Filmer thought it odd. He saw things too – he had seen an old woman's head in the middle of a fern. Yet he could be happy when he chose. They went to Hampton Court on top of a bus, and they were perfectly happy. All the little red and yellow flowers were out on the grass, like floating lamps he said, and talked and chattered and laughed, making up stories. Suddenly he said, 'Now we will kill ourselves,' when they were standing by the river, and he looked at it with a look which she had seen in his eyes when a train went by, or an omnibus – a look as if something fascinated him; and she felt he was going from her and she caught him by the arm. But going home he was perfectly quiet – perfectly reasonable. He would argue with her about killing themselves; and explain how wicked people were; how he could see them making up lies as they passed in the street. He knew all their thoughts, he said; he knew everything. He knew the meaning of the world, he said.

Then when they got back he could hardly walk. He lay on the sofa and made her hold his hand to prevent him from falling down, down, he cried, into the flames! and saw faces laughing at him, calling him horrible disgusting names, from the walls and hands pointing round the screen. Yet they were quite alone. But he began to talk aloud, answering people, arguing, laughing, crying, getting very excited and making her write things down. Perfect nonsense it was; about death; about Miss Isabel Pole. She could stand it no longer. She would go back.

She was close to him now, could see him staring at the sky, muttering, clasping his hands. Yet Dr Holmes said there was nothing the matter with him. What, then, had happened – why had he gone, then, why, when she sat by him, did he start, frown at her, move away, and point at her hand, take her hand, look at it terrified?

Was it that she had taken off her wedding ring? 'My hand has grown so thin,' she said; 'I have put it in my purse,' she told him.

He dropped her hand. Their marriage was over, he thought, with agony, with relief. The rope was cut; he mounted; he was free, as it was decreed that he, Septimus, the lord of men, should be free; alone (since his wife had thrown away her wedding ring; since she had left him), he Septimus, was alone, called forth in advance of the mass of men to hear the truth, to learn the meaning, which now at last, after all the toils of civilization – Greeks, Romans, Shakespeare, Darwin, and now himself – was to be given whole to ... 'To whom?' he asked aloud, 'To the Prime Minister,' the voices which rustled above his head replied. The supreme secret must be told to the Cabinet; first, that trees are alive; next, there is no crime; next, love, universal love, he muttered, gasping, trembling, painfully drawing out these profound truths which needed, so deep were they, so difficult, an immense effort to speak out, but the world was entirely changed by them for ever.

No crime; love; he repeated, fumbling for his card and pencil, when a Skye terrier snuffed his trousers and he started in an agony of fear. It was turning into a man! He could not watch it happen! It was horrible, terrible to see a dog become a man! At once the dog trotted away.

Heaven was divinely merciful, infinitely benignant. It spared him, pardoned his weakness. But what was the scientific explanation (for one must be scientific above all things)? Why could he see through bodies, see into the future, when dogs will become men? It was the heat wave presumably, operating upon a brain made sensitive by eons of evolution. Scientifically speaking, the flesh was melted off the world. His body was macerated until only the nerve fibres were left. It was spread like a veil upon a rock.

He lay back in his chair, exhausted but upheld. He lay resting, waiting, before he again interpreted, with effort, with agony, to mankind. He lay very high, on the back of the world. The earth thrilled beneath him. Red flowers grew through his flesh; their stiff leaves rustled by his head. Music began clanging against the rocks up here. It is a motor horn down in the street, he muttered; but up here it cannoned from rock to rock, divided, met in shocks of sound which rose in smooth columns (that music should be visible was a discovery) and became an anthem, an anthem twined round now by a shepherd boy's piping (That's an old man playing a penny whistle by the public-house, he muttered) which, as the boy stood still, came bubbling from his pipe, and then, as he climbed higher, made its exquisite plaint while the traffic passed beneath. This boy's elegy is played among the traffic, thought Septimus. Now he withdraws up into the snows, and roses hang about him – the thick red roses which grow on my bedroom wall, he reminded himself. The music stopped. He has his penny, he reasoned it out, and has gone on to the next public-house.

But he himself remained high on his rock, like a drowned sailor on a rock. I leant over the edge of the boat and fell down, he thought. I went under the sea. I have been dead, and yet am now alive, but let me rest still, he begged (he was talking to himself again – it was awful, awful!); and as, before waking, the voices of birds and the sound of wheels chime and chatter in a queer harmony, grow louder and louder, and the sleeper feels himself drawing to the shores of life, so he felt himself drawing towards life, the sun growing hotter, cries sounding louder, something tremendous about to happen.

He had only to open his eyes; but a weight was on them; a fear. He strained; he pushed; he looked; he saw Regent's

Park before him. Long streamers of sunlight fawned at his feet. The trees waved, brandished. We welcome, the world seemed to say; we accept; we create. Beauty, the world seemed to say. And as if to prove it (scientifically) wherever he looked, at the houses, at the railings, at the antelopes stretching over the palings, beauty sprang instantly. To watch a leaf quivering in the rush of air was an exquisite joy. Up in the sky swallows swooping, swerving, flinging themselves in and out, round and round, yet always with perfect control as if elastics held them; and the flies rising and falling; and the sun spotting now this leaf, now that, in mockery, dazzling it with soft gold in pure good temper; and now and again some chime (it might be a motor horn) tinkling divinely on the grass stalks – all of this, calm and reasonable as it was, made out of ordinary things as it was, was the truth now; beauty, that was the truth now. Beauty was everywhere.

'It is time,' said Rezia.

The word 'time' split its husk; poured its riches over him; and from his lips fell like shells, like shavings from a plane, without his making them, hard, white, imperishable, words, and flew to attach themselves to their places in an ode to Time; an immortal ode to Time. He sang. Evans answered from behind the tree. The dead were in Thessaly, Evans sang, among the orchids. There they waited till the War was over, and now the dead, now Evans himself –

'For God's sake don't come!' Septimus cried out. For he could not look upon the dead.

But the branches parted. A man in grey was actually walking towards them. It was Evans! But no mud was on him; no wounds; he was not changed. I must tell the whole world, Septimus cried, raising his hand (as the dead man in the grey suit came nearer), raising his hand like some colossal figure who has lamented the fate of man for ages in the desert alone with his hands pressed to his forehead, furrows of despair on his cheeks, and now sees light on the desert's edge which broadens and strikes the iron-black figure (and Septimus half rose from his chair), and with legions of men prostrate behind him he, the giant mourner, receives for one moment on his face the whole –

'But I am so unhappy, Septimus,' said Rezia, trying to make him sit down.

The millions lamented; for ages they had sorrowed. He would turn round, he would tell them in a few moments, only a few moments more, of this relief, of this joy, of this astonishing revelation –

'The time, Septimus,' Rezia repeated. 'What is the time?'

He was talking, he was starting, this man must notice him. He was looking at them.

'I will tell you the time,' said Septimus, very slowly, very drowsily, smiling mysteriously at the dead man in the grey suit. As he sat smiling, the quarter struck – the quarter to twelve.

And that is being young, Peter Walsh thought as he passed them. To be having an awful scene – the poor girl looked absolutely desperate – in the middle of the morning. But what was it about? he wondered; what had the young man in the overcoat been saying to her to make her look like that; what awful fix had they got themselves into, both to look so desperate as that on a fine summer morning? The amusing thing about coming back to England, after five years, was the way it made, anyhow the first days, things stand out as if one had never seen them before; lovers squabbling under a tree; the domestic family life of the parks. Never had he seen London look so enchanting – the softness of the distances; the richness; the greenness; the civilization, after India, he thought, strolling across the grass.

This susceptibility to impressions had been his undoing, no doubt. Still at his age he had, like a boy or a girl even, these alternations of mood; good days, bad days, for no reason whatever, happiness from a pretty face, downright misery at the sight of a frump. After India of course one fell in love with every woman one met. There was a freshness about them; even the poorest dressed better than five years ago surely; and to his eye the fashions had never been so becoming; the long black cloaks; the slimness; the elegance; and then the delicious and apparently universal habit of paint. Every woman, even the most respectable, had roses blooming under glass; lips cut with a knife; curls of Indian ink; there was design, art, everywhere; a change of some sort had undoubtedly taken place. What did the young people think about? Peter Walsh asked himself.

Those five years – 1918 to 1923 – had been, he suspected, somehow very important. People looked different. Newspapers seemed different. Now, for instance, there was a man writing quite openly in one of the respectable weeklies about water-closets. That you couldn't have done ten years ago – written quite openly about water-closets in a respectable weekly. And then this taking out a stick of rouge, or a powder-puff, and making up in public. On board ship coming home there were lots of young men and girls – Betty and Bertie he remembered in particular – carrying on quite openly; the old mother sitting and watching them with her knitting, cool as a cucumber. The girl would stand still and powder her nose in front of every one. And they weren't engaged; just having a good time; no feelings hurt on either side. As hard as nails she was – Betty Whatshername – but a thorough good sort. She would make a very good wife at thirty – she would marry when it suited her to marry; marry some rich man and live in a large house near Manchester.

Who was it now who had done that? Peter Walsh asked himself, turning into the Broad Walk – married a rich man and lived in a large house near Manchester? Somebody who had written him a long, gushing letter quite lately about 'blue hydrangeas'. It was seeing blue hydrangeas that made her think of him and the old days – Sally Seton, of course! It was Sally Seton – the last person in the world one would have expected to marry a rich man and live in a large house near Manchester, the wild, the daring, the romantic Sally!

But of all that ancient lot, Clarissa's friends – Whitbreads, Kindersleys, Cunninghams, Kinloch Jones's – Sally was probably the best. She tried to get hold of things by the right end anyhow. She saw through Hugh Whitbread anyhow – the admirable Hugh – when Clarissa and the rest were at his feet.

'The Whitbreads?' he could hear her saying. 'Who are the Whitbreads? Coal merchants. Respectable tradespeople.'

Hugh she detested for some reason. He thought of nothing but his own appearance, she said. He ought to have been a Duke. He would be certain to marry one of the Royal Princesses. And of course Hugh had the most extraordinary, the most natural, the most sublime respect for the British aristocracy of any human being he had ever come across. Even Clarissa had to own that. Oh, but he was such a dear, so unselfish, gave up shooting to please his old mother – remembered his aunts' birthdays, and so on.

Sally, to do her justice, saw through all that. One of the things he remembered best was an argument one Sunday morning at Bourton about women's rights (that antediluvian topic), when Sally suddenly lost her temper, flared up, and told Hugh that he represented all that was most detestable in British middle-class life. She told him that she considered him responsible for the state of 'those poor girls in Piccadilly' – Hugh, the perfect gentleman, poor Hugh! – never did a man look more horrified! She did it on purpose, she said afterwards (for they used to get together in the vegetable garden and compare notes). 'He's read nothing, thought nothing, felt nothing,' he could hear her saying in that very emphatic voice which carried so much farther than she knew. The stable boys had more life in them than Hugh, she said. He was a perfect specimen of the public-school type, she said. No country but England could have produced him. She was really spiteful, for some reason; had some grudge against him. Something had happened – he forgot what – in the smoking-room. He had insulted her – kissed her? Incredible! Nobody believed a word against Hugh, of course. Who could? Kissing Sally in the smoking-room! If it had been some Honourable Edith or Lady Violet, perhaps; but not that ragamuffin Sally without a penny to her name, and a father or a mother gambling at Monte Carlo. For of all the people he had ever met Hugh was the greatest snob – the most obsequious – no, he didn't cringe exactly. He was too much of a prig for that. A first-rate valet was the obvious comparison – somebody who walked behind carrying suitcases; could be trusted to send telegrams – indispensable to hostesses. And he'd found his job – married his Honourable

Evelyn; got some little post at Court, looked after the King's cellars, polished the Imperial shoe-buckles, went about in knee-breeches and lace ruffles. How remorseless life is! A little job at Court!

He had married this lady, the Honourable Evelyn, and they lived hereabouts, so he thought (looking at the pompous houses overlooking the Park), for he had lunched there once in a house which had, like all Hugh's possessions, something that no house could possibly have – linen cupboards it might have been. You had to go and look at them – you had to spend a great deal of time always admiring whatever it was – linen cupboards, pillow-cases, old oak furniture, pictures, which Hugh had picked up for an old song. But Mrs Hugh sometimes gave the show away. She was one of those obscure mouse-like little women who admire big men. She was almost negligible. Then suddenly she would say something quite unexpected – something sharp. She had the relics of the grand manner, perhaps. The steam coal was a little too strong for her – it made the atmosphere thick. And so there they lived, with their linen cupboards and their old masters and their pillow-cases fringed with real lace, at the rate of five or ten thousand a year presumably, while he, who was two years older than Hugh, cadged for a job.

At fifty-three he had to come and ask them to put him into some secretary's office, to find him some usher's job teaching little boys Latin, at the beck and call of some mandarin in an office, something that brought in five hundred a year; for if he married Daisy, even with his pension, they could never do on less. Whitbread could do it presumably; or Dalloway. He didn't mind what he asked Dalloway. He was a thorough good sort; a bit limited; a bit thick in the head; yes; but a thorough good sort. Whatever he took up he did in the same matter-of-fact sensible way; without a touch of imagination, without a spark of brilliancy, but with the inexplicable niceness of his type. He ought to have been a country gentleman – he was wasted on politics. He was at his best out of doors, with horses and dogs – how good he was, for instance, when that great shaggy dog of Clarissa's got caught in a trap and had its paw half torn off, and Clarissa turned faint and Dalloway did the whole thing; bandaged, made splints; told Clarissa not to be a fool. That was what she liked him for, perhaps – that was what she needed. 'Now, my dear, don't be a fool. Hold this – fetch that,' all the time talking to the dog as if it were a human being.

But how could she swallow all that stuff about poetry? How could she let him hold forth about Shakespeare? Seriously and solemnly Richard Dalloway got on his hind legs and said that no decent man ought to read Shakespeare's sonnets because it was like listening at keyholes (besides, the relationship was not one that he approved). No decent man ought to let his wife visit a deceased wife's sister. Incredible! The only thing to do was to pelt him with sugared almonds – it was at dinner. But Clarissa sucked it all in; thought it so honest of him; so independent of him; Heaven knows if she didn't think him the most original mind she'd ever met!

That was one of the bonds between Sally and himself. There was a garden where they used to walk, a walled-in place, with rose-bushes and giant cauliflowers – he could remember Sally tearing off a rose, stopping to exclaim at the beauty of the cabbage leaves in the moonlight (it was extraordinary how vividly it all came back to him, things he hadn't thought of for years), while she implored him, half laughing of course, to carry off Clarissa, to save her from the Hughs and the Dalloways and all the other 'perfect gentlemen' who would 'stifle her soul' (she wrote reams of poetry in those days), make a mere hostess of her, encourage her worldliness. But one must do Clarissa justice. She wasn't going to marry Hugh anyhow. She had a perfectly clear notion of what she wanted. Her emotions were all on the surface. Beneath, she was very shrewd – a far better judge of character than Sally, for instance, and with it all, purely feminine; with that extraordinary gift, that woman's gift, of making a world of her own wherever she happened to be. She came into a room; she stood, as he had often seen her, in a doorway with lots of people round her. But it was Clarissa one remembered. Not that she was striking; not beautiful at all; there was nothing picturesque about her; she never said anything specially clever; there she was, however; there she was.

No, no, no! He was not in love with her any more! He only felt, after seeing her that morning, among her scissors and silks, making ready for the party, unable to get away from the thought of her; she kept coming back and back like a sleeper jolting against him in a railway carriage; which was not being in love, of course; it was thinking of her, criticizing her, starting again, after thirty years, trying to explain her. The obvious thing to say of her was that she was worldly; cared too much for rank and society and getting on in the world – which was true in a sense; she had admitted it to him. (You could always get her to own up if you took the trouble; she was honest.) What she would say was that she hated frumps, fogies, failures, like himself presumably; thought people had no right to slouch about with their hands in their pockets; must do something, be something; and these great swells, these Duchesses, these hoary old Countesses one met in her drawing-room, unspeakably remote as he felt them to be from anything that mattered a straw, stood for something real to her. Lady Bexborough, she said once, held herself upright (so did Clarissa herself; she never lounged in any sense of the word; she was straight as a dart, a little rigid in fact). She said they had a kind of courage which the older she grew the more she respected. In all this there was a great deal of Dalloway, of course; a great deal of the public-spirited, British Empire, tariff-reform, governing-class spirit, which had grown on her, as it tends to do. With twice his wits, she had to see things through his eyes – one of the tragedies of married life. With a mind of her own, she must always be quoting Richard – as if one couldn't know to a tittle what Richard thought by reading the *Morning Post* of a morning! These parties, for example, were all for him, or for her idea of him (to do Richard justice he would have been happier farming in Norfolk). She made her drawing-room a sort of meeting-place; she had a genius for it. Over and over again he had seen her take some raw youth, twist him, turn him, wake him up; set him going. Infinite numbers of dull people conglomerated round her, of course. But odd unexpected people turned up; an artist sometimes; sometimes a writer; queer fish in that atmosphere. And behind it all was that network of visiting, leaving cards, being kind to people; running about with bunches of flowers, little presents; So-and-so was going to France – must have an air-cushion; a real drain on her strength; all that interminable traffic that women of her sort keep up; but she did it genuinely, from a natural instinct.

Oddly enough, she was one of the most thorough-going sceptics he had ever met, and possibly (this was a theory he used to make up to account for her, so transparent in some ways, so inscrutable in others), possibly she said to herself, As we are a doomed race, chained to a sinking ship (her favourite reading as a girl was Huxley and Tyndall, and they were fond of these nautical metaphors), as the whole thing is a bad joke, let us, at any rate, do our part; mitigate the sufferings of our fellow-prisoners (Huxley again); decorate the dungeon with flowers and air-cushions; be as decent as we possibly can. Those ruffians, the Gods, shan't have it all their own way – her notion being that the Gods, who never lost a chance of hurting, thwarting and spoiling human lives, were seriously put out if, all the same, you behaved like a lady. That phase came directly after Sylvia's death – that horrible affair. To see your own sister killed by a falling tree (all Justin Parry's fault – all his carelessness) before your very eyes, a girl too on the verge of life, the most gifted of them, Clarissa always said, was enough to turn one bitter. Later she wasn't so positive, perhaps; she thought there were no Gods; no one was to blame; and so she evolved this atheist's religion of doing good for the sake of goodness.

And of course she enjoyed life immensely. It was her nature to enjoy (though, goodness only knows, she had her reserves; it was a mere sketch, he often felt, that even he, after all these years, could make of Clarissa). Anyhow there was no bitterness in her; none of that sense of moral virtue which is so repulsive in good women. She enjoyed practically everything. If you walked with her in Hyde Park, now it was a bed of tulips, now a child in a perambulator, now some absurd little drama she made up on the spur of the moment. (Very likely she would have talked to those lovers, if she had thought them unhappy.) She had a sense of comedy that was really exquisite, but she needed people, always people, to bring it out, with the inevitable result that she frittered her time away, lunching, dining, giving these incessant parties of hers, talking nonsense, saying things she didn't mean, blunting the edge of her mind, losing her discrimination. There she would sit at the head of the table taking infinite pains with some old buffer who might be useful to Dalloway – they knew the most appalling bores in Europe – or in came Elizabeth and everything must give way to *her*. She was at a High School, at the inarticulate stage last time he was over, a round-eyed, pale-faced girl, with nothing of her mother in her, a silent, stolid creature, who took it all as a matter of course, let her mother make a fuss of her, and then said 'May I go now?' like a child of four; going off, Clarissa explained, with that mixture of amusement and pride which Dalloway himself seemed to rouse in her, to play hockey. And now Elizabeth was 'out', presumably; thought him an old fogy, laughed at her mother's friends. Ah well, so be it. The compensation of growing old, Peter Walsh thought, coming out of Regent's Park, and holding his hat in his hand, was simply this; that the passions remain as strong as ever, but one has gained – at last! – the power which adds the supreme flavour to existence – the power of taking hold of experience, of turning it round, slowly, in the light.

A terrible confession it was (he put his hat on again), but now, at the age of fifty-three, one scarcely needed people any more. Life itself, every moment of it, every drop of it, here, this instant, now, in the sun, in Regent's Park, was enough. Too much, indeed. A whole lifetime was too short to bring out, now that one had acquired the power, the full flavour; to extract every ounce of pleasure, every shade of meaning; which both were so much more solid than they used to be, so much less personal. It was impossible that he should ever suffer again as Clarissa had made him suffer. For hours at a time (pray God that one might say these things without being overheard!), for hours and days he never thought of Daisy.

Could it be that he was in love with her, then, remembering the misery, the torture, the extraordinary passion of those days? It was a different thing altogether – a much pleasanter thing – the truth being, of course, that now *she* was in love with *him*. And that perhaps was the reason why, when the ship actually sailed, he felt an extraordinary relief, wanted nothing so much as to be alone; was annoyed to find all her little attentions – cigars, notes, a rug for the voyage – in his cabin. Every one if they were honest would say the same; one doesn't want people after fifty; one doesn't want to go on telling women they are pretty; that's what most men of fifty would say, Peter Walsh thought, if they were honest.

But then these astonishing accesses of emotion – bursting into tears this morning, what was all that about? What could Clarissa have thought of him? thought him a fool presumably, not for the first time. It was jealousy that was at the bottom of it – jealousy which survives every other passion of mankind, Peter Walsh thought, holding his pocket-knife at arm's length. She had been meeting Major Orde, Daisy said in her last letter; said it on purpose, he knew; said it to make him jealous; he could see her wrinkling her forehead as she wrote, wondering what she could say to hurt him; and yet it made no difference; he was furious! All this pother of coming to England and seeing lawyers wasn't to marry her, but to prevent her from marrying anybody else. That was what tortured him, that was what came over him when he saw Clarissa so calm, so cold, so intent on her dress or whatever it was; realizing what she might have spared him, what she had reduced him to – a whimpering, snivelling old ass. But women, he thought, shutting his pocket-knife, don't know what passion is. They don't know the meaning of it to men. Clarissa was as cold as an icicle There she would sit on the sofa by his side, let him take her hand, give him one kiss on the cheek – Here he was at the crossing.

A sound interrupted him; a frail quivering sound, a voice

bubbling up without direction, vigour, beginning or end, running weakly and shrilly and with an absence of all human meaning into

> *ee um fah um so*
> *foo swee too eem oo –*

the voice of no age or sex, the voice of an ancient spring spouting from the earth; which issued, just opposite Regent's Park Tube Station, from a tall quivering shape, like a funnel, like a rusty pump, like a wind-beaten tree for ever barren of leaves which lets the wind run up and down its branches singing

> *ee um fah um so*
> *foo swee too eem oo,*

and rocks and creaks and moans in the eternal breeze.

Through all ages – when the pavement was grass, when it was swamp, through the age of tusk and mammoth, through the age of silent sunrise – the battered woman – for she wore a skirt – with her right hand exposed, her left clutching at her side, stood singing of love – love which has lasted a million years, she sang, love which prevails, and millions of years ago her lover, who had been dead these centuries, had walked, she crooned, with her in May; but in the course of ages, long as summer days, and flaming, she remembered, with nothing but red asters, he had gone; death's enormous sickle had swept those tremendous hills, and when at last she laid her hoary and immensely aged head on the earth, now become a mere cinder of ice, she implored the Gods to lay by her side a bunch of purple heather, there on her high burial place which the last rays of the last sun caressed; for then the pageant of the universe would be over.

As the ancient song bubbled up opposite Regent's Park Tube Station, still the earth seemed green and flowery; still, though it issued from so rude a mouth, a mere hole in the earth, muddy too, matted with root fibres and tangled grasses, still the old bubbling burbling song, soaking through the knotted roots of infinite ages, and skeletons and treasure, streamed away in rivulets over the pavement and all along the Marylebone Road, and down towards Euston, fertilising, leaving a damp stain.

Still remembering how once in some primeval May she had walked with her lover, this rusty pump, this battered old woman with one hand exposed for coppers, the other clutching her side, would still be there in ten million years, remembering how once she had walked in May, where the sea flows now, with whom it did not matter – he was a man, oh yes, a man who had loved her. But the passage of ages had blurred the clarity of that ancient May day; the bright-petalled flowers were hoar and silver frosted; and she no longer saw, when she implored him (as she did now quite clearly) 'look in my eyes with thy sweet eyes intently,' she no longer saw brown eyes, black whiskers or sunburnt face, but only a looming shape, a shadow shape, to which, with the bird-like freshness of the very aged, she still twittered 'give me your hand and let me press it gently' (Peter Walsh couldn't help giving the poor creature a coin as he stepped into his taxi), 'and if some one should see, what matter they?' she demanded; and her fist clutched at her side, and she smiled, pocketing her shilling, and all peering inquisitive eyes seemed blotted out, and the passing generations – the pavement was crowded with bustling middle-class people – vanished, like leaves, to be trodden under, to be soaked and steeped and made mould of by that eternal spring –

ee um fah um so
foo swee too eem oo.

'Poor old woman,' said Rezia Warren Smith.

Oh, poor old wretch! she said, waiting to cross.

Suppose it was a wet night? Suppose one's father, or somebody who had known one in better days had happened to pass, and saw one standing there in the gutter? And where did she sleep at night?

Cheerfully, almost gaily, the invincible thread of sound wound up into the air like the smoke from a cottage chimney, winding up clean beech trees and issuing in a tuft of blue smoke among the topmost leaves. 'And if some one should see, what matter they?'

Since she was so unhappy, for weeks and weeks now, Rezia had given meanings to things that happened, almost felt sometimes that she must stop people in the street, if they looked good, kind people, just to say to them 'I am unhappy'; and this old woman singing in the street 'if someone should see, what matter they?' made her suddenly quite sure that everything was going to be right. They were going to Sir William Bradshaw; she thought his name sounded nice; he would cure Septimus at once. And then there was a brewer's cart; and the grey horses had upright bristles of straw in their tails; there were newspaper placards. It was a silly, silly dream, being unhappy.

So they crossed, Mr and Mrs Septimus Warren Smith, and was there, after all, anything to draw attention to them, anything to make a passer-by suspect here is a young man who carries in him the greatest message in the world, and is, moreover, the happiest man in the world, and the most miserable? Perhaps they walked more slowly than other people, and there was something hesitating, trailing, in the man's walk, but what more natural for a clerk, who has not been in the West End on a week-day at this hour for years, than to keep looking at the sky, looking at this, that and the other, as if Portland Place were a room he had come into when the family are away, the chandeliers being hung in holland bags, and the caretaker, as she lets in long shafts of dusty light upon deserted, queer-looking arm-chairs, lifting one corner of the long blinds, explains to the visitors what a wonderful place it is; how wonderful, but at the same time, he thinks, how strange.

To look at, he might have been a clerk, but of the better sort; for he wore brown boots; his hands were educated; so, too, his profile – his angular, big-nosed, intelligent, sensitive profile; but not his lips altogether, for they were loose; and his eyes (as eyes tend to be), eyes merely; hazel; large; so that he was, on the whole, a border case, neither one thing nor the other; might end with a house at Purley and a motor car, or continue renting apartments in back streets all his life; one of those half-educated, self-educated men whose education is all learnt from books borrowed from public libraries, read in the evening after the day's work, on the advice of well-known authors consulted by letter.

As for the other experiences, the solitary ones, which people go through alone, in their bedrooms, in their offices, walking the fields and the streets of London, he had them; had left home, a mere boy, because of his mother; she lied; because he came down to tea for the fiftieth time with his hands unwashed; because he could see no future for a poet in Stroud; and so, making a confidant of his little sister, had gone to London leaving an absurd note behind him, such as great men have written, and the world has read later when the story of their struggles has become famous.

London has swallowed up many millions of young men called Smith; thought nothing of fantastic Christian names like Septimus with which their parents have thought to distinguish them. Lodging off the Euston Road, there were experiences, again experiences, such as change a face in two years from a pink innocent oval to a face lean, contracted, hostile. But of all this what could the most observant of friends have said except what a gardener says when he opens the conservatory door in the morning and finds a new blossom on his plant : It has flowered; flowered from vanity, ambition, idealism, passion, loneliness, courage, laziness, the usual seeds, which all muddled up (in a room off the Euston Road), made him shy, and stammering, made him anxious to improve himself, made him fall in love with Miss Isabel Pole, lecturing in the Waterloo Road upon Shakespeare.

Was he not like Keats? she asked; and reflected how she might give him a taste of *Antony and Cleopatra* and the rest; lent him books; wrote him scraps of letters; and lit in him such a fire as burns only once in a lifetime, without heat, flickering a red-gold flame infinitely ethereal and insubstantial over Miss Pole; *Antony and Cleopatra*; and the Waterloo Road. He thought her beautiful, believed her impeccably wise; dreamed of her, wrote poems to her, which, ignoring the subject, she corrected in red ink; he saw her, one summer evening, walking in a green dress in a square. 'It has flowered,' the gardener might have said, had he opened the door; had he come in, that is to say, any night about this time, and found him writing; found him tearing up his writing; found him finishing a masterpiece at three o'clock in the morning and running out to pace the streets, and visiting churches, and fasting one day, drinking another, devouring Shakespeare, Darwin, *The History of Civilization*, and Bernard Shaw.

Something was up, Mr Brewer knew; Mr Brewer, managing clerk at Sibleys and Arrowsmiths, auctioneers, valuers, land and estate agents; something was up, he thought, and, being paternal with his young men, and thinking very highly of Smith's abilities, and prophesying that he would, in ten or fifteen years, succeed to the leather arm-chair in the inner room under the skylight with the deed-boxes round him, 'if he keeps his health,' said Mr Brewer, and that was the danger – he looked weakly; advised football, invited him to supper and was seeing his way to consider recommending a rise of salary, when something happened which threw out many of Mr Brewer's calculations, took away his ablest young fellows, and eventually, so prying and insidious were the fingers of the European War, smashed a plaster cast of Ceres, ploughed a hole in the geranium beds, and utterly ruined the cook's nerves at Mr Brewer's establishment at Muswell Hill.

Septimus was one of the first to volunteer. He went to France to save an England which consisted almost entirely of Shakespeare's plays and Miss Isabel Pole in a green dress walking in a square. There in the trenches the change which Mr Brewer desired when he advised football was produced instantly; he developed manliness; he was promoted; he drew the attention, indeed the affection of his officer, Evans by name. It was a case of two dogs playing on a hearth-rug; one worrying a paper screw, snarling, snapping, giving a pinch, now and then, at the old dog's ear; the other lying somnolent, blinking at the fire, raising a paw, turning and growling good-temperedly. They had to be together, share with each other, fight with each other, quarrel with each other. But when Evans (Rezia, who had only seen him once, called him 'a quiet man', a sturdy red-haired man, undemonstrative in the company of women), when Evans was killed, just before the Armistice, in Italy, Septimus, far from show-ing any emotion or recognizing that here was the end of a friendship, congratulated himself upon feeling very little and very reasonably. The War had taught him. It was sub-lime. He had gone through the whole show, friendship, European War, death, had won promotion, was still under thirty and was bound to survive. He was right there. The last shells missed him. He watched them explode with in-difference. When peace came he was in Milan, billeted in the house of an innkeeper with a courtyard, flowers in tubs, little tables in the open, daughters making hats, and to Lucrezia, the younger daughter, he became engaged one evening when the panic was on him – that he could not feel.

For now that it was all over, truce signed, and the dead buried, he had, especially in the evening, these sudden thunder-claps of fear. He could not feel. As he opened the door of the room where the Italian girls sat making hats, he could see them; could hear them; they were rubbing wires among coloured beads in saucers; they were turning buck-ram shapes this way and that; the table was all strewn with feathers, spangles, silks, ribbons; scissors were rapping on the table; but something failed him; he could not feel. Still, scis-sors rapping, girls laughing, hats being made protected him; he was assured of safety; he had a refuge. But he could not sit there all night. There were moments of waking in the early morning. The bed was falling; he was falling. Oh for the scissors and the lamplight and the buckram shapes! He asked Lucrezia to marry him, the younger of the two, the gay, the frivolous, with those little artist's fingers that she would hold up and say 'It is all in them.' Silk, feathers, what not, were alive to them.

'It is the hat that matters most,' she would say, when they walked out together. Every hat that passed she would examine; and the cloak and the dress and the way the woman held herself. Ill-dressing, over-dressing she stigmat-ized, not savagely, rather with impatient movements of the hands, like those of a painter who puts from him some ob-vious well-meant glaring imposture; and then, generously, but always critically, she would welcome a shop-girl who had turned her little bit of stuff gallantly, or praise, wholly, with enthusiastic and professional understanding, a French lady descending from her carriage, in chinchilla, robes, pearls.

'Beautiful!' she would murmur, nudging Septimus, that he might see. But beauty was behind a pane of glass. Even taste (Rezia liked ices, chocolates, sweet things) had no relish to him. He put down his cup on the little marble table. He looked at people outside; happy they seemed, collecting in the middle of the street, shouting, laughing, squabbling over nothing. But he could not taste, he could not feel. In the tea-shop among the tables and the chattering waiters the appalling fear came over him – he could not feel. He could reason; he could read, Dante for example, quite easily ('Septimus, do put down your book,' said Rezia, gently shut-ing the *Inferno*), he could add up his bill; his brain was per-fect; it must be the fault of the world then – that he could not feel.

'The English are so silent,' Rezia said. She liked it, she said. She respected these Englishmen, and wanted to see London, and the English horses, and the tailor-made suits, and could remember hearing how wonderful the shops were, from an aunt who had married and lived in Soho.

It might be possible, Septimus thought, looking at Eng-land from the train window, as they left Newhaven; it might be possible that the world itself is without meaning.

At the office they advanced him to a post of considerable responsibility. They were proud of him; he had won crosses. 'You have done your duty; it is up to us –' began Mr Brewer; and could not finish, so pleasurable was his emotion. They took admirable lodgings off the Tottenham Court Road.

Here he opened Shakespeare once more. That boy's busi-ness of the intoxication of language – *Antony and Cleopatra* – had shrivelled utterly. How Shakespeare loathed humanity – the putting on of clothes, the getting of children, the sordidity of the mouth and the belly! This was now re-vealed to Septimus; the message hidden in the beauty of words. The secret signal which one generation passes, under disguise, to the next is loathing, hatred, despair. Dante the same. Aeschylus (translated) the same. There Rezia sat at the table trimming hats. She trimmed hats for Mrs Filmer's friends; she trimmed hats by the hour. She looked pale, mysterious, like a lily, drowned, under water, he thought.

'The English are so serious,' she would say, putting her arms round Septimus, her cheek against his.

Love between man and woman was repulsive to Shakespeare. The business of copulation was filth to him before the end. But, Rezia said, she must have children. They had been married five years.

They went to the Tower together; to the Victoria and Albert Museum; stood in the crowd to see the King open Parliament. And there were the shops – hat shops, dress shops, shops with leather bags in the window, where she would stand staring. But she must have a boy.

She must have a son like Septimus, she said. But nobody could be like Septimus; so gentle; so serious; so clever. Could she not read Shakespeare too? Was Shakespeare a difficult author? she asked.

One cannot bring children into a world like this. One cannot perpetuate suffering, or increase the breed of these lustful animals, who have no lasting emotions, but only whims and vanities, eddying them now this way, now that.

He watched her snip, shape, as one watches a bird hop, flit in the grass, without daring to move a finger. For the truth is (let her ignore it) that human beings have neither kindness, nor faith, nor charity beyond what serves to increase the pleasure of the moment. They hunt in packs. Their packs scour the desert and vanish screaming into the wilderness. They desert the fallen. They are plastered over with grimaces. There was Brewer at the office, with his waxed moustache, coral tie-pin, white slip, and pleasurable emotions – all coldness and clamminess within, – his geraniums ruined in the War – his cook's nerves destroyed; or Amelia Whatshername, handing round cups of tea punctually at five – a leering, sneering, obscene little harpy; and the Toms and Berties in their starched shirt fronts oozing thick drops of vice. They never saw him drawing pictures of them naked at their antics in his notebook. In the street, vans roared past him; brutality blared out on placards; men were trapped in mines; women burnt alive; and once a maimed file of lunatics being exercised or displayed for the diversion of the populace (who laughed aloud) ambled and nodded and grinned past him, in the Tottenham Court Road, each half apologetically, yet triumphantly, inflicting his hopeless woe. And would *he* go mad?

At tea Rezia told him that Mrs Filmer's daughter was expecting a baby. *She* could not grow old and have no children! She was very lonely, she was very unhappy! She cried for the first time since they were married. Far away he heard her sobbing; he heard it accurately, he noticed it distinctly; he compared it to a piston thumping. But he felt nothing.

His wife was crying, and he felt nothing; only each time she sobbed in this profound, this silent, this hopeless way, he descended another step into the pit.

At last, with a melodramatic gesture which he assumed mechanically and with complete consciousness of insincerity, he dropped his head on his hands. Now he had surrendered; now other people must help him. People must be sent for. He gave in.

Nothing could rouse him. Rezia put him to bed. She sent for a doctor – Mrs Filmer's Dr Holmes. Dr Holmes examined him. There was nothing whatever the matter, said Dr Holmes. Oh, what a relief! What a kind man, what a good man! thought Rezia. When he felt like that he went to the Music Hall, said Dr Holmes. He took a day off with his wife and played golf. Why not try two tabloids of bromide dissolved in a glass of water at bedtime? These old Bloomsbury houses, said Dr Holmes, tapping the wall, are often full of very fine panelling, which the landlords have the folly to paper over. Only the other day, visiting a patient, Sir Somebody Something, in Bedford Square –

So there was no excuse; nothing whatever the matter, except the sin for which human nature had condemned him to death; that he did not feel. He had not cared when Evans was killed; that was worst; but all the other crimes raised their heads and shook their fingers and jeered and sneered over the rail of the bed in the early hours of the morning at the prostrate body which lay realizing its degradation; how he had married his wife without loving her; had lied to her; seduced her; outraged Miss Isabel Pole, and was so pocked and marked with vice that women shuddered when they saw him in the street. The verdict of human nature on such a wretch was death.

Dr Holmes came again. Large, fresh-coloured, handsome, flicking his boots, looking in the glass, he brushed it all aside – headaches, sleeplessness, fears, dreams – nerve symptoms and nothing more, he said. If Dr Holmes found himself even half a pound below eleven stone six, he asked his wife for another plate of porridge at breakfast. (Rezia would learn to cook porridge.) But, he continued, health is largely a matter in our own control. Throw yourself into outside interests; take up some hobby. He opened Shakespeare – *Antony and Cleopatra*; pushed Shakespeare aside. Some hobby, said Dr Holmes, for did he not owe his own excellent health (and he worked as hard as any man in London) to the fact that he could always switch off from his patients on to old furniture? And what a very pretty comb, if he might say so, Mrs Warren Smith was wearing!

When the damned fool came again, Septimus refused to see him. Did he indeed? said Dr Holmes, smiling agreeably. Really he had to give that charming little lady, Mrs Smith, a friendly push before he could get past her into her husband's bedroom.

'So you're in a funk,' he said agreeably, sitting down by his patient's side. He had actually talked of killing himself to his wife, quite a girl, a foreigner, wasn't she? Didn't that give her a very odd idea of English husbands? Didn't one owe perhaps a duty to one's wife? Wouldn't it be better to do something instead of lying in bed? For he had had forty years' experience behind him; and Septimus could take Dr Holmes's word for it – there was nothing whatever the matter with him. And next time Dr Holmes came he hoped to find Smith out of bed and not making that charming little lady his wife anxious about him.

Human nature, in short, was on him – the repulsive brute,

with the blood-red nostrils. Holmes was on him. Dr Holmes came quite regularly every day. Once you stumble, Septimus wrote on the back of a postcard, human nature is on you. Holmes is on you. Their only chance was to escape, without letting Holmes know; to Italy – anywhere, anywhere, away from Dr Holmes.

But Rezia could not understand him. Dr Holmes was such a kind man. He was so interested in Septimus. He only wanted to help them, he said. He had four little children and he had asked her to tea, she told Septimus.

So he was deserted. The whole world was clamouring: Kill yourself, kill yourself, for our sakes. But why should he kill himself for their sakes? Food was pleasant; the sun hot; and this killing oneself, how does one set about it, with a table knife, uglily, with floods of blood, – by sucking a gas-pipe? He was too weak; he could scarcely raise his hand. Besides, now that he was quite alone, condemned, deserted, as those who are about to die are alone, there was a luxury in it, an isolation full of sublimity; a freedom which the at-tached can never know. Holmes had won of course; the brute with the red nostrils had won. But even Holmes him-self could not touch this last relic straying on the edge of the world, this outcast, who gazed back at the inhabited regions, who lay, like a drowned sailor, on the shore of the world.

It was at that moment (Rezia had gone shopping) that the great revelation took place. A voice spoke from behind the screen. Evans was speaking. The dead were with him.

'Evans, Evans!' he cried.

Mr Smith was talking aloud to himself, Agnes the servant girl cried to Mrs Filmer in the kitchen. 'Evans, Evans!' he had said as she brought in the tray. She jumped, she did. She scuttled downstairs.

And Rezia came in, with her flowers, and walked across the room, and put the roses in a vase, upon which the sun struck directly, and went laughing, leaping round the room.

She had had to buy the roses, Rezia said, from a poor man in the street. But they were almost dead already, she said, arranging the roses.

So there was a man outside; Evans presumably; and the roses, which Rezia said were half dead, had been picked by him in the fields of Greece. Communication is health; communication is happiness. Communication, he muttered.

'What are you saying, Septimus?' Rezia asked, wild with terror, for he was talking to himself.

She sent Agnes running for Dr Holmes. Her husband, she said, was mad. He scarcely knew her.

'You brute! You brute!' cried Septimus, seeing human nature, that is Dr Holmes, enter the room.

'Now what's all this about,' said Dr Holmes in the most amiable way in the world. 'Talking nonsense to frighten your wife?' But he would give him something to make him sleep. And if they were rich people, said Dr Holmes, looking ironically round the room, by all means let them go to Harley Street; if they had no confidence in him, said Dr Holmes, looking not quite so kind.

It was precisely twelve o'clock; twelve by Big Ben; whose stroke was wafted over the northern part of London; blent with that of other clocks, mixed in a thin ethereal way with the clouds and wisps of smoke and died up there among the seagulls – twelve o'clock struck as Clarissa Dalloway laid her green dress on her bed, and the Warren Smiths walked down Harley Street. Twelve was the hour of their appointment. Probably, Rezia thought, that was Sir William Bradshaw's house with the grey motor car in front of it. (The leaden circles dissolved in the air.)

Indeed it was – Sir William Bradshaw's motor car; low, powerful, grey with plain initials interlocked on the panel, as if the pomps of heraldry were incongruous, this man being the ghostly helper, the priest of science; and, as the motor car was grey, so, to match its sober suavity, grey furs, silver grey rugs were heaped in it, to keep her ladyship warm while she waited. For often Sir William would travel sixty miles or more down into the country to visit the rich, the afflicted, who could afford the very large fee which Sir William very properly charged for his advice. Her ladyship waited with the rugs about her knees an hour or more, leaning back, thinking sometimes of the patient, sometimes, excusably, of the wall of gold, mounting minute by minute while she waited; the wall of gold that was mounting between them and all shifts and anxieties (she had borne them bravely; they had had their struggles), until she felt wedged on a calm ocean, where only spice winds blow; respected, admired, envied, with scarcely anything left to wish for, though she regretted her stoutness; large dinner-parties every Thursday night to the profession; an occasional bazaar to be opened; Royalty greeted; too little time, alas, with her husband, whose work grew and grew; a boy doing well at Eton; she would have liked a daughter too; interests she had, however, in plenty; child welfare; the after-care of the epileptic, and photography, so that if there was a church building, or a church decaying, she bribed the sexton, got the key and took photographs, which were scarcely to be distinguished from the work of professionals, while she waited.

Sir William himself was no longer young. He had worked very hard; he had won his position by sheer ability (being the son of a shop-keeper); loved his profession; made a fine figurehead at ceremonies and spoke well – all of which had by the time he was knighted given him a heavy look, a weary look (the stream of patients being so incessant, the responsibilities and privileges of his profession so onerous), which weariness, together with his grey hairs, increased the extraordinary distinction of his presence and gave him the reputation (of the utmost importance in dealing with nerve cases) not merely of lightning skill and almost infallible accuracy in diagnosis, but of sympathy; tact; understanding of the human soul. He could see the first moment they came into the room (the Warren Smiths they were called); he was certain directly he saw the man; it was a case of extreme gravity. It was a case of complete breakdown – complete physical and nervous breakdown, with every symptom in an advanced stage, he ascertained in two or three minutes (writing answers to questions, murmured discreetly, on a pink card).

How long had Dr Holmes been attending him?

Six weeks.

Prescribed a little bromide? Said there was nothing the matter? Ah yes (those general practitioners! thought Sir William. It took half his time to undo their blunders. Some were irreparable).

'You served with great distinction in the War?'

The patient repeated the word 'war' interrogatively.

He was attaching meanings to words of a symbolical kind. A serious symptom to be noted on the card.

'The War?' the patient asked. The European War – that little shindy of schoolboys with gunpowder? Had he served with distinction? He really forgot. In the War itself he had failed.

'Yes, he served with the greatest distinction,' Rezia assured the doctor; 'he was promoted.'

'And they have the very highest opinion of you at your office?' Sir William murmured, glancing at Mr Brewer's very generously worded letter. 'So that you have nothing to worry you, no financial anxiety, nothing?'

He had committed an appalling crime and been condemned to death by human nature.

'I have – I have,' he began, 'committed a crime –'

'He has done nothing wrong whatever,' Rezia assured the doctor. If Mr Smith would wait, said Sir William, he would speak to Mrs Smith in the next room. Her husband was very seriously ill, Sir William said. Did he threaten to kill himself?

Oh, he did, she cried. But he did not mean it, she said. Of course not. It was merely a question of rest, said Sir William; of rest, rest, rest; a long rest in bed. There was a delightful home down in the country where her husband would be perfectly looked after. Away from her? she asked. Unfortunately, yes; the people we care for most are not good for us when we are ill. But he was not mad, was he? Sir William said he never spoke of 'madness'; he called it not having a sense of proportion. But her husband did not like doctors. He would refuse to go there. Shortly and kindly Sir William explained to her the state of the case. He had threatened to kill himself. There was no alternative. It was a question of law. He would lie in bed in a beautiful house in the country. The nurses were admirable. Sir William would visit him once a week. If Mrs Warren Smith was quite sure she had no more questions to ask – he never hurried his patients – they would return to her husband. She had nothing more to ask – not of Sir Wiliam.

So they returned to the most exalted of mankind; the criminal who faced his judges; the victim exposed on the heights; the fugitive; the drowned sailor; the poet of the immortal ode; the Lord who had gone from life to death; to Septimus Warren Smith, who sat in the arm-chair under the skylight staring at a photograph of Lady Bradshaw in Court dress, muttering messages about beauty.

'We have had our little talk,' said Sir William.

'He says that you are very, very ill,' Rezia cried.

'We have been arranging that you should go into a home,' said Sir William.

'One of Holmes's homes?' sneered Septimus.

The fellow made a distasteful impression. For there was in Sir William, whose father had been a tradesman, a natural respect for breeding and clothing, which shabbiness nettled; again, more profoundly, there was in Sir William, who had never had time for reading, a grudge, deeply buried, against cultivated people who came into his room and intimated that doctors, whose profession is a constant strain upon all the highest faculties, are not educated men.

'One of *my* homes, Mr Warren Smith,' he said 'where we will teach you to rest.'

And there was just one thing more.

He was quite certain that when Mr Warren Smith was well he was the last man in the world to frighten his wife. But he had talked of killing himself.

'We all have our moments of depression,' said Sir William.

Once you fall, Septimus repeated to himself, human nature is on you. Holmes and Bradshaw are on you. They scour the desert. They fly screaming into the wilderness. The rack and the thumbscrew are applied. Human nature is remorseless.

'Impulses came upon him sometimes?' Sir William asked, with his pencil on a pink card.

That was his own affair, said Septimus.

'Nobody lives for himself alone,' said Sir William, glancing at the photograph of his wife in Court dress.

'And you have a brilliant career before you,' said Sir William. There was Mr Brewer's letter on the table. 'An exceptionally brilliant career.'

But if he confessed? If he communicated? Would they let him off then, Holmes, Bradshaw?

'I – I –' he stammered.

But what was his crime? He could not remember it.

'Yes?' Sir William encouraged him. (But it was growing late.)

Love, trees, there is no crime – what was his message?

He could not remember it.

'I – I –' Septimus stammered.

'Try to think as little about yourself as possible,' said Sir William kindly. Really, he was not fit to be about.

Was there anything else they wished to ask him? Sir William would make all the arrangements (he murmured to Rezia) and he would let her know between five and six that evening.

'Trust everything to me,' he said, and dismissed them.

Never, never had Rezia felt such agony in her life! She had asked for help and been deserted! He had failed them! Sir William Bradshaw was not a nice man.

The upkeep of that motor car alone must cost him quite a lot, said Septimus, when they got out into the street.

She clung to his arm. They had been deserted.

But what more did she want?

To his patients he gave three-quarters of an hour; and if in this exacting science which has to do with what, after all, we know nothing about – the nervous system, the human brain – a doctor loses his sense of proportion, as a doctor he fails. Health we must have; and health is proportion; so that when a man comes into your room and says he is Christ (a common delusion), and has a message, as they mostly have, and threatens, as they often do, to kill himself, you invoke proportion; order rest in bed; rest in solitude; silence and rest; rest without friends, without books, without messages; six months' rest; until a man who went in weighing seven stone six comes out weighing twelve.

Proportion, divine proportion, Sir William's goddess, was acquired by Sir William walking hospitals, catching salmon, begetting one son in Harley Street by Lady Bradshaw, who caught salmon herself and took photographs scarcely to be distinguished from the work of professionals. Worshipping proportion, Sir William not only prospered himself but made England prosper, secluded her lunatics, forbade childbirth, penalized despair, made it impossible for the unfit to propagate their views until they, too, shared his sense of proportion – his, if they were men, Lady Bradshaw's if they were women (she embroidered, knitted, spent four nights out of seven at home with her son), so that not only did his colleagues respect him, his subordinates fear him, but the friends and relations of his patients felt for him the keenest gratitude for insisting that these prophetic Christs and Christesses, who prophesied the end of the world, or the advent of God, should drink milk in bed, as Sir William ordered; Sir William with his thirty years' experience of these kinds of cases, and his infallible instinct, this is madness, this sense; his sense of proportion.

But Proportion has a sister, less smiling, more formidable, a Goddess even now engaged – in the heat and sands of India, the mud and swamp of Africa, the purlieus of London, wherever, in short, the climate or the devil tempts men to fall from the true belief which is her own – is even now engaged in dashing down shrines, smashing idols, and setting up in their place her own stern countenance. Conversion is her name and she feasts on the wills of the weakly, loving to impress, to impose, adoring her own features stamped on the face of the populace. At Hyde Park Corner on a tub she stands preaching; shrouds herself in white and walks penitentially disguised as brotherly love through factories and parliaments; offers help, but desires power; smites out of her way roughly the dissentient, or dissatisfied; bestows her blessing on those who, looking upward, catch submissively from her eyes the light of their own. This lady too (Rezia Warren Smith divined it) had her dwelling in Sir William's heart, though concealed, as she mostly is, under some plausible disguise; some venerable name; love, duty, self-sacrifice. How he would work – how toil to raise funds, propagate reforms, initiate institutions! But conversion, fastidious Goddess, loves blood better than brick, and feasts most subtly on the human will. For example, Lady Bradshaw. Fifteen years ago she had gone under. It was nothing you could put your finger on; there had been no scene, no snap; only the slow sinking, water-logged, of her will into his. Sweet was her smile, swift her submission; dinner in Harley Street, numbering eight or nine courses, feeding ten or fifteen guests of the professional classes, was smooth and urbane. Only as the evening wore on a very slight dullness, or uneasiness perhaps, a nervous twitch, fumble, stumble and confusion indicated, what it was really painful to believe – that the poor lady lied. Once, long ago, she had caught salmon freely: now, quick to minister to the craving which lit her husband's eye so oilily for dominion, for power, she cramped, squeezed, pared, pruned, drew back, peeped through: so that without know-ing precisely what made the evening disagreeable, and caused this pressure on the top of the head (which might well be imputed to the professional conversation, or the fatigue of a great doctor whose life, Lady Bradshaw said, 'is not his own but his patient's'), disagreeable it was: so that guests, when the clock struck ten, breathed in the air of Harley Street even with rapture; which relief, however, was denied to his patients.

There in the grey room, with the pictures on the wall, and the valuable furniture, under the ground-glass skylight, they learnt the extent of their transgressions: huddled up in arm-chairs, they watched him go through, for their benefit, a curious exercise with the arms, which he shot out, brought sharply back to his hip, to prove (if the patient was obstinate) that Sir William was master of his own actions, which the patient was not. There some weakly broke down; sobbed, submitted; others, inspired by Heaven knows what

intemperate madness, called Sir William to his face a damnable humbug; questioned, even more imperiously, life itself.
Why live? they demanded. Sir William replied that life was
good. Certainly Lady Bradshaw in ostrich feathers hung
over the mantelpiece, and as for his income it was quite
twelve thousand a year. But to us, they protested, life has
given no such bounty. He acquiesced. They lacked a sense
of proportion. And perhaps, after all, there is no God? He
shrugged his shoulders. In short, this living or not living is
an affair of our own? But there they were mistaken. Sir
William had a friend in Surrey where they taught, what Sir
William frankly admitted was a difficult art — a sense of
proportion. There were, moreover, family affection; honour;
courage; and a brilliant career. All of these had in Sir
William a resolute champion. If they failed, he had to
support him police and the good of society, which, he
remarked very quietly, would take care, down in Surrey,
that these unsocial impulses, bred more than anything by
the lack of good blood, were held in control. And then
stole out from her hiding-place and mounted her throne
that Goddess whose lust is to override opposition, to stamp
indelibly in the sanctuaries of others the image of herself.
Naked, defenceless, the exhausted, the friendless received
the impress of Sir William's will. He swooped; he devoured.
He shut people up. It was this combination of decision and
humanity that endeared Sir William so greatly to the relations of his victims.

But Rezia Warren Smith cried, walking down Harley
Street, that she did not like that man.

Shredding and slicing, dividing and subdividing, the
clocks of Harley Street nibbled at the June day, counselled
submission, upheld authority, and pointed out in chorus
the supreme advantages of a sense of proportion, until the
mound of time was so far diminished that a commercial
clock, suspended above a shop in Oxford Street, announced,
genially and fraternally, as if it were a pleasure to Messrs
Rigby and Lowndes to give the information gratis, that it
was half-past one.

Looking up, it appeared that each letter of their names

stood for one of the hours; subconsciously one was grateful to Rigby and Lowndes for giving one time ratified by Greenwich; and this gratitude (so Hugh Whitbread ruminated, dallying there in front of the shop window) naturally took the form later of buying off Rigby and Lowndes socks or shoes. So he ruminated. It was his habit. He did not go deeply. He brushed surfaces; the dead languages, the living, life in Constantinople, Paris, Rome; riding, shooting, tennis, it had been once. The malicious asserted that he now kept guard at Buckingham Palace, dressed in silk stockings and knee-breeches, over what nobody knew. But he did it extremely efficiently. He had been afloat on the cream of English society for fifty-five years. He had known Prime Ministers. His affections were understood to be deep. And if it were true that he had not taken part in any of the great movements of the time or held important office, one or two humble reforms stood to his credit; an improvement in public shelters was one; the protection of owls in Norfolk another; servant girls had reason to be grateful to him; and his name at the end of letters to *The Times*, asking for funds, appealing to the public to protect, to preserve, to clear up litter, to abate smoke, and stamp out immorality in parks, commanded respect.

A magnificent figure he cut too, pausing for a moment (as the sound of the half-hour died away) to look critically, magisterially, at socks and shoes; impeccable, substantial, as if he beheld the world from a certain eminence, and dressed to match; but realized the obligations which size, wealth, health entail, and observed punctiliously, even when not absolutely necessary, little courtesies, old-fashioned ceremonies, which gave a quality to his manner, something to imitate, something to remember him by, for he would never lunch, for example, with Lady Bruton, whom he had known these twenty years, without bringing her in his outstretched hand a bunch of carnations, and asking Miss Brush, Lady Bruton's secretary, after her brother in South Africa, which, for some reason, Miss Brush, deficient though she was in every attribute of female charm, so much resented that she said 'Thank you, he's doing very well in South Africa,' when, for half-a-dozen years, he had been doing badly in Portsmouth.

Lady Bruton herself preferred Richard Dalloway, who arrived at the same moment. Indeed they met on the door-step.

Lady Bruton preferred Richard Dalloway of course. He was made of much finer material. But she wouldn't let them run down her poor dear Hugh. She could never forget his kindness – he had been really remarkably kind – she forgot precisely upon what occasion. But he had been – remark-ably kind. Anyhow, the difference between one man and another does not amount to much. She had never seen the sense of cutting people up, as Clarissa Dalloway did – cut-ting them up and sticking them together again; not at any rate when one was sixty-two. She took Hugh's carnations with her angular grim smile. There was nobody else coming, she said. She had got them there on false pretences, to help her out of a difficulty –

'But let us eat first,' she said.

And so there began a soundless and exquisite passing to and fro through swing doors of aproned, white-capped maids, handmaidens not of necessity, but adepts in a mys-tery or grand deception practised by hostesses in Mayfair from one-thirty to two, when, with a wave of the hand, the traffic ceases, and there rises instead this profound illusion in the first place about the food – how it is not paid for; and then that the table spreads itself voluntarily with glass and silver, little mats, saucers of red fruit; films of brown cream mask turbot; in casseroles severed chickens swim; coloured, undomestic, the fire burns; and with the wine and the coffee (not paid for) rise jocund visions before musing eyes; gently speculative eyes; eyes to whom life appears musical, mysterious; eyes now kindled to observe genially the beauty of the red carnations which Lady Bruton (whose movements were always angular) had laid beside her plate, so that Hugh Whitbread, feeling at peace with the entire universe and at the same time completely sure of his stand-ing, said, resting his fork :

'Wouldn't they look charming against your lace?'

Miss Brush resented this familiarity intensely. She

thought him an underbred fellow. She made Lady Bruton laugh.

Lady Bruton raised the carnations, holding them rather stiffly with much the same attitude with which the General held the scroll in the picture behind her; she remained fixed, tranced. Which was she now, the General's great-grand-daughter? great-great-granddaughter? Richard Dalloway asked himself. Sir Roderick, Sir Miles, Sir Talbot – that was it. It was remarkable how in that family the likeness per-sisted in the women. She should have been a general of dragoons herself. And Richard would have served under her, cheerfully; he had the greatest respect for her; he cherished these romantic views about well-set-up old women of pedigree, and would have liked, in his good-humoured way, to bring some young hot-heads of his acquaintance to lunch with her; as if a type like hers could be bred of amiable tea-drinking enthusiasts! He knew her country. He knew her people. There was a vine, still bear-ing, which either Lovelace or Herrick – she never read a word of poetry herself, but so the story ran – had sat under. Better to wait to put before them the question that bothered her (about making an appeal to the public; if so, in what terms and so on), better wait until they have had their coffee, Lady Bruton thought; and so laid the carnations down beside her plate.

'How's Clarissa?' she asked abruptly.

Clarissa always said that Lady Bruton did not like her. Indeed, Lady Bruton had the reputation of being more interested in politics than people; of talking like a man; of having had a finger in some notorious intrigue of the eighties, which was now beginning to be mentioned in memoirs. Certainly there was an alcove in her drawing-room, and a table in that alcove, and a photograph upon that table of General Talbot Moore, now deceased, who had written there (one evening in the eighties) in Lady Bruton's presence, with her cognisance, perhaps advice, a telegram ordering the British troops to advance upon an historical occasion. (She kept the pen and told the story.) Thus, when she said in her offhand way 'How's Clarissa?' husbands had difficulty in persuading their wives, and indeed, however devoted, were secretly doubtful themselves, of her interest in women who often got in their husbands' ways, prevented them from accepting posts abroad, and had to be taken to the seaside in the middle of the session to recover from influenza. Nevertheless her inquiry, 'How's Clarissa?' was well known by women infallibly to be a signal from a well-wisher, from an almost silent companion, whose utterances (half a dozen perhaps in the course of a lifetime) signified recognition of some feminine comradeship which went beneath masculine lunch parties and united Lady Bruton and Mrs Dalloway, who seldom met, and appeared when they did meet indifferent and even hostile, in a singular bond.

'I met Clarissa in the Park this morning,' said Hugh Whitbread, diving into the casserole, anxious to pay himself this little tribute, for he had only to come to London and he met everybody at once; but greedy, one of the greediest men she had ever known, Milly Brush thought, who observed men with unflinching rectitude, and was capable of everlasting devotion, to her own sex in particular, being knobbed, scraped, angular, and entirely without feminine charm.

'D'you know who's in town?' said Lady Bruton, suddenly bethinking her. 'Our old friend, Peter Walsh.'

They all smiled. Peter Walsh! And Mr Dalloway was genuinely glad, Milly Brush thought; and Mr Whitbread thought only of his chicken.

Peter Walsh! All three, Lady Bruton, Hugh Whitbread, and Richard Dalloway, remembered the same thing – how passionately Peter had been in love; been rejected; gone to India; come a cropper; made a mess of things; and Richard Dalloway had a very great liking for the dear old fellow too. Milly Brush saw that; saw a depth in the brown of his eyes; saw him hesitate; consider; which interested her, as Mr Dalloway always interested her, for what was he thinking, she wondered, about Peter Walsh?

That Peter Walsh had been in love with Clarissa; that he would go back directly after lunch and find Clarissa; that he would tell her, in so many words, that he loved her. Yes, he would say that.

Milly Brush once might almost have fallen in love with these silences; and Mr Dalloway was always so dependable; such a gentleman too. Now, being forty, Lady Bruton had only to nod, or turn her head a little abruptly, and Milly Brush took the signal, however deeply she might be sunk in these reflections of a detached spirit, of an uncorrupted soul whom life could not bamboozle, because life had not offered her a trinket of the slightest value; not a curl, smile, lip, cheek, nose; nothing whatever; Lady Bruton had only to nod, and Perkins was instructed to quicken the coffee.

'Yes; Peter Walsh has come back,' said Lady Bruton. It was vaguely flattering to them all. He had come back, battered, unsuccessful, to their secure shores. But to help him, they reflected, was impossible; there was some flaw in his character. Hugh Whitbread said one might of course mention his name to So-and-so. He wrinkled lugubriously, consequentially, at the thought of the letters he would write to the heads of Government offices about 'my old friend, Peter Walsh,' and so on. But it wouldn't lead to anything – not to anything permanent, because of his character.

'In trouble with some woman,' said Lady Bruton. They had all guessed that *that* was at the bottom of it.

'However,' said Lady Bruton, anxious to leave the subject, 'we shall hear the whole story from Peter himself.'

(The coffee was very slow in coming.)

'The address?' murmured Hugh Whitbread; and there was at once a ripple in the grey tide of service that washed round Lady Bruton day in, day out, collecting, intercepting, enveloping her in a fine tissue which broke concussions, mitigated interruptions, and spread round the house in Brook Street a fine net where things lodged and were picked out accurately, instantly by grey-haired Perkins, who had been with Lady Bruton these thirty years and now wrote down the address; handed it to Mr Whitbread, who took out his pocket-book, raised his eyebrows, and, slipping it in among documents of the highest importance, said that he would get Evelyn to ask him to lunch.

(They were waiting to bring the coffee until Mr Whitbread had finished.)

Hugh was very slow, Lady Bruton thought. He was getting fat, she noticed. Richard always kept himself in the pink of condition. She was getting impatient; the whole of her being was setting positively, undeniably, domineeringly brushing aside all this unnecessary trifling (Peter Walsh and his affairs) upon that subject which engaged her attention, and not merely her attention, but that fibre which was the ramrod of her soul, that essential part of her without which Millicent Bruton would not have been Millicent Bruton; that project for emigrating young people of both sexes born of respectable parents and setting them up with a fair prospect of doing well in Canada. She exaggerated. She had perhaps lost her sense of proportion. Emigration was not to others the obvious remedy, the sublime conception. It was not to them (not to Hugh, or Richard, or even to devoted Miss Brush) the liberator of the pent egotism, which a strong martial woman, well nourished, well descended, of direct impulses, downright feelings, and little introspective power (broad and simple – why could not every one be broad and simple? she asked), feels rise within her, once youth is past, and must eject upon some object – it may be Emigration, it may be Emancipation; but whatever it be, this object round which the essence of her soul is daily secreted becomes inevitably prismatic, lustrous, half looking-glass, half precious stone; now carefully hidden in case people should sneer at it; now proudly displayed. Emigration had become, in short, largely Lady Bruton.

But she had to write. And one letter to *The Times*, she used to say to Miss Brush, cost her more than to organise an expedition to South Africa (which she had done in the war). After a morning's battle, beginning, tearing up, beginning again, she used to feel the futility of her own womanhood as she felt it on no other occasion, and would turn gratefully to the thought of Hugh Whitbread who possessed – no one could doubt it – the art of writing letters to *The Times*.

A being so differently constituted from herself, with such a command of language; able to put things as editors liked them put; had passions which one could not call simply greed. Lady Bruton often suspended judgment upon men in deference to the mysterious accord in which they, but no woman, stood to the laws of the universe; knew how to put things; knew what was said; so that if Richard advised her, and Hugh wrote for her, she was sure of being somehow right. So she let Hugh eat his soufflé; asked after poor Evelyn; waited until they were smoking, and then said,

'Milly, would you fetch the papers?'

And Miss Brush went out, came back; laid papers on the table; and Hugh produced his fountain pen; his silver fountain pen, which had done twenty years' service, he said, unscrewing the cap. It was still in perfect order; he had shown it to the makers; there was no reason, they said, why it should ever wear out; which was somehow to Hugh's credit, and to the credit of the sentiments which his pen expressed (so Richard Dalloway felt) as Hugh began carefully writing capital letters with rings round them in the margin, and thus marvellously reduced Lady Bruton's tangles to sense, to grammar such as the editor of The Times, Lady Bruton felt, watching the marvellous transformation, must respect. Hugh was slow. Hugh was pertinacious. Richard said one must take risks. Hugh proposed modifications in deference to people's feelings, which, he said rather tartly when Richard laughed, 'had to be considered,' and read out 'how, therefore, we are of opinion that the times are ripe ... the superfluous youth of our ever-increasing population ... what we owe to the dead ...' which Richard thought all stuffing and bunkum, but no harm in it, of course, and Hugh went on drafting sentiments in alphabetical order of the highest nobility, brushing the cigar ash from his waistcoat, and summing up now and then the progress they had made until, finally, he read out the draft of a letter which Lady Bruton felt certain was a masterpiece. Could her own meaning sound like that?

Hugh could not guarantee that the editor would put it in; but he would be meeting somebody at luncheon.

Whereupon Lady Bruton, who seldom did a graceful

thing, stuffed all Hugh's carnations into the front of her dress, and flinging her hands out called him 'My Prime Minister!' What she would have done without them both she did not know. They rose. And Richard Dalloway strolled off as usual to have a look at the General's portrait, because he meant, whenever he had a moment of leisure, to write a history of Lady Bruton's family.

And Millicent Bruton was very proud of her family. But they could wait, they could wait, she said, looking at the picture; meaning that her family, of military men, administrators, admirals, had been men of action, who had done their duty; and Richard's first duty was to his country, but it was a fine face, she said; and all the papers were ready for Richard down at Aldmixton whenever the time came; the Labour Government, she meant. 'Ah, the news from India!' she cried.

And then, as they stood in the hall taking yellow gloves from the bowl on the malachite table and Hugh was offering Miss Brush with quite unnecessary courtesy some discarded ticket or other compliment, which she loathed from the depths of her heart and blushed brick red, Richard turned to Lady Bruton, with his hat in his hand, and said,

'We shall see you at our party to-night?' whereupon Lady Bruton resumed the magnificence which letter-writing had shattered. She might come; or she might not come. Clarissa had wonderful energy. Parties terrified Lady Bruton. But then, she was getting old. So she intimated, standing at her doorway; handsome; very erect; while her chow stretched behind her, and Miss Brush disappeared into the background with her hands full of papers.

And Lady Bruton went ponderously, majestically, up to her room, lay, one arm extended, on the sofa. She sighed, she snored, not that she was asleep, only drowsy and heavy, drowsy and heavy, like a field of clover in the sunshine this hot June day, with the bees going round and about and the yellow butterflies. Always she went back to those fields down in Devonshire, where she had jumped the brooks on Patty, her pony, with Mortimer and Tom, her brothers. And there were the dogs; there were the rats; there were her father and mother on the lawn under the trees, with the tea-things out, and the beds of dahlias, the hollyhocks, the pampas grass; and they, little wretches, always up to some mischief! stealing back through the shrubbery, so as not to be seen, all bedraggled from some roguery. What old nurse used to say about her frocks!

Ah dear, she remembered – it was Wednesday in Brook Street. Those kind good fellows, Richard Dalloway, Hugh Whitbread, had gone this hot day through the streets whose growl came up to her lying on the sofa. Power was hers, position, income. She had lived in the forefront of her time. She had had good friends; known the ablest men of her day. Murmuring London flowed up to her, and her hand, lying on the sofa back, curled upon some imaginary baton such as her grandfathers might have held, holding which she seemed, drowsy and heavy, to be commanding battalions marching to Canada, and those good fellows walking across London, that territory of theirs, that little bit of carpet, Mayfair.

And they went further and further from her, being attached to her by a thin thread (since they had lunched with her) which would stretch and stretch, get thinner and thinner as they walked across London; as if one's friends were attached to one's body, after lunching with them, by a thin thread, which (as she dozed there) became hazy with the sound of bells, striking the hour or ringing to service, as a single spider's thread is blotted with rain-drops, and, burdened, sags down. So she slept.

And Richard Dalloway and Hugh Whitbread hesitated at the corner of Conduit Street at the very moment that Millicent Bruton, lying on the sofa, let the thread snap; snored. Contrary winds buffeted at the street corner. They looked in at a shop window; they did not wish to buy or to talk but to part, only with contrary winds buffeting the street corner, with some sort of lapse in the tides of the body, two forces meeting in a swirl, morning and afternoon, they paused. Some newspaper placard went up in the air, gallantly, like a kite at first, then paused, swooped, fluttered; and a lady's veil hung. Yellow awnings trembled. The speed of the morning traffic slackened, and single carts rattled carelessly down half-empty streets. In Norfolk, of which Richard Dalloway was half thinking, a soft warm wind blew back the petals; confused the waters; ruffled the flowering grasses. Haymakers, who had pitched beneath hedges to sleep away the morning toil, parted curtains of green blades; moved trembling globes of cow parsley to see the sky; the blue, the steadfast, the blazing summer sky.

Aware that he was looking at a silver two-handled Jacobean mug, and that Hugh Whitbread admired condescendingly, with airs of connoisseurship, a Spanish necklace which he thought of asking the price of in case Evelyn might like it – still Richard was torpid; could not think or move. Life had thrown up this wreckage; shop windows full of coloured paste, and one stood stark with the lethargy of the old, stiff with the rigidity of the old, looking in. Evelyn Whitbread might like to buy this Spanish necklace – so she might. Yawn he must. Hugh was going into the shop.

'Right you are!' said Richard, following.

Goodness knows he didn't want to go buying necklaces with Hugh. But there are tides in the body. Morning meets afternoon. Borne like a frail shallop on deep, deep floods, Lady Bruton's great-grandfather and his memoir and his campaigns in North America were whelmed and sunk. And Millicent Bruton too. She went under. Richard didn't care a straw what became of Emigration; about that letter, whether the editor put it in or not. The necklace hung stretched between Hugh's admirable fingers. Let him give it to a girl, if he must buy jewels – any girl, any girl in the street. For the worthlessness of this life did strike Richard pretty forcibly – buying necklaces for Evelyn. If he'd had a boy he'd have said, Work, work. But he had his Elizabeth; he adored his Elizabeth.

'I should like to see Mr Dubonnet,' said Hugh in his curt worldly way. It appeared that this Dubonnet had the measurements of Mrs Whitbread's neck, or, more strangely still, knew her views upon Spanish jewellery and the extent of her possessions in that line (which Hugh could not remember). All of which seemed to Richard Dalloway awfully odd. For he never gave Clarissa presents, except a bracelet two or three years ago, which had not been a success. She never wore it. It pained him to remember that she never wore it. And as a single spider's thread after wavering here and there attaches itself to the point of a leaf, so Richard's mind, recovering from its lethargy, set now on his wife, Clarissa, whom Peter Walsh had loved so passionately; and Richard had had a sudden vision of her there at luncheon; of himself and Clarissa; of their life together; and he drew the tray of old jewels towards him, and taking up first this brooch, then that ring, 'How much is that?' he asked, but doubted his own taste. He wanted to open the drawing-room door and come in holding out something; a present for Clarissa. Only what? But Hugh was on his legs again. He was unspeakably pompous. Really, after dealing here for thirty-five years he was not going to be put off by a mere boy who did not know his business. For Dubonnet, it seemed, was out, and Hugh would not buy anything until Mr Dubonnet chose to be in; at which the youth flushed and bowed his correct little bow. It was all perfectly correct. And yet Richard couldn't have said that to save his life! Why these people stood that damned insolence he could not conceive. Hugh was becoming an intolerable ass. Richard Dalloway could not stand more than an hour of his society. And, flicking his bowler hat by way of farewell, Richard turned at the corner of Conduit Street eager, yes, very eager, to travel that spider's thread of attachment between himself and Clarissa; he would go straight to her, in Westminster.

But he wanted to come in holding something. Flowers? Yes, flowers, since he did not trust his taste in gold; any number of flowers, roses, orchids, to celebrate what was, reckoning things as you will, an event; this feeling about her when they spoke of Peter Walsh at luncheon; and they never spoke of it; not for years had they spoken of it; which, he thought, grasping his red and white roses together (a vast bunch in tissue paper), is the greatest mistake in the world. The time comes when it can't be said; one's too shy to say it, he thought, pocketing his sixpence or two of change, setting off with his great bunch held against his body to Westminster, to say straight out in so many words (whatever she might think of him), holding out his flowers, 'I love you.' Why not? Really it was a miracle thinking of the war, and thousands of poor chaps, with all their lives before them, shovelled together, already half forgotten; it was a miracle. Here he was walking across London to say to Clarissa in so many words that he loved her. Which one never does say, he thought. Partly one's lazy; partly one's shy. And Clarissa – it was difficult to think of her; except in starts, as at luncheon, when he saw her quite distinctly; their whole life. He stopped at the crossing; and repeated – being simple by nature, and undebauched, because he had tramped, and shot; being pertinacious and dogged, having championed the down-trodden and followed his instincts in the House of Commons; being preserved in his simplicity yet at the same time grown rather speechless, rather stiff – he repeated that it was a miracle that he should have married Clarissa; a miracle – his life had been a miracle, he thought; hesitating to cross. But it did make his blood boil to see little creatures of five or six crossing Piccadilly alone. The police ought to have stopped the traffic at once. He had no illusions about the London police. Indeed, he was collecting evidence of their malpractices; and those costermongers, not allowed to stand their barrows in the streets; and prostitutes, good Lord, the fault wasn't in them, nor in young men either, but in our detestable social system and so forth; all of which he considered, could be seen considering, grey, dogged, dapper, clean, as he walked across the Park to tell his wife that he loved her.

For he would say it in so many words, when he came into the room. Because it is a thousand pities never to say what one feels, he thought, crossing the Green Park and observing with pleasure how in the shade of the trees whole families, poor families, were sprawling; children kicking up their legs; sucking milk; paper bags thrown about, which could easily be picked up (if people objected) by one of those fat gentlemen in livery; for he was of opinion that every park, and every square, during the summer months should be open to children (the grass of the park flushed and faded, lighting up the poor mothers of Westminster and their crawling babies, as if a yellow lamp were moved beneath). But what could be done for female vagrants like that poor creature, stretched on her elbow (as if she had flung herself on the earth, rid of all ties, to observe curiously, to speculate boldly, to consider the whys and the wherefores, impudent, loose-lipped, humorous), he did not know. Bearing his flowers like a weapon, Richard Dalloway approached her; intent he passed her; still there was time for a spark between them — she laughed at the sight of him, he smiled good-humouredly, considering the problem of the female vagrant; not that they would ever speak. But he would tell Clarissa that he loved her, in so many words. He had, once upon a time, been jealous of Peter Walsh; jealous of him and Clarissa. But she had often said to him that she had been right not to marry Peter Walsh; which, knowing Clarissa, was obviously true; she wanted support. Not that she was weak; but she wanted support.

As for Buckingham Palace (like an old prima donna facing the audience all in white) you can't deny it a certain dignity, he considered, nor despise what does, after all, stand to millions of people (a little crowd was waiting at the gate to see the King drive out) for a symbol, absurd though it is; a child with a box of bricks could have done better, he thought; looking at the memorial to Queen Victoria (whom he could remember in her horn spectacles driving through Kensington), its white mound, its billowing motherliness; but he liked being ruled by the descendant of Horsa; he liked continuity; and the sense of handing on the traditions of the past. It was a great age in which to have lived. Indeed, his own life was a miracle; let him make no mistake about it; here he was, in the prime of life, walking to his house in Westminster to tell Clarissa that he loved her. Happiness is this, he thought.

It is this, he said, as he entered Dean's Yard. Big Ben was beginning to strike, first the warning, musical; then the hour, irrevocable. Lunch parties waste the entire afternoon, he thought, approaching his door.

The sound of Big Ben flooded Clarissa's drawing-room, where she sat, ever so annoyed, at her writing-table; worried; annoyed. It was perfectly true that she had not asked Ellie Henderson to her party; but she had done it on purpose. Now Mrs Marsham wrote: 'She had told Ellie Henderson she would ask Clarissa – Ellie so much wanted to come.'

But why should she invite all the dull women in London to her parties? Why should Mrs Marsham interfere? And there was Elizabeth closeted all this time with Doris Kilman. Anything more nauseating she could not conceive. Prayer at this hour with that woman. And the sound of the bell flooded the room with its melancholy wave; which receded, and gathered itself together to fall once more, when she heard, distractingly, something fumbling, something scratching at the door. Who at this hour? Three, good Heavens! Three already! For with overpowering directness and dignity the clock struck three; and she heard nothing else; but the door handle slipped round and in came Richard! What a surprise! In came Richard, holding out flowers. She had failed him, once at Constantinople; and Lady Bruton, whose lunch parties were said to be extraordinarily amusing, had not asked her. He was holding out flowers – roses, red and white roses. (But he could not bring himself to say he loved her; not in so many words.)

But how lovely, she said, taking his flowers. She understood; she understood without his speaking; his Clarissa. She put them in vases on the mantelpiece. How lovely they looked, she said. And was it amusing, she asked. Had Lady Bruton asked after her? Peter Walsh was back. Mrs Marsham had written. Must she ask Ellie Henderson? That woman Kilman was upstairs.

'But let us sit down for five minutes,' said Richard.

It all looked so empty. All the chairs were against the wall. What had they been doing? Oh, it was for the party; no, he had not forgotten the party. Peter Walsh was back. Oh yes; she had had him. And he was going to get a divorce; and he was in love with some woman out there. And he hadn't changed in the slightest. There she was, mending her dress. . . .

'Thinking of Bourton,' she said.

'Hugh was at lunch,' said Richard. She had met him too! Well, he was getting absolutely intolerable. Buying Evelyn necklaces; fatter than ever; an intolerable ass.

'And it came over me "I might have married you",' she said, thinking of Peter sitting there in his little bow-tie, with that knife, opening it, shutting it. 'Just as he always was, you know.'

They were talking about him at lunch, said Richard. (But he could not tell her he loved her. He held her hand. Happiness is this, he thought.) They had been writing a letter to *The Times* for Millicent Bruton. That was about all Hugh was fit for.

'And our dear Miss Kilman?' he asked. Clarissa thought the roses absolutely lovely; first bunched together; now of their own accord starting apart.

'Kilman arrives just after we've done lunch,' she said. 'Elizabeth turns pink. They shut themselves up. I suppose they're praying.'

Lord! He didn't like it; but these things pass over if you let them.

'In a mackintosh with an umbrella,' said Clarissa.

He had not said 'I love you'; but he held her hand. Happiness is this, is this, he thought.

'But why should I ask all the dull women in London to my parties?' said Clarissa. 'And if Mrs Marsham gave a party, did *she* invite her guests?'

'Poor Ellie Henderson,' said Richard – it was a very odd thing how much Clarissa minded about her parties, he thought.

But Richard had no notion of the look of a room. However – what was he going to say?

If she worried about these parties he would not let her give them. Did she wish she had married Peter? But he must go.

He must be off, he said, getting up. But he stood for a moment as if he were about to say something; and she wondered what? Why? There were the roses.

'Some Committee?' she asked, as he opened the door.

'Armenians,' he said; or perhaps it was 'Albanians.'

And there is a dignity in people; a solitude; even between husband and wife a gulf; and that one must respect, thought Clarissa, watching him open the door; for one would not part with it oneself, or take it, against his will, from one's husband, without losing one's independence, one's self-respect – something, after all, priceless.

He returned with a pillow and a quilt.

'An hour's complete rest after luncheon,' he said. And he went.

How like him! He would go on saying 'An hour's complete rest after luncheon' to the end of time, because a doctor had ordered it once. It was like him to take what doctors said literally; part of his adorable divine simplicity, which no one had to the same extent; which made him go and do the thing while she and Peter frittered their time away bickering. He was already half-way to the House of Commons, to his Armenians, his Albanians, having settled her on the sofa, looking at his roses. And people would say, 'Clarissa Dalloway is spoilt.' She cared much more for her roses than for the Armenians. Hunted out of existence, maimed, frozen, the victims of cruelty and injustice (she had heard Richard say so over and over again) – no, she could feel nothing for the Albanians, or was it the Armenians? but she loved her roses (didn't that help the Armenians?) – the only flowers she could bear to see cut. But Richard was already at the House of Commons; at his Committee, having settled all her difficulties. But no; alas, that was not true. He did not see the reasons against asking Ellie Henderson. She would do it, of course, as he wished it. Since he had brought the pillow, she would lie down. . . . But – but – why did she suddenly feel, for no reason that she could discover, desperately unhappy? As a person who has dropped some grain of pearl or diamond into the grass and parts the tall blades very carefully, this way and that, and searches here and there vainly, and at last spies it there at the roots, so she went through one thing and another; no, it was not Sally Seton saying that Richard would never be in the Cabinet because he had a second-class brain (it came back to her); no, she did not mind that; nor was it to do with Elizabeth either and Doris Kilman; those were the facts. It was a feeling, some unpleasant feeling, earlier in the day perhaps; something that Peter had said, combined with some depression of her own, in her bedroom, taking off her hat; and what Richard had said had added to it, but what had he said? There were his roses. Her parties! That was it! Her parties! Both of them criticized her very unfairly, laughed at her very unjustly, for her parties. That was it! That was it!

Well, how was she going to defend herself? Now that she knew what it was, she felt perfectly happy. They thought, or Peter at any rate thought, that she enjoyed imposing herself; liked to have famous people about her; great names; was simply a snob in short. Well, Peter might think so. Richard merely thought it foolish of her to like excitement when she knew it was bad for her heart. It was childish, he thought. And both were quite wrong. What she liked was simply life.

'That's what I do it for,' she said, speaking aloud, to life.

Since she was lying on the sofa, cloistered, exempt, the presence of this thing which she felt to be so obvious became physically existent; with robes of sound from the street, sunny, with hot breath, whispering, blowing out the blinds. But suppose Peter said to her, 'Yes, yes, but your parties – what's the sense of your parties?' all she could say was (and nobody could be expected to understand): They're an offering; which sounded horribly vague. But who was Peter to make out that life was all plain sailing? – Peter always in love, always in love with the wrong woman? What's your love? she might say to him. And she knew his answer; how it is the most important thing in the world and no woman possibly understood it. Very well. But could any man understand what she meant either? about life? She could not imagine Peter or Richard taking the trouble to give a party for no reason whatever.

But to go deeper, beneath what people said (and these judgements, how superficial, how fragmentary they are!)

in her own mind now, what did it mean to her, this thing called life? Oh, it was very queer. Here was So-and-so in South Kensington; some one up in Bayswater; and somebody else, say, in Mayfair. And she felt quite continuously a sense of their existence; and she felt what a waste; and she felt what a pity; and she felt if only they could be brought together; so she did it. And it was an offering; to combine, to create; but to whom?

An offering for the sake of offering, perhaps. Anyhow, it was her gift. Nothing else had she of the slightest importance; could not think, write, even play the piano. She muddled Armenians and Turks; loved success; hated discomfort; must be liked; talked oceans of nonsense; and to this day, ask her what the Equator was, and she did not know.

All the same, that one day should follow another; Wednesday, Thursday, Friday, Saturday; that one should wake up in the morning; see the sky; walk in the park; meet Hugh Whitbread; then suddenly in came Peter; then these roses; it was enough. After that, how unbelievable death was! – that it must end; and no one in the whole world would know how she had loved it all; how, every instant . . .

The door opened. Elizabeth knew that her mother was resting. She came in very quietly. She stood perfectly still. Was it that some Mongol had been wrecked on the coast of Norfolk (as Mrs Hilbery said), had mixed with the Dalloway ladies, perhaps a hundred years ago? For the Dalloways, in general, were fair-haired; blue-eyed; Elizabeth, on the contrary, was dark; had Chinese eyes in a pale face; an Oriental mystery; was gentle, considerate, still. As a child, she had had a perfect sense of humour; but now at seventeen, why, Clarissa could not in the least understand, she had become very serious; like a hyacinth sheathed in glossy green, with buds just tinted, a hyacinth which has had no sun.

She stood quite still and looked at her mother; but the door was ajar, and outside the door was Miss Kilman, as Clarissa knew; Miss Kilman in her mackintosh listening to whatever they said.

Yes, Miss Kilman stood on the landing, and wore a mackintosh; but had her reasons. First, it was cheap; second, she was over forty; and did not, after all, dress to please. She was poor, moreover; degradingly poor. Otherwise she would not be taking jobs from people like the Dalloways; from rich people, who liked to be kind. Mr Dalloway, to do him justice, had been kind. But Mrs Dalloway had not. She had been merely condescending. She came from the most worthless of all classes – the rich, with a smattering of culture. They had expensive things everywhere; pictures, carpets, lots of servants. She considered that she had a perfect right to anything that the Dalloways did for her.

She had been cheated. Yes, the word was no exaggeration, for surely a girl has a right to some kind of happiness? And she had never been happy, what with being so clumsy and so poor. And then, just as she might have had a chance at Miss Dolby's school, the war came; and she had never been able to tell lies. Miss Dolby thought she would be happier with people who shared her views about the Germans. She had had to go. It was true that the family was of German origin; spelt the name Kiehlman in the eighteenth century; but her brother had been killed. They turned her out because she would not pretend that the Germans were all villains – when she had German friends, when the only happy days of her life had been spent in Germany! And after all, she could read history. She had had to take whatever she could get. Mr Dalloway had come across her working for the Friends. He had allowed her (and that was really generous of him) to teach his daughter history. Also she did a little Extension lecturing and so on. Then Our Lord had come to her (and here she always bowed her head). She had seen the light two years and three months ago. Now she did not envy women like Clarissa Dalloway; she pitied them.

She pitied and despised them from the bottom of her heart, as she stood on the soft carpet, looking at the old engraving of a little girl with a muff. With all this luxury going on, what hope was there for a better state of things? Instead of lying on a sofa – 'My mother is resting,' Elizabeth had said – she should have been in a factory; behind a counter; Mrs Dalloway and all the other fine ladies!

Bitter and burning, Miss Kilman had turned into a church

two years three months ago. She had heard the Rev. Edward Whittaker preach; the boys sing; had seen the solemn lights descend, and whether it was the music, or the voices (she herself when alone in the evening found comfort in a violin; but the sound was excruciating; she had no ear), the hot and turbulent feelings which boiled and surged in her had been assuaged as she sat there, and she had wept copiously, and gone to call on Mr Whittaker at his private house in Kensington. It was the hand of God, he said. The Lord had shown her the way. So now, whenever the hot and painful feelings boiled within her, this hatred of Mrs Dalloway, this grudge against the world, she thought of God. She thought of Mr Whittaker. Rage was succeeded by calm. A sweet savour filled her veins, her lips parted, and, standing formidable upon the landing in her mackintosh, she looked with steady and sinister serenity at Mrs Dalloway, who came out with her daughter.

Elizabeth said she had forgotten her gloves. That was because Miss Kilman and her mother hated each other. She could not bear to see them together. She ran upstairs to find her gloves.

But Miss Kilman did not hate Mrs Dalloway. Turning her large gooseberry-coloured eyes upon Clarissa, observing her small pink face, her delicate body, her air of freshness and fashion, Miss Kilman felt, Fool! Simpleton! You who have known neither sorrow nor pleasure; who have trifled your life away! And there rose in her an overmastering desire to overcome her; to unmask her. If she could have felled her it would have eased her. But it was not the body; it was the soul and its mockery that she wished to subdue; make feel her mastery. If only she could make her weep; could ruin her; humiliate her; bring her to her knees crying, You are right! But this was God's will, not Miss Kilman's. It was to be a religious victory. So she glared; so she glowered.

Clarissa was really shocked. This a Christian – this woman! This woman had taken her daughter from her! She in touch with invisible presences! Heavy, ugly, commonplace, without kindness or grace, she know the meaning of life!

'You are taking Elizabeth to the Stores?' Mrs Dalloway said.

Miss Kilman said she was. They stood there. Miss Kilman was not going to make herself agreeable. She had always earned her living. Her knowledge of modern history was thorough in the extreme. She did, out of her meagre income, set aside so much for causes she believed in; whereas this woman did nothing, believed nothing; brought up her daughter – but here was Elizabeth, rather out of breath, the beautiful girl.

So they were going to the Stores. Odd it was, as Miss Kilman stood there (and stand she did, with the power and taciturnity of some prehistoric monster armoured for primeval warfare), how, second by second, the idea of her diminished, how hatred (which was for ideas, not people) crumbled, how she lost her malignity, her size, became second by second merely Miss Kilman, in a mackintosh, whom Heaven knows Clarissa would have liked to help.

At this dwindling of the monster, Clarissa laughed. Saying good-bye, she laughed.

Off they went together, Miss Kilman and Elizabeth, downstairs.

With a sudden impulse, with a violent anguish, for this woman was taking her daughter from her, Clarissa leant over the banisters and cried out, 'Remember the party! Remember our party to-night!'

But Elizabeth had already opened the front door; there was a van passing; she did not answer.

Love and religion! thought Clarissa, going back into the drawing-room, tingling all over. How detestable, how detestable they are! For now that the body of Miss Kilman was not before her, it overwhelmed her – the idea. The cruellest things in the world, she thought, seeing them clumsy, hot, domineering, hypocritical, eavesdropping, jealous, infinitely cruel and unscrupulous, dressed in a mackintosh coat, on the landing; love and religion. Had she ever tried to convert any one herself? Did she not wish everybody merely to be themselves? And she watched out of the window the old lady opposite climbing upstairs. Let her climb upstairs if she wanted to; let her stop; then let her, as Clarissa had often seen her, gain her bedroom, part her curtains, and disappear again into the background. Somehow one respected that – that old woman looking out of the window, quite unconscious that she was being watched. There was something solemn in it – but love and religion would destroy that, whatever it was, the privacy of the soul. The odious Kilman would destroy it. Yet it was a sight that made her want to cry.

Love destroyed too. Everything that was fine, everything that was true went. Take Peter Walsh now. There was a man, charming, clever, with ideas about everything. If you wanted to know about Pope, say, or Addison, or just to talk nonsense, what people were like, what things meant, Peter knew better than any one. It was Peter who had helped her; Peter who had lent her books. But look at the women he loved – vulgar, trivial, commonplace. Think of Peter in love – he came to see her after all these years, and what did he talk about? Himself. Horrible passion! she thought. Degrading passion! she thought, thinking of Kilman and her Elizabeth walking to the Army and Navy Stores.

Big Ben struck the half-hour.

How extraordinary it was, strange, yes, touching to see the old lady (they had been neighbours ever so many years) move away from the window, as if she were attached to that sound, that string. Gigantic as it was, it had something to do with her. Down, down, into the midst of ordinary things the finger fell, making the moment solemn. She was forced, so Clarissa imagined, by that sound, to move, to go – but where? Clarissa tried to follow her as she turned and disappeared, and could still just see her white cap moving at the back of the bedroom. She was still there, moving about at the other end of the room. Why creeds and prayers and mackintoshes? when, thought Clarissa, that's the miracle, that's the mystery; that old lady, she meant, whom she could see going from chest of drawers to dressing-table. She could still see her. And the supreme mystery which Kilman might say she had solved, or Peter might say he had solved, but Clarissa didn't believe either of them had the ghost of an idea of solving, was simply this: here was one room; there another. Did religion solve that, or love?

Love – but here the other clock, the clock which always struck two minutes after Big Ben, came shuffling in with its lap full of odds and ends, which it dumped down as if Big Ben were all very well with his majesty laying down the law, so solemn, so just, but she must remember all sorts of little things besides – Mrs Marsham, Ellie Henderson, glasses for ices – all sorts of little things came flooding and lapping and dancing in on the wake of that solemn stroke which lay flat like a bar of gold on the sea. Mrs Marsham, Ellie Henderson, glasses for ices. She must telephone now at once.

Volubly, troublously, the late clock sounded, coming in on the wake of Big Ben, with its lap full of trifles. Beaten up, broken up by the assault of carriages, the brutality of vans, the eager advance of myriads of angular men, of flaunting women, the domes and spires of offices and hospitals, the last relics of this lap full of odds and ends seemed to break, like the spray of an exhausted wave, upon the body of Miss Kilman standing still in the street for a moment to mutter 'It is the flesh.'

It was the flesh that she must control. Clarissa Dalloway had insulted her. That she expected. But she had not triumphed; she had not mastered the flesh. Ugly, clumsy, Clarissa Dalloway had laughed at her for being that; and had revived the fleshly desires, for she minded looking as she did beside Clarissa. Nor could she talk as she did. But why wish to resemble her? Why? She despised Mrs Dalloway from the bottom of her heart. She was not serious. She was not good. Her life was a tissue of vanity and deceit. Yet Doris Kilman had been overcome. She had, as a matter of fact, very nearly burst into tears when Clarissa Dalloway laughed at her. 'It is the flesh, it is the flesh,' she muttered (it being her habit to talk aloud), trying to subdue this turbulent and painful feeling as she walked down Victoria Street. She prayed to God. She could not help being ugly; she could not afford to buy pretty clothes. Clarissa Dalloway had laughed – but she would concentrate her mind upon something else until she had reached the pillar-box. At any rate she had got

Elizabeth. But she would think of something else; she would think of Russia; until she reached the pillar-box.

How nice it must be, she said, in the country, struggling, as Mr Whittaker had told her, with that violent grudge against the world which had scorned her, sneered at her, cast her off, beginning with this indignity – the infliction of her unlovable body which people could not bear to see. Do her hair as she might, her forehead remained like an egg, bald, white. No clothes suited here. She might buy anything. And for a woman, of course, that meant never meeting the opposite sex. Never would she come first with any one. Sometimes lately it had seemed to her that, except for Elizabeth, her food was all that she lived for; her comforts; her dinner, her tea; her hot-water bottle at night. But one must fight; vanquish; have faith in God. Mr Whittaker had said she was there for a purpose. But no one knew the agony! He said, pointing to the crucifix, that God knew. But why should she have to suffer when other women, like Clarissa Dalloway, escaped? Knowledge comes through suffering, said Mr Whittaker.

She had passed the pillar-box, and Elizabeth had turned into the cool brown tobacco department of the Army and Navy Stores while she was still muttering to herself what Mr Whittaker had said about knowledge coming through suffering and the flesh. 'The flesh,' she muttered.

What department did she want? Elizabeth interrupted her.

'Petticoats,' she said abruptly, and stalked straight on to the lift.

Up they went. Elizabeth guided her this way and that; guided her in her abstraction as if she had been a great child, an unwieldy battleship. There were the petticoats, brown, decorous, striped, frivolous, solid, flimsy; and she chose, in her abstraction, portentously, and the girl serving thought her mad.

Elizabeth rather wondered, as they did up the parcel, what Miss Kilman was thinking. They must have their tea, said Miss Kilman, rousing, collecting herself. They had their tea.

Elizabeth rather wondered whether Miss Kilman could be hungry. It was her way of eating, eating with intensity, then looking, again and again, at a plate of sugared cakes on the table next to them; then, when a lady and a child sat down and the child took the cake, could Miss Kilman really mind it? Yes, Miss Kilman did mind it. She had wanted that cake – the pink one. The pleasure of eating was almost the only pure pleasure left her, and then to be baffled even in that!

When people are happy they have a reserve, she had told Elizabeth, upon which to draw, whereas she was like a wheel without a tyre (she was fond of such metaphors), jolted by every pebble – so she would say, staying on after the lesson, standing by the fire-place with her bag of books, her 'satchel', she called it, on a Tuesday morning, after the lesson was over. And she talked too about the war. After all, there were people who did not think the English invariably right. There were books. There were meetings. There were other points of view. Would Elizabeth like to come with her to listen to So-and-so? (a most extraordinary-looking old man). Then Miss Kilman took her to some church in Kensington and they had tea with a clergyman. She had lent her books. Law, medicine, politics, all professions are open to women of your generation, said Miss Kilman. But for herself, her career was absolutely ruined, and was it her fault? Good gracious, said Elizabeth, no.

And her mother would come calling to say that a hamper had come from Bourton and would Miss Kilman like some flowers? To Miss Kilman she was always very, very nice, but Miss Kilman squashed the flowers all in a bunch, and hadn't any small talk, and what interested Miss Kilman bored her mother, and Miss Kilman and she were terrible together; and Miss Kilman swelled and looked very plain, but Miss Kilman was frightfully clever. Elizabeth had never thought about the poor. They lived with everything they wanted, – her mother had breakfast in bed every day; Lucy carried it up; and she liked old women because they were Duchesses, and being descended from some Lord. But Miss Kilman said (one of those Tuesday mornings when the lesson was over), 'My grandfather kept an oil and colour shop in Kensington.' Miss Kilman was quite different from any one she knew; she made one feel so small.

Miss Kilman took another cup of tea. Elizabeth, with her oriental bearing, her inscrutable mystery, sat perfectly upright; no, she did not want anything more. She looked for her gloves – her white gloves. They were under the table. Ah, but she must not go! Miss Kilman could not let her go! this youth, that was so beautiful! this girl, whom she genuinely loved! Her large hand opened and shut on the table.

But perhaps it was a little flat somehow, Elizabeth felt. And really she would like to go.

But said Miss Kilman, 'I've not quite finished yet.'

Of course, then, Elizabeth would wait. But it was rather stuffy in here.

'Are you going to the party to-night?' Miss Kilman said. Elizabeth supposed she was going; her mother wanted her to go. She must not let parties absorb her, Miss Kilman said, fingering the last two inches of a chocolate éclair.

She did not much like parties, Elizabeth said. Miss Kilman opened her mouth, slightly projected her chin, and swallowed down the last inches of the chocolate éclair, then wiped her fingers, and washed the tea round in her cup.

She was about to split asunder, she felt. The agony was so terrific. If she could grasp her, if she could clasp her, if she could make her hers absolutely and for ever and then die; that was all she wanted. But to sit here, unable to think of anything to say; to see Elizabeth turning against her; to be felt repulsive even by her – it was too much; she could not stand it. The thick fingers curled inwards.

'I never go to parties,' said Miss Kilman, just to keep Elizabeth from going. 'People don't ask me to parties' – and she knew as she said it that it was this egotism that was her undoing; Mr Whittaker had warned her; but she could not help it. She had suffered so horribly. 'Why should they ask me?' she said. 'I'm plain, I'm unhappy.' She knew it was idiotic. But it was all those people passing – people with parcels who despised her – who made her say it. However, she was Doris Kilman. She had her degree. She was a woman who had made her way in the world. Her knowledge of modern history was more than respectable.

'I don't pity myself,' she said. 'I pity' – she meant to say 'your mother,' but no, she could not, not to Elizabeth. 'I pity other people much more.'

Like some dumb creature who has been brought up to a gate for an unknown purpose, and stands there longing to gallop away, Elizabeth Dalloway sat silent. Was Miss Kilman going to say anything more?

'Don't quite forget me,' said Doris Kilman; her voice quivered. Right away to the end of the field the dumb creature galloped in terror.

The great hand opened and shut.

Elizabeth turned her head. The waitress came. One had to pay at the desk, Elizabeth said, and went off, drawing out, so Miss Kilman felt, the very entrails in her body, stretching them as she crossed the room, and then, with a final twist, bowing her head very politely, she went.

She had gone. Miss Kilman sat at the marble table among the éclairs, stricken once, twice, thrice by shocks of suffering. She had gone. Mrs Dalloway had triumphed. Elizabeth had gone. Beauty had gone; youth had gone.

So she sat. She got up, blundered off among the little tables, rocking slightly from side to side, and somebody came after her with her petticoat, and she lost her way, and was hemmed in by trunks specially prepared for taking to India; next got among the accouchement sets and baby linen; through all the commodities of the world, perishable and permanent, hams, drugs, flowers, stationery, variously smelling, now sweet, now sour, she lurched; saw herself thus lurching with her hat askew, very red in the face, full length in a looking-glass; and at last came out into the street.

The tower of Westminster Cathedral rose in front of her, the habitation of God. In the midst of the traffic, there was the habitation of God. Doggedly she set off with her parcel to that other sanctuary, the Abbey, where, raising her hands in a tent before her face, she sat beside those driven into shelter too; the variously assorted worshippers, now divested of social rank, almost of sex, as they raised their hands before their faces; but once they removed them, instantly reverent, middle-class, English men and women, some of them desirous of seeing the waxworks.

But Miss Kilman held her tent before her face. Now she was deserted; now rejoined. New worshippers came in from the street to replace the strollers, and still, as people gazed round and shuffled past the tomb of the Unknown Warrior, still she barred her eyes with her fingers and tried in this double darkness, for the light in the Abbey was bodiless, to aspire above the vanities, the desires, the commodities, to rid herself both of hatred and of love. Her hands twitched. She seemed to struggle. Yet to others God was accessible and the path to Him smooth. Mr Fletcher, retired, of the Treasury, Mrs Gorham, widow of the famous K.C., approached Him simply, and having done their praying, leant back, enjoyed the music (the organ pealed sweetly), and saw Miss Kilman at the end of the row, praying, praying, and, being still on the threshold of their underworld, thought of her sympathetically as a soul haunting the same territory; a soul cut out of immaterial substance; not a woman, a soul.

But Mr Fletcher had to go. He had to pass her, and being himself neat as a new pin, could not help being a little distressed by the poor lady's disorder; her hair down; her parcel on the floor. She did not at once let him pass. But, as he stood gazing about him, at the white marbles, grey window panes, and accumulated treasures (for he was extremely proud of the Abbey), her largeness, robustness, and power as she sat there shifting her knees from time to time (it was so rough the approach to her God – so tough her desires) impressed him, as they had impressed Mrs Dalloway (she could not get the thought of her out of her mind that afternoon), the Rev. Edward Whittaker, and Elizabeth too.

And Elizabeth waited in Victoria Street for an omnibus. It was so nice to be out of doors. She thought perhaps she need not go home just yet. It was so nice to be out in the air. So she would get on to an omnibus. And already, even as she stood there, in her very well-cut clothes, it was beginning. . . . People were beginning to compare her to poplar trees, early dawn, hyacinths, fawns, running water, and garden lilies; and it made her life a burden to her, for she so much preferred being left alone to do what she liked in the country, but they would compare her to lilies, and she had to go to parties, and London was so dreary compared with being alone in the country with her father and the dogs.

Buses swooped, settled, were off – garish caravans glistening with red and yellow varnish. But which should she get on to? She had no preferences. Of course, she would not push her way. She inclined to be passive. It was expression she needed, but her eyes were fine, Chinese, oriental, and, as her mother said, with such nice shoulders and holding herself so straight, she was always charming to look at; and lately, in the evening especially, when she was interested, for she never seemed excited, she looked almost beautiful, very stately, very serene. What could she be thinking? Every man fell in love with her, and she was really awfully bored. For it was beginning. Her mother could see that – the compliments were beginning. That she did not care more about it – for instance for her clothes – sometimes worried Clarissa, but perhaps it was as well with all those puppies and guinea pigs about having distemper, and it gave her a charm. And now there was this odd friendship with Miss Kilman. Well, thought Clarissa about three o'clock in the morning, reading Baron Marbot for she could not sleep, it proves she has a heart.

Suddenly Elizabeth stepped forward and most competently boarded the omnibus, in front of everybody. She took a seat on top. The impetuous creature – a pirate – started forward, sprang away; she had to hold the rail to steady herself, for a pirate it was, reckless, unscrupulous, bearing down ruthlessly, circumventing dangerously, boldly snatching a passenger, or ignoring a passenger, squeezing eel-like and arrogant in between, and then rushing insolently all sails spread up Whitehall. And did Elizabeth give one thought to poor Miss Kilman who loved her without jealousy, to whom she had been a fawn in the open, a moon in a glade? She was delighted to be free. The fresh air was so delicious. It had been so stuffy in the Army and Navy

Stores. And now it was like riding, to be rushing up White-hall; and to each movement of the omnibus the beautiful body in the fawn-coloured coat responded freely like a rider, like the figure-head of a ship, for the breeze slightly disarrayed her; the heat gave her cheeks the pallor of white painted wood; and her fine eyes, having no eyes to meet, gazed ahead, blank, bright, with the staring, incredible innocence of sculpture.

It was always talking about her own sufferings that made Miss Kilman so difficult. And was she right? If it was being on committees and giving up hours and hours every day (she hardly ever saw him in London) that helped the poor, her father did that, goodness knows – if that was what Miss Kilman meant about being a Christian; but it was so difficult to say. Oh, she would like to go a little farther. Another penny, was it, to the Strand? Here was another penny, then. She would go up the Strand.

She liked people who were ill. And every profession is open to the women of your generation, said Miss Kilman. So she might be a doctor. She might be a farmer. Animals are often ill. She might own a thousand acres and have people under her. She would go and see them in their cottages. This was Somerset House. One might be a very good farmer – and that, strangely enough, though Miss Kilman had her share in it, was almost entirely due to Somerset House. It looked so splendid, so serious, that great grey building. And she liked the feeling of people working. She liked those churches, like shapes of grey paper, breasting the stream of the Strand. It was quite different here from Westminster, she thought, getting off at Chancery Lane. It was so serious; it was so busy. In short, she would like to have a profession. She would become a doctor, a farmer, possibly go into Parliament if she found it necessary, all because of the Strand.

The feet of those people busy about their activities, hands putting stone to stone, minds eternally occupied not with trivial chatterings (comparing women to poplars – which was rather exciting, of course, but very silly), but with thoughts of ships, of business, of law, of administration, and with it all so stately (she was in the Temple), gay (there was the river), pious (there was the Church), made her quite determined, whatever her mother might say, to become either a farmer or a doctor. She was, of course, rather lazy.

And it was much better to say nothing about it. It seemed so silly. It was the sort of thing that did sometimes happen, when one was alone – buildings without architects' names, crowds of people coming back from the city having more power than single clergymen in Kensington, than any of the books Miss Kilman had lent her, to stimulate what lay slumbrous, clumsy, and shy on the mind's sandy floor, to break surface, as a child suddenly stretches its arms; it was just that, perhaps, a sigh, a stretch of the arms, an impulse, a revelation, which has its effects for ever, and then down again it went to the sandy floor. She must go home. She must dress for dinner. But what was the time? – where was a clock?

She looked up Fleet Street. She walked just a little way towards St Paul's, shyly, like some one penetrating on tiptoe, exploring a strange house by night with a candle, on edge lest the owner should suddenly fling wide his bedroom door and ask her business, nor did she dare wander off into queer alleys, tempting by-streets, any more than in a strange house open doors which might be bedroom doors, or sitting-room doors, or lead straight to the larder. For no Dalloways came down the Strand daily; she was a pioneer, a stray, venturing, trusting.

In many ways, her mother felt, she was extremely immature, like a child still, attached to dolls, to old slippers; a perfect baby; and that was charming. But then, of course, there was in the Dalloway family the tradition of public service. Abbesses, principals, head mistresses, dignitaries, in the republic of women – without being brilliant, any of them, they were that. She penetrated a little farther in the direction of St Paul's. She liked the geniality, sisterhood, motherhood, brotherhood of this uproar. It seemed to her good. The noise was tremendous; and suddenly there were trumpets (the unemployed) blaring, rattling about in the uproar; military music; as if people were marching; yet had they been dying – had some woman breathed her last, and whoever was watching, opening the window of the room where she had just brought off that act of supreme dignity, looked down on Fleet Street, that uproar, that military music would have come triumphing up to him, consolatory, indifferent.

It was not conscious. There was no recognition in it of one's fortune, or fate, and for that very reason even to those dazed with watching for the last shivers of consciousness on the faces of the dying, consoling.

Forgetfulness in people might wound, their ingratitude corrode, but this voice, pouring endlessly year in, year out, would take whatever it might be; this vow; this van; this life; this procession; would wrap them all about and carry them on, as in the rough stream of a glacier the ice holds a splinter of bone, a blue petal, some oak trees, and rolls them on.

But it was later than she thought. Her mother would not like her to be wandering off alone like this. She turned back down the Strand.

A puff of wind (in spite of the heat, there was quite a wind) blew a thin black veil over the sun and over the Strand. The faces faded; the omnibuses suddenly lost their glow. For although the clouds were of mountainous white so that one could fancy hacking hard chips off with a hatchet, with broad golden slopes, lawns of celestial pleasure gardens, on their flanks, and had all the appearance of settled habitations assembled for the conference of gods above the world, there was a perpetual movement among them. Signs were interchanged, when, as if to fulfil some scheme arranged already, now a summit dwindled, now a whole block of pyramidal size which had kept its station inalterably advanced into the midst or gravely led the procession to fresh anchorage. Fixed though they seemed at their posts, at rest in perfect unanimity, nothing could be fresher, freer, more sensitive superficially than the snow-white or gold-kindled surface; to change, to go, to dismantle the solemn assemblage was immediately possible; and in spite of the grave fixity, the accumulated robustness and solidity, now they struck light to the earth, now darkness.

Calmly and competently, Elizabeth Dalloway mounted the Westminster omnibus.

Going and coming, beckoning, signalling, so the light and shadow, which now made the wall grey, now the bananas bright yellow, now made the Strand grey, now made the omnibuses bright yellow, seemed to Septimus Warren Smith lying on the sofa in the sitting-room; watching the watery gold glow and fade with the astonishing sensibility of some live creature on the roses, on the wall-paper. Outside the trees dragged their leaves like nets through the depths of the air; the sound of water was in the room, and through the waves came the voices of birds singing. Every power poured its treasures on his head, and his hand lay there on the back of the sofa, as he had seen his hand lie when he was bathing, floating, on the top of the waves, while far away on shore he heard dogs barking and barking far away. Fear no more, says the heart in the body; fear no more.

He was not afraid. At every moment Nature signified by some laughing hint like that gold spot which went round the wall – there, there, there – her determination to show, by brandishing her plumes, shaking her tresses, flinging her mantle this way and that, beautifully, always beautifully, and standing close up to breathe through her hollowed hands Shakespeare's words, her meaning.

Rezia, sitting at the table twisting a hat in her hands, watched him; saw him smiling. He was happy, then. But she could not bear to see him smiling. It was not marriage; it was not being one's husband to look strange like that, always to be starting, laughing, sitting hour after hour silent, or clutching her and telling her to write. The table drawer was full of those writings; about war; about Shakespeare; about great discoveries; how there is no death. Lately he had become excited suddenly for no reason (and both Dr Holmes and Sir William Bradshaw said excitement was the worst thing for him), and waved his hands and cried out that he knew the truth! He knew everything! That man, his friend who was killed, Evans, had come, he said. He was singing behind the screen. She wrote it down just as he spoke it. Some things were very beautiful; others sheer nonsense. And he was always stopping in the middle, changing his mind; wanting to add something; hearing something new; listening with his hand up. But she heard nothing.

And once they found the girl who did the room reading one of these papers in fits of laughter. It was a dreadful pity. For that made Septimus cry out about human cruelty – how they tear each other to pieces. The fallen, he said, they tear to pieces. 'Holmes is on us,' he would say, and he would invent stories about Holmes; Holmes eating porridge; Holmes reading Shakespeare – making himself roar with laughter or rage, for Dr Holmes seemed to stand for something horrible to him. 'Human nature', he called him. Then there were the visions. He was drowned, he used to say, and lying on a cliff with the gulls screaming over him. He would look over the edge of the sofa down into the sea. Or he was hearing music. Really it was only a barrel organ or some man crying in the street. But 'Lovely!' he used to cry, and the tears would run down his cheeks, which was to her the most dreadful thing of all, to see a man like Septimus, who had fought, who was brave, crying. And he would lie listening until suddenly he would cry that he was falling down, down into the flames! Actually she would look for flames, it was so vivid. But there was nothing. They were alone in the room. It was a dream, she would tell him, and so quiet him at last, but sometimes she was frightened too. She sighed as she sat sewing.

Her sigh was tender and enchanting, like the wind outside a wood in the evening. Now she put down her scissors; now she turned to take something from the table. A little stir, a little crinkling, a little tapping built up something on the table there, where she sat sewing. Through his eyelashes he could see her blurred outline; her little black body; her face and hands; her turning movements at the table, as she took up a reel, or looked (she was apt to lose things) for her silk. She was making a hat for Mrs Filmer's married daughter, whose name was – he had forgotten her name.

'What is the name of Mrs Filmer's married daughter?' he asked.

'Mrs Peters,' said Rezia. She was afraid it was too small, she said, holding it before her. Mrs Peters was a big woman; but she did not like her. It was only because Mrs Filmer had been so good to them – 'She gave me grapes this morning,' she said – that Rezia wanted to do something to show that they were grateful. She had come into the room the other evening and found Mrs Peters, who thought they were out, playing the gramophone.

'Was it true?' he asked. She was playing the gramophone? Yes; she had told him about it at the time; she had found Mrs Peters playing the gramophone.

He began, very cautiously, to open his eyes, to see whether a gramophone was really there. But real things – real things were too exciting. He must be cautious. He would not go mad. First he looked at the fashion papers on the lower shelf, then gradually at the gramophone with the green trumpet. Nothing could be more exact. And so, gathering courage, he looked at the sideboard; the plate of bananas; the engraving of Queen Victoria and the Prince Consort; at the mantelpiece, with the jar of roses. None of these things moved. All were still; all were real.

'She is a woman with a spiteful tongue,' said Rezia.

'What does Mr Peters do?' Septimus asked.

'Ah,' said Rezia, trying to remember. She thought Mrs Filmer had said that he travelled for some company. 'Just now he is in Hull,' she said.

'Just now!' She said that with her Italian accent. She said that herself. He shaded his eyes so that he might see only a little of her face at a time, first the chin, then the nose, then the forehead, in case it were deformed, or had some terrible mark on it. But no, there she was, perfectly natural, sewing, with the pursed lips that women have, the set, the melancholy expression, when sewing. But there was nothing terrible about it, he assured himself, looking a second time, a third time at her face, her hands, for what was frightening or disgusting in her as she sat there in broad daylight, sewing? Mrs Peters had a spiteful tongue. Mr Peters was in Hull. Why, then, rage and prophesy? Why fly scourged and outcast? Why be made to tremble and sob by the clouds? Why seek truths and deliver messages when Rezia sat sticking pins into the front of her dress, and Mr Peters was in Hull? Miracles, revelations, agonies, loneliness, falling through the sea, down, down into the flames, all were burnt out, for he had a sense, as he watched Rezia trimming the straw hat for Mrs Peters, of a coverlet of flowers.

'It's too small for Mrs Peters,' said Septimus.

For the first time for days he was speaking as he used to do! Of course it was – absurdly small, she said. But Mrs Peters had chosen it.

He took it out of her hands. He said it was an organ grinder's monkey's hat.

How it rejoiced her, that! Not for weeks had they laughed like this together, poking fun privately like married people. What she meant was that if Mrs Filmer had come in, or Mrs Peters or anybody, they would not have understood what she and Septimus were laughing at.

'There,' she said, pinning a rose to one side of the hat. Never had she felt so happy! Never in her life!

But that was still more ridiculous, Septimus said. Now the poor woman looked like a pig at a fair. (Nobody ever made her laugh as Septimus did.)

What had she got in her work-box? She had ribbons and beads, tassels, artificial flowers. She tumbled them out on the table. He began putting odd colours together – for though he had no fingers, could not even do up a parcel, he had a wonderful eye, and often he was right, sometimes absurd, of course, but sometimes wonderfully right.

'She shall have a beautiful hat!' he murmured, taking up this and that, Rezia kneeling by his side, looking over his shoulder. Now it was finished – that is to say the design; she must stitch it together. But she must be very, very careful, he said, to keep it just as he had made it.

So she sewed. When she sewed, he thought, she made a sound like a kettle on the hob; bubbling, murmuring, always busy, her strong little pointed fingers pinching and poking; her needle flashing straight. The sun might go in and out, on the tassels, on the wall-paper, but he would wait, he thought, stretching out his feet, looking at his ringed sock at the end of the sofa; he would wait in this warm place, this pocket of still air, which one comes on at the edge of a wood sometimes in the evening, when because of a fall in the ground, or some arrangement of the trees (one must be scientific above all, scientific), warmth lingers, and the air buffets the cheek like the wing of a bird.

'There it is,' said Rezia, twirling Mrs Peters' hat on the tips of her fingers. 'That'll do for the moment. Later ...' her sentence bubbled away drip, drip, drip, like a contented tap left running.

It was wonderful. Never had he done anything which made him feel so proud. It was so real, it was so substantial, Mrs Peters' hat.

'Just look at it,' he said.

Yes, it would always make her happy to see that hat. He had become himself then, he had laughed then. They had been alone together. Always she would like that hat.

He told her to try it on.

'But I must look so queer!' she cried, running over to the glass and looking first this side, then that. Then she snatched it off again, for there was a tap at the door. Could it be Sir William Bradshaw? Had he sent already?

No! it was only the small girl with the evening paper.

What always happened, then happened – what happened every night of their lives. The small girl sucked her thumb at the door; Rezia went down on her knees; Rezia cooed and kissed; Rezia got a bag of sweets out of the table drawer. For so it always happened. First one thing, then another. So she built it up, first one thing and then another. Dancing, skipping, round and round the room they went. He took the paper. Surrey was all out, he read. There was a heat wave. Rezia repeated: Surrey was all out. There was a heat wave, making it part of the game she was playing with Mrs Filmer's grandchild, both of them laughing, chattering at the same time, at their game. He was very tired. He was very happy. He would sleep. He shut his eyes. But directly he saw nothing the sounds of the game became fainter and stranger and sounded like the cries of people seeking and not finding, and passing farther and farther away. They had lost him!

He started up in terror. What did he see? The plate of bananas on the sideboard. Nobody was there (Rezia had taken the child to its mother; it was bedtime). That was it: to be alone for ever. That was the doom pronounced in Milan when he came into the room and saw them cutting out buckram shapes with their scissors; to be alone for ever.

He was alone with the sideboard and the bananas. He was alone, exposed on this bleak eminence, stretched out – but not on a hill-top; not on a crag; on Mrs Filmer's sitting-room sofa. As for the visions, the faces, the voices of the dead, where were they? There was a screen in front of him, with black bulrushes and blue swallows. Where he had once seen mountains, where he had seen faces, where he had seen beauty, there was a screen.

'Evans!' he cried. There was no answer. A mouse had squeaked, or a curtain rustled. Those were the voices of the dead. The screen, the coal-scuttle, the sideboard remained to him. Let him, then, face the screen, the coal-scuttle and the sideboard ... but Rezia burst into the room chattering.

Some letter had come. Everybody's plans were changed. Mrs Filmer would not be able to go to Brighton after all. There was no time to let Mrs Williams know, and really Rezia thought it very, very annoying, when she caught sight of the hat and thought ... perhaps ... she ... might just make a little ... Her voice died out in contented melody.

'Ah, damn!' she cried (it was a joke of theirs, her swearing); the needle had broken. Hat, child, Brighton, needle. She built it up; first one thing, then another, she built it up, sewing.

She wanted him to say whether by moving the rose she had improved the hat. She sat on the end of the sofa. They were perfectly happy now, she said suddenly, putting the hat down. For she could say anything to him now. She could say whatever came into her head. That was almost the first thing she had felt about him, that night in the café when he had come in with his English friends. He had come in, rather shyly, looking round him, and his hat had fallen when he hung it up. That she could remember. She knew he was English, though not one of the large Englishmen her sister admired, for he was always thin; but he had a beautiful fresh colour; and with his big nose, his bright eyes, his way of sitting a little hunched, made her think, she had often told him, of a young hawk, that first evening she saw him, when they were playing dominoes, and he had come in – of a young hawk; but with her he was always very gentle. She had never seen him wild or drunk, only suffering sometimes through this terrible war, but even so, when she came in, he would put it all away. Anything, anything in the whole world, any little bother with her work, anything that struck her to say she would tell him, and he understood at once. Her own family even were not the same. Being older than she was and being so clever – how serious he was, wanting her to read Shakespeare before she could even read a child's story in English! – being so much more experienced, he could help her. And she, too, could help him.

But this hat now. And then (it was getting late) Sir William Bradshaw.

She held her hands to her head, waiting for him to say did he like the hat or not, and as she sat there, waiting, looking down, he could feel her mind, like a bird, falling from branch to branch, and always alighting, quite rightly; he could follow her mind, as she sat there in one of those loose lax poses that came to her naturally, and, if he should say anything, at once she smiled, like a bird alighting with all its claws firm upon the bough.

But he remembered. Bradshaw said, 'The people we are most fond of are not good for us when we are ill.' Bradshaw said he must be taught to rest. Bradshaw said they must be separated.

'Must', 'must', why 'must'? What power had Bradshaw over him? 'What right has Bradshaw to say "must" to me?' he demanded.

'It is because you talked of killing yourself,' said Rezia. (Mercifully, she could now say anything to Septimus.)

So he was in their power! Holmes and Bradshaw were on

him! The brute with the red nostrils was snuffling into every secret place! 'Must' it could say! Where were his papers? the things he had written?

She brought him his papers, the things he had written, things she had written for him. She tumbled them out on to the sofa. They looked at them together. Diagrams, designs, little men and women brandishing sticks for arms, with wings – were they? – on their backs; circles traced round shillings and sixpences – the suns and stars; zigzagging precipices with mountaineers ascending roped together, exactly like knives and forks; sea pieces with little faces laughing out of what might perhaps be waves : the map of the world. Burn them! he cried. Now for his writings; how the dead sing behind rhododendron bushes; odes to Time; conversations with Shakespeare; Evans, Evans, Evans – his messages from the dead; do not cut down trees; tell the Prime Minister. Universal love : the meaning of the world. Burn them! he cried.

But Rezia laid her hands on them. Some were very beautiful, she thought. She would tie them up (for she had no envelope) with a piece of silk.

Even if they took him, she said, she would go with him. They could not separate them against their wills, she said.

Shuffling the edges straight, she did up the papers, and tied the parcel almost without looking, sitting close, sitting beside him, he thought, as if all her petals were about her. She was a flowering tree; and through her branches looked out the face of a lawgiver, who had reached a sanctuary where she feared no one; not Holmes; not Bradshaw; a miracle, a triumph, the last and greatest. Staggering he saw her mount the appalling staircase, laden with Holmes and Bradshaw, men who never weighed less than eleven stone six, who sent their wives to court, men who made ten thousand a year and talked of proportion; who differed in their verdicts (for Holmes said one thing, Bradshaw another), yet judges they were; who mixed the vision and the sideboard; saw nothing clear, yet ruled, yet inflicted. Over them she triumphed.

'There!' she said. The papers were tied up. No one should

get at them. She would put them away.

And, she said, nothing should separate them. She sat down beside him and called him by the name of that hawk or crow which, being malicious and a great destroyer of crops, was precisely like him. No one could separate them, she said.

Then she got up to go into the bedroom to pack their things, but hearing voices downstairs and thinking that Dr Holmes had perhaps called, ran down to prevent him coming up.

Septimus could hear her talking to Holmes on the staircase.

'My dear lady, I have come as a friend,' Holmes was saying.

'No. I will not allow you to see my husband,' she said.

He could see her, like a little hen, with her wings spread barring his passage. But Holmes persevered.

'My dear lady, allow me ...' Holmes said, putting her aside (Holmes was a powerfully built man).

Holmes was coming upstairs. Holmes would burst open the door. Holmes would say, 'In a funk, eh?' Holmes would get him. But no; not Holmes; not Bradshaw. Getting up rather unsteadily, hopping indeed from foot to foot, he considered Mrs Filmer's nice clean bread-knife with 'Bread' carved on the handle. Ah, but one mustn't spoil that. The gas fire? But it was too late now. Holmes was coming. Razors he might have got, but Rezia, who always did that sort of thing, had packed them. There remained only the window, the large Bloomsbury lodging-house window; the tiresome, the troublesome, and rather melodramatic business of opening the window and throwing himself out. It was their idea of tragedy, not his or Rezia's (for she was with him). Holmes and Bradshaw liked that sort of thing. (He sat on the sill.) But he would wait till the very last moment. He did not want to die. Life was good. The sun hot. Only human beings? Coming down the staircase opposite an old man stopped and stared at him. Holmes was at the door. 'I'll give it you!' he cried, and flung himself vigorously, violently down on to Mrs Filmer's area railings.

'The coward!' cried Dr Holmes, bursting the door open. Rezia ran to the window, she saw; she understood. Dr Holmes and Mrs Filmer collided with each other. Mrs Filmer flapped her apron and made her hide her eyes in the bedroom. There was a great deal of running up and down stairs. Dr Holmes came in – white as a sheet, shaking all over, with a glass in his hand. She must be brave and drink something, he said (What was it? Something sweet), for her husband was horribly mangled, would not recover consciousness, she must not see him, must be spared as much as possible, would have the inquest to go through, poor young woman. Who could have foretold it? A sudden impulse, no one was in the least to blame (he told Mrs Filmer). And why the devil he did it, Dr Holmes could not conceive.

It seemed to her as she drank the sweet stuff that she was opening long windows, stepping out into some garden. But where? The clock was striking – one, two, three: how sensible the sound was; compared with all this thumping and whispering; like Septimus himself. She was falling asleep. But the clock went on striking, four, five, six, and Mrs Filmer waving her apron (they wouldn't bring the body in here, would they?) seemed part of that garden; or a flag. She had once seen a flag slowly rippling out from a mast when she stayed with her aunt at Venice. Men killed in battle were thus saluted, and Septimus had been through the War. Of her memories, most were happy.

She put on her hat, and ran through cornfields – where could it have been? – on to some hill, somewhere near the sea, for there were ships, gulls, butterflies; they sat on a cliff. In London, too, there they sat, and, half dreaming, came to her through the bedroom door, rain falling, whisperings, stirrings among dry corn, the caress of the sea, as it seemed to her, hollowing them in its arched shell and murmuring to her laid on shore, strewn she felt, like flying flowers over some tomb.

'He is dead,' she said, smiling at the poor old woman who guarded her with her honest light-blue eyes fixed on the door. (They wouldn't bring him in here, would they?) But Mrs Filmer pooh-poohed. Oh no, oh no! They were carrying him away now. Ought she not to be told? Married people ought to be together, Mrs Filmer thought. But they must do as the doctor said.

'Let her sleep,' said Dr Holmes, feeling her pulse. She saw the large outline of his body dark against the window. So that was Dr Holmes.

One of the triumphs of civilization, Peter Walsh thought. It is one of the triumphs of civilization, as the light high bell of the ambulance sounded. Swiftly, cleanly, the ambulance sped to the hospital, having picked up instantly, humanely, some poor devil; some one hit on the head, struck down by disease, knocked over perhaps a minute or so ago at one of these crossings, as might happen to oneself. That was civilization. It struck him coming back from the East – the efficiency, the organization, the communal spirit of London. Every cart or carriage of its own accord drew aside to let the ambulance pass. Perhaps it was morbid; or was it not touching rather, the respect which they showed this ambulance with its victim inside – busy men hurrying home, yet instantly bethinking them as it passed of some wife; or presumably how easily it might have been them there, stretched on a shelf with a doctor and a nurse.... Ah, but thinking became morbid, sentimental, directly one began conjuring up doctors, dead bodies; a little glow of pleasure, a sort of lust, too, over the visual impression warned one not to go on with that sort of thing any more – fatal to art, fatal to friendship. True. And yet, thought Peter Walsh, as the ambulance turned the corner, though the light high bell could be heard down the next street and still farther as it crossed the Tottenham Court Road, chiming constantly, it is the privilege of loneliness; in privacy one may do as one chooses. One might weep if no one saw. It had been his un-doing – this susceptibility – in Anglo-Indian society; not weeping at the right time, or laughing either. I have that in me, he thought, standing by the pillar-box, which could now dissolve in tears. Why, heaven knows. Beauty of some sort probably, and the weight of the day, which, beginning with that visit to Clarissa, had exhausted him with its heat, its intensity, and the drip, drip of one impression after another down into that cellar where they stood, deep, dark, and no one would ever know. Partly for that reason, its secrecy, complete and inviolable, he had found life like an unknown garden, full of turns and corners, surprising, yes; really it took one's breath away, these moments; there coming to him by the pillar-box opposite the British Museum one of them, a moment, in which things came together; this ambulance; and life and death. It was as if he were sucked up to some very high roof by that rush of emotion, and the rest of him, like a white shell-sprinkled beach, left bare. It had been his undoing in Anglo-Indian society – this susceptibility.

Clarissa once, going on top of an omnibus with him somewhere, Clarissa superficially at least, so easily moved, now in despair, now in the best of spirits, all aquiver in those days and such good company, spotting queer little scenes, names, people from the top of a bus, for they used to explore London and bring back bags full of treasures from the Caledonian market – Clarissa had a theory in those days – they had heaps of theories, always theories, as young people have. It was to explain the feeling they had of dissatisfaction; not knowing people; not being known. For how could they know each other? You met every day; then not for six months, or years. It was unsatisfactory, they agreed, how little one knew people. But she said, sitting on the bus going up Shaftesbury Avenue, she felt herself everywhere; not 'here, here, here'; and she tapped the back of the seat; but everywhere. She waved her hand, going up Shaftesbury Avenue. She was all that. So that to know her, or any one, one must seek out the people who completed them; even the places. Odd affinities she had with people she had never spoken to, some woman in the street, some man behind a counter – even trees, or barns. It ended in a transcendental theory which, with her horror of death, allowed her to believe, or say that she believed (for all her scepticism), that since our apparitions, the part of us which appears, are so momentary compared with the other, the unseen part of us, which spreads wide, the unseen might survive, be recovered somehow attached to this person or that, or even haunting certain places, after death. Perhaps – perhaps.

Looking back over that long friendship of almost thirty years her theory worked to this extent. Brief, broken, often painful as their actual meetings had been, what with his absences and interruptions (this morning, for instance, in came Elizabeth, like a long-legged colt, handsome, dumb, just as he was beginning to talk to Clarissa), the effect of them on his life was immeasurable. There was a mystery about it. You were given a sharp, acute, uncomfortable grain – the actual meeting; horribly painful as often as not; yet in absence, in the most unlikely places, it would flower out, open, shed its scent, let you touch, taste, look about you, get the whole feel of it and understanding, after years of lying lost. Thus she had come to him; on board ship; in the Himalayas; suggested by the oddest things (so Sally Seton, generous, enthusiastic goose! thought of *him* when she saw blue hydrangeas). She had influenced him more than any person he had ever known. And always in this way coming before him without his wishing it, cool, lady-like, critical; or ravishing, romantic, recalling some field or English harvest. He saw her most often in the country, not in London. One scene after another at Bourton. . . .

He had reached his hotel. He crossed the hall, with its mounds of reddish chairs and sofas, its spike-leaved, withered-looking plants. He got his key off the hook. The young lady handed him some letters. He went upstairs – he saw her most often at Bourton, in the late summer, when he stayed there for a week, or fortnight even, as people did in those days. First on top of some hill there she would stand, hands clapped to her hair, her cloak blowing out, pointing, crying to them – She saw the Severn beneath. Or in a wood, making the kettle boil – very ineffective with her fingers; the smoke curtseying, blowing in their faces; her little pink face showing through; begging water from an old woman in a cottage, who came to the door to watch them go. They walked always; the others drove. She was bored driving, disliked all animals, except that dog. They tramped miles along roads. She would break off to get her bearings, pilot him back across country; and all the time they argued, discussed poetry, discussed people, discussed politics (she was a Radical then); never noticing a thing except when she stopped, cried out at a view or a tree, and made him look with her; and so on again, through stubble fields, she walking ahead, with a flower for her aunt, never tired of walking for all her delicacy; to drop down on Bourton in the dusk. Then, after dinner, old Breitkopf would open the piano and sing without any voice, and they would lie sunk in arm-chairs, trying not to laugh, but always breaking down and laughing, laughing – laughing at nothing. Breitkopf was supposed not to see. And then in the morning, flirting up and down like a wagtail in front of the house....

Oh it was a letter from her! This blue envelope; that was her hand. And he would have to read it. Here was another of those meetings, bound to be painful! To read her letter needed the devil of an effort. 'How heavenly it was to see him. She must tell him that.' That was all.

But it upset him. It annoyed him. He wished she hadn't written it. Coming on top of his thoughts, it was like a nudge in the ribs. Why couldn't she let him be? After all, she had married Dalloway, and lived with him in perfect happiness all these years.

These hotels are not consoling places. Far from it. Any number of people had hung up their hats on those pegs. Even the flies, if you thought of it, had settled on other people's noses. As for the cleanliness which hit him in the face, it wasn't cleanliness, so much as bareness, frigidity; a thing that had to be. Some arid matron made her rounds at dawn sniffing, peering, causing blue-nosed maids to scour, for all the world as if the next visitor were a joint of meat to be served on a perfectly clean platter. For sleep, one bed; for sitting in, one arm-chair; for cleaning one's teeth and shaving one's chin, one tumbler, one looking-glass. Books, letters, dressing-gown, slipped about on the impersonality of the horse-hair like incongruous impertinences. And it was Clarissa's letter that made him see all this. 'Heavenly to see you. She must say so!' He folded the paper; pushed it away; nothing would induce him to read it again!

To get that letter to him by six o'clock she must have sat down and written it directly he left her; stamped it; sent somebody to the post. It was, as people say, very like her. She was upset by his visit. She had felt a great deal; had for a moment, when she kissed his hand, regretted, envied him even, remembered possibly (for he saw her look it) something he had said – how they would change the world if she married him perhaps; whereas, it was this; it was middle age; it was mediocrity; then forced herself with her indomitable vitality to put all that aside, there being in her a thread of life which for toughness, endurance, power to overcome obstacles and carry her triumphantly through he had never known the like of. Yes; but there would come a reaction directly he left the room. She would be frightfully sorry for him; she would think what in the world she could do to give him pleasure (short always of the one thing), and he could see her with the tears running down her cheeks going to her writing-table and dashing off that one line which he was to find greeting him.... 'Heavenly to see you!' And she meant it.

Peter Walsh had now unlaced his boots.

But it would not have been a success, their marriage. The other thing, after all, came so much more naturally.

It was odd; it was true; lots of people felt it. Peter Walsh, who had done just respectably, filled the usual posts adequately, was liked, but thought a little cranky, gave himself airs – it was odd that *he* should have had, especially now that his hair was grey, a contented look; a look of having reserves. It was this that made him attractive to women, who liked the sense that he was not altogether manly. There was something unusual about him, or something behind him. It might be that he was bookish – never came to see you without taking up the book on the table (he was now reading, with his bootlaces trailing on the floor); or that he was a gentleman, which showed itself in the way he knocked the ashes out of his pipe, and in his manners of course to women. For it was very charming and quite ridiculous how easily some girl without a grain of sense could twist him round her finger. But at her own risk. That is to say, though he might be ever so easy, and indeed with his gaiety and good-breeding fascinating to be with, it was only up to a point. She said something – no, no; he saw through that. He wouldn't stand that – no, no. Then he could shout and rock and hold his sides together over some joke with men. He was the best judge of cooking in India. He was a man. But not the sort of man one had to respect – which was a mercy; not like Major Simmons, for instance; not in the least, Daisy thought, when, in spite of her two small children, she used to compare them.

He pulled off his boots. He emptied his pockets. Out came with his pocket-knife a snapshot of Daisy on the verandah; Daisy all in white, with a fox-terrier on her knee; very charming, very dark; the best he had ever seen of her. It did come, after all, so naturally; so much more naturally than Clarissa. No fuss. No bother. No finicking and fidgeting. All plain sailing. And the dark, adorably pretty girl on the verandah exclaimed (he could hear her) Of course, of course she would give him everything! she cried (she had no sense of discretion), everything he wanted! she cried, running to meet him, whoever might be looking. And she was only twenty-four. And she had two children. Well, well!

Well indeed he had got himself into a mess at his age. And it came over him when he woke in the night pretty forcibly. Suppose they did marry? For him it would be all very well, but what about her? Mrs Burgess, a good sort and no chatterbox, in whom he had confided, thought this absence of his in England, ostensibly to see lawyers, might serve to make Daisy reconsider, think what it meant. It was a question of her position, Mrs Burgess said; the social barrier; giving up her children. She'd be a widow with a past one of these days, draggling about in the suburbs, or more likely, indiscriminate (you know, she said, what such women get like, with too much paint). But Peter Walsh pooh-poohed all that. He didn't mean to die yet. Anyhow, she must settle for herself; judge for herself, he thought, padding about the room in his socks, smoothing out his dress-shirt for he might go to Clarissa's party, or he might go to one of the Halls, or he might settle in and read an absorbing book written by a man he used to know at Oxford. And if he did retire, that's what he'd do – write books. He would go to Oxford and poke about in the Bodleian. Vainly the dark, adorably pretty girl ran to the end of the terrace; vainly waved her hand; vainly cried she didn't care a straw what people said. There he was, the man she thought the world of, the perfect gentleman, the fascinating, the distinguished (and his age made not the least difference to her), padding about in an hotel in Bloomsbury, shaving, washing, continuing, as he took up cans, put down razors, to poke about in the Bodleian, and get at the truth about one or two little matters that interested him. And he would have a chat with whoever it might be, and so come to disregard more and more precise hours for lunch, and miss engagements; and when Daisy asked him, as she would, for a kiss, a scene, fail to come up to the scratch (though he was genuinely devoted to her) – in short, it might be happier, as Mrs Burgess said, that she should forget him, or merely remember him as he was in August 1922, like a figure standing at the cross roads at dusk, which grows more and more remote as the dog-cart spins away, carrying her securely fastened to the back seat, though her arms are outstretched; and as she sees the figure dwindle and disappear, still she cries out how she would do anything in the world, anything, anything, anything. . . .

He never knew what people thought. It became more and more difficult for him to concentrate. He became absorbed; he became busied with his own concerns; now surly, now gay; dependent on women, absent-minded, moody, less and less able (so he thought as he shaved) to understand why Clarissa couldn't simply find them a lodging and be nice to Daisy; introduce her. And then he could just – just do what? just haunt and hover (he was at the moment actually engaged in sorting out various keys, papers), swoop and taste, be alone, in short, sufficient to himself; and yet nobody of course was more dependent upon others (he buttoned his waistcoat); it had been his undoing. He could not keep out of smoking-rooms, liked colonels, liked golf, liked bridge, and above all women's society, and the fineness of their companionship, and their faithfulness and audacity and greatness in loving which, though it had its drawbacks, seemed to him (and the dark, adorably pretty face was on the top of the envelopes) so wholly admirable, so splendid a flower to grow on the crest of human life, and yet he could not come up to the scratch, being always apt to see round things (Clarissa had sapped something in him permanently), and to tire very easily of mute devotion and to want variety in love, though it would make him furious if Daisy loved anybody else, furious! for he was jealous, uncontrollably jealous by temperament. He suffered tortures! But where was his knife; his watch; his seals, his note-case, and Clarissa's letter which he would not read again but liked to think of, and Daisy's photograph? And now for dinner.

They were eating.

Sitting at little tables round vases, dressed or not dressed, with their shawls and bags laid beside them, with their air of false composure, for they were not used to so many courses at dinner; and confidence, for they were able to pay for it; and strain, for they had been running about London all day shopping, sightseeing; and their natural curiosity, for they looked round and up as the nice-looking gentleman in horn-rimmed spectacles came in; and their good nature, for they would have been glad to do any little service, such as lend a time-table or impart useful information; and their desire, pulsing in them, tugging at them subterraneously, somehow to establish connections if it were only a birth-place (Liverpool, for example), in common or friends of the same name; with their furtive glances, odd silences, and sudden withdrawals into family jocularity and isolation; there they sat eating dinner when Mr Walsh came in and took his seat at a little table by the curtain.

It was not that he said anything, for being solitary he could only address himself to the waiter; it was his way of looking at the menu, of pointing his forefinger to a particular wine, of hitching himself up to the table, of addressing himself seriously, not gluttonously, to dinner, that won him their respect; which, having to remain unexpressed for the greater part of the meal, flared up at the table where the Morrises sat when Mr Walsh was heard to say at the end of the meal, 'Bartlett pears'. Why he should have spoken so moderately yet firmly, with the air of a disciplinarian well within his rights which are founded upon justice, neither young Charles Morris, nor old Charles, neither Miss Elaine nor Mrs Morris knew. But when he said, 'Bartlett pears,' sitting alone at his table, they felt that he counted on their support in some lawful demand; was champion of a cause which immediately became their own, so that their eyes met his eyes sympathetically, and when they all reached the smoking-room simultaneously, a little talk between them became inevitable.

It was not very profound – only to the effect that London was crowded; had changed in thirty years; that Mr Morris preferred Liverpool; that Mrs Morris had been to the Westminster flower-show, and that they had all seen the Prince of Wales. Yet, thought Peter Walsh, no family in the world can compare with the Morrises; none whatever; and their relations to each other are perfect, and they don't care a hang for the upper classes, and they like what they like, and Elaine is training for the family business, and the boy has won a scholarship at Leeds, and the old lady (who is about his own age) has three more children at home; and they have two motor cars, but Mr Morris still mends the boots on Sunday: it is superb, it is absolutely superb, thought Peter Walsh, swaying a little backwards and forwards with his liqueur glass in his hand among the hairy red chairs and ash-trays, feeling very well pleased with himself, for the Morrises liked him. Yes, they liked a man who said 'Bartlett pears'. They liked him, he felt.

He would go to Clarissa's party. (The Morrises moved off; but they would meet again.) He would go to Clarissa's party, because he wanted to ask Richard what they were doing in India – the conservative duffers. And what's being acted? And music.... Oh yes, and mere gossip.

For this is the truth about our soul, he thought, our self, who fish-like inhabits deep seas and plies among obscurities threading her way between the boles of giant weeds, over sun-flickered spaces and on and on into gloom, cold, deep, inscrutable; suddenly she shoots to the surface and sports on the wind-wrinkled waves; that is, has a positive need to brush, scrape, kindle herself, gossiping. What did the Government mean – Richard Dalloway would know – to do about India?

Since it was a very hot night and the paper boys went by with placards proclaiming in huge red letters that there was a heat-wave, wicker chairs were placed on the hotel steps and there, sipping, smoking, detached gentlemen sat. Peter Walsh sat there. One might fancy that day, the London day, was just beginning. Like a woman who had slipped off her print dress and white apron to array herself in blue and pearls, the day changed, put off stuff, took gauze, changed to evening, and with the same sigh of exhilaration that a woman breathes, tumbling petticoats on the floor, it too shed dust, heat, colour; the traffic thinned; motor cars, tinkling, darting, succeeded the lumber of vans; and here and there among the thick foliage of the squares an intense light hung. I resign, the evening seemed to say, as it paled and faded above the battlements and prominences, moulded, pointed, of hotel, flat, and block of shops, I fade, she was beginning, I disappear, but London would have none of it, and rushed her bayonets into the sky, pinioned her, constrained her to partnership in her revelry.

For the great revolution of Mr Willett's summer time had taken place since Peter Walsh's last visit to England. The prolonged evening was new to him. It was inspiriting, rather. For as the young people went by with their despatch-boxes, awfully glad to be free, proud too, dumbly, of stepping this famous pavement, joy of a kind, cheap, tinselly, if you like, but all the same rapture, flushed their faces. They dressed well too; pink stockings; pretty shoes. They would now have two hours at the pictures. It sharpened, it refined them, the yellow-blue evening light; and on the leaves in the square shone lurid, livid – they looked as if dipped in sea water – the foliage of a submerged city. He was astonished by the beauty; it was encouraging too, for where the returned Anglo-Indian sat by rights (he knew crowds of them) in the Oriental Club biliously summing up the ruin of the world, here was he, as young as ever; envying young people their summer time and the rest of it, and more than suspecting from the words of a girl, from a housemaid's laughter – intangible things you couldn't lay your hands on – that shift in the whole pyramidal accumulation which in his youth had seemed immovable. On top of them it had pressed; weighed them down, the women especially, like those flowers Clarissa's Aunt Helena used to press between sheets of grey blotting-paper with Littré's dictionary on top, sitting under the lamp after dinner. She was dead now. He had heard of her, from Clarissa, losing the sight of one eye. It seemed so fitting – one of nature's masterpieces – that old Miss Parry should turn to glass. She would die like some bird in a frost gripping her perch. She belonged to a different age, but being so entire, so complete, would always stand up on the horizon, stone-white, eminent, like a lighthouse marking some past stage on this adventurous, long, long voyage, this interminable – (he felt for a copper to buy a paper and read about Surrey and Yorkshire; he had held out that copper millions of times – Surrey was all out once more) – this interminable life. But cricket was no mere game. Cricket was important. He could never help reading about cricket. He read the scores in the stop press first, then how it was a hot day; then about a murder case. Having done things millions of times enriched them, though it might be said to take the surface off. The past enriched, and experience, and having cared for one or two people, and so having acquired the power which the young lack, of cutting short, doing what one likes, not caring a rap what people say and coming and going without any great expectations (he left his paper on the table and moved off), which however (and he looked for his hat and coat) was not altogether true of him, not to-night, for here he was starting to go to a party, at his age, with the belief upon him that he was about to have an experience. But what?

Beauty anyhow. Not the crude beauty of the eye. It was not beauty pure and simple – Bedford Place leading into Russell Square. It was straightness and emptiness of course;

the symmetry of a corridor; but it was also windows lit up, a piano, a gramophone sounding; a sense of pleasure-making hidden, but now and again emerging when, through the uncurtained window, the window left open, one saw parties sitting over tables, young people slowly circling, conversations between men and women, maids idly looking out (a strange comment theirs, when work was done), stockings drying on top ledges, a parrot, a few plants. Absorbing, mysterious, of infinite richness, this life. And in the large square where the cabs shot and swerved so quick, there were loitering couples, dallying, embracing, shrunk up under the shower of a tree; that was moving; so silent, so absorbed, that one passed, discreetly, timidly, as if in the presence of some sacred ceremony to interrupt which would have been impious. That was interesting. And so on into the flare and glare.

His light overcoat blew open, he stepped with indescribable idiosyncrasy, leant a little forward, tripped, with his hands behind his back and his eyes still a little hawk-like; he tripped through London, towards Westminster, observing.

Was everybody dining out, then? Doors were being opened here by a footman to let issue a high-stepping old dame, in buckled shoes, with three purple ostrich feathers in her hair. Door were being opened for ladies wrapped like mummies in shawls with bright flowers on them, ladies with bare heads. And in respectable quarters with stucco pillars through small front gardens, lightly swathed, with combs in their hair (having run up to see the children), women came; men waited for them, with their coats blowing open, and the motor started. Everybody was going out. What with these doors being opened, and the descent and the start, it seemed as if the whole of London were embarking in little boats moored to the bank, tossing on the waters, as if the whole place were floating off in carnival. And Whitehall was skated over, silver beaten as it was, skated over by spiders, and there was a sense of midges round the arc lamps; it was so hot that people stood about talking. And here in Westminster was a retired Judge, presumably, sitting four square at his house door dressed all in white. An Anglo-Indian presumably.

And here a shindy of brawling women, drunken women; here only a policeman and looming houses, high houses, domed houses, churches, parliaments, and the hoot of a steamer on the river, a hollow misty cry. But it was her street, this, Clarissa's; cabs were rushing round the corner, like water round the piers of a bridge, drawn together, it seemed to him, because they bore people going to her party, Clarissa's party.

The cold stream of visual impressions failed him now as if the eye were a cup that overflowed and let the rest run down its china walls unrecorded. The brain must wake now. The body must contract now, entering the house, the lighted house, where the door stood open, where the motor cars were standing, and bright women descending : the soul must brave itself to endure. He opened the big blade of his pocket-knife.

Lucy came running full tilt downstairs, having just nipped into the drawing-room to smooth a cover, to straighten a chair, to pause a moment and feel whoever came in must think how clean, how bright, how beautifully cared for, when they saw the beautiful silver, the brass fire-irons, the new chair-covers, and the curtains of yellow chintz : she appraised each; heard a roar of voices; people already coming up from dinner; she must fly!

The Prime Minister was coming, Agnes said : so she had heard them say in the dining-room, she said, coming in with a tray of glasses. Did it matter, did it matter in the least, one Prime Minister more or less? It made no difference at this hour of the night to Mrs Walker among the plates, saucepans, cullenders, frying-pans, chicken in aspic, ice-cream freezers, pared crusts of bread, lemons, soup tureens, and pudding basins which, however hard they washed up in the scullery, seemed to be all on top of her, on the kitchen table, on chairs, while the fire blared and roared, the electric lights glared, and still supper had to be laid. All she felt was, one Prime Minister more or less made not a scrap of difference to Mrs Walker.

The ladies were going upstairs already, said Lucy; the ladies were going up, one by one, Mrs Dalloway walking last and almost always sending back some message to the kitchen, 'My love to Mrs Walker,' that was it one night. Next morning they would go over the dishes – the soup, the salmon; the salmon, Mrs Walker knew, as usual underdone, for she always got nervous about the pudding and left it to Jenny; so it happened, the salmon was always underdone. But some lady with fair hair and silver ornaments had said, Lucy said, about the entrée, was it really made at home? But it was the salmon that bothered Mrs Walker, as she spun the plates round and round, and pushed in dampers and pulled out dampers; and there came a burst of laughter from the dining-room; a voice speaking; then another burst of laughter – the gentlemen enjoying themselves when the ladies had gone. The tokay, said Lucy, running in. Mr Dalloway had sent for the tokay, from the Emperor's cellars, the Imperial Tokay.

It was borne through the kitchen. Over her shoulder Lucy reported how Miss Elizabeth looked quite lovely; she couldn't take her eyes off her; in her pink dress, wearing the necklace Mr Dalloway had given her. Jenny must remember the dog, Miss Elizabeth's fox-terrier, which, since it bit, had to be shut up and might, Elizabeth thought, want something. Jenny must remember the dog. But Jenny was not going upstairs with all those people about. There was a motor at the door already! There was a ring at the bell – and the gentlemen still in the dining-room, drinking tokay!

There, they were going upstairs; that was the first to come, and now they would come faster and faster, so that Mrs Parkinson (hired for parties) would leave the hall door ajar, and the hall would be full of gentlemen waiting (they stood waiting, sleeking down their hair) while the ladies took their cloaks off in the room along the passage; where Mrs Barnet helped them, old Ellen Barnet, who had been with the family for forty years, and came every summer to help the ladies, and remembered mothers when they were girls, and though very unassuming did shake hands; said 'milady' very respectfully, yet had a humorous way with her, looking at the young ladies, and ever so tactfully helping Lady Lovejoy, who had some trouble with her under-bodice. And they could not help feeling, Lady Lovejoy and Miss Alice, that some little privilege in the matter of brush and comb was awarded them having known Mrs Barnet – 'thirty years, milady,' Mrs Barnet supplied her. Young ladies did not use to rouge, said Lady Lovejoy, when they stayed at Bourton in the old days. And Miss Alice didn't need rouge, said Mrs Barnet, looking at her fondly. There Mrs Barnet would sit, in the cloakroom, patting down the furs, smoothing out the Spanish shawls, tidying the dressing-table, and knowing perfectly well, in spite of the furs and the embroideries, which were nice ladies, which were not. The dear old body, said Lady Lovejoy, mounting the stairs, Clarissa's old nurse.

And then Lady Lovejoy stiffened. 'Lady and Miss Love-joy,' she said to Mr Wilkins (hired for parties). He had an admirable manner, as he bent and straightened himself, bent and straightened himself and announced with perfect im-partiality 'Lady and Miss Lovejoy ... Sir John and Lady Needham ... Miss Weld ... Mr Walsh.' His manner was admirable; his family life must be irreproachable, except that it seemed impossible that a being with greenish lips and shaven cheeks could ever have blundered into the nuisance of children.

'How delightful to see you!' said Clarissa. She said it to every one. How delightful to see you! She was at her worst – effusive, insincere. It was a great mistake to have come. He should have stayed at home and read his book, thought Peter Walsh; should have gone to a music hall; he should have stayed at home, for he knew no one.

Oh dear, it was going to be a failure; a complete failure, Clarissa felt it in her bones as dear old Lord Lexham stood there apologizing for his wife who had caught a cold at the Buckingham Palace garden party. She could see Peter out of the tail of her eye, criticizing her, there, in that corner. Why, after all, did she do these things? Why seek pinnacles and stand drenched in fire? Might it consume her anyhow!

Burn her to cinders! Better anything, better brandish one's torch and hurl it to earth than taper and dwindle away like some Ellie Henderson! It was extraordinary how Peter put her into these states just by coming and standing in a corner. He made her see herself; exaggerate. It was idiotic. But why did he come, then, merely to criticize? Why always take, never give? Why not risk one's one little point of view? There he was wandering off, and she must speak to him. But she would not get the chance. Life was that – humiliation, renunciation. What Lord Lexham was saying was that his wife would not wear her furs at the garden party because 'my dear, you ladies are all alike' – Lady Lexham being seventy-five at least! It was delicious, how they petted each other, that old couple. She did like old Lord Lexham. She did think it mattered, her party, and it made her feel quite sick to know that it was all going wrong, all falling flat. Anything, any explosion, any horror was better than people wandering aimlessly, standing in a bunch at a corner like Ellie Henderson, not even caring to hold themselves upright.

Gently the yellow curtain with all the birds of Paradise blew out and it seemed as if there were a flight of wings into the room, right out, then sucked back. (For the windows were open.) Was it draughty, Ellie Henderson wondered? She was subject to chills. But it did not matter that she should come down sneezing tomorrow; it was the girls with their naked shoulders she thought of, being trained to think of others by an old father, an invalid, late vicar of Bourton, but he was dead now; and her chills never went to her chest, never. It was the girls she thought of, the young girls with their bare shoulders, she herself having always been a wisp of a creature, with her thin hair and meagre profile; though now, past fifty, there was beginning to shine through some mild beam, something purified into distinction by years of self-abnegation but obscured again, perpetually, by her distressing gentility, her panic fear, which arose from three hundred pounds income, and her weaponless state (she could not earn a penny) and it made her timid, and more and more disqualified year by year to meet well-dressed people who did this sort of thing every night of the season, merely telling their maids 'I'll wear so and so,' whereas Ellie Henderson ran out nervously and bought cheap pink flowers, half-a-dozen, and then threw a shawl over her old black dress. For her invitation to Clarissa's party had come at the last moment. She was not quite happy about it. She had a sort of feeling that Clarissa had not meant to ask her this year.

Why should she? There was no reason really, except that they had always known each other. Indeed, they were cousins. But naturally they had rather drifted apart, Clarissa being so sought after. It was an event to her, going to a party. It was quite a treat just to see the lovely clothes. Wasn't that Elizabeth, grown up, with her hair done in the fashionable way, in the pink dress? Yet she could not be more than seventeen. She was very, very handsome. But girls when they first came out didn't seem to wear white as they used. (She must remember everything to tell Edith.) Girls wore straight frocks, perfectly tight, with skirts well above the ankles. It was not becoming, she thought.

So, with her weak eyesight, Ellie Henderson craned rather forward, and it wasn't so much she who minded not having any one to talk to (she hardly knew anybody there), for she felt that they were all such interesting people to watch; politicians presumably; Richard Dalloway's friends; but it was Richard himself who felt that he could not let the poor creature go on standing there all the evening by herself.

'Well, Ellie, and how's the world treating *you*?' he said in his genial way, and Ellie Henderson, getting nervous and flushing and feeling that it was extraordinarily nice of him to come and talk to her, said that many people really felt the heat more than the cold.

'Yes, they do,' said Richard Dalloway. 'Yes.'

But what more did one say?

'Hullo, Richard,' said somebody, taking him by the elbow, and, good Lord, there was old Peter, old Peter Walsh. He was delighted to see him – ever so pleased to see him! He hadn't changed a bit. And off they went together walking right across the room, giving each other little pats, as if they hadn't met for a long time, Ellie Henderson thought, watching them go, certain she knew that man's face. A tall man, middle aged, rather fine eyes, dark, wearing spectacles, with a look of John Burrows. Edith would be sure to know.

The curtain with its flight of birds of Paradise blew out again. And Clarissa saw – she saw Ralph Lyon beat it back, and go on talking. So it wasn't a failure after all! it was going to be all right now – her party. It had begun. It had started. But it was still touch and go. She must stand there for the present. People seemed to come in a rush.

Colonel and Mrs Garrod ... Mr Hugh Whitbread ... Mr Bowley ... Mrs Hilbery ... Lady Mary Maddox ... Mr Quin ... intoned Wilkins. She had six or seven words with each, and they went on, they went into the rooms; into something now, not nothing, since Ralph Lyon had beat back the curtain.

And yet for her own part, it was too much of an effort. She was not enjoying it. It was too much like being – just anybody, standing there; anybody could do it; yet this anybody she did a little admire, couldn't help feeling that she had, anyhow, made this happen, that it marked a stage, this post that she felt herself to have become, for oddly enough she had quite forgotten what she looked like, but felt herself a stake driven in at the top of her stairs. Every time she gave a party she had this feeling of being something not herself, and that every one was unreal in one way; much more real in another. It was, she thought, partly their clothes, partly being taken out of their ordinary ways, partly the background; it was possible to say things you couldn't say anyhow else, things that needed an effort; possible to go much deeper. But not for her; not yet anyhow.

'How delightful to see you!' she said. Dear old Sir Harry! He would know every one.

And what was so odd about it was the sense one had as they came up the stairs one after another, Mrs Mount and Celia, Herbert Ainsty, Mrs Dakers – oh, and Lady Bruton!

'How awfully good of you to come!' she said, and she meant it – it was odd how standing there one felt them going on, going on, some quite old, some ...

What name? Lady Rosseter? But who on earth was Lady Rosseter?

'Clarissa!' That voice! It was Sally Seton! Sally Seton! after all these years! She loomed through a mist. For she hadn't looked like *that*, Sally Seton, when Clarissa grasped the hot-water can. To think of her under this roof, under this roof! Not like that!

All on top of each other, embarrassed, laughing, words tumbled out – passing through London; heard from Clara Haydon; what a chance of seeing you! So I thrust myself in – without an invitation....

One might put down the hot-water can quite composedly. The lustre had left her. Yet it was extraordinary to see her again, older, happier, less lovely. They kissed each other, first this cheek, then that, by the drawing-room door, and Clarissa turned, with Sally's hand in hers, saw her rooms full, heard the roar of voices, saw the candlesticks, the blowing curtains, and the roses which Richard had given her.

'I have five enormous boys,' said Sally.

She had the simplest egotism, the most open desire to be thought first always, and Clarissa loved her for being still like that. 'I can't believe it!' she cried, kindling all over with pleasure at the thought of the past.

But alas, Wilkins; Wilkins wanted her; Wilkins was emitting in a voice of commanding authority, as if the whole company must be admonished and the hostess reclaimed from frivolity, one name:

'The Prime Minister,' said Peter Walsh.

The Prime Minister? Was it really? Ellie Henderson marvelled. What a thing to tell Edith!

One couldn't laugh at him. He looked so ordinary. You might have stood him behind a counter and bought biscuits – poor chap, all rigged up in gold lace. And to be fair, as he went his rounds, first with Clarissa, then with Richard escorting him, he did it very well. He tried to look somebody. It was amusing to watch. Nobody looked at him. They just went on talking, yet it was perfectly plain that they all knew, felt to the marrow of their bones, this majesty passing; this symbol of what they all stood for, English society. Old Lady Bruton, and she looked very fine too, very stalwart in her lace, swam up, and they withdrew into a little room which at once became spied upon, guarded, and a sort of stir and rustle rippled through every one openly : the Prime Minister!

Lord, lord, the snobbery of the English! thought Peter Walsh, standing in the corner. How they loved dressing up in gold lace and doing homage! There! That must be – by Jove it was – Hugh Whitbread, snuffing around the precincts of the great, grown rather fatter, rather whiter, the admirable Hugh!

He looked always as if he were on duty, thought Peter, a privileged but secretive being, hoarding secrets which he would die to defend, though it was only some little piece of tittle-tattle dropped by a court footman which would be in all the papers to-morrow. Such were his rattles, his baubles, in playing with which he had grown white, come to the verge of old age, enjoying the respect and affection of all who had the privilege of knowing this type of the English public-school man. Inevitably one made up things like that about Hugh; that was his style; the style of those admirable letters which Peter had read thousands of miles across the sea in *The Times*, and had thanked God he was out of that pernicious hubble-bubble if it were only to hear baboons chatter and coolies beat their wives. An olive-skinned youth from one of the Universities stood obsequiously by. Him he would patronize, initiate, teach how to get on. For he liked nothing better than doing kindnesses, making the hearts of old ladies palpitate with the joy of being thought of in their age, their affliction, thinking themselves quite forgotten, yet here was dear Hugh driving up and spending an hour talking of the past, remembering trifles, praising the home-made cake, though Hugh might eat cake with a Duchess any day of his life, and, to look at him, probably did spend a good deal of time in that agreeable occupation. The All-judging, the All-merciful, might excuse. Peter Walsh had no mercy. Villains there must be, and, God knows, the rascals who get hanged for battering the brains of a girl out in a train do less harm on the whole than Hugh Whitbread and his kindness! Look at him now, on tip-toe, dancing forward, bowing and scraping, as the Prime Minister and Lady Bruton emerged, intimating for all the world to see that he was privileged to say something, something private, to Lady Bruton as she passed. She stopped. She wagged her fine old head. She was thanking him presumably for some piece of servility. She had her toadies, minor officials in Government offices who ran about putting through little jobs on her behalf, in return for which she gave them luncheon. But she derived from the eighteenth century. She was all right.

And now Clarissa escorted her Prime Minister down the room, prancing, sparkling, with the stateliness of her grey hair. She wore ear-rings, and a silver-green mermaid's dress. Lolloping on the waves and braiding her tresses she seemed, having that gift still; to be; to exist; to sum it all up in the moment as she passed; turned, caught her scarf in some other woman's dress, unhitched it, laughed, all with the most perfect ease and air of a creature floating in its element. But age had brushed her; even as a mermaid might behold in her glass the setting sun on some very clear evening over the waves. There was a breath of tenderness; her severity, her prudery, her woodenness were all warmed through now, and she had about her as she said good-bye to the thick gold-laced man who was doing his best, and good luck to him, to look important, an inexpressible dignity; an exquisite cordiality; as if she wished the whole world well, and must now, being on the very verge and rim of things, take her leave. So she made him think. (But he was not in love.)

Indeed, Clarissa felt, the Prime Minister had been good to come. And, walking down the room with him, with Sally there and Peter there and Richard very pleased, with all those people rather inclined, perhaps, to envy, she had felt that intoxication of the moment, that dilatation of the nerves of the heart itself till it seemed to quiver, steeped, upright; – yes, but after all it was what other people felt, that; for, though she loved it and felt it tingle and sting, still these semblances, these triumphs (dear old Peter, for example, thinking her so brilliant), had a hollowness; at arm's length they were, not in the heart; and it might be that she was growing old, but they satisfied her no longer as they used; and suddenly, as she saw the Prime Minister go down the stairs, the gilt rim of the Sir Joshua picture of the little girl with a muff brought back Kilman with a rush; Kilman her enemy. That was satisfying; that was real. Ah, how she hated her – hot, hypocritical, corrupt; with all that power; Elizabeth's seducer; the woman who had crept in to steal and defile (Richard would say, What nonsense!). She hated her: she loved her. It was enemies one wanted not friends – not Mrs Durrant and Clara, Sir William and Lady Bradshaw, Miss Truelock and Eleanor Gibson (whom she saw coming upstairs). They must find her if they wanted her. She was for the party!

There was her old friend Sir Harry.

'Dear Sir Harry!' she said, going up to the fine old fellow who had produced more bad pictures than any other two Academicians in the whole of St John's Wood (they were always of cattle, standing in sunset pools absorbing moisture, or signifying, for he had a certain range of gesture, by the raising of one foreleg and the toss of the antlers, 'the Approach of the Stranger' – all his activities, dining out, racing, were founded on cattle standing absorbing moisture in sunset pools).

'What are you laughing at?' she asked him. For Willie Titcomb and Sir Harry and Herbert Ainsty were all laughing. But no. Sir Harry could not tell Clarissa Dalloway (much though he liked her; of her type he thought her perfect, and threatened to paint her) his stories of the music-hall stage. He chaffed her about her party. He missed his brandy. These circles, he said, were above him. But he liked her; respected her, in spite of her damnable, difficult, upper-class refinement, which made it impossible to ask Clarissa Dalloway to sit on his knee. And up came that wandering will-o'-the-wisp, that vagous phosphorescence, old Mrs Hilbery, stretching her hands to the blaze of his laughter (about the Duke and the Lady), which, as she heard it across the room, seemed to reassure her on a point which sometimes bothered her if she woke early in the morning and did not like to call her maid for a cup of tea : how it is certain we must die.

'They won't tell us their stories,' said Clarissa.

'Dear Clarissa!' exclaimed Mrs Hilbery. She looked tonight, she said, so like her mother as she first saw her walking in a garden in a grey hat.

And really Clarissa's eyes filled with tears. Her mother, walking in a garden! But alas, she must go.

For there was Professor Brierly, who lectured on Milton, talking to little Jim Hutton (who was unable even for a party like this to compass both tie and waistcoat or make his hair lie flat), and even at this distance they were quarrelling, she could see. For Professor Brierly was a very queer fish. With all those degrees, honours, lectureships between him and the scribblers, he suspected instantly an atmosphere not favourable to his queer compound; his prodigious learning and timidity; his wintry charm without cordiality; his innocence blent with snobbery; he quivered if made conscious, by a lady's unkempt hair, a youth's boots, of an underworld, very creditable doubtless, of rebels, of ardent young people; of would-be geniuses, and intimated with a little toss of the head, with a sniff – Humph! – the value of moderation; of some slight training in the classics in order to appreciate Milton. Professor Brierly (Clarissa could see) wasn't hitting it off with little Jim Hutton (who wore red socks, his black being at the laundry) about Milton. She interrupted.

She said she loved Bach. So did Hutton. That was the bond between them, and Hutton (a very bad poet) always felt that Mrs Dalloway was far the best of the great ladies who took an interest in art. It was odd how strict she was. About music she was purely impersonal. She was rather a prig. But how charming to look at! She made her house so nice, if it weren't for her Professors. Clarissa had half a mind to snatch him off and set him down at the piano in the back room. For he played divinely.

'But the noise!' she said. 'The noise!'

'The sign of a successful party.' Nodding urbanely, the Professor stepped delicately off.

'He knows everything in the whole world about Milton,' said Clarissa.

'Does he indeed?' said Hutton, who would imitate the Professor throughout Hampstead: the Professor on Milton; the Professor on moderation; the Professor stepping delicately off.

But she must speak to that couple, said Clarissa, Lord Gayton and Nancy Blow.

Not that *they* added perceptibly to the noise of the party. They were not talking (perceptibly) as they stood side by side by the yellow curtains. They would soon be off elsewhere, together; and never had very much to say in any circumstances. They looked; that was all. That was enough. They looked so clean, so sound, she with an apricot bloom of powder and paint, but he scrubbed, rinsed, with the eyes of a bird, so that no ball could pass him or stroke surprise him. He struck, he leapt, accurately, on the spot. Ponies' mouths quivered at the end of his reins. He had his honours, ancestral monuments, banners hanging in the church at home. He had his duties; his tenants; a mother and sisters; had been all day at Lord's, and that was what they were talking about – cricket, cousins, the movies – when Mrs Dalloway came up. Lord Gayton liked her most awfully. So did Miss Blow. She had such charming manners.

'It is angelic – it is delicious of you to have come!' she said. She loved Lord's; she loved youth, and Nancy, dressed at enormous expense by the greatest artists in Paris, stood there looking as if her body had merely put forth, of its own accord, a green frill.

'I had meant to have dancing,' said Clarissa.

For the young people could not talk. And why should they? Shout, embrace, swing, be up at dawn; carry sugar to ponies; kiss and caress the snouts of adorable chows; and then, all tingling and streaming, plunge and swim. But the enormous resources of the English language, the power it bestows, after all, of communicating feelings (at their age, she and Peter would have been arguing all evening), was not for them. They would solidify young. They would be good beyond measure to the people on the estate, but alone, perhaps, rather dull.

'What a pity!' she said. 'I had hoped to have dancing.'

It was so extraordinarily nice of them to have come! But talk of dancing! The rooms were packed.

There was old Aunt Helena in her shawl. Alas, she must leave them – Lord Gayton and Nancy Blow. There was old Miss Parry, her aunt.

For Miss Helena Parry was not dead: Miss Parry was alive. She was past eighty. She ascended staircases slowly with a stick. She was placed in a chair (Richard had seen to it). People who had known Burma in the 'seventies were always led up to her. Where had Peter got to? They used to be such friends. For at the mention of India, or even Ceylon, her eyes (only one was glass) slowly deepened, became blue, beheld, not human beings – she had no tender memories, no proud illusions about Viceroys, Generals, Mutinies – it was orchids she saw, and mountain passes, and herself carried on the backs of coolies in the 'sixties over solitary peaks; or descending to uproot orchids (startling blossoms, never beheld before) which she painted in water-colour; an indomitable Englishwoman, fretful if disturbed by the war, say, which dropped a bomb at her very door, from her deep meditation over orchids and her own figure journeying in the 'sixties in India – but here was Peter.

'Come and talk to Aunt Helena about Burma,' said Clarissa.

And yet he had not had a word with her all the evening!

'We will talk later,' said Clarissa, leading him up to Aunt Helena, in her white shawl, with her stick.

'Peter Walsh,' said Clarissa.

That meant nothing.

Clarissa had asked her. It was tiring; it was noisy; but Clarissa had asked her. So she had come. It was a pity that they lived in London – Richard and Clarissa. If only for Clarissa's health it would have been better to live in the country. But Clarissa had always been fond of society.

'He has been in Burma,' said Clarissa.

Ah! She could not resist recalling what Charles Darwin had said about her little book on the orchids of Burma.

(Clarissa must speak to Lady Bruton.)

No doubt it was forgotten now, her book on the orchids of Burma, but it went into three editions before 1870, she told Peter. She remembered him now. He had been at Bourton (and he had left her, Peter Walsh remembered, without a word in the drawing-room that night when Clarissa had asked him to come boating).

'Richard so much enjoyed his lunch party,' said Clarissa to Lady Bruton.

'Richard was the greatest possible help,' Lady Bruton replied. 'He helped me to write a letter. And how are you?'

'Oh, perfectly well!' said Clarissa. (Lady Bruton detested illness in the wives of politicians.)

'And there's Peter Walsh!' said Lady Bruton (for she could never think of anything to say to Clarissa; though she liked her. She had lots of fine qualities; but they had nothing in common – she and Clarissa. It might have been better if Richard had married a woman with less charm, who would have helped him more in his work. He had lost his chance of the Cabinet). 'There's Peter Walsh!' she said, shaking hands with that agreeable sinner, that very able fellow who should have made a name for himself but hadn't (always in difficulties with women), and, of course, old Miss Parry. Wonderful old lady!

Lady Bruton stood by Miss Parry's chair, a spectral grenadier, draped in black, inviting Peter Walsh to lunch; cordial; but without small talk, remembering nothing whatever about the flora or fauna of India. She had been there, of course; had stayed with three Viceroys; thought some of the Indian civilians uncommonly fine fellows; but what a tragedy it was – the state of India! The Prime Minister had just been telling her (old Miss Parry, huddled up in her shawl, did not care what the Prime Minister had just been telling her), and Lady Bruton would like to have Peter Walsh's opinion, he being fresh from the centre, and she would get Sir Sampson to meet him, for really it prevented her from sleeping at night, the folly of it, the wickedness she might say, being a soldier's daughter. She was an old woman now, not good for much. But her house, her servants, her good friend Milly Brush – did he remember her? – were all there only asking to be used if – if they could be of help, in short. For she never spoke of England, but this isle of men, this dear, dear land, was in her blood (without reading Shakespeare), and if ever a woman could have worn the helmet and shot the arrow, could have led troops to attack, ruled with indomitable justice barbarian hordes and lain under a shield noseless in a church, or made a green grass mound on some primeval hillside, that woman was Millicent Bruton. Debarred by her sex, and some truancy, too, of the logical faculty (she found it impossible to write a letter to *The Times*), she had the thought of Empire always at hand, and had acquired from her association with that armoured goddess her ramrod bearing, her robustness of demeanour, so that one could not figure her even in death parted from the earth or roaming territories over which, in some spiritual shape, the Union Jack had ceased to fly. To be not English even among the dead – no, no! Impossible!

But was it Lady Bruton? (whom she used to know). Was it Peter Walsh grown grey? Lady Rosseter asked herself (who had been Sally Seton). It was old Miss Parry certainly – the old aunt who used to be so cross when she stayed at Bourton. Never should she forget running along the passage naked, and being sent for by Miss Parry! And Clarissa! oh Clarissa! Sally caught her by the arm.

Clarissa stopped beside them.

'But I can't stay,' she said. 'I shall come later. Wait,' she said, looking at Peter and Sally. They must wait, she meant, until all these people had gone.

'I shall come back,' she said, looking at her old friends, Sally and Peter, who were shaking hands, and Sally, remembering the past no doubt, was laughing.

But her voice was wrung of its old ravishing richness; her eyes not aglow as they used to be, when she smoked cigars, when she ran down the passage to fetch her sponge bag without a stitch of clothing on her, and Ellen Atkins asked, What if the gentlemen had met her? But everybody forgave her. She stole a chicken from the larder because she was hungry in the night; she smoked cigars in her bedroom; she left a priceless book in the punt. But everybody adored her (except perhaps Papa). It was her warmth; her vitality – she would paint, she would write. Old women in the village never to this day forgot to ask after 'your friend in the red cloak who seemed so bright'. She accused Hugh Whitbread, of all people (and there he was, her old friend Hugh, talking to the Portuguese Ambassador), of kissing her in the smoking-room to punish her for saying that women should have votes. Vulgar men did, she said. And Clarissa remembered having to persuade her not to denounce him at family prayers – which she was capable of doing with her daring, her recklessness, her melodramatic love of being the centre of everything and creating scenes, and it was bound, Clarissa used to think, to end in some awful tragedy; her death; her martyrdom; instead of which she had married, quite unexpectedly, a bald man with a large buttonhole who owned, it was said, cotton mills at Manchester. And she had five boys!

She and Peter had settled down together. They were talking: it seemed so familiar – that they should be talking. They would discuss the past. With the two of them (more even than with Richard) she shared her past; the garden; the trees; old Joseph Breitkopf singing Brahms without any voice; the drawing-room wallpaper; the smell of the mats. A part of this Sally must always be; Peter must always be. But she must leave them. There were the Bradshaws, whom she disliked.

She must go up to Lady Bradshaw (in grey and silver, balancing like a sea-lion at the edge of its tank, barking for invitations, Duchesses, the typical successful man's wife), she must go up to Lady Bradshaw and say . . .

But Lady Bradshaw anticipated her.

'We are shockingly late, dear Mrs Dalloway; we hardly dared to come in,' she said.

And Sir William, who looked very distinguished, with his grey hair and blue eyes, said yes: they had not been able to resist the temptation. He was talking to Richard about that Bill probably, which they wanted to get through the Commons. Why did the sight of him, talking to Richard, curl her up? He looked what he was, a great doctor. A man absolutely at the head of his profession, very powerful, rather worn. For think what cases came before him – people in the uttermost depths of misery; people on the verge of insanity; husbands and wives. He had to decide questions of appalling difficulty. Yet – what she felt was, one wouldn't like Sir William to see one unhappy. No; not that man.

'How is your son at Eton?' she asked Lady Bradshaw.

He had just missed his eleven, said Lady Bradshaw, because of the mumps. His father minded even more than he did, she thought, 'being,' she said, 'nothing but a great boy himself.'

Clarissa looked at Sir William, talking to Richard. He did not look like a boy – not in the least like a boy.

She had once gone with some one to ask his advice. He had been perfectly right; extremely sensible. But Heavens – what a relief to get out to the street again! There was some poor wretch sobbing, she remembered, in the waiting-room. But she did not know what it was about Sir William; what exactly she disliked. Only Richard agreed with her, 'didn't like his taste, didn't like his smell.' But he was extraordinarily able. They were talking about this Bill. Some case Sir William was mentioning, lowering his voice. It had its bearing upon what he was saying about the deferred effects of shell shock. There must be some provision in the Bill.

Sinking her voice, drawing Mrs Dalloway into the shelter of a common femininity, a common pride in the illustrious qualities of husbands and their sad tendency to overwork, Lady Bradshaw (poor goose – one didn't dislike her) murmured how, 'just as we were starting, my husband was called up on the telephone, a very sad case. A young man (that is what Sir William is telling Mr Dalloway) had killed himself. He had been in the army.' Oh! thought Clarissa, in the middle of my party, here's death, she thought.

She went on, into the little room where the Prime Minister had gone with Lady Bruton. Perhaps there was somebody there. But there was nobody. The chairs still kept the impress of the Prime Minister and Lady Bruton, she turned deferentially, he sitting four-square, authoritatively. They had been talking about India. There was nobody. The party's splendour fell to the floor, so strange it was to come in alone in her finery.

What business had the Bradshaws to talk of death at her party? A young man had killed himself. And they talked of it at her party – the Bradshaws talked of death. He had killed himself – but how? Always her body went through it, when she was told, first, suddenly, of an accident; her dress flamed, her body burnt. He had thrown himself from a window. Up had flashed the ground; through him, blundering, bruising, went the rusty spikes. There he lay with a thud, thud, thud in his brain, and then a suffocation of blackness. So she saw it. But why had he done it? And the Bradshaws talked of it at her party!

She had once thrown a shilling into the Serpentine, never anything more. But he had flung it away. They went on living (she would have to go back; the rooms were still crowded; people kept on coming). They (all day she had been thinking of Bourton, of Peter, of Sally), they would grow old. A thing there was that mattered; a thing, wreathed about with chatter, defaced, obscured in her own life, let drop every day in corruption, lies, chatter. This he had preserved. Death was defiance. Death was an attempt to communicate, people feeling the impossibility of reaching the centre which, mystically, evaded them; closeness drew apart; rapture faded; one was alone. There was an embrace in death.

But this young man who had killed himself – had he plunged holding his treasure? 'If it were now to die, 'twere now to be most happy,' she had said to herself once, coming down, in white.

Or there were the poets and thinkers. Suppose he had had that passion, and had gone to Sir William Bradshaw, a great doctor, yet to her obscurely evil, without sex or lust, extremely polite to women, but capable of some indescribable outrage – forcing your soul, that was it – if this young man had gone to him, and Sir William had impressed him, like that, with his power, might he not have then said (indeed she felt it now), Life is made intolerable; they make life intolerable, men like that?

Then (she had felt it only this morning) there was the terror; the overwhelming incapacity, one's parents giving it into one's hands, this life, to be lived to the end, to be walked with serenely; there was in the depths of her heart an awful fear. Even now, quite often if Richard had not been there reading *The Times*, so that she could crouch like a bird and gradually revive, send roaring up that immeasurable delight, rubbing stick to stick, one thing with another, she must have perished. She had escaped. But that young man had killed himself.

Somehow it was her disaster – her disgrace. It was her punishment to see sink and disappear here a man, there a woman, in this profound darkness, and she forced to stand here in her evening dress. She had schemed; she had pilfered. She was never wholly admirable. She had wanted success, Lady Bexborough and the rest of it. And once she had walked on the terrace at Bourton.

Odd, incredible; she had never been so happy. Nothing could be slow enough; nothing last too long. No pleasure could equal, she thought, straightening the chairs, pushing in one book on the shelf, this having done with the triumphs of youth, lost herself in the process of living, to find it, with a shock of delight, as the sun rose, as the day sank. Many a time had she gone, at Bourton when they were all talking, to look at the sky; or seen it between people's shoulders at dinner; seen it in London when she could not sleep. She walked to the window.

It held, foolish as the idea was, something of her own in it, this country sky, this sky above Westminster. She parted the curtains; she looked. Oh, but how surprising! – in the room opposite the old lady stared straight at her! She was going to bed. And the sky. It will be a solemn sky, she had thought, it will be a dusky sky, turning away its cheek in beauty. But there it was – ashen pale, raced over quickly by tapering vast clouds. It was new to her. The wind must have risen. She was going to bed, in the room opposite. It was fascinating to watch her, moving about, that old lady, crossing the room, coming to the window. Could she see her? It was fascinating, with people still laughing and shouting in the drawing-room, to watch that old woman, quite quietly, going to bed alone. She pulled the blind now. The clock began striking. The young man had killed himself; but she did not pity him; with the clock striking the hour, one, two, three, she did not pity him, with all this going on. There! the old lady had put out her light! the whole house was dark now with this going on, she repeated, and the words came to her, Fear no more the heat of the sun. She must go back to them. But what an extraordinary night! She felt somehow very like him – the young man who had killed himself. She felt glad that he had done it; thrown it away while they went on living. The clock was striking. The leaden circles dissolved in the air. But she must go back. She must assemble. She must find Sally and Peter. And she came in from the little room.

'But where is Clarissa?' said Peter. He was sitting on the sofa with Sally. (After all these years he really could not call her 'Lady Rosseter'.) 'Where's the woman gone to?' he asked. 'Where's Clarissa?'

Sally supposed, and so did Peter for the matter of that, that there were people of importance, politicians, whom neither of them knew unless by sight in the picture papers, whom Clarissa had to be nice to, had to talk to. She was with them. Yet there was Richard Dalloway not in the Cabinet. He hadn't been a success, Sally supposed? For herself, she scarcely ever read the papers. She sometimes saw his name mentioned. But then – well, she lived a very solitary life, in the wilds, Clarissa would say, among great merchants, great manufacturers, men after all, who did things. She had done things too!

'I have five sons!' she told him.

Lord, lord, what a change had come over her! the softness of motherhood; its egotism too. Last time they met, Peter remembered, had been among the cauliflowers in the moonlight, the leaves 'like rough bronze' she had said, with her literary turn; and she had picked a rose. She had marched him up and down that awful night, after the scene by the fountain; he was to catch the midnight train. Heavens, he had wept!

That was his old trick, opening a pocket-knife, thought Sally, always opening and shutting a knife when he got excited. They had been very, very intimate, she and Peter Walsh, when he was in love with Clarissa, and there was that dreadful, ridiculous scene over Richard Dalloway at lunch. She had called Richard 'Wickham'. Why not call Richard 'Wickham'? Clarissa had flared up! and indeed they had never seen each other since, she and Clarissa, not more than half-a-dozen times perhaps in the last ten years. And Peter Walsh had gone off to India, and she had heard vaguely that he had made an unhappy marriage, and she didn't know whether he had any children, and she couldn't ask him, for he had changed. He was rather shrivelled-looking, but kinder, she felt, and she had a real affection for him, for he was connected with her youth, and she had still a little Emily Brontë he had given her, and he was to write, surely? In those days he was to write.

'Have you written?' she asked him, spreading her hand, her firm and shapely hand, on her knee in a way he recalled.

'Not a word!' said Peter Walsh, and she laughed.

She was still attractive, still a personage, Sally Seton. But who was this Rosseter? He wore two camellias on his wedding day – that was all Peter knew of him. 'They have myriads of servants, miles of conservatories,' Clarissa wrote; something like that. Sally owned it with a shout of laughter.

'Yes, I have ten thousand a year' – whether before the tax was paid or after, she couldn't remember, for her husband, 'whom you must meet,' she said, 'whom you would like,' she said, did all that for her.

And Sally used to be in rags and tatters. She had pawned her great-grandfather's ring which Marie Antoinette had given him – had he got it right? – to come to Bourton.

Oh yes, Sally remembered; she had it still, a ruby ring

which Marie Antoinette had given her great-grandfather. She never had a penny to her name in those days, and going to Bourton always meant some frightful pinch. But going to Bourton had meant so much to her – had kept her sane, she believed, so unhappy had she been at home. But that was all a thing of the past – all over now, she said. And Mr Parry was dead; and Miss Parry was still alive. Never had he had such a shock in his life! said Peter. He had been quite certain she was dead. And the marriage had been, Sally supposed, a success? And that very handsome, very self-possessed young woman was Elizabeth, over there, by the curtains, in pink.

(She was like a poplar, she was like a river, she was like a hyacinth, Willie Titcomb was thinking. Oh how much nicer to be in the country and do what she liked! She could hear the poor dog howling, Elizabeth was certain.) She was not a bit like Clarissa, Peter Walsh said.

'Oh, Clarissa!' said Sally.

What Sally felt was simply this. She had owed Clarissa an enormous amount. They had been friends, not acquaintances, friends, and she still saw Clarissa all in white going about the house with her hands full of flowers – to this day tobacco plants made her think of Bourton. But – did Peter understand? – she lacked something. Lacked what was it? She had charm; she had extraordinary charm. But to be frank (and she felt that Peter was an old friend, a real friend – did absence matter? did distance matter? She had often wanted to write to him, but torn it up, yet felt he understood, for people understand without things being said, as one realizes growing old, and old she was, had been that afternoon to see her sons at Eton, where they had the mumps), to be quite frank, then, how could Clarissa have done it? – married Richard Dalloway? a sportsman, a man who cared only for dogs. Literally, when he came into the room he smelt of the stables. And then all this? She waved her hand.

Hugh Whitbread it was, strolling past in his white waist-coat, dim, fat, blind, past everything he looked, except self-esteem and comfort.

'He's not going to recognize *us*,' said Sally, and really she hadn't the courage – so that was Hugh! the admirable Hugh!

'And what does he do?' she asked Peter.

He blacked the King's boots or counted bottles at Windsor, Peter told her. Peter kept his sharp tongue still! But Sally must be frank, Peter said. That kiss now, Hugh's.

On the lips, she assured him, in the smoking-room one evening. She went straight to Clarissa in a rage. Hugh didn't do such things! Clarissa said, the admirable Hugh! Hugh's socks were without exception the most beautiful she had ever seen – and now his evening dress. Perfect! And had he children?

'Everybody in the room has six sons at Eton,' Peter told her, except himself. He, thank God, had none. No sons, no daughters, no wife. Well, he didn't seem to mind, said Sally. He looked younger, she thought, than any of them.

But it had been a silly thing to do, in many ways, Peter said, to marry like that; 'a perfect goose she was,' he said, but, he said, 'we had a splendid time of it,' but how could that be? Sally wondered; what did he mean? and how odd it was to know him and yet not know a single thing that had happened to him. And did he say it out of pride? Very likely, for after all it must be galling for him (though he was an oddity, a sort of sprite, not at all an ordinary man), it must be lonely at his age to have no home, nowhere to go to. But he must stay with them for weeks and weeks. Of course he would; he would love to stay with them, and that was how it came out. All these years the Dalloways had never been once. Time after time they had asked them. Clarissa (for it was Clarissa of course) would not come. For, said Sally, Clarissa was at heart a snob – one had to admit it, a snob. And it was that that was between them, she was convinced. Clarissa thought she had married beneath her, her husband being – she was proud of it – a miner's son. Every penny they had he had earned. As a little boy (her voice trembled) he had carried great sacks.

(And so she would go on, Peter felt, hour after hour; the miner's son; people thought she had married beneath her;

her five sons; and what was the other thing – plants, hydrangeas, syringas, very very rare hibiscus lilies that never grow north of the Suez Canal, but she, with one gardener in a suburb near Manchester, had beds of them, positively beds! Now all that Clarissa had escaped, unmaternal as she was.)

A snob was she? Yes, in many ways. Where was she, all this time? It was getting late.

'Yes,' said Sally, 'when I heard Clarissa was giving a party, I felt I couldn't *not* come – must see her again (and I'm staying in Victoria Street, practically next door). So I just came without an invitation. But,' she whispered, 'tell me, do. Who is this?'

It was Mrs Hilbery, looking for the door. For how late it was getting! And, she murmured, as the night grew later, as people went, one found old friends; quiet nooks and corners; and the loveliest views. Did they know, she asked, that they were surrounded by an enchanted garden? Lights and trees and wonderful gleaming lakes and the sky. Just a few fairy lamps, Clarissa Dalloway had said, in the back garden! But she was a magician! It was a park.... And she didn't know their names, but friends she knew they were, friends without names, songs without words, always the best. But there were so many doors, such unexpected places, she could not find her way.

'Old Mrs Hilbery,' said Peter; but who was that? that lady standing by the curtain all the evening, without speaking? He knew her face; connected her with Bourton. Surely she used to cut up underclothes at the large table in the window? Davidson, was that her name?

'Oh, that is Ellie Henderson,' said Sally. Clarissa was really very hard on her. She was a cousin, very poor. Clarissa *was* hard on people.

She was rather, said Peter. Yet, said Sally, in her emotional way, with a rush of that enthusiasm which Peter used to love her for, yet dreaded a little now, so effusive she might become – how generous to her friends Clarissa was! and what a rare quality one found it, and how sometimes at night or on Christmas Day, when she counted up her blessings, she put that friendship first. They were young; that was it. Clarissa was pure-hearted; that was it. Peter would think her sentimental. So she was. For she had come to feel that it was the only thing worth saying – what one felt. Cleverness was silly. One must say simply what one felt.

'But I do not know,' said Peter Walsh, 'what I feel.'

Poor Peter, thought Sally. Why did not Clarissa come and talk to them? That was what he was longing for. She knew it. All the time he was thinking only of Clarissa, and was fidgeting with his knife.

He had not found life simple, Peter said. His relations with Clarissa had not been simple. It had spoilt his life, he said. (They had been so intimate – he and Sally Seton, it was absurd not to say it.) One could not be in love twice, he said. And what could she say? Still, it is better to have loved (but he would think her sentimental – he used to be so sharp). He must come and stay with them in Manchester. That is all very true, he said. All very true. He would love to come and stay with them, directly he had done what he had to do in London.

And Clarissa had cared for him more than she had ever cared for Richard, Sally was positive of that.

'No, no, no!' said Peter (Sally should not have said that – she went too far). That good fellow – there he was at the end of the room, holding forth, the same as ever, dear old Richard. Who was he talking to? Sally asked, that very distinguished-looking man? Living in the wilds as she did, she had an insatiable curiosity to know who people were. But Peter did not know. He did not like his looks, he said, probably a Cabinet Minister. Of them all, Richard seemed to him the best, he said – the most disinterested.

'But what has he done?' Sally asked. Public work, she supposed. And were they happy together? Sally asked (she herself was extremely happy); for, she admitted, she knew nothing about them, only jumped to conclusions, as one does, for what can one know even of the people one lives with every day? she asked. Are we not all prisoners? She had read a wonderful play about a man who scratched on the wall of his cell, and she had felt that was true of life – one scratched on the wall. Despairing of human relationships (people were so difficult), she often went into her garden and got from her flowers a peace which men and women never gave her. But no; he did not like cabbages; he preferred human beings, Peter said. Indeed, the young are beautiful, Sally said, watching Elizabeth cross the room. How unlike Clarissa at her age! Could he make anything of her? She would not open her lips. Not much, not yet, Peter admitted. She was like a lily, Sally said, a lily by the side of a pool. But Peter did not agree that we know nothing. We know everything, he said; at least he did.

But these two, Sally whispered, these two coming now (and really she must go, if Clarissa did not come soon), this distinguished-looking man and his rather common-looking wife who had been talking to Richard – what could one know about people like that?

'That they're damnable humbugs,' said Peter, looking at them casually. He made Sally laugh.

But Sir William Bradshaw stopped at the door to look at a picture. He looked in the corner for the engraver's name. His wife looked too. Sir William Bradshaw was so interested in art.

When one was young, said Peter, one was too much excited to know people. Now that one was old, fifty-two to be precise (Sally was fifty-five, in body, she said, but her heart was like a girl's of twenty); now that one was mature then, said Peter, one could watch, one could understand, and one did not lose the power of feeling, he said. No, that is true, said Sally. She felt more deeply, more passionately, every year. It increased, he said, alas, perhaps, but one should be glad of it – it went on increasing in his experience. There was some one in India. He would like to tell Sally about her. He would like Sally to know her. She was married, he said. She had two small children. They must all come to Manchester, said Sally – he must promise before they left.

'There's Elizabeth,' he said, 'she feels not half what we feel, not yet.' 'But,' said Sally, watching Elizabeth go to her father, 'one can see they are devoted to each other.' She could feel it by the way Elizabeth went to her father.

For her father had been looking at her, as he stood talking

to the Bradshaws, and he had thought to himself who is that lovely girl? And suddenly he realized that it was his Elizabeth, and he had not recognized her, she looked so lovely in her pink frock! Elizabeth had felt him looking at her as she talked to Willie Titcomb. So she went to him and they stood together, now that the party was almost over, looking at the people going, and the rooms getting emptier and emptier, with things scattered on the floor. Even Ellie Henderson was going, nearly last of all, though no one had spoken to her, but she had wanted to see everything, to tell Edith. And Richard and Elizabeth were rather glad it was over, but Richard was proud of his daughter. And he had not meant to tell her, but he could not help telling her. He had looked at her, he said, and he had wondered, who is that lovely girl? and it was his daughter! That did make her happy. But her poor dog was howling.

'Richard has improved. You are right,' said Sally. 'I shall go and talk to him. I shall say good-night. What does the brain matter,' said Lady Rosseter, getting up, 'compared with the heart?'

'I will come,' said Peter, but he sat on for a moment. What is this terror? what is this ecstasy? he thought to himself. What is it that fills me with extraordinary excitement?

It is Clarissa, he said.

For there she was.

JACOB'S ROOM

The manner in which Virginia Woolf describes the reality of Jacob's life from boyhood to early maturity is entirely her own, for this is the novel in which, for the first time, she broke from the conventions of the English novel, and found the style described by Bernard Blackstone as 'free, conversational, musical, the short phrases following each other like waves of the sea'.

95p

A ROOM OF ONE'S OWN

Based on two papers read to women students at Cambridge in October 1928, *A Room of One's Own* is Virginia Woolf's finest piece of non-fiction. It is a book for everyone who has ever wondered why it is that women are largely absent from the history books, unless they are queens, mothers or mistresses. Here is feminism infused with humour and subtlety – and optimism for what the liberated mind can achieve.

£1.25

Night and Day	£1.95 ☐
Between the Acts	£1.25 ☐
The Voyage Out	£1.95 ☐
The Years	£1.50 ☐
To the Lighthouse	£1.25 ☐
The Waves	£1.50 ☐
Jacob's Room	95p ☐
Orlando	£1.50 ☐
A Room of One's Own	£1.25 ☐
Moments of Being	£1.35 ☐
A Writer's Diary	£1.95 ☐

All these books are available to your local bookshop or newsagent, or can be ordered direct from the publisher. Just tick the titles you want and fill in the form below.

Name ....

Address ....

....

Write to Granada Cash Sales, PO Box 11, Falmouth, Cornwall TR10 9EN

Please enclose remittance to the value of the cover price plus:

UK: 40p for the first book, 18p for the second book plus 13p per copy for each additional book ordered to a maximum charge of £1.49.

BFPO and EIRE: 40p for the first book, 18p for the second book plus 13p per copy for the next 7 books, thereafter 7p per book.

OVERSEAS: 60p for the first book and 18p for each additional book.

Granada Publishing reserve the right to show new retail prices on covers, which may differ from those previously advertised in the text or elsewhere.

ALSO BY IAN McEWAN

First Love, Last Rites
In Between the Sheets
The Cement Garden
The Comfort of Strangers
The Child in Time
The Innocent
Black Dogs
The Daydreamer
Enduring Love
Amsterdam
Atonement
Saturday
On Chesil Beach
Solar
The Children Act

IAN McEWAN

Sweet Tooth

VINTAGE

13

Vintage
20 Vauxhall Bridge Road,
London SW1V 2SA

Vintage is part of the Penguin Random House group of companies
whose addresses can be found at global.penguinrandomhouse.com

Penguin
Random House
UK

Ian McEwan is an unlimited company registered
in England and Wales number 7473219

This edition reissued in Vintage in 2016
First published by Vintage in 2013
First published in Great Britain by Jonathan Cape in 2012

penguin.co.uk/vintage

A CIP catalogue record for this book is available
from the British Library

ISBN 9780099578789

Printed and bound in Great Britain by Clays Ltd, St Ives plc

Penguin Random House is committed to a sustainable future for our
business, our readers and our planet. This book is made from Forest
Stewardship Council® certified paper.

MIX
Paper from
responsible sources
FSC
www.fsc.org   FSC® C018179

To Christopher Hitchens
1949–2011

If only I had met, on this search, a single clearly evil person.

Timothy Garton Ash, *The File*

1

My name is Serena Frome (rhymes with plume) and almost forty years ago I was sent on a secret mission for the British security service. I didn't return safely. Within eighteen months of joining I was sacked, having disgraced myself and ruined my lover, though he certainly had a hand in his own undoing.

I won't waste much time on my childhood and teenage years. I'm the daughter of an Anglican bishop and grew up with a sister in the cathedral precinct of a charming small city in the east of England. My home was genial, polished, orderly, book-filled. My parents liked each other well enough and loved me, and I them. My sister Lucy and I were a year and a half apart and though we fought shrilly during our adolescence, there was no lasting harm and we became closer in adult life. Our father's belief in God was muted and reasonable, did not intrude much on our lives and was just sufficient to raise him smoothly through the Church hierarchy and install us in a comfortable Queen Anne house. It overlooked an enclosed garden with ancient herbaceous borders that were well known, and still are, to those who know about plants. So, all stable, enviable, idyllic even. We grew up inside a walled garden, with all the pleasures and limitations that implies.

The late sixties lightened but did not disrupt our existence. I never missed a day at my local grammar school unless I was ill. In my late teens there slipped over the garden wall some heavy petting, as they used to call it, experiments with tobacco, alcohol and a little hashish, rock and roll records, brighter colours and warmer relations all round. At seventeen my friends and I were timidly and delightedly rebellious, but we did our school work, we memorised and disgorged the irregular verbs, the equations, the motives of fictional characters. We liked to think of ourselves as bad girls, but actually we were rather good. It pleased us, the general excitement in the air in 1969. It was inseparable from the expectation that soon it would be time to leave home for another education elsewhere. Nothing strange or terrible happened to me during my first eighteen years and that is why I'll skip them.

Left to myself I would have chosen to do a lazy English degree at a provincial university far to the north or west of my home. I enjoyed reading novels. I went fast – I could get through two or three a week – and doing that for three years would have suited me just fine. But at the time I was considered something of a freak of nature – a girl who happened to have a talent for mathematics. I wasn't interested in the subject, I took little pleasure in it, but I enjoyed being top, and getting there without much work. I knew the answers to questions before I even knew how I had got to them. While my friends struggled and calculated, I reached a solution by a set of floating steps that were partly visual, partly just a feeling for what was right. It was hard to explain how I knew what I knew. Obviously, an exam in maths was far less effort than one in English literature. And in my final year I was captain of the school chess team. You must exercise some historical imagination to understand what it meant for a girl in those times to travel to a neighbouring school and knock from his perch some condescending smirking squit of a boy. However, maths and chess, along with hockey, pleated skirts and hymn-singing, I considered mere school stuff. I reckoned it was time to put away these childish things when I began to think about applying to university. But I reckoned without my mother.

She was the quintessence, or parody, of a vicar's then a bishop's wife – a formidable memory for parishoners' names and faces and gripes, a way of sailing down a street in her Hermès scarf, a kindly but unbending manner with the daily and the gardener. Faultless charm on any social scale, in any key. How knowingly she could level with the tight-faced, chain-smoking women from the housing estates when they came for the Mothers' and Babies' Club in the crypt. How compellingly she read the Christmas Eve story to the Barnardo's children gathered at her feet in our drawing room. With what natural authority she put the Archbishop of Canterbury at his ease when he came through once for tea and Jaffa cakes after blessing the restored cathedral font. Lucy and I were banished upstairs for the duration of his visit. All this – and here is the difficult part – combined with utter devotion and subordination to my father's cause. She promoted him, served him, eased his way at every turn.

From boxed socks and ironed surplice hanging in the wardrobe, to his dustless study, to the profoundest Saturday silence in the house when he wrote his sermon. All she demanded in return – my guess, of course – was that he love her or, at least, never leave her.

But what I hadn't understood about my mother was that buried deep beneath this conventional exterior was the hardy little seed of a feminist. I'm sure that word never passed her lips, but it made no difference. Her certainty frightened me. She said it was my duty as a woman to go to Cambridge to study maths. As a woman? In those days, in our milieu, no one ever spoke like that. No woman did anything 'as a woman'. She told me she would not permit me to waste my talent. I was to excel and become extraordinary. I must have a proper career in science or engineering or economics. She allowed herself the world–oyster cliché. It was unfair on my sister that I was both clever and beautiful when she was neither. It would compound the injustice if I failed to aim high. I didn't follow the logic of this, but I said nothing. My mother told me she would never forgive me and she would never forgive herself if I went off to read English and became no more than a slightly better educated housewife than she was. I was in danger of *wasting my life*. Those were her words, and they represented an admission. This was the only time she expressed or implied dissatisfaction with her lot.

Then she enlisted my father – 'the Bishop' was what my sister and I called him. When I came in from school one afternoon my mother told me he was waiting for me in his study. In my green blazer with its heraldic crest and emblazoned motto – *Nisi Dominus Vanum* (Without the Lord All Is in Vain) – I sulkily lolled in his clubbish leather

4

armchair while he presided at his desk, shuffling papers, humming to himself as he ordered his thoughts. I thought he was about to rehearse for me the parable of the talents, but he took a surprising and practical line. He had made some enquiries. Cambridge was anxious to be seen to be 'opening its gates to the modern egalitarian world'. With my burden of triple misfortune – a grammar school, a girl, an all-male subject – I was certain to get in. If, however, I applied to do English there (never my intention; the Bishop was always poor on detail) I would have a far harder time. Within a week my mother had spoken to my headmaster. Certain subject teachers were deployed and used all my parents' arguments as well as some of their own, and of course I had to give way.

So I abandoned my ambition to read English at Durham or Aberystwyth, where I am sure I would have been happy, and went instead to Newnham College, Cambridge, to learn at my first tutorial, which took place at Trinity, what a mediocrity I was in mathematics. My Michaelmas term depressed me and I almost left. Gawky boys, unblessed by charm or other human attributes like empathy and generative grammar, cleverer cousins of the fools I had smashed at chess, leered as I struggled with concepts they took for granted. 'Ah, the serene Miss Frome,' one tutor would exclaim sarcastically as I entered his room each Tuesday morning. '*Serenissima*. Blue-eyed one! Come and enlighten us!' It was obvious to my tutors and fellow students that I could not succeed precisely because I was a good-looking girl in a mini-skirt, with blonde hair curling past her shoulder blades. The truth was that I couldn't succeed because I was like nearly all the rest of humanity – not much good at maths, not at this level. I did my best to transfer out to English or French or even anthropology, but no one wanted me. In those days the rules were tightly observed. To shorten a long, unhappy story, I stuck it out and by the end managed a third.

If I've rushed through my childhood and teenage years, then I'll certainly condense my time as an undergraduate. I never went in a punt, with or without a wind-up gramophone, or visited the Footlights – theatre embarrasses me – or got myself arrested at the Garden House riots. But I lost my virginity in my first term, several times over it seemed, the general style being so wordless and clumsy, and had a pleasant succession of boyfriends, six or seven or eight over the nine terms, depending on your definitions of carnality. I made a handful of good friends from among the Newnham women. I played tennis and I read books. All thanks to my mother, I was studying the wrong subject, but I didn't stop reading. I'd never read much poetry or any plays at school, but I think I had more pleasure out of novels than my university friends, who were obliged to sweat over weekly essays on *Middlemarch* or *Vanity Fair*. I raced through the same books, chatted about them perhaps, if there was someone around who could tolerate my base level of discourse, then I moved on. Reading was my way of not thinking about maths. More than that (or do I mean less?), it was my way of not thinking.

I've said I was fast. *The Way We Live Now* in four afternoons lying on my bed! I could take in a block of text or a whole paragraph in one visual gulp. It was a matter of letting my eyes and thoughts go soft, like wax, to take the impression fresh off the page. To the irritation of those around me, I'd turn a page every few seconds with an impatient snap of the wrist. My needs were simple. I didn't bother much with themes or felicitous phrases and skipped fine descriptions of weather, landscapes and interiors. I wanted characters I could believe in, and I wanted to be made curious about what was to happen to them. Generally, I preferred people to be falling in and out of love, but I didn't mind so much if they tried their hand at something else. It was vulgar to want it, but I liked someone to say 'Marry me' by the end. Novels without female characters were a lifeless desert. Conrad was beyond my consideration, as were most stories by Kipling and Hemingway. Nor was I impressed by reputations. I read anything I saw lying around. Pulp fiction, great literature and everything in between – I gave them all the same rough treatment.

What famous novel pithily begins like this? *The temperature hit ninety degrees the day she arrived.* Isn't it punchy? Don't you know it? I caused amusement among my Newnham friends studying English when I told them that *Valley of the Dolls* was as good as anything Jane Austen ever wrote. They laughed, they teased me for months. And they hadn't read a line of Susann's work. But who cared? Who really minded about the unformed opinions of a failing mathematician? Not me, not my friends. To this extent at least I was free.

The matter of my undergraduate reading habits is not a digression. Those books delivered me to my career in intelligence. In my final year my friend Rona Kemp started up a weekly magazine called *?Quis?*. Such projects rose and fell by the dozen, but hers was ahead of its time with its high–low mix. Poetry and pop music, political theory and gossip, string quartets and student fashion, *nouvelle*

7

vague and football. Ten years later the formula was everywhere. Rona may not have invented it but she was among the first to see its attractions. She went on to *Vogue* by way of the *TLS* and then to an incendiary rise and fall, starting new magazines in Manhattan and Rio. The double question marks in this, her first title, were an innovation that helped ensure a run of eleven issues. Remembering my Susann moment, she asked me to write a regular column, 'What I Read Last Week'. My brief was to be 'chatty and omnivorous'. Easy! I wrote as I talked, usually doing little more than summarising the plots of the books I had just raced through, and, in conscious self-parody, I heightened the occasional verdict with a row of exclamation marks. My light-headed alliterative prose went down well. On a couple of occasions strangers approached me in the street to tell me so. Even my facetious maths tutor made a complimentary remark. It was the closest I ever came to a taste of that sweet and heady elixir, student fame.

I had written half a dozen jaunty pieces when something went wrong. Like many writers who come by a little success, I began to take myself too seriously. I was a girl with untutored tastes, I was an empty mind, ripe for a takeover. I was waiting, as they said in some of the novels I was reading, for Mr Right to come along and sweep me off my feet. My Mr Right was a stern Russian. I discovered an author and a subject and became an enthusiast. Suddenly I had a theme, and a mission to persuade. I began to indulge myself with lengthy rewrites. Instead of talking straight onto the page, I was doing second and then third drafts. In my modest view, my column had become a vital public service. I got up in the night to delete whole paragraphs and draw arrows and balloons across the pages. I went for important walks. I knew my popular appeal would dwindle, but I didn't care. The dwindling proved my point, it was the heroic price I knew I must pay. The wrong people had been reading me. I didn't care when Rona remonstrated. In fact, I felt vindicated. 'This isn't exactly chatty,' she said coolly as she handed back my copy in the Copper Kettle one afternoon. 'This isn't what we agreed.' She was right. My breeziness and exclamation marks had dissolved as anger and urgency narrowed my interests and destroyed my style.

My decline was initiated by the fifty minutes I spent with Aleksandr Solzhenitsyn's *One Day in the Life of Ivan Denisovich* in the new translation by Gillon Aitken. I picked it up straight after finishing Ian Fleming's *Octopussy*. The transition was harsh. I knew nothing of the Soviet labour camps and had never heard the word 'gulag'. Growing up in a cathedral precinct, what did I know of the cruel absurdities of communism, of how brave men and women in bleak and remote penal colonies were reduced to thinking day by day of nothing else beyond their own survival? Hundreds of thousands transported to the Siberian wastes for fighting for their country in a foreign land, for having been a prisoner of war, for upsetting a party official, for being a party official, for wearing glasses, for being a Jew, a homosexual, a peasant who owned a cow, a poet. Who was speaking out for all this lost humanity? I had never troubled myself with politics before. I knew nothing of the arguments and disillusionment of an older generation. Nor had I heard of the 'left opposition'. Beyond school, my education had been confined to some extra maths and piles of paperback novels. I was an innocent and my outrage was moral. I didn't use, and hadn't even heard, the word 'totalitarianism'. I probably would have thought it had something to do with refusing a drink. I believed I was seeing through a veil, that I was breaking new ground as I filed dispatches from an obscure front.

Within a week I'd read Solzhenitsyn's *The First Circle*. The title came from Dante. His first circle of hell was reserved for Greek philosophers and consisted, as it happened, of a pleasant *walled garden* surrounded by hellish suffering, a garden from which escape and access to paradise was forbidden. I made the enthusiast's mistake of assuming that everyone shared my previous ignorance. My column became a harangue. Did smug Cambridge not know what had gone on, was still going on, three thousand miles to the east, had it not noticed the damage this failed utopia of food queues, awful clothes and restricted travel was doing to the human spirit? What was to be done?

?Quis? tolerated four rounds of my anti-communism. My interests extended to Koestler's *Darkness at Noon*, Nabokov's *Bend Sinister* and that fine treatise by Milosz, *The Captive Mind*. I was also the first person in the world to understand Orwell's *Nineteen Eighty-Four*. But my heart was always with my first love, Aleksandr. The forehead that rose like an Orthodox dome, the hillbilly pastor's wedge of beard, the grim, gulag-conferred authority, his stubborn immunity to politicians. Even his religious convictions could not deter me. I forgave him when he said that men had forgotten God. *He* was God. Who could match him? Who could deny him his Nobel Prize? Gazing at his photograph, I wanted to be his lover. I would have served him as my mother did my father. Box his socks? I would have knelt to wash his feet. With my tongue!

In those days, dwelling on the iniquities of the Soviet

system was routine for Western politicians and editorials in most newspapers. In the context of student life and politics, it was just a little distasteful. If the CIA was against communism, there must be something to be said for it. Sections of the Labour Party still held a candle for the ageing, square-jawed Kremlin brutes and their grisly project, still sang the Internationale at the annual conference, still dispatched students on goodwill exchanges. In the Cold War years of binary thinking, it would not do to find yourself agreeing about the Soviet Union with an American President waging war in Vietnam. But at that teatime rendezvous in the Copper Kettle, Rona, even then so polished, perfumed, precise, said it was not the politics of my column that troubled her. My sin was to be earnest. The next issue of her magazine didn't carry my byline. My space was taken up by an interview with the Incredible String Band. And then *?Quis?* folded.

Within days of my sacking I started on a Colette phase, which consumed me for months. And I had other urgent concerns. Finals were only weeks away and I had a new boyfriend, a historian called Jeremy Mott. He was of a certain old-fashioned type – lanky, large-nosed, with an outsized Adam's apple. He was unkempt, clever in an understated way, and extremely polite. I'd noticed quite a few of his sort around. They all seemed to be descended from a single family and come from public schools in the north of England, where they were issued with the same clothes. These were the last men on earth still wearing Harris tweed jackets with leather patches on the elbows and trim on the cuffs. I learned, though not from Jeremy, that he was expected to get a first and that he had already

11

published an article in a scholarly journal of sixteenth-century studies.

He turned out to be a tender and considerate lover, despite his unfortunate, sharply angled pubic bone, which first time hurt like hell. He apologised for it, as one might for a mad but distant relative. By which I mean he was not particularly embarrassed. We settled the matter by making love with a folded towel between us, a remedy I sensed he had often used before. He was truly attentive and skilful, and could keep going for as long as I wanted, and beyond, until I could bear no more. But his own orgasms were elusive, despite my efforts, and I began to suspect that there was something he wanted me to be saying or doing. He wouldn't tell me what it was. Or rather, he insisted that there was nothing to tell. I didn't believe him. I wanted him to have a secret and shameful desire that only I could satisfy. I wanted to make this lofty, courteous man all mine. Did he want to smack my back-side, or have me smack his? Was he wanting to try on my underwear? This mystery obsessed me when I was away from him, and made it all the harder to stop thinking about him when I was supposed to be concentrating on the maths. Colette was my escape.

One afternoon in early April, after a session with the folded towel in Jeremy's rooms, we were crossing the road by the old Corn Exchange, I in a haze of contentment and some related pain from a pulled muscle in the small of my back, and he – well, I wasn't sure. As we walked along I was wondering whether I should broach the subject once more. He was being pleasant, with his arm heavily around my shoulders as he told me about his essay on the Star Chamber. I was convinced that he wasn't properly fulfilled.

I thought I heard it in the tightness of his voice, his nervous pace. In days of lovemaking he had not been blessed with a single orgasm. I wanted to help him, and I was genuinely curious. I was also troubled by the thought that I might be failing him. I aroused him, that much was clear, but perhaps he didn't quite desire me sufficiently. We went past the Corn Exchange in the twilight chill of a damp spring, my lover's arm was about me like a fox fur, my happiness faintly compromised by a muscular twinge and only a little more by the enigma of Jeremy's desires.

Suddenly, from out of an alley, there appeared before us under the inadequate street lighting Jeremy's history tutor, Tony Canning. When we were introduced he shook my hand, and held on to it far too lingeringly, I thought. He was in his early fifties – about my father's age – and I knew only what Jeremy had already told me. He was a professor, a one-time friend of the Home Secretary, Reggie Maudling, who had been to dine in his college. The two men had fallen out one drunken evening over the policy of internment without trial in Northern Ireland. Professor Canning had chaired a commission on historical sites, sat on various advisory boards, was a trustee of the British Museum and had written a highly regarded book about the Congress of Vienna.

He was of the great and good, a type vaguely familiar to me. Men like him came to our house to visit the Bishop from time to time. They were annoying of course to anyone under twenty-five in that post-sixties period, but I rather liked them too. They could be charming, even witty, and the whiff they trailed of cigars and brandy made the world seem orderly and rich. They thought much of themselves, but they didn't seem dishonest, and they had, or gave the

13

impression they had, a strong sense of public service. They took their pleasures seriously (wine, food, fishing, bridge, etc.) and apparently some had fought an interesting war. I had memories of childhood Christmases when one or two of them would tip my sister and me a ten-bob note. Let these men rule the world. There were others far worse.

Canning had a relatively subdued grand manner, perhaps to match his modest public roles. I noted the wavy hair, finely parted, and moist fleshy lips and a small cleft in the centre of his chin, which I thought was endearing because I could see, even in poor light, that he had some trouble shaving it clean. Ungovernable dark hairs protruded from the vertical trough of skin. He was a good-looking man.

When the introductions were over, Canning asked me some questions about myself. They were polite and innocent enough – about my degree, Newnham, the principal, who was a good friend of his, my home town, the cathedral. Jeremy cut in with some small talk and then Canning interrupted in turn to thank him for showing him my last three articles for *?Quis?*.

He turned to me again. 'Bloody good pieces. You've quite a talent, my dear. Are you going into journalism?'

?Quis? was a student rag, not intended for serious eyes. I was gratified by the praise, but too young to know how to take a compliment. I mumbled something modest but it sounded dismissive, then I clumsily tried to correct myself and became flustered. The professor took pity on me and invited us to tea and we accepted, or Jeremy did. And so we followed Canning back across the market towards his college.

His rooms were smaller, dingier, more chaotic than I

14

expected, and I was surprised to see him making a mess of the tea, partly rinsing the chunky brown-stained mugs and slopping hot water from a filthy electric kettle over papers and books. None of this fitted with what I came to know of him later. He sat behind his desk, we sat on armchairs and he continued to ask questions. It could have been a tutorial. Now that I was nibbling his Fortnum & Mason chocolate biscuits, I felt obliged to answer him more fully. Jeremy was encouraging me, nodding stupidly at everything I said. The professor asked about my parents, and what it was like growing up 'in the shadow of a cathedral' – I said, wittily, I thought, that there was no shadow because the cathedral was to the north of our house. Both men laughed and I wondered if my joke had implied more than I understood. We moved on to nuclear weapons and calls in the Labour Party for unilateral disarmament. I repeated a phrase I'd read somewhere – a cliché I realised later. It would be impossible 'to put the genie back in the bottle'. Nuclear weapons would have to be managed, not banned. So much for youthful idealism. Actually, I had no particular views on the subject. In another context, I could have spoken up for nuclear disarmament. I would have denied it, but I was trying to please, to give the right answers, to be interesting. I liked the way Tony Canning leaned forwards when I spoke, I was encouraged by his little smile of approbation, which stretched but did not quite part his plump lips, and his way of saying 'I see' or 'Quite . . .' whenever I paused.

Perhaps it should have been obvious to me where this was leading. In a tiny, hothouse world of undergraduate journalism, I'd announced myself as a trainee Cold

Warrior. It must be obvious now. This was Cambridge, after all. Why else would I recount the meeting? At the time the encounter had no significance for me at all. We had been on our way to a bookshop and instead we were taking tea with Jeremy's tutor. Nothing very strange in that. Recruitment methods in those days were changing, but only a little. The Western world may have been undergoing a steady transformation, the young may have thought they had discovered a new way of talking to each other, the old barriers were said to be crumbling from the base. But the famous 'hand on the shoulder' was still applied, perhaps less frequently, perhaps with less pressure. In the university context certain dons continued to look out for promising material and pass names on for interview. Certain successful candidates in the Civil Service exams were still taken aside and asked if they had ever thought of 'another' department. Mostly, people were quietly approached once they'd been out in the world a few years. No one ever needed to spell it out, but background remained important, and having the Bishop in mine was no disadvantage. It's often been remarked how long it took for the Burgess, Maclean and Philby cases to dislodge the assumption that a certain class of person was more likely to be loyal to his country than the rest. In the seventies those famous betrayals still resounded, but the old enlistment methods were robust.

Generally, both hand and shoulder belonged to men. It was unusual for a woman to be approached in that much-described, time-honoured way. And though it was strictly true that Tony Canning ended up recruiting me for MI5, his motives were complicated and he had no official sanction. If the fact that I was young and attractive was important to him, it took a while to discover the full pathos of that. (Now that the mirror tells a different story, I can say it and get it out of the way. I really was *pretty*. More than that. As Jeremy once wrote in a rare effusive letter, I was 'actually rather gorgeous'.) Even the elevated greybeards on the fifth floor, whom I never met and rarely saw in my brief period of service, had no idea why I'd been sent to them. They hedged their bets, but they never guessed that Professor Canning, an old MI5 hand himself, thought he was making them a gift in the spirit of expiation. His case was more complex and sadder than anyone knew. He would change my life and behave with selfless cruelty as he prepared to set out on a journey with no hope of return. If I know so little about him even now, it's because I accompanied him only a very small part of the way.

2

My affair with Tony Canning lasted a few months. At first I was also seeing Jeremy, but by late June, after finals, he moved to Edinburgh to start work on a PhD. My life became less fraught, though it still troubled me that I hadn't cracked his secret by the time he left and couldn't give him satisfaction. He had never complained or looked sorry for himself. Some weeks later he wrote a tender, regretful letter to say that he had fallen in love with a violinist he'd heard one evening at the Usher Hall playing a Bruch concerto, a young German from Düsseldorf with an exquisite tone, especially in the slow movement. His name was Manfred. Of course. If I'd been a little more old-fashioned in my thinking, I would have guessed it, for there was a time when every man's sexual problem had only one cause.

How convenient. The mystery was solved, and I could stop worrying about Jeremy's happiness. He was sweetly concerned for my feelings, even offering to travel down and meet me to explain things. I wrote back to congratulate him, and felt mature as I exaggerated my delight for his benefit. Such liaisons had only been legal for five years and were a novelty to me. I told him that there was no need to come all the way to Cambridge, that I'd always have the fondest memories, that he was the loveliest of men, and I looked forward to meeting Manfred one day, please let's keep in touch, Goodbye! I would have liked to thank him for introducing me to Tony, but I saw no point in creating suspicion. Nor did I tell Tony about his former student. Everyone knew as much as they needed to know to be happy.

And we were. We kept our tryst each weekend in an isolated cottage not far from Bury St Edmunds in Suffolk. You turned off a quiet narrow lane onto an indistinct track that crossed a field, you stopped at the edge of an ancient pollarded wood, and there, hidden by a tangle of hawthorn bushes, was a small white picket gate. A flagstone path curved through an overgrown country garden (lupins, hollyhocks, giant poppies) to a heavy oak door studded with rivets or nails. When you opened that door you were in the dining room, a place of giant flagstones and worm-holed beams half buried in the plaster. On the wall opposite was a bright Mediterranean scene of whitewashed houses and sheets drying on a line. It was a watercolour by Winston Churchill, painted in Marrakech during a break from the Conference in 1943. I never learned how it came into Tony's possession.

Frieda Canning, an art dealer who travelled abroad a good deal, didn't like coming here. She complained about the damp and the smell of mildew and the dozens of tasks associated with a second home. As it happened, the smell vanished as soon as the place warmed up, and it was her husband who did all the tasks. They required special knowledge and skills: how to light the stubborn Rayburn stove and force open the kitchen window, how to activate the bathroom plumbing and dispose of the broken-backed mice in the traps. I didn't even have to cook much. For all his sloppy tea-making, Tony fancied himself in the kitchen. I was sometimes his sous chef, and he taught me a good deal. He cooked in the Italian style, learned during four years as a lecturer at an institute in Siena. His back played up, so at the beginning of each visit I humped hessian sacks of food and wine through the garden from his ancient MGA parked in the field.

It was a decent summer by English standards and Tony set a stately pace to the day. We often ate our lunch in the shade of an ancient cotoneaster in the garden. Generally, when he woke from his after-lunch nap, he took a bath and then, if it was warm, he read in a hammock slung between two birch trees. And, if it was really hot, he sometimes suffered from nosebleeds and had to lie on his back indoors with a flannel and ice cubes pressed to his face. Some evenings we took a picnic into the woods, with a bottle of white wine wrapped in a crisp tea towel, wine glasses in a cedarwood container, and a flask of coffee. This was high table *sur l'herbe*. Saucers as well as cups, damask tablecloth, porcelain plates, silverware and one collapsible aluminium-and-canvas chair – I carried everything without complaint. Later in the summer we didn't go far along the footpaths because Tony said it hurt to walk, and he tired easily. In the evenings he liked to play opera on an old gramophone and though he urgently explained the characters and intrigues of *Aida*, *Così Fan Tutte* and *L'Elisir d'Amore*, those reedy yearning voices meant little to me. The quaint hiss and crackle of the blunted needle as it gently rose and fell with the warp of the album sounded like the ether, through which the dead were hopelessly calling to us.

He liked talking to me about his childhood. His father had been a naval commander in the first war and was an expert yachtsman. In the late twenties, family holidays consisted of island hopping in the Baltic and this was how his parents came across and bought a stone cottage on the remote island of Kumlinge. It became one of those child-hood paradise places burnished by nostalgia. Tony and his older brother roamed free, building fires and camps on the beaches, rowing out to an uninhabited islet to steal sea-bird eggs. He had cracked box-camera snaps to prove that the dream was real.

One afternoon in late August we went into the woods. We often did, but on this occasion Tony turned off the footpath and I blindly followed. We barged through the undergrowth, and I assumed we were going to make love in some secret place he knew. The leaves were dry enough. But he was thinking only of mushrooms, ceps. I concealed my disappointment and learned the identi-fying tricks – pores not gills, a fine filigree on the stem, no staining when you pushed your thumb into the flesh. That evening he cooked up a big pan of what he preferred to call porcini, with olive oil, pepper, salt and pancetta, and we ate them with grilled polenta, salad and red wine, a Barolo. This was exotic food in the seventies. I remember everything – the scrubbed pine table with dented legs of faded duck-egg blue, the wide faience bowl of slippery ceps, the disc of polenta beaming like a miniature sun from a pale green plate with a cracked glaze, the dusty

21

black bottle of wine, the peppery rugola in a chipped white bowl, and Tony making the dressing in seconds, tipping oil and squeezing half a lemon in his fist even, so it seemed, as he carried the salad to the table. (My mother concocted her dressings at eye level, like an industrial chemist.) Tony and I ate many similar meals at that table, but this one can stand for the rest. What simplicity, what taste, what a man of the world! That night the wind was up and the bough of an ash thumped and scraped across the thatched roof. After dinner there would be reading, then talking to be sure, but only after love-making, and that only after another glass of wine.

As a lover? Well, obviously not as energetic and inexhaustible as Jeremy. And though Tony was in good shape for his age, I was a little put out first time to see what fifty-four years could do to a body. He was sitting on the edge of the bed, bending to remove a sock. His poor naked foot looked like a worn-out old shoe. I saw folds of flesh in improbable places, even under his arms. How strange, that in my surprise, quickly suppressed, it didn't occur to me that I was looking at my own future. I was twenty-one. What I took to be the norm – taut, smooth, supple – was the transient special case of youth. To me, the old were a separate species, like sparrows or foxes. And now, what I would give to be fifty-four again! The body's largest organ bears the brunt – the old no longer fit their skin. It hangs off them, off us, like a room-for-growth school blazer. Or pyjamas. And in a certain light, though it may have been the bedroom curtains, Tony had a yellowish look, like an old paperback, one in which you could read of various misfortunes – of overeating, scars from knee and appendicitis operations, of a dog bite, a rock-climbing accident and a childhood disaster with a breakfast frying pan which had left him bereft of a patch of pubic hair. There was a white four-inch scar to the right of his chest reaching towards his neck, whose history he would never explain. But if he was slightly . . . foxed, and resembled at times my frayed old teddy back home in the cathedral close, he was also a worldly, a gentlemanly, lover. His style was courtly. I warmed to the way he undressed me, and draped my clothes over his forearm, like a swimming-pool attendant, and the way he sometimes wanted me to sit astride his face – as new to me as rugola salad, that one.

I also had reservations. He could be hasty, impatient to get on to the next thing – the passions of his life were drinking and talking. Later, I sometimes thought he was selfish, definitely old school, racing towards his own moment, which he always gained with a wheezy shout. And too obsessed by my breasts, which were lovely then, I'm sure, but it didn't feel right to have a man the Bishop's age fixated in a near infantile way, virtually nursing there with a strange whimpering sound. He was one of those Englishmen wrenched aged seven from Mummy and driven into numbing boarding-school exile. They never acknowledge the damage, these poor fellows, they just live it. But these were minor complaints. It was all new, an adventure that proved my own maturity. A knowing, older man doted on me. I forgave him everything. And I loved those soft-cushioned lips. He kissed beautifully.

Still, I liked him most when he was back in his clothes, with his fine parting restored (he used hair oil and a steel comb), when he was great and good once more, settling me in an armchair, deftly drawing the cork from a Pinot Grigio, directing my reading. And there was something

I've since noticed over the years – the mountain range that separates the naked from the clothed man. Two men on one passport. Again, it hardly mattered, it was all one – sex and cooking, wine and short walks, talking. And we were also studious. In the early days, in the spring and early summer of that year, I was working for my finals. Tony could give me no help there. He sat across from me, writing a monograph about John Dee.

He had scores of friends but, of course, he never invited anyone round when I was there. Only once did we have visitors. They came one afternoon in a car with a driver, two men in dark suits, in their forties, I guessed. Rather too curtly, Tony asked me if I would go for a longish walk in the woods. When I came back an hour and a half later, the men had gone. Tony gave no explanation and that night we went back to Cambridge.

The cottage was the only place where we saw each other. Cambridge was too much of a village; Tony was too well known there. I had to hike with my holdall to a remote corner of town on the edge of a housing estate and wait in a bus shelter for him to come by in his ailing sports car. It was supposed to be a convertible but the concertina metal bits that supported the canvas top were too rusted to fold back. This old MGA had a map light on a chrome stem, and quivering dials. It smelled of engine oil and friction heat, the way a 1940s Spitfire might. You felt the warm tin floor vibrate beneath your feet. It was a thrill to step out of the bus queue, resentfully observed by ordinary passengers, while I turned from frog to princess and stooped to crawl in beside the professor. It was like getting into bed, in public. I shoved my bag into the tiny space behind me, and felt the seat's cracked leather snag faintly against the silk of my blouse – one he had bought me in Liberty's – as I leaned across to receive my kiss.

When exams were over Tony said he was taking charge of my reading. Enough novels! He was appalled by my ignorance of what he called 'our island story'. He was right to be. I'd studied no history at school beyond the age of fourteen. Now I was twenty-one, blessed with a privileged education, but Agincourt, the Divine Right of Kings, the Hundred Years War were mere phrases to me. The very word 'history' conjured a dull succession of thrones and murderous clerical wrangling. But I submitted to the tutelage. The material was more interesting than maths and my reading list was short – Winston Churchill and G.M. Trevelyan. The rest my professor would talk me through.

My first tutorial was conducted in the garden under the cotoneaster. I learned that since the sixteenth century the foundation of English then British policy in Europe was the pursuit of the balance of power. I was required to read up on the Congress of Vienna of 1815. Tony was insistent that an equilibrium between nations was the foundation of a lawful international system of peaceful diplomacy. It was vital that nations held one another in check.

I often did my reading alone after lunch while Tony took his nap – these sleeps became longer as the summer wore on and I should have taken notice. Initially, I impressed him with my speed-reading. Two hundred pages in a couple of hours! Then I disappointed him. I couldn't answer his questions clearly, I wasn't retaining information. He made me go back through Churchill's version of the Glorious Revolution, tested me, groaned theatrically – You bloody sieve! – made me read again, asked more questions. These oral exams happened during walks in the woods, and over glasses of wine after the suppers he cooked. I resented his persistence. I wanted us to be lovers, not teacher and pupil. I was annoyed with him as well as myself when I didn't know the answers. And then, a few querulous sessions later, I began to feel some pride, and not simply in my improved performance. I started to take note of the story itself. Here was something precious and it seemed as if I'd discovered it on my own, like Soviet oppression. Wasn't England at the end of the seventeenth century the freest and most inquisitive society the world had ever known? Wasn't the English Enlightenment of more consequence than the French? Wasn't it right that England should have set itself apart to struggle against the Catholic despotisms on the Continent? And surely, we were the inheritors of that freedom.

I was easily led. I was being groomed for my first interview, which was to take place in September. He had an idea of the kind of Englishwoman they would want to take on, or that he would want, and he worried that my narrow education would let me down. He believed, wrongly as it turned out, that one of his old students would be among my interviewers. He insisted I read a newspaper every day, by which of course he meant *The Times*, which in those days was still the august paper of record. I hadn't bothered much with the press before, and I had never even heard of a leader. Apparently, this was the 'living heart' of a newspaper. At first glance, the prose resembled a chess problem. So I was hooked. I admired those orotund and lordly pronouncements on matters of public concern. The judgements were somewhat opaque and never above a reference to Tacitus or Virgil. So mature! I thought any of these anonymous writers was fit to be World President.

And what were the concerns of the day? In the leaders, grand subordinate clauses orbited elliptically about their starry main verbs, but in the letters pages no one was in any doubt. The planets were out of kilter and the letter writers knew in their anxious hearts that the country was sinking into despair and rage and desperate self-harm. The United Kingdom had succumbed, one letter announced, to a frenzy of *akrasia* – which was, Tony reminded me, the Greek word for acting against one's better judgement. (Had I not read Plato's *Protagoras*?) A useful word. I stored it away. But there *was* no better judgement, nothing to act against. Everyone had gone mad, so everyone said. The archaic word 'strife' was in heavy use in those rackety days, with inflation provoking strikes, pay settlements driving inflation, thick-headed, two-bottle-lunch management, bloody-minded unions with insurrectionary ambitions, weak government, energy crises and power cuts, skinheads, filthy streets, the Troubles, nukes. Decadence, decay, decline, dull inefficiency and apocalypse . . .

Among the favoured topics in letters to *The Times* were the miners, 'a workers' state', the bipolar world of Enoch Powell and Tony Benn, flying pickets, and the Battle for Saltley. A letter from a retired rear admiral said the country resembled a rusting battleship holed below the waterline. Tony read the letter over breakfast and shook his copy noisily at me – newsprint was crinkly and loud back then.

'Battleship?' he fumed. 'It isn't even a corvette. This is a bloody rowing boat going down!'

That year, 1972, was just the beginning. When I started reading the paper the three-day week, the next power cuts, the government's *fifth* state of emergency were not so far ahead of us. I believed what I read, but it seemed remote. Cambridge looked much the same, and so did the woods around the Cannings' cottage. Despite my history lessons I felt I had no stake in the nation's fate. I owned one suitcase of clothes, fewer than fifty books, some childhood things in my bedroom at home. I had a lover who adored me and cooked for me and never threatened to leave his wife. I had one obligation, a job interview – *weeks* away. I was free. So what was I doing, applying to the Security Service to help maintain this ailing state, this sick man of Europe? Nothing, I was doing nothing. I didn't know. A chance had come my way and I was taking it. Tony wanted it so I wanted it and I had little else going on. So why not?

Besides, I still regarded myself as accountable to my parents and they were pleased to hear that I was considering a respectable wing of the Civil Service, the Department of Health and Social Security. It may not have been the atom-smashing my mother had in mind, but its solidity in turbulent times must have soothed her. She wanted to know why I had not come to live at home after finals, and I was able to tell her that a kindly older tutor was preparing me for my 'board'. It made sense, surely, to take a tiny cheap room by Jesus Green and 'work my socks off', even at weekends.

My mother might have expressed some scepticism if my sister Lucy hadn't created a diversion by getting herself into such trouble that summer. She was always louder, feistier, a bigger risk-taker, and had been far more

28

convinced than I was by the liberating sixties as they limped into the next decade. She was also two inches taller now and was the first person I ever saw wearing 'cut-off' jeans. Loosen up, Serena, be free! Let's go travelling! She caught hippiedom just as it was going out of fashion, but that's how it was in provincial market towns. She was also telling the world that her sole aim in life was to be a doctor, a general practitioner or perhaps a paediatrician.

She pursued her ambitions by a roundabout route. That July she was a foot passenger off the Calais to Dover ferry and was interrupted by a customs official, or rather, by his dog, a barking bloodhound suddenly excited by the aroma of her backpack. Inside, wrapped in unlaundered T-shirts and dog-proof layers of plastic, was half a pound of Turkish hashish. And inside Lucy, though this was also not declared, was a developing embryo. The identity of the father was uncertain.

My mother had to devote a good portion of every day for the next few months to a quadruple mission. The first was to save Lucy from prison, the second, to keep her story out of the newspapers, the third, to prevent her being sent down from Manchester, where she was a second-year medical student, and the fourth, after not much agonising, was to arrange the termination. As far as I could tell from my crisis visit home (Lucy smelling of patchouli and sobbing as she crushed me in her sun-tanned arms), the Bishop was prepared to bow his head and take whatever the heavens had prepared for him. But my mother was already at the controls, fiercely activating the networks that extend locally and nationally from any twelfth-century cathedral. For example, the Chief Constable for our county was a regular lay preacher and knew of old his counterpart, the Chief Constable of Kent. A Conservative Association friend was acquainted with the Dover magistrate before whom Lucy made her first appearance. The editor of our local paper was wanting to get his tone-deaf twin sons into the cathedral choir. Pitch of course was relative, but nothing could be taken for granted, and it was, my mother assured me, *all jolly hard work*, and none of it more so than the abortion, medically routine but, to Lucy's surprise, deeply upsetting. Eventually she received a six-month suspended sentence, nothing appeared in the press, and a Mancunian university rector or some such eminence was assured of my father's support on an arcane matter at the upcoming Synod. My sister returned to her studies in September. Two months later she dropped out.

So I was left in peace during July and August to loll about Jesus Green, reading Churchill, bored, waiting for the weekend and the hike to the bus stop on the city boundary. It would not be long before I enshrined the summer of '72 as a golden age, a precious idyll, but it was only Friday to Sunday evening that held the pleasures. Those weekends were an extended tutorial in how to live, how and what to eat and drink, how to read newspapers and hold up my end of an argument and how to 'gut' a book. I knew I had an interview coming up, but it never crossed my mind to ask why Tony took such trouble over me. If I had I would have probably thought that such attentions were part of what it meant to have an affair with an older man.

Of course, the situation couldn't last and it all came apart during a stormy half-hour by a busy main road, two days before I was due at my interview in London. The precise sequence of events is worth recording. There was a silk blouse, the one I've already mentioned, bought for me by Tony in early July. It was well chosen. I liked the expensive feel of it on a warm evening and Tony told me more than once how he liked the plain loose cut of it on me. I was touched. He was the first man in my life to buy me an article of clothing. A sugar daddy. (I don't think the Bishop had ever been in a shop.) It was an old-fashioned thing, this present, with a touch of kitsch about it, and awfully girlish, but I loved it. When I wore it I was in his embrace. The pale blue copperplate words on the label appeared distinctly erotic – 'wild silk hand wash'. Round the neck and cuffs were bands of *broderie anglaise*, and two pleats on the shoulder were matched by two little tucks at the back. This gift was an emblem, I suppose. When it was time to come away, I would bring it back to my bedsit, wash it in the basin, and iron and fold it so that it would be ready for the next visit. Like me.

But on this occasion in September we were in the bedroom and I was packing my things away when Tony interrupted what he was saying – he was talking about Idi Amin of Uganda – to tell me to chuck the blouse in the laundry basket along with one of his shirts. It made sense. We would be back soon and the housekeeper, Mrs Travers, would be in the following day to take care of everything. Mrs Canning was in Vienna for ten days. I remembered the moment well because it gave me such pleasure. That our love was routine, taken for granted, with an immediate future measured in three or four days was comforting. I was often lonely in Cambridge, waiting for Tony's call to the payphone in the hallway. In a passing moment of something like wifely entitlement, I lifted the wicker lid and dropped my blouse on top of his shirt and thought no more about it. Sarah Travers came in three times a week from the nearest village. We once spent a pleasant half-hour shelling peas together at the kitchen table and she told me about her son, gone off to be a hippie in Afghanistan. She said it with pride, as though he'd joined the army for a necessary and dangerous war. I didn't like to think about it too closely, but I assumed she had seen a succession of Tony's women friends pass through the cottage. I don't think she cared, as long as she was paid.

Back on Jesus Green four days went by and I heard nothing. Obediently, I read up on the Factory Acts and the Corn Laws and studied the newspaper. I saw some friends who were passing through, but never wandered far from the phone. On the fifth day I went to Tony's college, left a note with the porter and hurried home, worried that I might have missed his call. I couldn't ring him – my lover had taken care not to give me his home phone number. He rang that evening. His voice was flat. Without greeting, he instructed me to be at the bus stop the following morning at ten. I was halfway through asking him a plaintive question when he hung up. Naturally, I didn't sleep much that night. Amazing to think that I lay awake worrying about *him*, when I should have known in my silly heart that I was for the chop.

At dawn I took a bath and made myself fragrant. By seven I was ready. What a hopeful fool, to have packed a bag with the underwear he liked (black of course, and purple) and plimsolls for walking in the woods. I was at the bus stop by nine twenty-five, worried that he'd be early and disappointed not to find me there. He came around ten fifteen. He pushed open the passenger door and I crawled in, but there was no kiss. Instead he kept both hands on the wheel and pulled away hard from the kerb. We drove ten miles or so and he wouldn't speak to me. His knuckles were white from his grip and he would only look ahead. What was the matter? He wouldn't tell me. And I was frantic, intimidated by the way he swung his little car out across the lanes, overtaking recklessly on rises and bends, as if to warn me of the storm to come.

He doubled back towards Cambridge on a roundabout and pulled into a lay-by off the A45, a place of oily, littered grass with a kiosk on worn bare ground that sold hot dogs and burgers to lorry drivers. At this time in the morning the stall was shuttered and padlocked and no one else was parked there. We got out. It was the worst kind of day at the end of summer – sunny, windy, dusty. To our right was a widely spaced row of parched sycamore saplings and on the other side of it the traffic was whining and roaring. It was like being on the edge of a race track. The lay-by was a couple of hundred yards long. He set off along it and I kept by his side. To talk we almost had to shout.

The first thing he said was, 'So your little trick didn't work.'

'What trick?'

I quickly turned over the recent past. Since there was no trick, I was suddenly hopeful that there was a simple matter we could straighten out in seconds. We could be laughing about this, I even thought. We could be making love before noon.

We reached the point where the lay-by joined the road. 'Get this clear,' he said, and we stopped. 'You'll never get between Frieda and me.'

'Tony, *what trick?*'

He turned back again in the direction of his car and I followed. 'Bloody nightmare.' He was talking to himself.

I called out over the din. 'Tony. Tell me!'

'Aren't you pleased? Last night we had our worst row in twenty-five years. Aren't you excited by your success?'

Even I, inexperienced and baffled and horrified as I was, could sense the absurdity of this. He was going to tell me in his own way, so I said nothing and waited. We walked back past his car and the closed-up kiosk. To our right was a hedge of high dusty hawthorns. Gaily coloured sweet wrappers and crisp packets were trapped in the spiky branches. There was a used condom, ridiculously long, lying on the grass. A fine place to end an affair.

'Serena, how could you be so stupid?'

I did feel stupid. We stopped again and I said in a quavering voice I couldn't control, 'I honestly don't understand.'

'You wanted her to find your blouse. Well, she found your blouse. You thought she'd be furious and you were right. You thought you could break up my marriage and move in but you were wrong.'

The injustice of this overwhelmed me and it was hard to speak. Somewhere just behind and above the root of my tongue my throat was beginning to tighten. In case there were tears I turned away quickly. I didn't want him to see.

'Of course, you're young and all that. But you should be ashamed.'

When I found it, I hated my croaky pleading voice. 'Tony, you said to put it in your laundry basket.'

'Come on now. You know I said nothing of the sort.'

He said it gently, almost lovingly, like a caring father,

one I was about to lose. We should have been having a row, bigger than any he'd ever had with Frieda, I should have been flying at him. But inconveniently I thought I was about to start crying and I was determined not to. I don't cry easily, and when I do I want to be alone. But that soft plummy voice of authority pierced me. It was so confident and kind that I was close to believing it. I already sensed I could never alter his recollection of the previous Sunday or prevent him from dismissing me. I also knew I was in danger of behaving as though I was guilty. Like a shoplifter, crying with relief at being caught. So unfair, so hopeless. I couldn't speak to make my case. Those hours of waiting by the phone and the sleepless night had undone me. The back of my throat went on tightening, other muscles lower down my neck joined in, tugging at my lips, trying to stretch them over my teeth. Something was going to snap, but I couldn't let it, not in front of him. Not when he was so wrong. The only way to hold it down and keep my dignity was to remain silent. To speak would have been to let go. And I was desperate to speak. I needed to tell him how unjust he was being, how he was risking everything between us for a lapse in memory. It was one of those familiar occasions when the mind wants one thing, the body another. Like wanting sex during an exam, or being sick at a wedding. The more I struggled in silence to stay on top of my feelings, the more I hated myself and the calmer he became.

'It was underhand, Serena. I thought you were better than that. I don't find this easy to say, but I'm deeply disappointed.'

He went on in this way while I remained with my back turned. How he had trusted me, encouraged me, had high hopes for me, and I had let him down. It must have been easier for him, talking to the back of my head, not having to look me in the eye. I was beginning to suspect that this was not about a simple mistake, a commonplace failure of memory in a busy, important older man. I thought I saw it all plainly enough. Frieda had come back early from Vienna. For some reason, perhaps a nasty hunch, she had gone out to the cottage. Or they had gone there together. In the bedroom was my laundered blouse. Then came the scene in Suffolk or Cambridge, and her ultimatum – get rid of the girl, or march. So Tony had made the obvious decision. But here's the point. He had made another choice too. He had decided to cast himself as the victim, the wronged, the deceived, the rightly furious. He had persuaded himself that he had said nothing to me about the laundry basket. The memory had been erased, and for a purpose. But now he didn't even know he'd erased it. He wasn't even pretending. He actually believed in his disappointment. He really did think that I had done something devious and mean. He was protecting himself from the idea that he'd had a choice. Weak, self-deluding, pompous? All those, but above all, a failure of *reasoning*. High table, monographs, government commissions – meaningless. His reasoning had deserted him. As I saw it, Professor Canning was suffering from a gross intel-lectual malfunction.

I groped for a tissue in the tight pocket of my jeans and blew my nose with a sad honking sound. I still could not trust myself to speak.

Tony was saying, 'You know where this all has to lead, don't you?'

Still in his soft-voiced therapeutic mode. I nodded. I

knew exactly. He told me anyway. As he did, I watched a van draw up at speed and stop with a clever drifting skid on the gravel by the kiosk. Pop music was playing loudly from the cabin. A young guy with a ponytail and drummer's T-shirt that showed off his muscled brown arms got out and slung two big polythene bags of hamburger buns onto the dirt by the kiosk. Then he was gone with a roar and a cloud of blue smoke which the wind brought straight to us. Yes, I was being dumped, like the buns. I suddenly understood why we were here in this lay-by. Tony was expecting a scene. He didn't want to have it in his tiny car. How would he eject a hysterical girl from the passenger seat? So why not have it here, where he could drive away and leave me to hitch a ride back into town?

Why should I tolerate that? I walked away from him towards his car. I knew what I had to do. We could both remain in the lay-by. Forced into my company for an extra hour, he might be brought to his senses. Or not. It didn't matter. I had my plan. I reached the driver's door, pulled it open and took the keys from the ignition. His whole life on a chunky ring, a big busy masculine array of Chubbs, Banhams and Yales, his office, his house, his second home, his mailbox, safe and second car, and all the other parts of his existence he had kept from me. I drew back my arm to throw the ensemble over the hawthorn hedge. If he could find a way in, let him go through the field on hands and knees among the cows and shit puddles and look for the keys to his life while I watched.

After three years of Newnham tennis my throw would have been reasonably strong. But I wasn't able to show it off. My arm was at the limit of its backswing when I felt his fingers curl round my wrist and tighten. He had the keys off me in seconds. He wasn't rough and I put up no struggle. He pushed round me and got into his car without speaking. He had said enough, and besides, I had just confirmed the worst of his expectations. He tossed my bag onto the ground, slammed the door and started the engine. Now that I had my voice back, what did I say? Again, I was pathetic. I didn't want him to leave. I called stupidly through the car's canvas top, 'Tony, stop pretending that you don't know the truth.'

How ridiculous. Of course he wasn't pretending. That was precisely his failure. He gunned the engine a couple of times in case there was anything else I wanted to say that needed drowning out. Then he pulled forward – slowly at first, concerned perhaps that I would throw myself over the windscreen or under the wheels. But I stood there like a tragic fool and I watched him go. I saw his brake lights come on as he slowed to join the traffic. Then he was gone, and it was over.

3

I didn't cancel my appointment with MI5. I had nothing else in my life now, and with Lucy's affairs settled for the moment, even the Bishop was encouraging about my career prospects in Health and Social Security. Two days after the lay-by scene I went to my interview in Great Marlborough Street, on the western edge of Soho. I waited on a hard chair set down for me by a mutely disapproving secretary in a dim corridor with a concrete floor. I don't think I'd ever been in such a depressing building. Along from where I sat was a row of iron-framed windows formed out of the sort of bubbled glass bricks I associated with basements. But it was the dirt, inside and out, not the bricks, that deterred the light. On the window ledge nearest me were piles of newspapers covered in black grit. I wondered whether the job, if I was offered it, would turn out to be a form of sustained punishment adminis-tered at a distance by Tony. There was a complex odour drifting up a stairwell. I passed the time trying to identify its multiple sources. Perfume, cigarettes, ammonia-based cleaning fluid and something organic, perhaps once edible.

My first interview, with a brisk and friendly woman called Joan, consisted mostly of form-filling and answering simple biographical questions. An hour later I was back in the same room with Joan and an army type called Harry Tapp, who had a sandy toothbrush moustache and chain-smoked from a slim gold case. I took to his old-fashioned clipped voice, and the way he softly drummed the yellow fingers of his right hand whenever he spoke and rested them when he listened. In the course of fifty minutes the three of us colluded in the construction of a character profile for me. I was essentially a mathematician with other suitable interests. But how on earth had I ended up with a third? I lied or distorted as required and said that in my final year I had, quite foolishly, given my workload, become interested in writing, in the Soviet Union and in the work of Solzhenitsyn. Mr Tapp was intrigued to hear my views, which I recited, having read through my old pieces as advised by my departed lover. And beyond university, the self I invented was derived entirely from my summer with him. Who else did I have? Sometimes I *was* Tony. I had a passion, it turned out, for the English countryside, in particular Suffolk, and for one glorious ancient pollarded wood, where I liked to ramble and pick ceps in the autumn. Joan knew about ceps and while Tapp looked on impatiently, we quickly swapped recipes. She had never heard of pancetta. Tapp asked me if I had ever taken an interest in encryption. No, but I confessed a weakness for current affairs. We hurried through the issues of the day – the miners' and dockers' strikes, the Common Market, the mayhem in Belfast. I spoke the language of a

Times leader, echoing patrician, thoughtful-sounding opinions that could hardly be opposed. For example, when we arrived at the 'permissive society' I cited *The Times*'s view that the sexual freedom of individuals had to be balanced against the needs of children for security and love. Who could take a stand against that? I was getting into my stride. Then there was my passion for English history. Again, Harry Tapp perked up. What in particular? The Glorious Revolution. Ah now, that was very interesting indeed! And then, later, who was my intellectual hero? I talked of Churchill, not as a politician, but as a historian (I summarised the 'incomparable' account of Trafalgar), as the Nobel Laureate for Literature, and then as the watercolourist. I'd always had a particular fondness for the little-known *Marrakech Rooftop Laundry*, which I believed was now in a private collection.

Prompted by something that Tapp said, I daubed onto my self-portrait a passion for chess without mentioning that I hadn't played in more than three years. He asked me if I was familiar with the Zilber–Tal endgame of 1958. I wasn't but I could plausibly elaborate on the famous Saavedra position. In fact, I had never in my life been so clever as during that interview. And not since my articles in *?Quis?* had I been so pleased with myself. There was little I could not talk about. I could give my ignorance on any matter a certain shine. My voice was Tony's. I spoke like a master of a college, the chairman of a government committee of inquiry, a country squire. Join MI5? I was ready to lead it. It was no surprise then, after I had been asked to leave the room and called back five minutes later, to hear Mr Tapp tell me he had decided to offer me a job. What else could he do?

For several seconds I didn't take in what he was saying. And when I did, I thought he was teasing or testing me. I was to fill the post of junior assistant officer. I already knew that in Civil Service rankings this was the lowest of the low. My principal duties would be in filing, indexing and related library work. With hard work and in time, I might rise to assistant officer. I didn't allow my expression to betray what I suddenly understood – that I'd made a terrible mistake, or Tony had. Or that this really was the punishment he had devised for me. I was not being recruited as an 'officer'. Not a spy then, no front-line work. Pretending to be pleased, I enquired tentatively, and it was confirmed by Joan as a routine fact of life: men and women had separate career tracks and only men became officers. Of course, of course, I said. Of course I knew that. I was the clever young woman who knew everything. I was too proud to let them see how misinformed I had been or how put out I was. I heard myself accept with enthusiasm. Marvellous! Thank you! I was given a start date. Can't wait! We stood and Mr Tapp shook my hand and drifted away. As Joan walked me down to the entrance, she explained that his offer was subject to the usual vetting procedures. If I was accepted, I would be working over in Curzon Street. I would be obliged to sign the Official Secrets Act and be bound by its strict provisions. Of course, I kept saying. Marvellous. Thank you.

I left the building in a disturbed and dark state of mind. Even before I said goodbye to Joan I'd decided I didn't want the job. It was an insult, a lowly secretarial position at two-thirds the usual rate. With tips I could have earned double as a waitress. They could keep their job. I'd write them a note. However disappointing, that at least seemed clear. I felt emptied out, I had no idea what I was supposed

42

to be doing or where I should go. My money was running out for my Cambridge room. No choice then but to go back to my parents, become a daughter again, a child, and face the Bishop's indifference and my mother's organising zeal. Worse though than that prospect was this sudden fit of lover's grief. Impersonating Tony for an hour and raiding memories of our summer for my own use had brought the affair to life in my thoughts. I had talked myself into understanding the full measure of my loss. It was as though we'd been having a long conversation and he'd abruptly turned away, leaving me with an overpowering sense of his absence. I missed him and yearned for him, and knew I'd never get him back.

Desolate, I went slowly along Great Marlborough Street. The job and Tony were twin aspects of one thing, a summer's sentimental education, and it had disintegrated around me in forty-eight hours. He was back with his wife and his college, and I had nothing. No love, no job. Only the chill of loneliness. And the sorrow was compounded by the memory of the way he'd turned on me. So unfair! I glanced across the road and by a nasty coincidence found myself approaching the mock Tudor facade of Liberty's, where Tony had bought the blouse.

Trying not to feel crushed, I quickly turned down Carnaby Street and picked my way through the crowds. Whining guitar music and the scent of patchouli from a basement shop made me think of my sister and all the trouble at home. Ranks of 'psychedelic' shirts and Sergeant Pepper-ish tasselled military suits hung on long racks on the pavement. Available for like-minded hordes desperate to express their individuality. Well, my mood was sour. I went down Regent Street, then turned left, penetrating deeper into Soho, and walked along streets filthy with litter and abandoned snacks, ketchup-streaked burgers and hotdogs and cartons squelched into the pavement and gutter, and rubbish sacks heaped around lamp posts. The word 'adult' was everywhere in red neon. In windows, items on mock-velvet plinths, whips, dildoes, erotic ointments, a studded mask. A fat guy in a leather jacket, some kind of strip-joint barker, called out to me from a doorway a single indistinct word that sounded like Toy! Perhaps it was Oi! Someone whistled at me. I hurried on, careful to look no one in the eye. I was still thinking of Lucy. Unfair to associate this quarter with her, but the new spirit of liberation that had got my sister arrested and pregnant had also permitted these shops (and, I might have added, my own affair with an older man). Lucy had told me more than once that the past was a burden, that it was time to tear everything down. A lot of people were thinking that way. A seedy, careless insurrection was in the air. But thanks to Tony I now knew with what trouble it had been assembled, Western civilisation, imperfect as it was. We suffered from faulty governance, our freedoms were incomplete. But in this part of the world our rulers no longer had absolute power, savagery was mostly a private affair. Whatever was under my feet in the streets of Soho, we had raised ourselves above filth. The cathedrals, the parliaments, the paintings, the courts of law, the libraries and the labs – far too precious to pull down.

Perhaps it was Cambridge and the cumulative effect of so many ancient buildings and lawns, of seeing how kind time was to stone, or perhaps I simply lacked youthful courage and was cautious and prim. But this inglorious revolution wasn't for me. I didn't want a sex shop in every town, I didn't want my sister's kind of life, I didn't want history put to the torch. Come travelling? I wanted to travel with civilised men like Tony Canning, who took for granted the importance of laws and institutions and thought constantly of how to improve them. If only he wanted to travel with *me*. If only he wasn't such a bastard.

The half-hour it took me to wander from Regent Street to the Charing Cross Road arranged my fate for me. I changed my mind, I decided to take the job after all and have order and purpose in my life and some independence. There may have been a passing touch of masochism in my decision – as a rejected lover I deserved no more than to be an office skivvy. And nothing else was on offer. I could leave behind Cambridge and its association with Tony, and I could lose myself in London's crowds – there was something pleasingly tragic about that. I would tell my parents I had a proper Civil Service job in the Department of Health and Social Security. It turned out that I needn't have been so secretive, but at the time it rather thrilled me to mislead them.

I returned to my bedsit that afternoon, gave notice to my landlord and began to pack up my room. The following day I arrived home in the cathedral close with all my belongings. My mother was delighted for me and embraced me lovingly. To my astonishment, the Bishop gave me a twenty-pound note. Three weeks later I started my new life in London.

Did I know Millie Trimingham, the single mother who would one day become Director General? When, in later years, it became permissible to tell everyone that you once worked for MI5, I was often asked this question. If it irritated me it was because I suspected it concealed another: with my Cambridge connections why didn't I rise nearly as high? I joined three years after she did, and, it's true, I started out following her path, the one she describes in her memoir – same grim building in Mayfair, same training section in a long, thin, ill-lit room, same tasks, both meaningless and intriguing. But when I joined in 1972 Trimingham was already a legend among the new girls. Remember, we were in our early twenties, she was in her mid-thirties. My new friend Shirley Shilling pointed her out to me. Trimingham was at the end of a corridor, back-lit by a grubby window, a wedge of files under one arm, in urgent conference with an anonymous man who looked to be from the cloudy summits of authority. She seemed at ease, almost an equal, clearly empowered to make a joke, causing him to give out a shout of a laugh and place his hand on her forearm briefly, as if to say, restrain that wit of yours or you'll make my life impossible.

She was admired by us new-joiners because we'd heard that she'd mastered the filing system and the intricacies of the Registry so quickly that she was moved on in less than two months. Some said it was weeks, even days. We believed there was a hint of rebellion in the clothes she wore, bright prints and scarves, authentic, bought in Pakistan, where she'd worked for the Service in some lawless outpost. This was what we told ourselves. We should have asked her. A lifetime later I read in her memoir that she did clerical work in the Islamabad office. I still don't know if she took part in the Women's Revolt of that year, when female graduates in MI5 started campaigning for better prospects. They wanted to be allowed to run agents themselves, like male desk officers. My guess is that Trimingham would have been sympathetic to the aims, but wary of collective action, speeches and resolutions. I've never understood why word of the Revolt never reached our intake. Perhaps we were considered too junior. Above all, it was the spirit of the age that slowly changed the Service, but she was the first to break out, first to dig the hole in the ceiling of the women's block. She did it quietly, with tact. The rest of us scrambled up noisily behind her. I was one of the last. And when she had been transferred out of the training section, it was to confront the hard new future – IRA terrorism – whereas many of us who followed lingered a while, fighting the old battles with the Soviet Union.

Most of the ground floor was taken up by the Registry, that vast memory bank where more than three hundred well-born secretaries toiled like slaves on the pyramids, processing file requests, returning or distributing files to desk case officers round the building and sorting incoming material. The system was thought to work so well that it held out far too long against the computer age. This was the last redoubt, the ultimate tyranny of paper. Just as an army recruit is made to embrace his new life by peeling spuds and scouring the parade ground with a toothbrush, so I passed my first few months compiling members' lists of provincial branches of the Communist Party of Great Britain and opening files on all those not already accounted for. My special concern was Gloucestershire. (In her time, Trimingham had Yorkshire.) In my first month I opened a file on the headmaster of a grammar school in Stroud who had attended an open meeting of his local branch one Saturday evening in July 1972. He wrote his name on a sheet of paper that was circulated by the comrades, but then he must have decided not to join. He was on none of the subscription lists that had been procured for us. But I chose to start a file on him because he was in a position to influence young minds. This was on my own initiative, my very first, and that's why I remember his name, Harold Templeman, and his year of birth. If Templeman had decided to get out of schoolmastering (he was only forty-three) and apply for a Civil Service job that brought him into contact with classified information, the vetting procedure would have led someone to his file. Templeman would have been questioned about that evening in July (surely he would have been impressed) or his application would have been dismissed and he would never have known why. Perfect. In theory, at least. We were still learning the demanding protocols that determined what was acceptable material for a file. During the early months of 1973 such a closed, functioning system, however pointless, was a comfort to me. All twelve of us working in that room knew well enough that any agent run by the Soviet Centre was never going to announce himself to us by joining the Communist Party of Great Britain. I didn't care.

On my way to work I used to reflect on the immensity that separated my job description from the reality. I could say to myself – since I could say it to no one else – that I worked for MI5. That had a certain ring. Even now it stirs me a little, to think of that pale little thing wanting to do her bit for the country. But I was just one more office girl in a mini-skirt, jammed in with the rest, thousands of us pouring down the filthy connecting Tube tunnels at the change for Green Park, where the litter and grit and stinking subterranean gales that we took as our due slapped our faces and restyled our hair. (London is so much cleaner now.) And when I got to work, I was still an office girl, typing straight-backed on a giant Remington in a smoky room like hundreds of thousands across the capital, fetching files, deciphering male handwriting, hurrying back from my lunch break. I even earned less than most. And just like the working girl in a Betjeman poem Tony once read to me, I too washed my smalls in the hand basin of my bedsit.

As a clerical officer of the lowest grade my first week's pay after deductions was fourteen pounds thirty pence, in the novel decimal currency, which had not yet lost its unserious, half-baked, fraudulent air. I paid four pounds a week for my room, and an extra pound for electricity. My travel cost just over a pound, leaving me eight pounds for food and all else. I present these details not to complain, but in the spirit of Jane Austen, whose novels I had once raced through at Cambridge. How can one understand the inner life of a character, real or fictional, without knowing the state of her finances? *Miss Frome, newly installed in diminutive lodgings at number seventy St Augustine's Road, London North West One, had less than one thousand a year and a heavy heart.* I managed week to week, but I did not feel part of a glamorous clandestine world.

Still, I was young, and maintaining a heavy heart all moments of the day was beyond me. My chum, at lunch breaks and evenings out, was Shirley Shilling, whose alliterative name in the dependable old currency caught something of her plump lopsided smile and old-fashioned taste for fun. She was in trouble with our chain-smoking supervisor, Miss Ling, in the very first week for 'taking too long in the lavatory'. Actually, Shirley had hurried out of the building at ten o'clock to buy herself a frock for a party that night, had run all the way to a department store in Oxford Street, found the very thing, tried it on, tried the next size up, paid and got a bus back – in twenty minutes. There would have been no time at lunch because she planned to try on shoes. None of the rest of us new girls would have dared so much.

So what did we make of her? The cultural changes of the past several years may have seemed profound but they had clipped no one's social antennae. Within a minute, no, less, by the time Shirley had uttered three words, we would have known that she was of humble origins. Her father owned a bed and sofa shop in Ilford called Bedworld, her school was a giant local comprehensive, her university was Nottingham. She was the first in her family to stay on at school past the age of sixteen. MI5 may have been wanting to demonstrate a more open recruitment policy, but Shirley happened to be exceptional. She typed at twice the speed of the best of us, her memory – for faces, files, conversations, procedures – was sharper than ours, she asked fearless, interesting questions. It was a sign of the times that a large minority of the girls admired her – her mild Cockney had a touch of modern glamour, her voice and manner reminded us of Twiggy or Keith Richards or Bobby Moore. In fact her brother was a professional footballer who played for the Wolverhampton Wanderers reserves. This club, so we were obliged to learn, had reached the final of the newfangled EUFA Cup that year. Shirley was exotic, she represented a confident new world.

50

Some girls were snobbish about Shirley, but none of us was as worldly and cool. Many of our intake would have been presentable at court to Queen Elizabeth as debutantes if the practice hadn't been terminated fifteen years earlier. A few were the daughters or nieces of serving or retired officers. Two-thirds of us had degrees from the older universities. We spoke in identical tones, we were socially confident and could have passed muster at a country house weekend. But there was always a trace of an apology in our style, a polite impulse to defer, especially when one of the senior officers, one of the ex-colonial types, came through our crepuscular room. Then most of us (I exclude myself, of course) were the mistresses of the lowered gaze and the compliant near-smile. Among the new-joiners a low-level unacknowledged search was on for a decent husband from the right sort of background.

Shirley, however, was unapologetically loud and, being in no mood to marry, looked everyone in the eye. She had a knack or weakness for laughing boisterously at her own anecdotes – not, I thought, because she found herself funny, but because she thought that life needed celebrating and wanted others to join in. Loud people, especially loud women, always attract enemies and Shirley had one or two who despised her heartily, but in general she breezed her way into our affections, mine especially. It may have helped her, not to have been threateningly beautiful. She was large, at least thirty pounds overweight, size sixteen to my ten, and she actually told us that the word we must use of her was 'willowy'. Then she laughed. Her round, somewhat pudgy face was rescued, even blessed, by being rarely at rest, she was so animated. Her best feature was the slightly unusual combination of black hair, naturally curled, with pale freckles across the bridge of her nose, and greyish-blue eyes. And her smile tilted downwards to the right, giving her a look I can't quite find the word for. Somewhere between *rakish* and *game*. Despite her limited circumstances, she had been around more than most of us. In the year after university she hitchhiked alone to Istanbul, sold her blood, bought a motorbike, broke her leg, shoulder and elbow, fell in love with a Syrian doctor, had an abortion, and was brought home to England from Anatolia on a private yacht in return for a little on-board cooking.

But from my point of view none of these adventures was as exotic as the notebook she carried with her always, a childish pink plastic-covered thing with a short pencil tucked into the spine. For a while she wouldn't say what she wrote, but one evening in a Muswell Hill pub she owned up to jotting down 'the clever or funny or daft stuff' people said. She also wrote 'tiny stories about stories' and otherwise just 'thoughts'. The notebook was always within reach and she'd write in it mid-conversation. The other girls in the office teased her about it, and I was curious to know if she had wider writing ambitions. I talked to her about the books I was reading, and though she listened politely, even intently, she never offered an opinion of her own. I wasn't sure she did any reading at all. Either that or she was protecting a big secret.

She lodged just a mile to the north of me in a tiny third-floor room that overlooked the thunderous Holloway Road. Within a week of introducing ourselves we started meeting in the evenings. Soon afterwards I discovered that our friendship had earned us the office nickname 'Laurel and Hardy', the reference being to our relative sizes, not a taste for slapstick. I didn't tell Shirley. It never occurred to her that a night out should take place anywhere other than in pubs, by preference noisy ones with music. She had no interest in the places round Mayfair. Within a few months I was familiar with the human ecology, the gradations of decency and decay, of the pubs around Camden, Kentish Town and Islington.

It was in Kentish Town, on our first excursion, that I saw in an Irish pub a terrible fight. In films a punch to the jaw is banal but it's extraordinary to witness in reality, though the sound, the bony crunch, is far more muted and wet. To a sheltered young woman, it looked reckless beyond belief, so careless of retaliation, of prospects, of life itself, those fists that wielded a pickaxe by day for Murphy the builders, pile-driving into a face. We watched from our bar stools. I saw something curve through the air past a beer-pump handle – a button or a tooth. More people were joining in, there was a fair amount of shouting, and the barman, a handy-looking fellow himself with a caduceus tattooed above his wrist, was speaking into the phone. Shirley put an arm about my shoulders and propelled me towards the door. Our rum-and-Cokes with melting ice were behind us on the bar.

'Police on their way, might want witnesses. Best to go.' Out in the street we remembered her coat. 'Ah forget it,' she said with a wave of her hand. She was already walking on. 'I *ate* that coat.'

We weren't looking for men on our nights out. Instead, we talked a good deal – about our families, about our lives so far. She spoke of her Syrian doctor, I spoke of Jeremy Mott, but not of Tony Canning. Office gossip was strictly forbidden, even to us lowly beginners, and it was a matter of pride to obey instructions. Besides, I had the impression that Shirley was already doing more important work than me. It was bad form to ask. When our pub conversation was interrupted, when men did approach us, they came looking for me and got Shirley instead. I was content to be mute at her side as she took over. They couldn't get past the banter and laughter, the bright chatty questions about what they did and where they were from, and they retreated after subsidising a round or two of rum-and-Cokes. In the hippie pubs around Camden Lock, which was not yet a tourist attraction, the long-haired men were more insidious and persistent with softer come-ons about their inner feminine spirit, the collective uncon-scious, the transit of Venus and related hokum. Shirley repelled them with uncomprehending friendliness while I shrank from these reminders of my sister.

We would be in that part of town for the music, drinking our way towards the Dublin Castle on Parkway. Shirley had a boyish passion for rock and roll and in the early seventies the best bands played in pubs, often cavernous Victorian establishments. I surprised myself by developing a passing taste for this racy, unpretentious music. My bedsit was dull and I was glad to have something to do in the evenings apart from reading novels. One evening, when we knew each other better, Shirley and I had a conversation about our ideal man. She told me about her dream, an introspec-tive bony guy, just over six feet, jeans, black T-shirt, cropped hair and hollow cheeks and a guitar round his neck. We must have seen two dozen versions of this archetype as she escorted me to all pub venues between Canvey Island and Shepherd's Bush. We heard Bees Make Honey (my favourite), Roogalator (hers) – and Dr Feelgood, Ducks Deluxe, Kilburn and the High Roads. Not like me at all, to be standing in a sweaty crowd with a half pint in my hand, my ears buzzing with the din. It gave me some innocent pleasure to think how horrified the counterculture crowd around us would be, to know that we were the ultimate enemy from the 'straight' grey world of MI5. Laurel and Hardy, the new shock troops of internal security.

4

Towards the end of winter in 1973 I received a letter forwarded by my mother from my old friend Jeremy Mott. He was still in Edinburgh, still happy with his doctoral work and his new life of semi-secretive affairs, each one ending, so he claimed, without much trouble or remorse. I read the letter one morning on my way to work on one of the rare occasions when I'd managed to push through the packed fetid carriage and find myself a seat. The important paragraph began halfway down the second page. To Jeremy it would have been no more than an item of serious gossip.

You remember my tutor, Tony Canning. We went to his rooms once for tea. Last September he left his wife, Frieda. They were married for more than thirty years. No explanation apparently. There'd been rumours around the college that he'd been seeing a younger woman out at his cottage in Suffolk. But that wasn't it. The word was he dumped her too. I had a letter from a friend last month. He heard it from the Master's mouth. All this has been an open secret around the college but no one thought to tell me. Canning was ill. Why not say it? He had something badly wrong and he was beyond treatment. In October he resigned his fellowship and took himself off to an island in the Baltic, where he rented a small house. He was looked after by a local woman, who may have been a little more than a housekeeper. Towards the end he was moved to a cottage hospital on another island. His son visited him there and Frieda went too. I'm assuming you didn't see the obituary in *The Times* in February. I'm sure I would have heard from you if you had. I never knew he was in the SOE towards the end of the war. Quite the hero, parachuting into Bulgaria by night and getting seriously wounded in the chest during an ambush. Then four years in MI5 in the late forties. Our fathers' generation – their lives were so much more meaningful than ours, don't you think? Tony was awfully good to me. I wish someone had let me know. At least I could have written to him. Why don't you come and cheer me up? There's a sweet little spare room off the kitchen. But I think I've told you that before.

Why not say it? Cancer. In the early seventies it was only just coming to an end, the time when people used to drop their voices at the word. Cancer was a disgrace, the victim's that is, a form of failure, a smear and a dirty defect, of personality rather than flesh. Back then I'm sure I'd have taken for granted Tony's need to creep away without explanation, to winter with his awful secret by a cold sea. The

57

sand dunes of his childhood, bitter winds, treeless inland marshes, and Tony walking by the empty beach hunched in his donkey jacket with his shame, his nasty secret and his increasing need for another nap. Sleep coming in like a tide. Of course he needed to be alone. I'm sure I didn't question any of that. What impressed and shocked me was the planning. Telling me to put my blouse in the laundry basket, then pretending to forget that he had in order to make himself obnoxious to me so I wouldn't follow him and complicate his last months. Did it really have to be so elaborate? Or severe?

On my way to work I blushed to remember how I'd thought my reasoning about feelings was superior to his. I blushed just before I started to cry. Passengers nearest me on the crowded Tube decently looked away. He must have known how much past I would have to rewrite when I heard the real story. There must have been some comfort in believing that I would forgive him then. That seemed very sad. But why had there been no posthumous letter, explaining, remembering something between us, saying goodbye, acknowledging me, giving me something to live with, anything to replace our last scene? For weeks afterwards I tormented myself with suspicions that such a letter would have been intercepted by the 'housekeeper' or Frieda.

Tony in exile, trudging the lonely beaches, without the playmate-brother who'd shared the carefree years – Terence Canning was killed in the D-Day landings – and without his college, his friends, his wife. Above all, without me. Tony could have been looked after by Frieda, he could have been in the cottage or in his bedroom at home, with his books, with visits from his friends and his son. Even

I could have sneaked in somehow, disguised as a former student. Flowers, champagne, family and old friends, old photographs – wasn't that how people try to organise their deaths, at least when they were not fighting for breath or writhing in pain or dumbly immobilised by terror?

In the weeks that followed, I replayed scores of small moments. Those afternoon naps that made me so impatient, that grey morning face I couldn't bear to look at. At the time I'd thought it was simply how it had to be, when you were fifty-four. There was one exchange in particular I kept returning to – those few seconds in the bedroom by the laundry basket when he was telling me about Idi Amin and the expelled Ugandan Asians. It was a big story at the time. The vicious dictator was driving his countrymen out, they had British passports, and Ted Heath's government, ignoring the outrage in the tabloids, was insisting, decently enough, that they must be allowed to settle here. That was Tony's view too. He interrupted himself and without drawing breath said quickly, 'Just drop it in there with mine. We'll be back soon.' Just that, a mundane domestic instruction, and then he continued with his line of thought. Now wasn't that ingenious, when his body was already failing and his plans were taking shape? To orchestrate the moment, see a chance and take it on the wing. Or work something up afterwards. Perhaps less of a trick, more a habit of mind picked up in his time with the SOE. A trick of the trade. As a device, a deception, it was cleverly managed. He threw me off and I was too injured to pursue him. I don't think I really loved him at the time, during those months out at the cottage, but when I heard of his death I soon convinced myself that I did. The trick, his deceit, was far more duplicitous than any married man's love affair. Even then, I admired him for it, but I couldn't quite forgive him.

I went to Holborn public library, where back issues of *The Times* were kept, and looked up the obituary. Idiotically, I skimmed it, scanning it for my name, and then I started again. A whole life in a few columns, and not even a photograph. The Dragon School in Oxford, Marlborough, then Balliol, the Guards, action in the Western Desert, an unexplained gap, and then SOE as Jeremy had described it, followed by four years in the Security Service from 1948. How uncurious I'd been about Tony's war and post war, though I knew he had good connections in MI5. The piece briefly summarised the fifties onwards – journalism, books, public service, Cambridge, death.

And for me, nothing changed. I went on working in Curzon Street while I tended the little shrine of my secret grief. Tony had chosen my profession for me, lent me his woods, ceps, opinions, worldliness. But I had no proof, no tokens, no photograph of him, no letters, not even a scrap of a note because our meetings were arranged by phone. Diligently, I'd returned all the books he lent me as I read them, except one, R.H. Tawney's *Religion and the Rise of Capitalism*. I looked for it everywhere, and went back many times to search forlornly in the same places again. It had sun-faded soft green boards with a cup stain that looped through the author's initials, and a simple 'Canning' in imperious purple ink on the first endpaper, and throughout, on almost every page, his marginalia in hard pencil. So precious. But it had melted away, as only books can, perhaps when I moved out of my Jesus Green room. My surviving keepsakes were a carelessly donated bookmark, of which more later, and my job. He had dispatched me to this grubby office in Leconfield House. I didn't like it, but it was the legacy and I could not have tolerated being anywhere else.

Working patiently, without complaint, humbly submitting to the disparagements of Miss Ling – this was how I kept the flame. If I failed to be efficient, if I arrived late or complained or thought about leaving MI5, I would have been letting him down. I persuaded myself of a great love in ruins, and so I racked up the pain. *Akrasia*! Whenever I took extra care in turning some desk officer's scrawl into an error-free typed memo in triplicate, it was because it was my duty to honour the memory of the man I had loved.

There were twelve in our intake, including three men. Of these, two were married businessmen in their thirties and of no interest to anyone. There was a third, Greatorex, on whom ambitious parents had conferred the name Maximilian. He was about thirty, had jutting ears and was extremely reticent, whether from shyness or superiority none of us was certain. He'd been transferred across from MI6 and was already desk officer status, merely sitting in with us new-joiners to see how our systems worked. The other two men, the business types, were also not so far now from officer status. Whatever I'd felt at the interview, I no longer minded so much. As our chaotic training proceeded, I absorbed the general spirit of the place and, taking my cue from the other girls, began to accept that in this small part of the adult world, and unlike in the rest of the Civil Service, women were of a lower caste.

We were spending even more time now with the scores

of other girls in the Registry, learning the strict rules of file retrieval and discovering, without being told, that there were concentric circles of security clearance and that we languished in outer darkness. The clattering temperamental trolleys on their tracks delivered files to the various departments around the building. Whenever one of them went wrong, Greatorex knew how to fix it with a set of miniature screwdrivers he kept on him. Among the more snobbish girls this earned him the nickname 'Handyman', confirming him as a ridiculous prospect. That was fortunate for me because, even in my condition of mourning, I was beginning to take an interest in Maximilian Greatorex.

Occasionally, in the late afternoon, we would be 'invited' to attend a lecture. It would have been unthinkable not to go. The subject never wandered far from communism, its theory and practice, the geopolitical struggle, the naked intent of the Soviet Union to attain world dominance. I'm making these talks sound more interesting than they were. The theory and practice element was by far the largest, and most of that was theory. This was because the talks were given by an ex-RAF man, Archibald Jowell, who had gone into the whole thing, perhaps in an evening class, and was anxious to share what he knew of dialectics and related concepts. If you were to close your eyes, as many did, you could easily imagine that you were at a Communist Party meeting in somewhere like Stroud, for it was not Jowell's intention or remit to demolish Marxist–Leninist thought, or even express scepticism. He wanted us to understand the mind of the enemy 'from the inside', and to know thoroughly the theoretical base from which it worked. Coming at the end of a day of typing and of trying to learn what constituted a file-worthy fact in the mind of the fearsome Miss Ling, Jowell's earnest, haranguing delivery had a deadly, soporific effect on most of the intake. Everyone believed that to be caught out in a shameful moment when neck muscles relax and the head snaps forward might damage career prospects. But believing was not quite enough. Heavy eyelids in the late afternoon had their own logic, their own peculiar weight.

So what was wrong with me that I sat upright and alert for the entire hour on the edge of my chair, legs crossed, notebook pressed against my bare knee as I wrote my notes? I was a mathematician and a former chess player, and I was a girl in need of comfort. Dialectical materialism was a safely enclosed system, like the vetting procedures, but more rigorous and intricate. More like an equation of Leibniz or Hilbert. Human aspirations, societies, history, and a method of analysis in an entanglement as expressive and inhumanly perfect as a Bach fugue. Who could sleep through it? The answer was everyone but myself and Greatorex. He would sit a knight's move ahead of me and to my left, with the visible page of his notebook covered in dense loopy writing.

Once, my attention drifted from the lecture as I considered him. It was the case that his ears protruded from strange hillocks of bone at the sides of his skull and those ears were awfully pink. But the effect was much exaggerated by his old-fashioned haircut, the standard military short back and sides, a style which revealed a deep groove down his nape. He reminded me of Jeremy and, less comfortably, of some of the undergraduate mathematicians at Cambridge, the ones who had humiliated me in tutorials. But his facial appearance was misleading, for his body looked lean and strong. In my thoughts I restyled his hair, growing it out so that it filled the space between the tips of his ears and his head, and covered the top of his collar, perfectly permissible now even in Leconfield House. The mustard-coloured check tweed jacket should go. Even from my oblique angle I could see that his tie knot was too small. He needed to start calling himself Max and keep his screwdrivers in a drawer. He was writing in brown ink. That too would have to change.

'And so I return to my starting point,' ex-Flight Commander Jowell was saying in conclusion. 'Ultimately the power and endurance of Marxism, as with any other theoretical scheme, rests with its capacity to seduce intelligent men and women. And this one most certainly can. Thank you.'

Our bleary group roused itself to stand respectfully as the lecturer left the room. When he was gone Max turned and looked right at me. It was as if the vertical groove at the base of his skull was telepathically sensitive. He knew I'd been rearranging his entire being.

I was the one who looked away.

He indicated the pen in my hand. 'Taking lots of notes.'

I said, 'It was fascinating.'

He started to say something, then changed his mind and with an impatient downward gesture with his hand he turned from me and left the room.

But we became friends. Because he reminded me of Jeremy, I lazily assumed that he preferred men, though I hoped I was wrong. I hardly expected him to speak of it, especially in these offices. The security world despised homosexuals, at least outwardly, which made them vulnerable to blackmail, which made them unemployable in the intelligence services and therefore despicable. But while I fantasised about Max I could at least tell myself that I must be getting over Tony. And Max, as I tried to make everyone call him, was a good addition. I thought at first we might make a threesome around town with Shirley, but she told me he was creepy and not to be trusted. And he didn't like pubs or cigarette smoke, or loud music, so we often sat after work on a bench in Hyde Park or Berkeley Square. He couldn't talk about it and I wouldn't ask, but my impression was that he'd worked for a while at Cheltenham, in signals intelligence. He was thirty-two and lived alone in one part of the wing of a country house near Egham, on a bend in the Thames. He said more than once I should come and visit, but there was never a specific invitation. He came from a family of academics, was educated at Winchester and Harvard, where he did a law degree and then another in psychology, but he was haunted by the idea that he had made the wrong choices, that he should have been studying something practical like engineering. At one point he had thought of apprenticing himself to a watch designer in Geneva, but his parents talked him out of it. His father was a philosopher, his mother a social anthropologist, and Maximilian was their only child. They wanted him to have a life of the mind and thought he shouldn't be fiddling about with his hands. After a short unhappy spell teaching at a crammer, some freelance journalism and travelling, he came into the Service through a business friend of an uncle.

It was a warm spring that year and our friendship blossomed with the trees and shrubs around our various benches. Early on, in my eagerness, I ran ahead of our intimacy and asked if pressure from academic parents bearing down on an only child might have caused him to be shy. The question offended him, as though I'd insulted his family. He had a typically English distaste for psychological explanation. His manner was stiff as he explained that he didn't recognise himself in the term. If he held back with strangers it was because he believed that it was best to go carefully until he understood what he was dealing with. He was perfectly at ease with people he knew and liked. And so it turned out. Gently prompted, I told him everything – my family, my Cambridge, my poor maths degree, my column in *?Quis?*.

'I heard about your column,' he said, to my surprise. Then he added something that pleased me. 'The word around the place is that you've read everything worth reading. You're up on modern literature and all that.'

It was a release to talk to someone at last about Tony. Max had even heard of him, and remembered a government commission, a history book and one or two other scraps, one of which was a public argument over funding for the arts.

'What did you say his island was called?'

At that point, my mind emptied. I had known the name so well. It was synonymous with death. I said, 'It's suddenly gone from me.'

'Finnish? Swedish?'

'Finnish. In the Åland archipelago.'

'Was it Lemland?'

'Doesn't sound right. It'll come to me.'

'Let me know when it does.'

I was surprised by his insistence. 'Why does it matter?'

'D'you know, I've been around the Baltic a bit. Tens of thousands of islands. One of the best-kept secrets of modern tourism. Thank God everybody flees south in summer. Clearly, your Canning was a man of taste.'

We left it at that. But a month or so later, we were sitting in Berkeley Square trying to reconstruct the lyrics of the famous song about a nightingale singing there. Max had told me he was a self-taught pianist who liked to play show tunes and soppy crooning songs from the forties and fifties, music as unfashionable then as his haircut. I happened to know this particular song from a school revue. We were partly singing, partly speaking the charming words, *I may be right, I may be wrong/But I'm perfectly willing to swear/That when you turned and smiled at me/A nightingale . . .* when Max broke off and said, 'Was it Kumlinge?'

'Yes, that's it. How did you know?'

'Well, I've heard it's very beautiful.'

'I think he liked the isolation.'

'He must have.'

As the spring wore on I grew even fonder of Max, to the point of mild obsession. When I wasn't with him, when I was out in the evening with Shirley, I felt incomplete and restless. It was a relief to be back at work, where I could see him across the desks, his head bent over his papers. But that was never enough and soon I would be trying to arrange our next encounter. It had to be faced, I had a taste for a certain ill-dressed, old-fashioned kind of man (Tony didn't count), big-boned and thin and awkwardly intelligent. There was something remote and upright in Max's manner. His automatic restraint made me feel clumsy and overemphatic. I worried that he didn't actually like me and was too civil to say so. I imagined that he had all manner of private rules, hidden notions of correctness that I was constantly transgressing. My unease sharpened my interest in him. What animated

67

him, the subject that breathed warmth into his manner, was Soviet communism. He was a Cold Warrior of a superior sort. Where others loathed and raged, Max believed that good intentions had combined with human nature to devise a tragedy of sullen entrapment. The happiness and fulfilment of hundreds of millions across the Russian empire had been fatally compromised. No one, not even its leaders, would have chosen what they now had. The trick was to offer escape by degrees, without loss of face, by patient coaxing and incentives, by building trust while standing firm against what he called a truly terrible idea.

He was certainly not the sort I could question about his love life. I wondered if he had a male lover living with him in Egham. I even formed an idea of going down there to take a look. That's how bad things were getting. Wanting what I assumed I could not have heightened my feelings. But I also wondered if he might, like Jeremy, be able to give a woman pleasure without getting much for himself. Not ideal, not reciprocal, but it wouldn't be so bad for me. Better than pointless longing.

We were walking in the park one early evening after work. The subject was the Provisional IRA – I suspected he had some insider knowledge. He was telling me about an article he'd read when, on an impulse, I took his arm and asked if he wanted to kiss me.

'Not particularly.'

'I'd like you to.'

We stopped in the centre of the path where it went between two trees, obliging people to squeeze around us. It was a deep, passionate kiss, or a good imitation of one. I thought he might be compensating for a lack of desire.

When he drew away, I tried to pull him back towards me, but he resisted.

'That's it for now,' he said, touching the tip of my nose with his forefinger, acting the firm parent talking down to a demanding child. So, playing along, I made a sulky moue and meekly put my hand in his and we walked on. I knew the kiss was going to make things harder for me, but at least we were holding hands for the first time. He disengaged a few minutes later.

We sat on the grass, well away from other people, and returned to the Provos. There had been bombs in Whitehall and at Scotland Yard the previous month. The Service was continuing to reorganise itself. A handful, the more promising handful, Shirley included, of our intake had been moved on from nursery-level Registry work, and had probably been absorbed into the new concern. Rooms had been taken over, meetings went on late behind closed doors. I had been left behind. I displaced my frustration by complaining, as I had before, about being stuck with the old battle. The lectures were fascinating in the way a dead language was. The world was securely settled into its two camps, I argued. Soviet communism had as much evangelical fervour for expansion as you'd find in the Church of England. The Russian empire was repressive and corrupt, but comatose. The new threat was terrorism. I'd read an article in *Time* magazine and regarded myself as well informed. It wasn't just the Provisional IRA, or the various Palestinian groups. Underground anarchist and far-left factions across mainland Europe were already setting off bombs and kidnapping politicians and industrialists. The Red Brigades, the Baader–Meinhof Group, and in South America the Tupamaros and scores like them, in the United States the Symbionese Liberation Army – these blood-thirsty nihilists and narcissists were well connected across borders and soon they'd represent an internal threat here. We'd had the Angry Brigade, others far worse would follow. What were we doing, still piling most of our resources into cat-and-mouse business with irrelevant time-servers in Soviet trade delegations?

Most of our resources? What could a mere trainee know about allocations within the Service? But I tried to make myself sound confident. I was stirred up by a kiss, I wanted to impress Max. He was watching me closely, tolerantly amused.

'I'm glad you're up on your grisly factions. But, Serena, the year before last we threw out a hundred and five Soviet agents. They were crawling all over us. Educating White-hall to do the right thing was a big moment for the Service. The gossip was that it was awfully difficult to bring the Home Secretary on board.'

'He was Tony's friend until they . . .'

'It all came out of Oleg Lyalin's defection. He was supposed to be responsible for organising sabotage in the UK in the event of a crisis. There was a statement in the Commons. You must have read about it at the time.'

'Yes, I remember.'

Of course I didn't. The expulsions had failed to make it into my *?Quis?* columns. I didn't then have Tony around to make me read newspapers.

'My point is,' Max said, 'that comatose isn't quite right, is it?'

He was still regarding me in a particular way, as if he expected the conversation to lead somewhere significant.

I said, 'I suppose not.' I was feeling uneasy, all the more so because I sensed that he intended me to be. Our friendship was so recent and sudden. I knew nothing about him and now he looked like a stranger to me, his outsized ears cupped in my direction like radar dishes to catch my softest, least honest whisper, his thin, intense face tightly concentrated on mine. I worried that he wanted something from me and that, even if he got it, I wouldn't know what it was.

'Would you like me to kiss you again?'

It was as long as the first, this stranger's kiss, and because it broke the tension between us, all the more pleasurable. I felt myself relaxing, even *dissolving*, the way people do in romantic novels. I could no longer bear to think that he was pretending.

He drew back and said quietly, 'Did Canning ever mention Lyalin to you?' Before I could reply, he kissed me again, just a glancing touch of lips and tongues. I was tempted to say yes because it was what he wanted.

'No, he didn't. Why are you asking?'

'Just curious. Did he introduce you to Maudling?'

'No. Why?'

'I would have been interested to hear your impressions, that's all.'

We kissed again. We were reclining on the grass. My hand was on his thigh and I let it slip towards his groin. I wanted to know if he was genuinely aroused by me. I didn't want him to be a brilliant pretender. But just as my fingertips were inches from the hard proof, he twisted away, extracted himself and stood, then stooped to brush dried grass from his trousers. The gesture looked fussy. He offered a hand to pull me up.

'I should get my train. I'm cooking dinner for a friend.'

'Oh, really.'

We walked on. He had caught the hostility in my voice and his touch on my arm was tentative, or apologetic. He said, 'Did you ever go to Kumlinge to visit his grave?'

'No.'

'Did you read the obituary?'

Because of this 'friend' our evening was going nowhere.

'Yes.'

'Was it *The Times* or *Telegraph*?'

'Max, are you interrogating me?'

'Don't be silly. I'm just terribly nosy. Please forgive me.'

'Then leave me alone.'

We walked in silence. He didn't know what to say. An only child, a boys' boarding school – he didn't know how to talk to a woman when things went awry. And I said nothing. I was angry, but I didn't want to drive him away. I was calmer by the time we stopped to say our goodbyes on the pavement just beyond the park railings.

'Serena, you do realise that I'm becoming very attached to you.'

I was pleased, I was very pleased, but I didn't show it and said nothing, waiting for him to say more. He seemed about to, then he changed the subject.

'By the way. Don't be impatient about the work. I happen to know there's a really interesting project coming through. Sweet Tooth. Right up your street. I've put in a good word for you.'

He didn't wait for a response. He pursed his lips and shrugged, then set off along Park Lane in the direction of Marble Arch, while I stood there watching him, wondering whether he was telling the truth.

5

My room in St Augustine's Road faced north over the street with a view into the branches of a horse chestnut tree. As it came into leaf that spring the room grew darker by the day. My bed, which was about half the size of the room, was a rickety affair with walnut veneer headboard and mattress of boggy softness. With the bed came a musty yellow candlewick bedcover. I took it to the launderette a couple of times but never completely purged it of a clammy intimate scent, of dog perhaps, or very unhappy human. The only other furniture was a chest of drawers with a tilting bevelled mirror on top. The whole piece stood in front of a miniature fireplace, which exuded a sour, sooty smell on warm days. With the tree in full blossom there wasn't enough natural light to read by when it was cloudy, so I bought an art deco lamp for thirty pence from a junk shop on the Camden Road. A day later I went back and paid one pound twenty pence for a compact boxy armchair to read in without having to sink into the bed. The shop owner carried the chair home for me on his back, half a mile and up two flights of stairs for what we agreed was the price of a pint – thirteen pence. But I gave him fifteen pence.

Most of the houses in the street were subdivided and unmodernised, though I don't remember anyone using that word then or thinking in those terms. Heating was by electric fire, the floors were covered in ancient brown lino in the corridors and kitchen, and elsewhere with floral carpeting that was sticky underfoot. Small improvements probably dated from the twenties or thirties – the wiring was contained in dusty pipes screwed to the walls, the telephone confined to the draughty hallway, the electric immersion heater, fed by a hungry meter, delivered water at near boiling point to a tiny cold bathroom with no shower, shared by four women. These houses had not yet escaped their inheritance of Victorian gloom, but I never heard anyone complain. As I remember it, even in the seventies ordinary people who happened to live in these old places were only just beginning to wake up to the idea that they could be more comfortable further out of town if prices here kept on rising. The houses in the back streets of Camden Town awaited a new and vigorous class of people to move in and get to work, installing radiators and, for reasons no one could explain, stripping the pine skirting and floorboards and every last door of all vestiges of paintwork or covering.

I was lucky in my housemates – Pauline, Bridget, Tricia – three working-class girls from Stoke-on-Trent, who knew each other from childhood, passed all their school exams and somehow remained together during their legal training, which was almost complete. They were boring, ambitious, ferociously tidy. The house ran smoothly, the kitchen was always clean, the tiny fridge was full. If there were boyfriends, I never saw them. No drunkenness, no drugs, no loud music. In those days, a more likely household would have had people like my sister in it. Tricia was studying for the bar, Pauline was specialising in company law and Bridget was going into property. They each told me in their different defiant ways that they were never going back. And they weren't speaking of Stoke in purely geographical terms. But I didn't enquire too closely. I was adapting to my new job and wasn't much interested in their class struggle or upward mobility. They thought I was a dull civil servant, I thought they were dull trainee solicitors. Perfect. We had different schedules and we rarely ate together. No one bothered much with the sitting room – the only comfortable communal space. Even the TV was mostly silent. They studied in their rooms in the evening, I read in mine, or I went out with Shirley.

I kept up the reading in the same old style, three or four books a week. That year it was mostly modern stuff in paperbacks I bought from charity and second-hand shops in the High Street or, when I thought I could afford it, from Compendium near Camden Lock. I went at things in my usual hungry way, and there was an element of boredom too, which I was trying to keep at bay, and not succeeding. Anyone watching me might have thought I was consulting a reference book, I turned the pages so fast. And I suppose I was, in my mindless way, looking for something, a version of myself, a heroine I could slip inside as one might a pair of favourite old shoes. Or a wild silk blouse. For it was my best self I wanted, not the girl hunched in the evenings in her junk-shop chair over a cracked-spine paperback, but a fast young woman

75

pulling open the passenger door of a sports car, leaning over to receive her lover's kiss, speeding towards a rural hideout. I would not admit to myself that I should have been reading a lower grade of fiction, like a mass-market romance. I had finally managed to absorb a degree of taste or snobbery from Cambridge, or from Tony. I no longer promoted Jacqueline Susann over Jane Austen. Sometimes my alter ego shimmered fleetingly between the lines, she floated towards me like a friendly ghost from the pages of Doris Lessing, or Margaret Drabble or Iris Murdoch. Then she was gone – their versions were too educated or too clever, or not quite lonely enough in the world to be me. I suppose I would not have been satisfied until I had in my hands a novel about a girl in a Camden bedsit who occupied a lowly position in MI5 and was without a man.

I craved a form of naive realism. I paid special attention, I craned my readerly neck whenever a London street I knew was mentioned, or a style of frock, a real public person, even a make of car. Then, I thought, I had a measure, I could gauge the quality of the writing by its accuracy, by the extent to which it aligned with my own impressions, or improved upon them. I was fortunate that most English writing of the time was in the form of un-demanding social documentary. I wasn't impressed by those writers (they were spread between South and North America) who infiltrated their own pages as part of the cast, determined to remind the poor reader that all the characters and even they themselves were pure inventions and that there was a difference between fiction and life. Or, to the contrary, to insist that life was a fiction anyway. Only writers, I thought, were ever in danger of confusing the two. I was a born empiricist. I believed that writers were paid to pretend, and where appropriate should make use of the real world, the one we all shared, to give plausibility to whatever they had made up. So, no tricksy haggling over the limits of their art, no showing disloyalty to the reader by appearing to cross and recross in disguise the borders of the imaginary. No room in the books I liked for the double agent. That year I tried and discarded the authors that sophisticated friends in Cambridge had pressed on me – Borges and Barth, Pynchon and Cortázar and Gaddis. Not an Englishman among them, I noted, and no women of any race. I was rather like people of my parents' generation who not only disliked the taste and smell of garlic, but distrusted all those who consumed it.

During our summer of love Tony Canning used to tell me off for leaving books lying around open and face down. It ruined the spine, causing a book to spring open at a certain page, which was a random and irrelevant intrusion on a writer's intentions and another reader's judgement. And so he presented me with a bookmark. It wasn't much of a gift. He must have pulled it out of the bottom of a drawer. It was a strip of green leather with crenellated ends and embossed in gold with the name of some Welsh castle or ramparts. It was holiday gift-shop kitsch from the days when he and his wife were happy, or happy enough to take excursions together. I only faintly resented it, this tongue of leather that spoke so insidiously of another life elsewhere, without me. I don't think I ever used it then. I memorised my page number and stopped damaging spines. Months after the affair I found the bookmark lying curled and sticky with a chocolate wrapper at the bottom of a duffel bag.

I've said that after his death I had no love tokens. But

I had this. I cleaned it up, straightened it out, and started to treasure and use it. Writers are said to have superstitions and little rituals. Readers have them too. Mine was to hold my bookmark curled between my fingers and stroke it with my thumb as I read. Late at night, when the time came to put my book away, my ritual was to touch the bookmark to my lips, and set it between the pages before closing the book and putting it on the floor by my chair, where I could reach for it easily next time. Tony would have approved.

One evening in early May, more than a week after our first kisses, I stayed later than usual talking with Max in Berkeley Square. He'd been in a particularly communicative mood, telling me about an eighteenth-century clock he thought he might write about one day. By the time I got back to St Augustine's Road the house was dark. I remembered that this was the second day of some obscure legal holiday. Pauline, Bridget and Tricia, for all their disavowals, had gone back to Stoke for a long weekend. I put on the lights in the hall and in the passage to the kitchen. I bolted the front door and went up towards my room. I suddenly missed that trio of sensible girls from the north and the wedge of light under the doors of their rooms, and I was uneasy. But I was sensible too. I had no supernatural fears, and I scoffed at reverential talk of intuitional knowledge and a sixth sense. My raised pulse, I reassured myself, was due to my exertions on the stairs. But when I reached my own door, I paused on the threshold before turning on the overhead light, restrained by the faintest of anxieties at being alone in a large old house. There had been a pavement knifing in Camden Square a month before, a motiveless attack by a thirty-year-old schizophrenic man. I was sure there was no intruder in the house, but news of a terrible event like that acts on you viscerally, in ways you're hardly aware of. It sharpens the senses. I stood still and listened and heard, beyond the tinnitus hiss of silence, the city's hum and, nearer, creaks and clicks as the shell of the building cooled and contracted in the night air.

I reached out and pushed down the Bakelite switch and saw immediately that the room was undisturbed. Or so I thought. I stepped in, put down my bag. The book I'd been reading the night before – *Eating People is Wrong*, by Malcolm Bradbury – was in its proper position, on the floor by the chair. But the bookmark was lying on the seat of my armchair. And no one had been in the house since I'd left that morning.

Naturally, my first assumption was that I had broken with my ritual the night before. Easy enough when you're tired. I could have stood and let the bookmark fall as I crossed to the basin to wash. My memory, however, was distinct. The novel was short enough for me to read in two sittings. But my eyes were heavy. I was less than halfway when I kissed the scrap of leather and placed it between pages ninety-eight and ninety-nine. I even recalled the last phrase I read because I glanced at it again before I closed the book. It was a line of dialogue. 'Intelligentsias are by no means always liberal in outlook.'

I went about the room looking for other signs of disturbance. Since I had no bookshelves, my books were in piles against the wall, divided between the read and the unread. On top of the latter, next in line, was A.S. Byatt's *The Game*. All was in order. I went through the chest of drawers, through my wash bag, I looked at the bed and under it

– nothing had been moved or stolen. I came back to the chair and stared down a good while, as if that would solve the mystery. I knew I should go downstairs and look for signs of a break-in, but I didn't want to. The title of Bradbury's novel stared up at me and seemed now an ineffective protest against a prevailing ethic. I picked up the book and riffled through the pages and found the place where I had left off. Out on the landing I leaned over the banister and heard nothing unusual, but I still did not dare go down.

There was no lock or bolt on my door. I dragged the chest of drawers across it and went to bed with the light on. For most of the night I lay on my back with the covers pulled up to my chin, listening, thinking in circles, waiting for the dawn to come like a soothing mother and make things better. And when it did, they were. At first light I was persuaded that tiredness had fogged my memory, that I was confusing the intention with the act, that I had put the book down without the bookmark. I'd been frightening myself with my own shadow. Daylight seemed then to be the physical manifestation of common sense. I needed some rest because the next day I had an important lecture to attend. Enough ambiguity had gathered around the bookmark to let me sleep the two and a half hours before the alarm went off.

The next day I earned a black mark from MI5, or rather, Shirley Shilling earned it for me. I was the sort of girl who could occasionally speak her mind, but my stronger impulse was for advancement and for approval from my seniors. Shirley had something combative, even reckless, about her that was alien to my nature. But we were a duo, after all, Laurel and Hardy, and perhaps it was inevitable that I would be drawn into the general ambience of her cockiness and be cast as the sidekick who was bound to take the blame.

It happened in the afternoon when we attended the lecture in Leconfield House, with the title 'Economic Anarchy, Civic Unrest'. The meeting was well attended. By an unspoken convention, whenever we had a distinguished visitor, the seating arranged itself by status. Right up in the front were various grand figures from the fifth floor. Three rows back was Harry Tapp, sitting with Millie Trimingham. Two rows behind them was Max, talking to a man I'd never seen before. Then there were the packed ranks of women below assistant desk officer status. And finally, Shirley and I, the naughty girls, had the back row to ourselves. I, at least, had a notebook at the ready.

The Director General came forward to introduce the visiting speaker, a brigadier, as someone with long experience in counter-insurgency, who was now in a consultative role with the Service. From scattered parts of the room there was applause for a military man. He spoke with a trace of the clipped manner we associate now with old British movies and 1940s wireless commentaries. There were still a few around among our seniors who exuded that flinty seriousness derived from their experience of a prolonged and total war.

But the brigadier also had a taste for the occasional flowery phrase. He said he was aware that there was a good number of ex-servicemen in the room and he hoped they would forgive him for stating facts well known to them but not to others. And the first of those facts was this – our soldiers were fighting a war, but no politician had the courage to give it that name. Men sent in to keep apart factions divided by obscure and ancient sectarian hatred found themselves attacked by both sides. Rules of engagement were such that trained soldiers were not allowed to respond in the way they knew best. Nineteen-year-old squaddies from Northumberland or Surrey, who may once have thought their mission was to come and protect the Catholic minority from the Protestant ascendancy, lay bleeding their lives, their futures, into the gutters of Belfast and Derry while Catholic children and teenage yobs taunted them and cheered. These men were being felled by sniper fire, often from tower blocks, and generally by IRA gunmen working under cover of coordinated riot or street disturbance. As for last year's Bloody Sunday, the Paras were under intolerable pressure from those same well-tried tactics – Derry hooligans backed up by sniper fire. The Widgery Report last April, produced with commendable speed, had confirmed the facts. That said, it was clearly an operational error to have an aggressive and highly motivated outfit like the Paras policing a civil-rights march. It should have been the task of the Royal Ulster Constabulary. Even the Royal Anglians would have been a calmer influence.

But it was done, and the net effect of killing thirteen civilians on that day was to endear both wings of the IRA to the world. Money, arms and recruits were as rivers of honey in spate. Sentimental and ignorant Americans, many of Protestant rather than Catholic descent, were feeding the fires with their foolish dollars donated to the Republican cause through fundraisers like NORAID. Not until the United States had its own terrorist attacks would it even begin to understand. To right the tragedy of Derry's wasted lives, the Official IRA slaughtered five cleaning ladies, a gardener and a Catholic priest in Aldershot, while the Provisionals murdered mothers and children in Belfast's Abercorn restaurant, some of them Catholics. And during the national strike our boys confronted ugly Protestant mobs, spurred on by the Ulster Vanguard, as nasty a bunch as one could hope to meet. Then the ceasefire, and when that failed, utter savagery dispensed to the Ulster public by psychopathic gun and bomb toters of both persuasions, and thousands of armed robberies and indiscriminate nail bombings, knee cappings, punishment beatings, five thousand seriously injured, several hundred killed by loyalist and Republican militias, and quite a few by the British army – though not, of course, intentionally. Such were the tallies for 1972.

The brigadier sighed theatrically. He was a big man, with eyes too small for the bony mass of his head. Neither a lifetime of spit and polish nor his tailored dark suit and breast-pocket handkerchief could contain the shaggy, shambling six-foot-three bulk of him. He appeared ready to dispatch a score of psychopaths with his own bare hands. Now, he told us, the Provisional IRA had organised itself into cells on the mainland in classic terrorist style. After eighteen months of lethal attacks, the word was they were about to get worse. The pretence of going for purely military assets had long been dropped. The game was terror. As in Northern Ireland, children, shoppers, ordinary working men were all suitable targets. Bombs in department stores and pubs would have even more impact in the context of the widely anticipated social breakdown brought on by industrial decline, high unemployment, rising inflation and an energy crisis.

It was to our collective dishonour that we had failed

to expose the terrorist cells or disrupt their lines of supply. And this was to be his main point – there was one overriding reason for our failure, which was the lack of coordinated intelligence. Too many agencies, too many bureaucracies defending their corners, too many points of demarcation, insufficient centralised control.

The only sound was a creak of chairs and whispers, and I saw in front of me a restrained movement of heads tilting or turning minimally, of shoulders canting slightly towards a neighbour. The brigadier had touched upon a common complaint in Leconfield House. Even I had heard some of it, from Max. No flow of information across the borders of the jealous empires. But was our visitor going to tell the room what it wanted to hear, was he on our side? He was. He said MI6 was operating where it was not supposed to be, in Belfast and Londonderry, in the United Kingdom. With its remit of foreign intelligence, Six had a historical claim which dated back before Partition and was now irrelevant. This was a domestic issue. The territory therefore belonged to Five. Army Intelligence was over-staffed, mired in procedural antecedents. The RUC Special Branch, which considered itself the owner of the turf, was clumsy, under-resourced and, more to the point, part of the problem – a Protestant fiefdom. And who else could have made such a mess of internment in '71?

Five had been right to keep its distance from the dubious interrogation techniques, torture in anyone's book. Now it was doing its best in a crowded field. But even if each agency was staffed by geniuses and paragons of efficiency, four in collaboration could never defeat the monolithic entity of the Provisional IRA, one of the most formidable terrorist groups the world had ever known. Northern

Ireland was a vital concern of domestic security. The Service must get a grip and advance its claim through the Whitehall corridors, suborn the other players to its will, become the rightful inheritor of the estate, and move in on the root of the problem.

There was no applause, partly because the brigadier's tone was close to exhortation, and that sort of thing didn't go down well here. And everyone knew that an assault on Whitehall's corridors would hardly be enough. I didn't take notes during the discussion between the brigadier and the Director General. From the question session I recorded only one of the questions, or ran a couple together as representative of the general drift. They came from the ex-colonial officers – one in particular I remember was Jack MacGregor, who had a dry, gingerish look and the tightly swallowed vowels of a South African, though he originally came from Surrey. He and some of his colleagues were particularly interested in the proper response to social breakdown. What would be the role of the Service? And what about the army? Could we stand aside and watch public order break down in the event that the government couldn't hold the line?

The Director General answered – curtly and with excessive politeness. The Service was accountable to the Joint Intelligence Committee and the Home Secretary, the army to the Ministry of Defence, and that was how it would remain. The emergency powers were sufficient to meet any threat and were something of a challenge to democracy in themselves.

A few minutes later, the question returned in a more pointed form from another ex-colonial. Suppose at the next general election a Labour government was returned.

And suppose its left wing made common cause with radical union elements and one saw a direct threat to parliamentary democracy. Surely some form of contingency planning would be in order.

I wrote down the DG's exact words. 'I rather think I've made the position perfectly clear. Restoring democracy, as it's called, is what the army and security services might do in Paraguay. Not here.'

I thought the DG was embarrassed to have what he would have thought of as ranchers and tea planters reveal their colours before an outsider, who was nodding gravely.

It was at this point that Shirley startled the room by calling out from her back-row seat next to mine, 'These berks want to stage a coup!'

There was a collective gasp and all heads turned to look at us. She had broken several rules at a stroke. She had spoken unbidden by the Director General, and had used a dubious word like 'berk', whose provenance as rhyming slang some must have known. She had thereby insulted decorum and two desk officers far senior to herself. She had been uncouth in front of a visitor. And, she was lowly, and she was a woman. And, worst of all, she was probably right. None of that would have mattered to me but for the fact that Shirley sat nonchalantly before the collective glare, while I blushed, and the more I blushed the more certain everyone was that I was the one who had spoken. Aware of what they were thinking, I blushed even more, until my neck was hot. Their eyes were no longer fixed on us, but on me. I wanted to crawl under my chair. My shame rose in my throat for the crime I had not committed. I fiddled with my notebook – those notes I had hoped would earn me respect – and lowered my eyes, stared at my knees and so provided yet more evidence of my guilt.

The Director General brought the occasion back to its formal proprieties by thanking the brigadier. There was applause, the brigadier and the DG left the room and people stood to go, and turned to look at me again.

Suddenly Max was right in front of me. He said quietly, 'Serena, that wasn't a good idea.'

I turned to appeal to Shirley but she was in the crowd going out through the door. I don't know how I came by such a masochistic code of honour that prevented me from insisting I wasn't the one who had called out. And yet I was sure that by now the DG would be asking for my name, and someone like Harry Tapp would be telling him.

Later, when I caught up with Shirley and confronted her, she told me the whole thing was trivial and hilarious. I shouldn't worry, she told me. It would do me no harm for people to think I had a mind of my own. But I knew that the opposite was true. It would do me a lot of harm. People at our level were not supposed to have minds of their own. This was my first black mark, and it was not the last.

6

I was expecting a reprimand, but instead my moment came – I was sent out of the building on a secret mission, and Shirley went with me. We received our instructions one morning from a desk officer called Tim Le Prevost. I'd seen him about the place but he'd never spoken to us before. We were summoned to his office and invited to listen carefully. He was a small-lipped tightly buttoned chap with narrow shoulders and a rigid expression, almost certainly ex-army. A van was parked in a locked garage off a Mayfair street half a mile away. We were to drive to an address in Fulham. It was a safe house, of course, and in the brown envelope he tossed across his desk were various keys. In the back of the van we would find cleaning materials, a Hoover and vinyl aprons, which we were to put on before we set off. Our cover was that we worked for a firm called Springklene.

When we arrived at our destination we were to give the place 'a damned good going over', which would include changing the sheets on all the beds and cleaning the windows. Clean linen had already been delivered. One of the mattresses on a single bed needed to be turned. It should have been replaced long ago. The lavatories and bath needed particular attention. The rotten food in the fridge was to be disposed of. All ashtrays were to be emptied. Le Prevost enunciated these homely details with much distaste. Before the day was out, we were to go to a small supermarket on the Fulham Road and buy basic provisions and three meals a day for two persons for three days. A separate trip was to be made to an off-licence, where we should buy four bottles of Johnnie Walker Red Label. We were to settle for nothing else. Here was another envelope with fifty pounds in fivers. He wanted receipts and change. We were to remember to triple lock the front door on our way out with the three Banhams. Above all, we should never in our lives mention this address, not even to colleagues in this building.

'Or,' Le Prevost said, with a twist of his little mouth, 'do I mean *especially*?'

We were dismissed and when were out of the building, heading along Curzon Street, it was Shirley, not me, who was scathing.

'Our *cover*,' she kept saying in a loud whisper. 'Our bloody cover. Cleaning ladies pretending to be *cleaning ladies*!'

It was an insult, of course, though less of one then than it would be now. I didn't say the obvious, that the Service could hardly bring in outside cleaners to a safe house, any more than it could call on our male colleagues – they were not only too grand, but they would have made a terrible job. I surprised myself with my stoicism. I think I must have absorbed the general spirit of camaraderie and cheerful devotion to duty among the women. I was becoming like my mother. She had the Bishop, I had the Service. Like her I had my own strong-minded inclination to obey. I did worry, however, whether this was the job that Max had said was right up my street. If it was, I'd never talk to him again.

We found the garage and put on our aprons. Shirley, wedged in tight behind the wheel, was still muttering mutinously as we pulled out into Piccadilly. The van was pre-war – it had spoked wheels and a running board and must have been among the last of the sit-up-and-beg contraptions on the road. The name of our firm was written on the sides in art deco lettering. The 'k' of 'Springklene' was done up as a gleeful housemaid wielding a feather duster. I thought we looked far too conspicuous. Shirley drove with surprising confidence, swinging us at speed round Hyde Park Corner and demonstrating a flashy technique with the gear stick, known, she told me, as double declutching, necessary on such an ancient crate.

The flat occupied the ground floor of a Georgian house in a quiet side street and was grander than I expected. All the windows were barred. Once we were in with our mops, fluids and buckets, we made a tour. The squalor was even more depressing than Le Prevost had implied and was of the obvious male sort, right down to a once-sodden cigar stub on the edge of the bath, and a foot-high pile of *The Times*, with some copies roughly quartered, moonlighting as lavatory paper. The sitting room had an abandoned late-night air – drawn curtains, empty bottles of vodka and Scotch, heaped ashtrays, four glasses. There were three bedrooms, the smallest of which had a single bed. On its mattress, which was stripped, was a wide patch of dried blood, just where a head might rest. Shirley was loudly disgusted, I was rather thrilled. Someone had been intensively interrogated. Those Registry files were connected to real fates.

As we went round taking in the mess, she continued to complain and exclaim, and clearly wanted me to join in. I tried, but my heart wasn't in it. If my small part in the war against the totalitarian mind was bagging up decaying food and scraping down hardened bathtub scum, then I was for it. It was only a little duller than typing up a memo.

It turned out that I had a better understanding of the work involved – odd, considering my cosseted childhood with nanny and daily. I suggested we did the filthiest stuff first, lavatories, bathroom, kitchen, clearing the rubbish, then we could start on the surfaces, then the floors and finally the beds. But before all else, we turned the mattress, for Shirley's sake. There was a radio in the sitting room and we decided that it would be consistent with our cover to have pop music playing. We went at it for two hours, then I took one of the fivers and went out to buy the wherewithal for a tea break. On the way back I used some change to feed the parking meter. When I returned to the house, Shirley was perched on the edge of one of the double beds, writing in her little pink book. We sat in the kitchen, drank tea, smoked and ate chocolate biscuits. The radio was playing, there was fresh air and sunlight through the open windows and Shirley was restored to a good mood and told me a surprising story about herself while she finished off all the biscuits.

Her English teacher at the Ilford comprehensive, a force in her life the way certain teachers can be, was a

Labour councillor, probably ex-Communist Party, and it was through him that she found herself at the age of sixteen on an exchange with German students. That is, she went to communist East Germany with a school group, to a village an hour's bus ride from Leipzig.

'I thought it was going to be shit. Everyone said it would be. Serena, it was fucking paradise.'

'The GDR?'

She lodged with a family on the edge of the village. The house was an ugly, cramped two-bedroom bungalow but there was a half-acre of orchard and a stream, and not far away a forest big enough to get lost in. The father was a TV engineer, the mother a doctor, and there were two little girls under five years who fell in love with the lodger and used to climb into her bed early in the morning. The sun always shone in East Germany – it was April, and by chance there was a heatwave. There were expeditions into the forest to hunt for morels, there were friendly neighbours, everyone encouraged her German, someone had a guitar and knew some Dylan songs, there was a good-looking boy with three fingers on one hand who was keen on her. He took her to Leipzig one afternoon to see a serious football match.

'No one had much. But they had enough. At the end of ten days I thought, no, this really works, this is better than Ilford.'

'Maybe everywhere is. Especially in the countryside. Shirley, you could have had a good experience just outside Dorking.'

'Honestly, this was different. People cared about each other.'

What she was saying was familiar. There had been

pieces in the newspaper and a TV documentary reporting in triumph that East Germany had finally overtaken Britain in living standards. Years later, when the Wall came down and the books were opened, it turned out to be nonsense. The GDR was a disaster. The facts and figures people had believed, and had wanted to believe, were the Party's own. But in the seventies, the British mood was self-lacerating, and there was a general willingness to assume that every country in the world, Upper Volta included, was about to leave us far behind.

I said, 'People care about each other here as well.'

'Well, fine. We all care about each other. So what are we fighting against?'

'A paranoid one-party state, no free press, no freedom to travel. A nation as prison camp, that sort of thing.' I heard Tony at my shoulder.

'*This* is a one-party state. Our press is a joke. And the poor can't travel anywhere.'

'Oh, Shirley, really!'

'Parliament's our single party. Heath and Wilson belong to the same elite.'

'What nonsense!'

We had never talked politics before. It had always been music, families, personal tastes. I assumed that all my colleagues had roughly the same sort of views. I was looking at her closely to see if she was teasing me. She looked away, reached roughly across the table for another cigarette. She was angry. I didn't want a full-on row with my new friend. Lowering my tone I said softly, 'But if you think that, Shirley, why join this lot?'

'I dunno. Partly to please my dad. I mean, I've told him it's the Civil Service. I didn't think they'd let me in. When they did everyone was proud. Including me. It felt like a victory. But you know how it is – they had to have one non-Oxbridge type. I'm just your token prole. So.' She stood. 'Better get on with our crucial work.'

I stood too. The conversation was embarrassing and I was glad it was over.

'I'll finish off in the sitting room,' she said, and then paused in the kitchen doorway. She looked a sad figure, bulging under her plastic apron, her hair, still damp from her exertions before our tea break, sticking to her forehead.

She said, 'Come on, Serena, you can't think all this is so simple. That we just happen to be on the side of the angels.'

I shrugged. Actually, in relative terms I thought we were, but her tone was so scathing that I didn't want to say so. I said, 'If people had a free vote across Eastern Europe, including your GDR, they'd kick the Russians out, and the CP wouldn't stand a chance. They're there by force. That's what I'm against.'

'You think people here wouldn't kick the Americans off their bases? You must have noticed – the choice isn't on offer.'

I was about to reply when Shirley snatched up her duster and a lavender canister of spray-on polish and left, calling out as she went down the hall, 'You've soaked up all the propaganda, girl. Reality isn't always middle class.'

Now I was angry, too angry to speak. In the last minute or so Shirley had upped her Cockney accent, the better to use some notion of working-class integrity against me. How dare she condescend like that? Reality isn't always middle class! Intolerable. Her 'reality' had been ludicrously glottal. How could she traduce our friendship and say she was my token prole? And I'd never given a moment's thought to the college she was at, except to think that I would have been happier at hers. As for her politics – the outworn orthodoxy of *idiots*. I felt I could have run after her and shouted at her. My mind was filled with withering retorts, and I wanted to use them all at once. But I stood in silence and walked around the kitchen table a couple of times, then I picked up the vacuum cleaner, a heavy-duty affair, and went to the small bedroom, the one with the bloody mattress.

That was how I came to clean the room so thoroughly. I went at it in a fury, running the conversation over and over again, merging what I'd said with what I wished I'd said. Just before our break I had filled a bucket to clean the woodwork round the windows. I decided I would clean the skirting boards first. And if I was going to be kneeling on the floor, I would need to vacuum the carpet. To do that properly I carried out into the corridor a few pieces of furniture – a bedside locker and two wooden chairs that were by the bed. The only electric socket in the room was low down on the wall under the bed and a reading lamp was already plugged in. I had to lie on my side on the floor and reach in at full stretch. No one had cleaned under there in a long time. There were dust balls, a couple of used tissues and one dirty white sock. Because the plug was a tight fit it took an effort to pull and jiggle it clear. My thoughts were still on Shirley and what I would say to her next. I'm a coward in important confrontations. I suspected we would both choose the English solution and pretend that the conversation had never happened. That made me angrier still.

Then my wrist brushed against a piece of paper concealed by one of the legs of the bed. It was triangular, no more than three inches along the hypotenuse, torn from the right-hand top corner of *The Times*. On one side was the familiar lettering – 'Olympic Games: Complete programme, page 5'. On the reverse, faint pencil writing under one of the straight edges. I backed out and sat down on the bed to take a closer look. I peered and understood nothing until I realised I was holding the scrap upside down. What I saw first were two letters in lower case. 'tc'. The line of the tear sliced right through the word below. The writing was faint, as though there had been minimal downward pressure, but the letters were clearly formed: 'umlinge'. Just before the 'u' was a stroke that could only have been the foot of the letter 'k'. I turned the piece of paper upside down again, hoping to make the letters do something else for me, demonstrate that I was simply projecting. But there was no ambiguity. His initials, his island. But not his handwriting. In a matter of seconds my mood had shifted from intense irritation to a more complex mix – of bafflement and unfocused anxiety.

Naturally, one of my first thoughts was of Max. He was the only one I knew who knew the name of the island. The obituary had made no mention of it and Jeremy Mott probably didn't know. But Tony had plenty of old connections in the Service, though very few were active now. Perhaps a couple of very senior figures. They surely wouldn't have known of Kumlinge. As for Max, I sensed it would be a bad idea to ask him for an explanation. I would have been giving away something I should hold on to. He wouldn't tell me the truth if it didn't suit him. If he knew anything worth telling, then he had already deceived me by keeping silent. I thought back to our conversation in the park and his persistent questions. I looked at the scrap of paper again. It looked old, faintly yellowish. If this was a significant mystery, I didn't have enough information to solve it. Into this vacancy came an irrelevant thought. The 'k' on the side of our van was the missing letter, dressed up like a housemaid – just like me. Yes, everything was connected! Now that I was being really stupid, it was almost a relief.

I stood up. I was tempted to turn the mattress back just to look at the blood again. It was right under where I'd just been sitting. Was it as old as the piece of paper? I didn't know how blood aged. But that was it, here was the simplest formulation of the mystery and the core of my unease: did the name of the island and Tony's initials have anything to do with the blood?

I put the paper in the pocket of my apron and went along the hallway to the lavatory, hoping I didn't run into Shirley. I locked the door, knelt by the pile of newspapers and began sorting through it. Not every day was there – the safe house must have stood empty for longish periods. So the copies reached back many months. The Munich games were last summer, ten months ago. Who could forget, eleven Israeli athletes massacred by Palestinian guerrillas? I found the copy with the missing corner only a couple of inches from the bottom and pulled it clear. There was the first half of the word 'programme'. August 25th, 1972. 'Unemployment at its highest level for August since 1939'. I faintly remembered the story, not for the jobless headline but for the article about my old hero Solzhenitsyn across the top of the page. His 1970 Nobel Prize acceptance speech had just surfaced. He attacked the United Nations for failing to make acceptance of the declaration of human rights a condition of membership. I thought that was right, Tony thought it was naive. I was stirred by the lines about 'the shadows of the fallen' and 'the vision of art that sprang from the pain and solitude of the Siberian waste'. And I especially liked the line, 'Woe to the nation whose literature is disturbed by the intervention of power.'

Yes, we'd spent some time talking about that speech, and disagreeing. And that would have been not long before our parting scene in the lay-by. Might he have come here afterwards when his plans for retreat had already taken shape? But why? And whose blood? I had solved nothing, but I felt clever in making progress. And feeling clever, I've always thought, is just a sigh away from being cheerful. I heard Shirley coming and quickly put the pile in order, flushed the lavatory, washed my hands and opened the door.

I said, 'We should remember to put lavatory rolls on the list.'

She was standing well back along the corridor and I don't think she heard me. She was looking contrite and I felt suddenly warm towards her.

'I'm sorry about just now. Serena, I don't know why I do this. Bloody stupid. I go right over the top for the sake of argument.' And then she added as a jokey softener, 'It's only because I like you!'

I noted that she deliberately sounded the 't' of 'right', in itself a muted apology.

I said, 'It was nothing,' and meant it. What had passed between us was nothing to what I had just found. I'd already decided not to discuss it. I'd never said much to her about Tony. I'd saved all that for Max. I might have got this the wrong way round, but there was nothing to be gained from confiding in her now. The piece of paper was tucked deep into my pocket. We chatted in our usual friendly way for a while and then we went back to work. It was a long day and we were not completely done, cleaning and shopping, until after six. I came away with the August copy of *The Times* in case I could learn more from it. When we dropped off the van in Mayfair that evening and parted, I thought Shirley and I were once more the best of friends.

7

The following morning I received an eleven o'clock invitation to Harry Tapp's office. I was still expecting to have my wrists slapped for Shirley's indiscretion at the lecture. At ten to eleven I went to the ladies' to check on my appearance and as I combed my hair I imagined myself taking the train home after being sacked, and preparing a story for my mother. Would the Bishop even notice I'd been away? I went up two floors to a part of the building that was new to me. It was only slightly less dingy – the corridors were carpeted, the cream and green paint on the walls was not peeling. I tapped timidly on a door. A man came out – he looked even younger than me – and told me in a nervous, pleasant way that I should wait. He indicated one of the bright orange plastic moulded chairs that were then spreading through the offices. A quarter of an hour passed before he appeared again and held the door open for me.

In a sense, this was when the story began, at the point at which I entered the office and had my mission explained.

Tapp was sitting behind his desk and nodded expressionlessly at me. There were three others in the room besides the fellow who had shown me in. One, by far the oldest, with swept-back silver hair, was sprawled in a scuffed leather armchair, the others were on hard office chairs. Max was there and pursed his lips in greeting. I wasn't surprised to see him and simply smiled. There was a large combination safe in one corner. The air was thick with smoke and moist with breath. They had been in conference a good while. There were no introductions.

I was shown onto one of the hard seats and we sat in a horseshoe facing the desk.

Tapp said, 'So, Serena. How are you settling in?'

I said I thought I had settled in well and that I was happy with the work. I was aware that Max knew it wasn't so, but I didn't care. I added, 'Am I here because you think I'm not up to scratch, sir?'

Tapp said, 'It wouldn't take five of us to tell you that.'

There were low chuckles all round and I took care to join in. 'Up to scratch' was a phrase I'd never used before.

There followed a session of small talk. Someone asked me about my lodgings, another about my commute. There was a discussion about the irregularities of the Northern line. Canteen food was gently mocked. The more this went on, the more nervous I became. The man in the armchair said nothing, but he was watching me over the steeple he formed with his fingers, with his thumbs tucked under his chin. I tried not to look in his direction. Guided by Tapp, the conversation shifted to the events of the day. Inevitably, we came to the Prime Minister and the miners. I said that free trade unions were important institutions. But their remit should be the pay and conditions of their members. They

101

should not be politicised and it was not their business to remove democratically elected governments. This was the right answer. I was prompted to speak of Britain's recent entry to the Common Market. I said I was for it, that it would be good for business, dissolve our insularity, improve our food. I didn't really know what to think, but decided it was better to sound decisive. This time I knew that I'd parted company with the room. We progressed to the Channel Tunnel. There had been a White Paper, and Heath had just signed a preliminary agreement with Pompidou. I was all for it – imagine catching the London–Paris express! I surprised myself with a burst of enthusiasm. Again, I was alone. The man in the armchair grimaced and looked away. I guessed that in his youth he had been prepared to give his life to defend the realm against the political passions of Continentals. A tunnel was a security threat.

So we went on. I was being interviewed, but I had no idea to what end. Automatically I strove to please, more so whenever I sensed that I was not succeeding. I assumed that the whole business was being conducted for the benefit of the silver-haired man. Apart from that single look of displeasure, he communicated nothing. His hands remained in their praying position, with the tips of his forefingers just touching his nose. It was a conscious effort not to look at him. I was annoyed with myself for wanting his approval. Whatever he had in mind for me, I wanted it too. I wanted him to want me. I couldn't look at him, but when my gaze moved across the room to meet the eye of another speaker, I caught just a glimpse, and learned nothing.

We came to a break in the conversation. Tapp indicated a lacquered box on the desk and cigarettes were offered around. I expected to be sent out of the room as before. But some quiet signal must have emanated from the silvery gentleman because Tapp cleared his throat to mark a fresh start and said, 'Well then, Serena. We understand from Max here that on top of your maths you're rather well up on modern writing – literature, novels, that sort of thing – bang up to date on, what's the word?'

'Contemporary literature,' Max supplied.

'Yes, awfully well read and quite in with the scene.'

I hesitated, and said, 'I like reading in my spare time, sir.'

'No need for "sir". And you're up to date on this contemporary stuff that's coming out now.'

'I read novels in second-hand paperbacks mostly, a couple of years after they've appeared in hardback. The hardbacks are a bit beyond my budget.'

This hair-splitting distinction seemed to baffle or irritate Tapp. He leaned back in his chair and closed his eyes for several seconds and waited for the confusion to disperse. He didn't open them again until he was halfway through his next sentence. 'So if I said to you the names of Kingsley Amis or David Storey or . . .' he glanced down at a sheet of paper, 'William Golding, you'd know exactly what I was talking about.'

'I've read those writers.'

'And you know how to talk about them.'

'I think so.'

'How would you rank them?'

'Rank them?'

'Yes, you know, best to worst.'

'They're very different kinds of writer . . . Amis is a comic novelist, brilliantly observant with something quite merciless about his humour. Storey is a chronicler of working-class life, marvellous in his way and, uh, Golding is harder to define, probably a genius . . .'

'So then?'

'For pure reading pleasure I'd put Amis at the top, then Golding because I'm sure he's profound, and Storey third.'

Tapp checked his notes, then looked up with a brisk smile. 'Exactly what I've got down here.'

My accuracy evinced a rumble of approval. It didn't seem much of an achievement to me. There were, after all, only six ways to organise such a list.

'And do you know personally any of these writers?'

'No.'

'Do you know any writers at all, or publishers or anyone else connected with the business?'

'No.'

'Have you ever actually met a writer, or been in a room with one?'

'No, never.'

'Or written to one, as it were, a fan letter?'

'No.'

'Any Cambridge friends determined to be writers?'

I thought carefully. Among the Eng Lit set at Newnham there had been a fair amount of longing in this direction, but as far as I knew my female acquaintance had settled for various combinations of finding respectable jobs, marrying, getting pregnant, disappearing abroad or retreating into the remnants of the counterculture in a haze of pot smoke.

'No.'

Tapp looked up expectantly. 'Peter?'

At last the man in the armchair lowered his hands and

spoke. 'I'm Peter Nutting by the way. Miss Frome, have you ever heard of a magazine called *Encounter*?'

Nutting's nose was revealed as beakish. His voice was a light tenor – somehow surprising. I thought I had heard of a nudist lonely-hearts small-ads news-sheet of that name, but I wasn't sure. Before I could speak he continued, 'It doesn't matter if you haven't. It's a monthly, intellectual stuff, politics, literature, general cultural matters. Pretty good, well respected, or it was, with a fairly wide range of opinion. Let's say centre left to centre right, and mostly the latter. But here's the point. Unlike most intellectual periodicals it's been sceptical or downright hostile when it comes to communism, especially of the Soviet sort. It spoke up for the unfashionable causes – freedom of speech, democracy and so on. Actually, it still does. And it soft-pedals rather on American foreign policy. Ring any bells with you? No? Five or six years ago it came out, in an obscure American magazine and then the *New York Times* I think it was, that *Encounter* was funded by the CIA. There was a stink, a lot of arm-waving and shouting, various writers took flight with their consciences. The name Melvin Lasky means nothing to you? No reason why it should. The CIA has been backing its own highbrow notion of culture since the end of the forties. They've generally worked at one remove through various foundations. The idea has been to try to lure left-of-centre European intellectuals away from the Marxist perspective and make it intellectually respectable to speak up for the Free World. Our friends have sloshed a lot of cash around by way of various fronts. Ever hear of the Congress of Cultural Freedom? Never mind.

'So that's been the American way and basically, since

105

the *Encounter* affair, it's a busted flush. When a Mr X pops up from some giant foundation offering a six-figure sum, everyone runs screaming. But still, this is a culture war, not just a political and military affair, and the effort's worthwhile. The Soviets know it and they spend on exchange schemes, visits, conferences, the Bolshoi Ballet. That's on top of the money they channel into the National Union of Mineworkers strike fund by way of . . .'

'Peter,' Tapp murmured, 'let's not go down that pit again.'

'All right. Thank you. Now the dust is settling, we've decided to push ahead with our own scheme. Modest budget, no international festivals, no first-class flights, no twenty-pantechnicon orchestral tours, no bean feasts. We can't afford it and we don't want to. What we intend is pinpointed, long-term and cheap. And that's why you're here. Are there any questions so far?'

'No.'

'You might know of the Information Research Department over at the Foreign Office.'

I didn't, but I nodded.

'So you'll know this kind of thing has a long history. IRD have worked with us and MI6 for years, cultivating writers, newspapers, publishers. George Orwell on his deathbed gave IRD a list of thirty-eight communist fellow-travellers. And IRD helped *Animal Farm* into eighteen languages and did a lot of good work for *Nineteen Eighty-Four*. And some marvellous publishing ventures over the years. Ever heard of Background Books? – that was an IRD outfit, paid for with the Secret Vote. Superb stuff. Bertrand Russell, Guy Wint, Vic Feather. But these days . . .'

He sighed and looked around the room. I sensed a common grievance.

'IRD has lost its way. Too many silly ideas, too close to Six – in fact, one of their own is in charge. D'you know, Carlton House Terrace is full of nice hard-working girls like you, and when people from Six visit, some fool has to run ahead through the offices shouting, "Faces to the wall, everybody!" Can you imagine such a thing? You can bet those girls peep through their fingers, eh?'

He looked around expectantly. There were obliging chuckles.

'So we want to start afresh. Our idea is to concentrate on suitable young writers, academics and journalists mostly, people at the start of their careers, when they need financial support. Typically, they'll have a book they want to write and need to take time off from a demanding job. And we thought it might be interesting to have a novelist on the list . . .'

Harry Tapp cut in, unusually excited. 'Makes it a little less heavy, more, you know, a bit of light-hearted fun. Frothy. Someone the newspapers will take an interest in.'

Nutting continued. 'Since you like that sort of thing, we thought you might want to be involved. We're not interested in the decline of the West, or down with progress or any other modish pessimism. Do you see what I mean?'

I nodded. I thought I did.

'Your corner's going to be a little trickier than the rest. You know as well as I do, it's not straightforward to deduce an author's views from his novels. That's why we've been looking for a novelist who also writes journalism. We're looking out for the sort who might spare a moment for his hard-pressed fellows in the Eastern bloc, travels out there perhaps to lend support or sends books, signs petitions for persecuted writers, engages his mendacious Marxist colleagues here, isn't afraid to talk publicly about writers in prison in Castro's Cuba. Generally swims against the orthodox flow. It takes courage, Miss Frome.'

'Yes, sir. I mean, yes.'

'Especially if you're young.'

'Yes.'

'Free speech, freedom of assembly, legal rights, democratic process – not much cherished these days by a lot of intellectuals.'

'No.'

'We need to encourage the right people.'

'Yes.'

A silence settled on the room. Tapp again offered round cigarettes from his case, first to me, then to the rest. We all smoked and waited for Nutting. I was aware of Max's eyes on me. When I met his look he made the slightest inclination of his head, as if to say, 'Keep it up.'

With some initial difficulty, Nutting levered himself out of his armchair, went across to Tapp's desk and picked up the notes. He turned the pages until he found what he wanted.

'The people we're looking for will be of your generation. They'll cost us less, that's for sure. The sort of stipend we'll be offering through our front organisation will be enough to keep a chap from having to do a day job for a year or two, even three. We know we can't be in a hurry and that we're not going to see results next week. We're expecting to have ten subjects, but all you need to think about is this one. And one proposal . . .'

He looked down through half-moon specs that hung by a cord around his neck.

'His name is Thomas Haley, or T.H. Haley as he prefers it in print. Degree in English at the University of Sussex, got a first, still there now, studied for an MA in international relations under Peter Calvocoressi, now doing a doctorate in literature. We took a peek at Haley's medical record. Nothing much to report. He's published a few short stories and some journalism. He's looking for a publisher. But he also needs to find himself a proper job once his studies are over. Calvocoressi rates him highly, which should be enough for anyone. Benjamin here has put together a file and we'd like your opinion. Assuming you're happy, we'd like you to get on the train to Brighton and take a look at him. If you give the thumbs up, we'll take him on. Otherwise, we'll look somewhere else. It'll be on your say-so. You'll precede your visit, of course, with an introductory letter.'

They were all watching me. Tapp, whose elbows rested on his desk, had made his own finger-steeple. Then, without parting his palms, he drummed his fingers together soundlessly.

I felt obliged to make some form of intelligent objection. 'Won't I be like your Mr X, popping up with a chequebook? He might run at the sight of me.'

'At the sight of you? I rather doubt it, my dear.'

Again, low chuckles all round. I blushed and was annoyed. Nutting was smiling at me and I made myself smile back.

He said, 'The sums are going to be attractive. We'll channel funds through a cut-out, an existing Foundation. Not a huge or well-known outfit, but it's one where we have some reliable contacts. If Haley or any of the others decides to check, it'll stand up nicely. I'll let you know its name as soon as it's settled. Obviously, you'll be the Foundation's representative. They'll let us know when letters come for you. And we'll get you some of their headed paper.'

'Wouldn't it be possible to simply make some friendly recommendations to the, you know, the government department that hands out money to artists?'

'The Arts Council?' Nutting let out a pantomime shout of a bitter laugh. Everyone else was grinning. 'My dear girl. I envy your innocence. But you're right. It should have been possible! It's a novelist in charge of the literature section, Angus Wilson. Know of him? On paper just the sort we could have worked with. Member of the Athenaeum, naval attaché in the war, worked on secret stuff in the famous Hut Eight on the uh, at, well, I'm not allowed to say. I took him to lunch, then saw him a week later in his office. I started to explain what I wanted. D'you know, Miss Frome, he all but threw me out of a third-floor window.'

He had told this story before and delighted in telling it again, embellished.

'One moment he was behind his desk, nice white linen suit, lavender bow tie, clever jokes, the next his face was puce and he had hold of my lapels and was pushing me out of his office. What he said I can't repeat in front of a lady. And camp as a tent peg. God knows how they let him near naval codes in 'forty-two.'

'There you go,' Tapp said. 'It's filthy propaganda when we do it, and then they're sold out at the Albert Hall for the Red Army Chorus.'

'Max here rather wishes Wilson *had* tossed me out of the window,' Nutting said, and to my surprise winked at me. 'Isn't that right, Max?'

110

'I've had my say,' Max said. 'Now I'm on board.'

'Good.' Nutting nodded at Benjamin, the young man who had shown me in. He opened the folder on his lap.

'I'm sure this is everything he's published. Not easy to track down, some of it. I suggest you look at the journalism first. I should direct your attention towards an article he wrote for the *Listener*, deploring the way newspapers romanticise villains. It's mostly about the Great Train Robbery – he objects to the word "great" – but there's a robust aside about Burgess and Maclean and the number of deaths they were responsible for. You'll see he's a member of the Readers and Writers Educational Trust, an organisation that supports dissidents in Eastern Europe. He wrote a piece for the Trust's journal last year. You might look at the longish article he wrote for *History Today* about the East German uprising of 'fifty-three. There's a goodish piece about the Berlin Wall in *Encounter*. Generally, the journalism is sound. But it's the short stories you'll be writing to him about, and they're his thing. Five in all, as Peter said. Actually, one in *Encounter*, and then things you've never heard of – the *Paris Review*, the *New American Review*, *Kenyon Review* and *Transatlantic Review*.'

'Geniuses with the titles, these creative types,' Tapp said.

'Worth noting that those four are based in the States,' Benjamin went on. 'An Atlanticist at heart. We've asked around and people describe him as promising. Though one insider told us that's a standard description for any young writer. He's been turned down three times by a Penguin short-story series. He's also been turned down by the *New Yorker*, the *London Magazine* and *Esquire*.'

Tapp said, 'As a matter of interest, how did you come by all this?'

111

'It's a long story. First I met a former . . .'

'Keep going,' Nutting said. 'I'm due upstairs at eleven thirty. And by the way. Calvocoressi has told a friend that Haley's a personable fellow, decently turned out. So, a good role model for the young. I'm sorry, Benjamin. Carry on.'

'A well-known publishing house has said they like the stories but won't publish them in a collection until he comes up with a novel. Short stories don't sell. Publishers usually do these collections as a favour to their well-established authors. He needs to write something longer. This is important to know because a novel takes a while and it's hard to do when you've got a full-time job. And he's keen to write a novel, says he has an idea for one apparently. Another thing, he doesn't have an agent and is looking for one.'

'*Agent?*'

'Altogether different fish, Harry. Sells the work, does the contracts, takes a cut.'

Benjamin handed me the folder. 'That's about it. Obviously, don't leave it lying around.'

The man who had not yet spoken, a greyish shrunken-looking fellow with oily centre-parted hair, said, 'Are we expecting to have at least a little influence over what any of these people write?'

Nutting said, 'It would never work. We have to trust in our choices and hope Haley and the rest turn out well and become, you know, important. This is a slow-burn thing. We aim to show the Americans how it's done. But there's no reason why we can't give him a leg-up along the way. You know, people who owe us a favour or three. In Haley's case, well, sooner or later one of our own is going to be chairing this new Booker Prize committee.

And we might look into that agent business. But as for the stuff itself, they have to feel free.'

He was standing up and looking at his watch. Then he looked at me. 'Any more background questions, Benjamin's your man. Operationally, it's Max. The codename is Sweet Tooth. Right then? That'll be all.'

I was taking a risk, but I had begun to feel indispensable. Over-confident, perhaps. But who else in this room apart from me had ever, as an adult, read a short story in his leisure time? I couldn't hold back. I was eager and hungry. I said, 'This is a little awkward for me, and no offence to Max, but if I'm reporting directly to him, I wonder if it might be helpful if I could have some clarification of my own status.'

Peter Nutting sat down again. 'My dear girl. What can you mean?'

I stood in front of him humbly, as I used to in front of my father in his study. 'It's a great challenge and I'm thrilled to be asked. The Haley case is fascinating, and it's also delicate. You're asking me, in effect, to run Haley. I'm honoured. But agent-running . . . well, I'd like to be clear then about where I stand.'

There followed an embarrassed silence of the sort only a woman can impose on a roomful of men. Then Nutting muttered, 'Well, yes, quite . . .'

He turned in desperation to Tapp. 'Harry?'

Tapp slipped his gold cigarette case into the inside pocket of his jacket as he stood. 'Simple, Peter. You and I will go downstairs after lunch and talk to Personnel. I don't foresee any objection. Serena can be made up to assistant desk officer. It's time she was.'

'There you are, Miss Frome.'

'Thank you.'

We all stood. Max was looking at me with what I thought was new respect. I heard a singing sound in my ears, like a polyphonic chorus. I had been in the Service only nine months and even if I was among the last in my intake to be promoted, I'd reached as high as any woman could go. Tony would have been so proud of me. He would have taken me out for a celebratory dinner at his club. Wasn't it the same as Nutting's? The least I could do, I thought, as we filed out of Tapp's office, was to phone my mother and let her know how well I was doing at the Department of Health and Social Security.

8

I settled myself into my armchair, angled my new reading lamp and took up my bookmark fetish. I had a pencil at the ready, as though preparing for a tutorial. My dream had come true – I was studying English, not maths. I was free of my mother's ambitions for me. The folder was on my lap, buff coloured, HMSO, closed with loops of string. What a transgression, and how privileged I was, to have a file at home. It had been hammered into us in our early training – files were sacred. Nothing was to be removed from a file, no file was to be removed from the building. Benjamin had accompanied me to the front entrance, and was made to open up the folder to prove that it wasn't a Registry Personal File, even though it was the same colour as one. As he explained to the P Branch duty officer on the desk, it was mere background information. But that night it gave me pleasure to think of it as the Haley file.

I count those first hours with his fiction as among the happiest in my time at Five. All my needs beyond the sexual met and merged: I was reading, I was doing it for

115

a higher purpose that gave me professional pride, and I was soon to meet the author. Did I have doubts or moral qualms about the project? Not at that stage. I was pleased to have been chosen. I thought I could do the job well. I thought I might earn praise from the higher floors in the building – I was a girl who liked to be praised. If someone had asked, I would have said we were nothing more than a clandestine Arts Council. The opportunities we offered were as good as any.

The story had been published in the *Kenyon Review* in the winter of 1970 and the whole issue was there, with a protruding purchase slip from a specialist bookshop in Longacre, Covent Garden. It concerned the formidably named Edmund Alfredus, an academic teacher of medieval social history who becomes in his mid-forties a Labour MP in a tough east London constituency, having been a local councillor there for a dozen years. He's well to the left of his party and *something of a trouble-maker, an intellectual dandy, a serial adulterer and a brilliant public speaker* with good connections to powerful members of the Tube train drivers' union. He happens to have an identical twin brother, Giles, a milder figure, an Anglican vicar with a pleasant living in rural West Sussex within cycling distance of Petworth House, where Turner once painted. His small, elderly congregation gathers in *a pre-Norman church whose pargeted uneven walls bore the palimpsests of Saxon murals depicting a suffering Christ overlaid by a gyre of ascending angels, whose awkward grace and simplicity spoke to Giles of mysteries beyond the reach of an industrial, scientific age.*

They are also beyond the reach of Edmund, a strict atheist who in private is scornful of Giles's comfortable life and improbable beliefs. For his part, the vicar is embarrassed that Edmund has not outgrown his adolescent Bolshevik views. But the brothers are close and usually manage to avoid religious or political disputes. They lost their mother to breast cancer when they were eight and were sent away by their emotionally remote father to boarding prep school, where they clung to each other for comfort, and so were bound for life.

Both men married in their late twenties and have children. But a year after Edmund takes his seat in the House of Commons, the patience of his wife, Molly, breaks on account of one affair too many and she throws him out. Looking for shelter from the storm of domestic ruin and divorce proceedings, and nascent press interest, Edmund heads to the Sussex vicarage to spend a long weekend, and here is where the story proper begins. Brother Giles is in distress. That Sunday he is due to deliver the sermon in his church in the presence of the Bishop of Ch—, well known for being a prickly, intolerant sort. (Naturally, I projected my father into the role.) His Grace will not be pleased to be told that the vicar, whose performance he intends to inspect, has come down with a bad dose of flu complicated by laryngitis.

On his arrival, Edmund is directed by the vicar's wife, his sister-in-law, straight up to the old nursery on the top floor, where Giles has been quarantined. Even in their forties and for all their differences, the Alfredus twins share a taste for mischief. With Giles sweating, and croaking to be heard, they confer for half an hour and make their decision. For Edmund it's a useful distraction from the trouble at home, to spend all the next day, Saturday, learning the liturgy and the order of service and thinking about his sermon. The theme, announced to the bishop in advance, is from I Corinthians 13, the famous verses in the King James translation declaring that of faith, hope and charity, 'the greatest of these is charity'. Giles has insisted that in line with modern scholarship, Edmund is to substitute 'love' for 'charity'. No disagreement here. As a medievalist, Edmund knows his Bible, and he admires the Authorised Version. And yes, he is happy to talk of love. On Sunday morning he puts on his brother's surplice and, after combing his hair in imitation of Giles's neat side parting, slips out of the house and makes his way across the graveyard to the church.

News of the bishop's visit *had swollen the congregation to almost forty*. Prayers and hymns follow in the usual order. Everything proceeds smoothly. An ancient canon, *his gaze wrenched downward by osteoporosis*, assists efficiently in the service without noticing that Giles is Edmund. At the correct moment Edmund mounts the carved stone pulpit. Even the ageing regulars in the pews are aware that their soft-spoken vicar appears particularly confident, forthright even, no doubt keen to impress the distinguished visitor. Edmund begins by repeating from the first reading selected passages from Corinthians, speaking the lines with actorly rotundity – close, some might have thought, if they had ever been to a theatre (so Haley adds in aside), to a parody of Olivier. Edmund's words resound in the near-empty church, and with tongue thrust between teeth he relishes the 'th' sound in the verbs. *Love suffereth long, and is kind; love envieth not; love vaunteth not itself, is not puffed up, doth not behave itself unseemly, seeketh not her own, is not easily provoked, thinketh no evil; rejoiceth not in iniquity, but rejoiceth in the truth . . .*

Then he begins a passionate disquisition on love, driven

118

in part by shame at his recent betrayals and sorrow for the wife and two children he has left behind, and the warm memories of all the good women he has known, and by the sheer pleasure in performance that a good public speaker feels. The generous acoustic and his raised position in the pulpit also help him to fresh turns of rhetorical extravagance. Deploying the very debating skills that have helped bring out the Tube train drivers on three one-day strikes in as many weeks, he sets out the case that love as we know and celebrate it today is a Christian invention. In the harsh Iron Age world of the Old Testament, ethics were pitiless, its jealous God was ruthless and His most cherished values were revenge, domination, enslavement, genocide and rape. Here some noted the bishop swallowing hard.

Against such a background, Edmund says, we see how radical the new religion was in putting love at its centre. Uniquely in human history, a quite different principle of social organisation was proposed. In fact, a new civilisation takes root. However short it may fall of these ideals, a fresh direction is set. Jesus's idea is irresistible and irreversible. Even unbelievers must live within it. For love doesn't stand alone, nor can it, *but trails like a blazing comet, bringing with it other shining goods – forgiveness, kindness, tolerance, fairness, companionability and friendship, all bound to the love which is at the heart of Jesus's message.*

It is not done, in an Anglican church in West Sussex, to applaud a sermon. But when Edmund has finished, having quoted from memory lines of Shakespeare, Herrick, Christina Rossetti, Wilfred Owen and Auden, the impulse to cheer is palpable in the pews. The vicar, in sonorous falling tones which breathe wisdom and sadness down the nave, leads the congregation into prayer. When the bishop straightens, purplish from the effort of leaning forwards, he's beaming and everyone else, the retired colonels and horse breeders and the ex-captain of the polo team and all their wives beam too, and beam again as they file out through the porch, where they shake Edmund's hand. The bishop actually pumps his hand, is fulsome, then, mercifully, regrets he has another appointment and cannot stay for coffee. The canon shuffles off without a word, and soon everyone is heading towards their Sunday lunch, and Edmund, feeling the lightness of triumph in his step, fairly skips through the graveyard, back to the vicarage to tell his brother all about it.

Here, on the eighteenth of thirty-nine pages, was a space between the paragraphs adorned with a single asterisk. I stared into it to prevent my gaze slipping down the page and revealing the writer's next move. Sentimentally, I hoped that Edmund's high-flown talk of love would deliver him back to his wife and children. Not much chance of that in a modern story. Or he might talk himself into becoming a Christian. Or Giles could lose his faith when he hears how his congregation is stirred by clever rhetoric from the mouth of an atheist. I was drawn to the possibility of the narrative following the bishop home to witness him that night lying in the bath, brooding steamily on what he had heard. That was because I didn't want my father the Bishop to disappear from the scene. In fact, the ecclesiastical trappings entranced me – the Norman church, the smells of brass polish, lavender wax, old stone and dust that Haley evoked, the black, white and red bell ropes behind the font with the wonky oak lid held together by iron rivets and ties across a massive split, and above all the vicarage with the chaotic back hall beyond the kitchen, where Edmund dumps his bag on the chessboard lino, and the nursery on the top floor, just like ours. I felt faintly homesick. If only Haley had gone, or made Edmund go, into the bathroom to see the waist-high tongue-and-groove panelling painted baby blue and the giant bath, stained by blue-green algae beneath the taps, standing four-square on rusty lion's feet. And into the lavatory, where a faded bathtime duck hung from the end of the cistern chain. I was the basest of readers. All I wanted was my own world, and myself in it, given back to me in artful shapes and accessible form.

I was drawn to mild-mannered Giles by the same associations, but it was Edmund I wanted. Wanted? To travel with. I wanted Haley to examine Edmund's mind for me, to open it up for my inspection, and to explain it to me, man to woman. Edmund reminded me of Max, and of Jeremy. And of Tony most of all. These clever, amoral, inventive, destructive men, single-minded, selfish, emotionally cool, coolly attractive. I think I preferred them to the love of Jesus. They were so necessary, and not only to me. Without them we would still be living in mud huts, waiting to invent the wheel. Three-crop rotation would never have come to pass. Such impermissible thoughts at the dawn of feminism's second wave. I stared into the asterisk. Haley had got under my skin, and I wondered if he was one of those necessary men. I felt violated by him, and homesick and curious, all at once. So far I hadn't made a single pencil mark. It wasn't fair that such a shit as Edmund should give a brilliant cynical speech and be praised, but it was right, it seemed true. That image of him dancing in joy among the graves on his way back to tell his brother how well he has performed suggested hubris. Haley was intimating that punishment or downfall must follow. I didn't want it to. Tony had been punished and that was enough for me. Writers owed their readers a duty of care, of mercy. The *Kenyon Review*'s asterisk was beginning to rotate beneath my fixed gaze. I blinked it to a standstill and read on.

It had not occurred to me that with almost half of the story told, Haley would introduce another important character. But she was there all through the service, sitting at the end of the third row, right against the wall by the piled-up hymnbooks, unnoticed by Edmund. Her name is Jean Alise. It is quickly established that she is thirty-five, lives locally, is a widow and somewhat wealthy, is devout, more so since the death of her husband in a motorbike accident, has some psychiatric illness in her past and is, of course, beautiful. Edmund's sermon has a profound, even devastating, effect upon her. She loves its message and understands its truth, she loves the poetry and is powerfully drawn to the man who speaks it. She stays up all that night wondering what to do. She doesn't actually want to, but she's falling in love and is prepared to go to the vicarage and say so. She cannot help it, she's ready to wreck the vicar's marriage.

At nine the following morning she rings the vicarage doorbell and it is Giles in his dressing gown who answers. He's making the beginnings of a recovery, but he's still pale and shaky. To my relief, Jean knows right away that this is not her man. She establishes that there is a brother and follows him to London, to the address that Giles has innocently provided. It's a small furnished flat in Chalk

Farm, where Edmund is setting up a temporary base while he goes through his divorce.

It's a stressful time and he is not able to resist a beautiful woman who appears desperate to give him everything he wants. She stays for an unbroken two weeks and Edmund makes passionate love to her – Haley describes their intimacy in detail I found difficult. Her clitoris is *monstrous, the size of a prepubertal boy's penis.* He has never known such a generous lover. Jean soon decides that she is bound to Edmund for the rest of her life. Once she has learned that her man is an atheist, she understands that the task granted to her is to bring him to the light of God. Wisely, she doesn't mention her mission and bides her time. It takes her only a few days to forgive him the blasphemous impersonation of his brother.

Edmund meanwhile is reading and re-reading in private a letter from Molly which hints strongly at a reconciliation. She loves him, and if he could only cease his affairs there might be a way they could be a family again. The children are missing him sorely. It is going to be hard to extricate himself, but he knows what he must do. Fortunately, Jean pops down to her moated house in Sussex to attend to her horses and dogs and other matters. Edmund arrives at the family home and has an hour with his wife. It goes well, she looks wonderful, he makes promises he is certain he can keep. The children come home from school and they have tea together. It's like old times.

When he tells Jean the next day, over a fry-up breakfast in a local greasy spoon, that he is going back to his wife, he sets off a frightening psychiatric episode. He didn't realise up until this point quite how fragile her mental health is. After breaking the plate he was eating off, she runs screaming from the cafe into the street. He decides not to go after her. Instead, he hurries to the flat and packs up his belongings, leaves what he thinks is a kindly note to Jean and moves back in with Molly. The bliss of reunion lasts three days, until Jean re-enters his life with a vengeance.

The nightmare begins with her calling at the house and making a scene in front of Molly and the kids. She writes letters to Molly as well as Edmund, she accosts the children on their way to school, she phones several times every day and often in the small hours. Daily she stands outside the house, waiting to talk to any member of the family who dares come out. The police will do nothing because they say that Jean is not breaking any law. She follows Molly to her work – she's a headmistress at a primary school – and makes one of her awesome scenes in the playground.

Two months pass. *A stalker can as easily bind a family in solidarity as break it apart.* But in the Alfredus marriage, the bonds are still too weak, the damage of past years has not yet been repaired. This affliction, Molly tells Edmund in their final heart to heart, is what he has brought down on their family. She must protect the children as well as her own sanity and her job. Once more, she asks him to leave. He acknowledges an intolerable situation. As he steps out of the house with his bags, Jean is waiting for him on the pavement. He hails a cab. After a violent scuffle, witnessed by Molly from a bedroom window, Jean forces her way in beside her man, whose face she has badly scratched. He weeps for his marriage all the way to Chalk Farm, back to the apartment she has kept on as a shrine to their love. He is not aware of her comforting arm around his shoulder and her promise to love him and be with him always.

Now they are together, she is sane, practical and loving. For a while it is hard to imagine those terrible episodes ever took place, and it is easy in his distress, submitting to her kindly ministrations, to become her lover again. But now and then *she drifted up towards the dark clouds where these tornadoes of emotion were formed.* Even the legal confirmation of his divorce fails to bring Jean contentment. He dreads her explosive moments and does everything he can to avert them. What sets her off? When she suspects he is thinking of, or looking at, another woman, when he stays too late at the House for an all-night sitting, when he's out drinking with his left-wing friends, when he delays yet again the registry-office wedding. *He hated confrontations and was innately lazy, so by degrees her jealous eruptions trained him to her will.* It happens slowly. He finds it easier to stay away from old lovers who have become friends, or from female colleagues in general, easier to ignore the division bell and the demands of the Whips' Office and his constituents, and easier in fact to marry than face the consequences – those terrifying storms – of continuing to put off the day.

In the 1970 election that brings Edward Heath to power, Edmund loses his seat and is taken aside by his agent and told that the Party will not nominate him next time round. The newly married couple move to her lovely home in Sussex. He has become financially dependent on Jean. He carries no weight these days with the Tube train drivers' union or other friends on the left. Just as well, because his opulent surroundings embarrass him. Visits from his children seem to precipitate nasty scenes and so, by degrees, he joins *that sorry legion of passive men who abandon their children in order to placate their second wives.* Easier too to attend weekly church services than have yet more shouting matches. As he advances into his fifties he begins to take an interest in the roses within the estate's walled garden and becomes an expert on the carp in the moat. He learns to ride, though he can never shake off the feeling that he looks ridiculous on a horse. However, his relations with his brother Giles have never been better. As for Jean, in church when she sees through furtive partly opened eyes Edmund kneeling at her side during the blessing that follows the Reverend Alfredus's sermon, she knows that *though the way had been hard and she had suffered for her pains, she was bringing her husband ever closer to Jesus and this, her single most important achievement in life, had only been possible through the redeeming and enduring power of love.*

There it was. Only as I reached the end did I realise that I had failed to take in the title. 'This Is love'. He seemed too worldly, too knowing, this twenty-seven-year-old who was to be my innocent target. Here was a man who knew what it was to love a destructive woman afflicted by mood storms, a man who had noted the lid of an ancient font, who knew that the wealthy stocked their moats with carp and the downtrodden kept their stuff in supermarket trolleys – both supermarkets and trolleys were recent additions to life in Britain. If Jean's mutant genitalia were not an invention but a memory, then I already felt belittled or outclassed. Was I a touch jealous of his affair?

I was packing away the file, too tired to face another story. I'd experienced a peculiar form of wilful narrative sadism. Alfredus may have earned the narrowing of his life, but Haley had driven him into the ground. Misanthropy or self-loathing – were they entirely distinct? – must be part of his make-up. I was discovering that the experience of reading is skewed when you know, or are about to know, the author. I had been inside a stranger's mind. Vulgar curiosity made me wonder if every sentence confirmed or denied or masked a secret intention. I felt closer to Tom Haley than I would if he'd been a colleague in the Registry these past nine months. But if I sensed intimacy, it was hard to say exactly what I knew. I needed an instrument, some measuring device, the narrative equivalent of movable compass points with which to gauge the distance between Haley and Edmund Alfredus. The author may have been keeping his own demons at arm's length. Perhaps Alfredus – not a necessary man after all – represented the kind of person Haley feared he could become. Or he may have punished Alfredus in the spirit of moral primness for adultery and presuming to impersonate a pious man. Haley might be a prig, even a religious prig, or he could be a man with many fears. And priggishness and fear could be twin aspects of a single larger character defect. If I hadn't wasted three years being bad at maths at Cambridge, I might have done English and learned how to read. But would I have known how to read T.H. Haley?

9

The following night I had a date with Shirley at the Hope and Anchor in Islington to hear Bees Make Honey. I was half an hour late. She was sitting alone at the bar smoking, hunched over her notebook, with a couple of inches of beer in her pint glass. It was warm outside but it had been raining heavily and the place had a canine smell of damp jeans and hair. Amp lights glowed in a corner where a lone roadie was setting up. The crowd, which probably included the band and their pals, was hardly more than two dozen. In those days, at least in my circle, even women didn't embrace on greeting. I slipped onto the bar stool beside Shirley and ordered drinks. It was still something back then for two girls to assume a pub was as much theirs as any man's and to drink at the bar. In the Hope and Anchor and a handful of other places in London no one cared. The revolution had arrived and you could get away with it. We pretended to take it for granted, but it was still a kick. Elsewhere across the kingdom they would have taken us for whores, or treated us as though we were.

At work we ate our lunches together but there was still something between us, a little piece of gritty residue from that brief dispute. If her politics were so infantile or bone-headed, how much of a friend could she be? But at other times I believed that time would settle the matter and that, by simple contagion at work, her political views would mature. Sometimes *not* talking is the best way through a difficulty. The fad for personal 'truth' and confrontation was doing great damage in my view and blighting many friendships and marriages.

Not long before our date, Shirley had gone missing from her desk for most of one day and part of the next. She wasn't ill. Someone had seen her getting into the lift and had seen the button she pushed. The gossip was she'd been summoned to the fifth floor, the misty heights where our masters conducted their unknowable business. The gossip also hinted that since she was smarter than the rest of us, she was up for some unusual form of promotion. From the large debutante faction this provoked some amiable snobbery of the 'Oh, if only *I'd* been born into the working class' sort. I checked my own feelings. Would I feel jealous at being left behind by my best friend? I thought I would.

When she was back among us she ignored questions and told us nothing, didn't even lie, which was taken by most as confirmation of superior advancement. I wasn't so sure. Her plumpness sometimes made her expression hard to read, her subcutaneous fat being the mask she lived behind. Which would have made this line of work a good choice for her, if only the women were sent out to do more than clean houses. But I thought I knew her well enough. There was no triumph there. Did I feel just a tiny bit relieved? I thought so.

This was our first meeting outside the building since then. I was determined not to ask questions about the fifth floor. It would have looked undignified. Besides, I now had my own assignment and promotion, even if they emanated from two floors below hers. She switched to gin and orange, a large one, and I had the same. In low voices we talked office gossip for the first quarter of an hour. Now that we were no longer new girls, we felt at liberty to ignore some of the rules. There was a substantial new item. One of our intake, Lisa – Oxford High, St Anne's, bright and charming – had just announced her engagement to a desk officer called Andrew – Eton, King's, boyish and intellectual. It was the fourth such alliance in nine months. If Poland had joined NATO it would not have caused more excitement in the ranks than these bilateral negotiations. Part of the interest was speculating who would be next. 'Who whom?' as some Leninist wag put it. Early on, I'd been spotted on the bench in Berkeley Square with Max. I used to feel a thrill in my stomach when I heard our names fed through the mill, but lately we'd been dropped for more tangible outcomes. So Shirley and I discussed Lisa and the consensus that her wedding date was too remote, and then touched on Wendy's prospects with a figure who may have been too grand – her Oliver was an assistant head of section. But I thought there was something flat or routine in our exchange. I sensed that Shirley was putting something off, lifting her glass too frequently, as if summoning her courage.

Sure enough, she ordered another gin, took a swig, hesitated, then said, 'I have to tell you something. But first you have to do something for me.'

'Yes.'

'Smile, like you were just now.'

'What?'

'Just do as I say. We're being watched. Put on a smile. We're having a happy conversation. OK?'

I stretched my lips.

'You can do better than that. Don't freeze.'

I tried harder, I nodded and shrugged, trying to look animated.

Shirley said, 'I've been sacked.'

'Impossible!'

'As of today.'

'Shirley!'

'Just keep smiling. You mustn't tell anyone.'

'OK, but why?'

'I can't tell you everything.'

'You can't have been sacked. It doesn't make sense. You're better than all of us.'

'I could have told you somewhere private. But our rooms aren't secure. And I want them to see me talking to you.'

The lead guitarist had strapped on his guitar. He and the drummer were with the roadie now, all three bent over some piece of equipment on the floor. There was a howl of feedback, quickly subdued. I stared at the crowd, knots of people with their backs to us, mostly men, standing about with their pints waiting for the band to start. Could one or two be from A4, the Watchers? I was sceptical.

I said, 'Do you really think you're being followed?'

'No, not me. *You.*'

My laughter was genuine. 'That's ridiculous.'

'Seriously. The Watchers. Ever since you joined. They've

probably been into your room. Put in a mike. Serena, don't stop smiling.'

I turned back to the crowd. Shoulder-length hair for men was by then a minority taste, and the terrible moustaches and big sideburns were still some while ahead. So, plenty of ambiguous-looking types, plenty of candidates. I thought I could see a possible half-dozen. Then, suddenly, everyone in the room looked a possibility.

'But Shirley. Why?'

'I thought you could tell me.'

'There's nothing. You've made this up.'

'Look, I've got something to tell you. I did something stupid and I'm really ashamed. I don't know how to say it. I was going to do it yesterday, then my nerve failed. But I need to be honest about this. I've fucked up.'

She took a deep breath and reached for another cigarette. Her hands were shaking. We looked over towards the band. The drummer was sitting in, adjusting the hi-hat, showing off a tricky little turn with the brushes.

Shirley said at last, 'Before we went to clean that house, they called me in. Peter Nutting, Tapp, that creepy kid, Benjamin someone.'

'Jesus. Why?'

'They laid it on. Said I was doing well, possibility of promotion, softening me up like. Then they said they knew we were close friends. Nutting asked if you ever said anything unusual or suspicious. I said no. They asked what we talked about.'

'Christ. What did you say?'

'I should have told them to get stuffed. I didn't have the courage. There was nothing to hide so I told them the truth. I said we talked about music, friends, family,

132

the past, chit-chat, nothing much at all.' She looked at me a touch accusingly. 'You would've done the same.'

'I'm not sure.'

'If I'd said nothing they'd have been even more suspicious.'

'All right. Then what?'

'Tapp asked me if we ever spoke about politics and I said no. He said he found that hard to believe, I said it was a fact. We went round and round for a bit. Then they said OK, they were going to ask me something delicate. But it was very important and they'd be deeply appreciative, etc., if I could see my way to oblige, on and on, you know the greasy way they talk.'

'I think so.'

'They wanted me to get into a political conversation with you, and to come on like a real closet leftie, draw you out and see where you stood and . . .'

'Let them know.'

'I know. I'm ashamed. But don't get sour. I'm trying to be straight with you. And remember to smile.'

I stared at her, at her fat face and its scattered freckles. I was trying to hate her. Almost there. I said, '*You* smile. Faking's your thing.'

'I'm sorry.'

'So that whole conversation . . . you were on the job.'

'Listen, Serena, I voted for *Heath*. So yes, I was on the job, and I hate myself for it.'

'That workers' paradise near Leipzig was a lie?'

'No, it was a real school trip. Boring as shit. And I was homesick, wept like a baby. But listen, you did all right, you said all the right things.'

'Which you reported back!'

She was looking at me sorrowfully, shaking her head. 'That's the point. I didn't. I went to see them that evening and told them I couldn't do it, I wasn't playing. I didn't even tell them we'd had the conversation. I said I wasn't going to inform on a friend.'

I looked away. Now I was really confused, because I rather wished she had told them what I'd said. But I couldn't say that to Shirley. We drank our gin in silence for half a minute. The bass player was on now and the thing on the floor, some sort of junction box, was still giving trouble. I glanced around. No one in the pub was looking in our direction.

I said, 'If they know that we're friends they must have guessed that you'd tell me what they asked you to do.'

'Exactly. They're sending you a message. Perhaps they're warning you off something. I've been straight with you. Now you tell me. Why are they interested in you?'

Of course, I had no idea. But I was angry with her. I didn't want to look ignorant – no, more than that, I wanted her to believe that there were matters I preferred not to discuss. And I wasn't sure I believed anything she was saying.

I turned the question back to her. 'So they sacked you because you wouldn't inform on a colleague? That doesn't sound plausible to me.'

She took a long time getting out her cigarettes, offering one, lighting them. We ordered more drinks. I didn't want another gin, but my thoughts were too disordered, I couldn't think of what else to have. So we had the same again. I was almost out of money.

'Well,' she said, 'I don't want to talk about it. So there you are. This career is over. I never thought it would last anyway. I'm going to live at home and look after my dad. He's acting a bit confused lately. I'll help out in the shop. And I might even do some writing. But listen. I wish you'd tell me what was going on.'

And then, in a sudden gesture of affection, conjuring up the old days of our friendship she took the lapel of my cotton jacket and shook it. Shaking sense into me. 'You've got yourself caught up in something. It's crazy, Serena. They look and talk like a bunch of stuffed shirts, and they *are*, but they can be mean. It's what they're good at. They're *mean*.'

I said, 'We'll see.'

I was anxious and completely baffled, but I wanted to punish her, make her worry about me. I could almost fool myself that I really had a secret.

'Serena. You can tell me.'

'Too complicated. And why should I tell you anything? What could you do about it anyway? You're bottom of the heap like me. Or you were.'

'Are you talking to the other side?'

It was a shocking question. In that reckless tipsy moment I wished I did have a Russian controller and a double life, and dead-letter drops on Hampstead Heath, or better, that I was a double agent, feeding useless truths and destructive lies into an alien system. At least I had T.H. Haley. And why would they give me him if I was under suspicion?

'Shirley, *you're* the other side.'

Her reply was lost to the opening chords of 'Knee Trembler', an old favourite with us, but we didn't enjoy it this time round. It was the end of our conversation. Stalemate. She wouldn't tell me why she was sacked, I wouldn't tell

135

her the secret I didn't have. A minute later, she slid from her bar stool and left without saying or miming goodbye. I wouldn't have responded anyway. I sat there a while, trying to enjoy the band, trying to calm myself and think straight. When I'd finished my gin, I drank the remains of Shirley's. I didn't know which upset me more, my good friend or my employers snooping on me. Shirley's betrayal was unforgivable, my employers' frightening. If I was under suspicion, there must have been an administrative error, but that didn't make Nutting and Co. any less frightening. It was no comfort to learn they had sent the Watchers into my room and that, in a moment's incompetence, someone had dropped my bookmark.

Without a pause the band cruised straight into their second song, 'My Rockin' Days'. If they really were there, down among the punters and their pints, the Watchers would have been far closer to the speakers than I was. I guessed that this wouldn't have been their kind of music. Those stolid A4 types would be more the easy-listening sort. They'd hate this throbbing jangling din. There was some comfort in that, but not in much else.

I decided to go home and read another story.

No one knew how Neil Carder came by his money or what he was doing living alone in an eight-bedroom Highgate mansion. Most neighbours who passed him occasionally in the street didn't even know his name. He was a plain-looking fellow in his late thirties, with a narrow pale face, very shy and with an awkward manner, and no gift for the kind of easy small talk that might have led him towards the beginnings of some local acquaintance. But he caused no trouble, and kept his house and garden in good order.

If his name came up in the rounds of gossip, what generally featured was the large white 1959 Bentley he kept parked outside the house. What was a mousy fellow like Carder doing with a showy vehicle like that? Another item of speculation was the young, cheerful, colourfully dressed Nigerian housekeeper who came in six days a week. Abeje shopped, laundered, cooked, she was attractive, and was popular with the watchful housewives. But was she also Mr Carder's lover? It seemed so unlikely that people were tempted to think it might even be true. Those pale silent men, you never knew . . . But then, they were never seen together, she was never in his car, she always left just after teatime and waited at the top of the street for her bus back to Willesden. If Neil Carder had a sex life it was indoors and strictly nine till five.

The circumstances of a brief marriage, a large and surprising inheritance and an inward, unadventurous nature had combined to empty Carder's life. It had been a mistake to buy so large a house in an unfamiliar part of London, but he couldn't motivate himself to move out and buy another. What would be the point? His few friends and Civil Service colleagues had been repelled by his sudden enormous wealth. Perhaps they were jealous. Either way, people were not queuing up to help him spend his money. Beyond the house and car he had no great material ambitions, no passionate interests he could at last fulfil, no philanthropic impulses, and travelling abroad didn't appeal. Abeje was certainly a bonus, and he fantasised about her a fair bit, but she was married with two small children. Her husband, also a Nigerian, had once kept goal for the national soccer team. One glance at a snapshot of him and Carder knew he was no match, he was not Abeje's type.

Neil Carder was a dull fellow and his life was making him duller. He slept late, checked on his portfolio and spoke with his stockbroker, read a bit, watched TV, walked on the Heath now and then, occasionally went to bars and clubs, hoping to meet someone. But he was too shy to make approaches and nothing ever happened. He felt he was held in suspension, he was waiting for a new life to begin, but he felt incapable of taking an initiative. And when at last it did begin, it was in a most unexceptional way. He was walking along Oxford Street, at the Marble Arch end, on his way from his dentist in Wigmore Street when he passed a department store with immense plate-glass windows behind which was an array of mannequins in various poses, modelling evening wear. He paused a moment to look in, felt self-conscious, walked on a few paces, hesitated, and went back. The dummies – he came to hate that term – were disposed in such a way as to suggest a sophisticated gathering at cocktail hour. One woman leaned forwards, as though to divulge a secret, another held up a stiff white arm in amused disbelief, a third, languorously bored, looked across her shoulder towards a doorway, where a rugged fellow in a dinner jacket leaned with his unlit cigarette.

But Neil wasn't interested in any of these. He was looking at a young woman who had turned away from the entire group. She was contemplating an engraving – a view of Venice – on the wall. But not quite. Through an error of alignment by the window dresser, or, as he suddenly found himself imagining, *a degree of stubbornness in the woman herself, her gaze was off the picture by several inches and was angled straight into the corner. She was pursuing a thought, an idea, and she didn't care how she appeared.* She didn't want to be there. She wore an orange silk dress of simple folds and, unlike all the rest, she was barefoot. Her shoes – they must have been her shoes – were lying on their sides by the door, discarded as she came in. She loved freedom. In one hand she held *a small black and orange beaded purse, while the other trailed at her side, wrist turned outwards as she lost herself to her idea. Or perhaps a memory. Her head was slightly lowered to reveal the pure line of her neck. Her lips were parted, but only just, as though she was formulating a thought, a word, a name . . . Neil.*

He shrugged himself out of his daydream. He knew it was absurd and walked on purposefully, glancing at his watch to convince himself that he did indeed have a purpose. But he didn't. All that waited for him was the empty house in Highgate. Abeje would have gone by the time he got home. He wouldn't even have the benefit of the latest bulletin on her toddler children. He forced himself to keep walking, well aware that a form of madness was lying in wait, for an idea was forming, and becoming pressing. It said something for his strength of mind that he made it all the way to Oxford Circus before he turned around. Not so good, though, that he hurried all the way back to the store. This time he felt no embarrassment standing by her, gazing into this private moment of hers. What he saw now was her face. So thoughtful, so sad, so beautiful. She was so apart, so alone. The conversation around her was shallow, she had heard it all before, these were not her people, this was not her milieu. How was she to break out? It was a sweet fantasy and an enjoyable one, and at this stage Carder had no difficulty acknowledging that it *was* a fantasy. That token of sanity left him all the freer to indulge himself as the shopping crowds stepped around him on the pavement.

Later, he was not able to remember actually weighing up or making a decision. With a sense of a destiny already formed, he went into the shop, spoke to one person, was referred up to another, then a more senior third who refused outright. Quite out of order. A sum was mentioned, eyebrows were raised, a superior summoned, the sum was doubled and the matter agreed. By the end of the week? No, it had to be now, and the dress must come too, and he wished to buy several others of the correct size. *The assistants and the managers stood around him. Here they had on their hands, not for the first time, an eccentric. A man in love. All present knew that a mighty purchase was under way.* For such dresses were not cheap, and nor were several pairs of matching shoes, and the shot silk underwear. And then – how calm and decisive the fellow was – the jewellery. And, an afterthought, the perfume. All done in two and a half hours. A delivery van was made immediately available, the address in Highgate was written down, the payment made.

That evening, no one saw her arrive in the arms of the driver.

At this point I got myself out of my reading chair and went downstairs to make tea. I was still a little drunk, still troubled by my conversation with Shirley. I felt that I would doubt my own sanity if I started looking for a hidden microphone in my room. I also felt vulnerable to Neil Carder's loose grip on reality. It could loosen my own. And was he yet another character to be ground under Haley's narrative heel for getting everything wrong? With some reluctance, I carried my tea upstairs and sat on the edge of my bed, willing myself to pick up another of

Haley's pages. Clearly, the reader was intended to have no relief from the millionaire's madness, no chance to stand outside it and see it for what it was. There was no possibility of this clammy tale ending well.

At last I returned to the chair and learned that the mannequin's name was Hermione, which happened to be the name of Carder's ex-wife. She had walked out on him one morning after less than a year. That evening, while Hermione lay naked on the bed, he cleared a wardrobe for her in the dressing room and hung her clothes and stowed her shoes. He took a shower, then they dressed for dinner. He went downstairs to arrange on two plates the meal Abeje had prepared for him. It only needed reheating. Then he went back to the bedroom to fetch her down to the splendid dining room. They ate in silence. In fact, she didn't touch her food and wouldn't meet his eye. He understood why. The tension between them was almost unbearable – one reason why he drank two bottles of wine. *He was so drunk he had to carry her up the stairs.*

What a night! He was one of those men *for whom passivity in a woman was a goad, a piercing enticement.* Even in rapture he saw the boredom in her eyes that brought him to fresh heights of ecstasy. Finally, not long before dawn, they rolled apart, sated, immobilised by a profound exhaustion. Hours later, aroused by sunlight through the curtains, he managed to turn onto his side. It touched him profoundly that she had slept the night through on her back. *He delighted in her stillness. Her inwardness was so intense that it rolled back upon itself to become its opposite, a force that overwhelmed and consumed him and drove his love onwards to constant sensuous obsession.* What had started as an idle fantasy outside a shop window was now an intact inner world, a vertiginous reality he preserved with the fervour of a religious fanatic. He couldn't allow himself to consider her inanimate because his pleasure in love depended on a masochistic understanding that she was *ignoring him, she disdained him and thought he was not worthy of her kisses, of her caresses, or even of her conversation.*

When Abeje came in to tidy and clean the bedroom, she was surprised to find Hermione in a corner staring out of the window, wearing a dress of torn silk. But the housekeeper was pleased to discover in one of the wardrobes a rack of fine dresses. She was an intelligent woman of the world and she had been aware of, and somewhat oppressed by, her employer's lingering, ineffectual gaze as she went about her work. Now he had a lover. What a relief. If his woman imported a dummy to hang her clothes on, who cared? As the extreme disorder of the bedlinen suggested, and as she relayed it in her native Yoruba that night to embolden her muscular husband, *They are truly singing.*

Even in the most richly communicative and reciprocal love affairs, it is nearly impossible to sustain that initial state of rapture beyond a few weeks. Historically, a resourceful few may have managed months. *But when the sexual terrain is tended by one mind alone, one lonely figure tilling the frontiers of a wilderness, the fall must come in days.* What nourished Carder's love – Hermione's silence – was bound to destroy it. She had been living with him less than a week when he observed a shift in her mood, a near imperceptible recalibration of her silence that contained the faint but constant note, almost beyond hearing, of dissatisfaction. Driven by this tinnitus of doubt, he strove harder to please her. That night, when they were upstairs, a suspicion passed through his mind and he experienced a thrill – it really was a thrill – of horror. *She was thinking about someone else.* She had that same look he had observed through the store window as she stood apart from the guests and gazed into the corner. She wanted to be elsewhere. When he made love to her, the agony of this realisation was inseparable from the pleasure, sharp as a surgeon's scalpel, that seemed to slice his heart in two. But it was only a suspicion after all, he thought as he retreated to his side of the bed. He slept deeply that night.

What revived his doubts the next morning was a parallel shift in Abeje's attitude as she served him his breakfast (Hermione always stayed in bed until noon). His housekeeper was both brisk and evasive. She wouldn't meet his eye. The coffee was lukewarm and weak and when he complained, he thought she was surly. When she brought in another pot, hot and strong, so she said as she put it down, it came to him. It was simple. The truth was always simple. They were lovers, Hermione and Abeje. Furtive and fleeting. Whenever he was out of the house. For who else had Hermione seen since she arrived? Hence that look of distracted longing. Hence Abeje's abrupt performance this morning. Hence everything. He was a fool, an innocent fool.

The unravelling was swift. That night the surgeon's knife was sharper, cut deeper, with a twist. And he knew Hermione knew. He saw it in the blankness of her terror. *Her crime was his reckless empowerment. He tore into her with all the savagery of disappointed love, and his fingers were round her throat as she came, as they both came. And when he was done, her arms and legs and head had parted company with her torso, which he dashed against the bedroom wall. She lay in all corners, a ruined woman.* This time there was no consoling sleep. In the morning he concealed her body parts in a plastic sack and carried her and all her belongings to the dustbins. In a daze he wrote a note (he was in no mood for further confrontation) to Abeje to inform her of her dismissal 'forthwith' and left on the kitchen table her wages to the end of the month. He went for a long and purging walk across the Heath. That night, Abeje opened up the plastic bags she had retrieved from the bins and modelled the outfits for her husband – the jewels and shoes as well as the silky frocks. She told him haltingly in his native Kanuri (they had married out of their tribes), *She left him and it broke him up.*

Thereafter, Carder lived alone and 'did' for himself and shrank into middle age with minimal dignity. The whole experience bequeathed him nothing. There were no lessons for him, no reckoning, *for though he, an ordinary fellow, had discovered for himself the awesome power of the imagination, he tried not to think of what had happened. He decided to banish the affair utterly, and such is the efficiency of the compartmentalised mind, he succeeded. He forgot all about her. And he never lived so intensely again.*

10

Max had told me his new office was smaller than a broom cupboard, but it was slightly larger. More than a dozen brooms could have been stored vertically between the desk and the door, and a few more between his chair and the walls. However, there was no space for a window. The room formed a narrow triangle, with Max squeezed in at the apex while I sat with my back to the base. The door wouldn't close properly, so there was no real privacy. Since it opened inwards, I would have had to stand and push my chair under the desk if someone had wanted to come in. On the desk was a pile of headed paper with Freedom International Foundation's address in Upper Regent Street, and a Picassoesque ascending dove holding an open book in its beak. We each had in front of us a copy of the Foundation's brochure, whose cover bore the single word 'freedom' at a slant in uneven red lettering that suggested a rubber stamp. Freedom International, a registered charity, promoted 'excellence and freedom of expression in the arts everywhere in the world'. It was not easily dismissed. It had subsidised or supported by translation or roundabout means writers in Yugoslavia, Brazil, Chile, Cuba, Syria, Romania and Hungary, a dance troupe in Paraguay, journalists in Franco's Spain and Salazar's Portugal and poets in the Soviet Union. It had given money to an actors' collective in Harlem, New York, a baroque orchestra in Alabama, and successfully campaigned for the abolition of the Lord Chamberlain's power over the British theatre.

'It's a decent outfit,' Max said. 'I hope you'll agree. They take their stands everywhere. No one's going to confuse them with those IRD apparatchiks. Altogether more subtle.'

He was wearing a dark blue suit. Far better than the mustard jacket he'd been wearing every other day. And because he was growing his hair, his ears looked less protuberant. The only light source in the room, a high single bulb under a tin shade, picked out his cheekbones and the bow of his lips. He looked sleek and beautiful and quite incongruous in the narrow room, like an animal trapped in an undersized cage.

I said, 'Why was Shirley Shilling sacked?'

He didn't blink at the change of subject. 'I was hoping you might know.'

'Something to do with me?'

'Look, the thing about working in places like this . . . you have all these colleagues, they're pleasant, charming, good backgrounds and all that. Unless you do operations together you don't know what they're up to, what their work is and whether they're any good at it. You don't know whether they're beaming idiots or friendly geniuses. Suddenly they're promoted or sacked and you've no idea why. That's how it is.'

I didn't believe he knew nothing. There was a silence as we let the matter rest. Since Max told me by the gates of Hyde Park that he was becoming attached to me we had spent very little time together. I sensed he was moving up the hierarchy, out of my reach.

He said, 'I got the impression at the meeting the other day that you don't know much about IRD. Information Research Department. It doesn't officially exist. Set up in 'forty-eight, part of the Foreign Office, works out of Carlton Terrace, the idea being to feed information about the Soviet Union into the public domain through friendly journalists, news agencies, put out fact sheets, issue rebuttals, encourage certain publications. So – labour camps, no rule of law, rotten standards of living, repression of dissent, usual stuff. Generally helping out the NCL, the non-communist left, and anything to puncture fantasies here about life in the East. But IRD is drifting. Last year it was trying to persuade the left that we need to join Europe. Ridiculous. And thank God we're taking Northern Ireland off them. It did good work in its day. Now it's too bloated and crude. And rather irrelevant. The word is that it's going to be cut soon. But what matters in this building is that IRD's become the creature of MI6, got itself sucked into black propaganda, deception exercises that deceive no one. Their reports come out of dodgy sources. IRD and its so-called Action Desk have been helping Six to relive the last war. It's Boy Scout nonsense they go in for. That's why everyone in Five likes that "faces to the wall" story Peter Nutting told.'

I said, 'Is it true?'

'I doubt it. But it makes Six look idiotic and pompous, so it goes down well here. Anyway, the idea with Sweet

Tooth is to strike out on our own, independently of Six or the Americans. Having a novelist was an afterthought, Peter's whim. Personally, I think it's a mistake – too unpredictable. But this is what we're doing. The writer doesn't have to be a Cold War fanatic. Just be sceptical about utopias in the East or looming catastrophe in the West – you know the sort of thing.'

'What happens when the writer discovers we've been paying his rent? He's going to be furious.'

Max looked away. I thought I'd asked a stupid question. But after a moment's silence he said, 'The link between us and Freedom International works at several removes. Even if you knew exactly where to look, you'd have your work cut out. The calculation is that, if anything comes out, writers will prefer to avoid the embarrassment. They'll stay quiet. And if they don't, we'll explain there are ways of proving that they always knew where the money was coming from. And the money will keep on flowing. A fellow can get used to a certain way of living and be reluctant to lose it.'

'Blackmail then.'

He shrugged. 'Look, the IRD in its heyday never told Orwell or Koestler what to put in their books. But it did what it could to make sure their ideas got the best circulation around the world. We're dealing with free spirits. We don't tell them what to think. We enable them to do their work. Over there free spirits used to be marched to the gulags. Now Soviet psychiatry's the new State terror. To oppose the system is to be criminally insane. Here we've got some Labour Party and union people and university profs and students and so-called intellectuals who'll tell you the US is no better—'

'Bombing Vietnam.'

'Well, all right. But across the Third World there are whole populations who think the Soviet Union has something to teach them about liberty. The fight isn't over yet. We want to encourage the right good thing. As Peter sees it, Serena, you love literature, you love your country. He thinks this is perfect for you.'

'But you don't.'

'I think we should stick to non-fiction.'

I couldn't work him out. There was something impersonal in his manner. He didn't like Sweet Tooth, or my bit of it, but he was calm about it, even bland. He was like a bored shop assistant encouraging me to buy a dress he knew wasn't right. I wanted to throw him off balance, bring him closer. He was taking me through the details. I was to use my real name. I was to go to Upper Regent Street and meet the Foundation staff. As they understood it, I worked for the organisation called Word Unpenned, which was donating funds to Freedom International to distribute to recommended writers. When I eventually travelled to Brighton I was to make sure that I took nothing with me that would connect me to Leconfield House.

I wondered if Max thought I was stupid. I interrupted him and said, 'What if I like Haley?'

'Fine. We'll sign him up.'

'I mean, really like him.'

He looked up sharply from his check list. 'If you think you'd rather not take this on . . .' His tone was cold and I was pleased.

'Max,' I said, 'it was a joke.'

'Let's talk about your letter to him. I'll need to see a draft.'

So we discussed that and other arrangements and I realised that as far as he was concerned, we were no longer close friends. I could no longer ask him to kiss me. But I wasn't prepared to accept that. I picked up my handbag from the floor and opened it and took out a packet of paper tissues. It was only the year before that I'd stopped using cotton handkerchiefs with broderie anglaise edging and my initials monogrammed in pink in one corner – a Christmas present from my mother. Paper tissues were becoming ubiquitous, like supermarket trolleys. The world was starting to become seriously disposable. I dabbed at a corner of my eye, trying to make my decision. Resting curled in my bag was the triangle of paper with the pencil marks. I'd changed my mind. It was exactly the right thing to do, to show it to Max. Or it was exactly the wrong thing. There was nothing in between.

'Are you all right?'

'Touch of hayfever.'

Finally I thought what I had thought many times before, that it was better, or at least more interesting, to have Max lie to me, than to know nothing at all. I took out the fragment of newsprint and slid it across the desk towards him. He glanced at it, turned it over, turned it back, set it down and looked fixedly at me.

'Well?'

I said, 'Canning and the island whose name you so cleverly guessed.'

'Where did you get it?'

'If I tell you, are you going to be straight with me?'

He said nothing, so I told him anyway, about the Fulham safe house and the single bed and its mattress.

'Who was with you?'

I told him and he said 'Ah' quietly into his hands. Then he said, 'So they sacked her.'

'Meaning?'

He pulled his hands apart in a gesture of helplessness. I wasn't cleared to know.

'May I hold on to this?'

'Certainly not.' I snatched it off the desk before he could move his hand and stowed it in my bag.

He softly cleared his throat. 'Then we should move to the next item. The stories. What are you going to say to him?'

'Very excited, brilliant new talent, extraordinary range, lovely sinuous prose, deeply sensitive, especially about women, seems to know and understand them from the inside, unlike most men, dying to know him better and—'

'Serena, enough!'

'And sure that he has a great future, one that the Foundation would like to be a part of. Especially if he'll consider writing a novel. Prepared to pay – how much?'

'Two thousand a year.'

'For how many—'

'Two years. Renewable.'

'My God. How's he going to refuse?'

'Because a complete stranger will be sitting on his lap licking his face. Be cooler. Make him come to you. The Foundation is interested, considering his case, lots of other candidates, what are his future plans, etc.?'

'Fine. I play hard to get. Then I'll give him everything.'

Max sat back, folded his arms, glanced at the ceiling and said, 'Serena, I'm sorry you're upset. I honestly don't know why Shilling was sacked, I don't know about your piece of paper. That's it. But look, it's only fair that I tell you something about myself.'

He was about to tell me what I already suspected, that he was a homosexual. Now I was ashamed. I hadn't wanted to force a confession out of him.

'I'm telling you because we've been good friends.'

'Yes.'

'But it mustn't leave this room.'

'No!'

'I'm engaged to be married.'

I suspected that in the fraction of a second it took me to rearrange my expression, he glimpsed the heart of my confusion.

'But that's fantastic news. Who's—'

'She's not in Five. Ruth's a doctor at Guy's. Our families have always been very close.'

My words were out before I could snatch them back. 'An arranged marriage!'

But Max only laughed shyly and there may have been the hint of a blush, hard to detect in the yellowish light. So perhaps I was right, the parents who had chosen his studies, who wouldn't let him work with his hands, had chosen his wife. Remembering that vulnerability in him I felt the first chill of sorrow. I had missed out. And there was self-pity too. People told me I was beautiful and I believed them. I should have been wafted through life with the special dispensation that beauty bestows, discarding men at every turn. Instead, they abandoned me, or died on me. Or married.

Max said, 'I thought I should tell you.'

'Yes. Thanks.'

'We won't be announcing it for another couple of months.'

'Of course not.'

Max briskly squared his notes against the desk. The distasteful business was concluded and we could continue. He said, 'What did you really think of the stories? That one about the twin brothers.'

'I thought it was very good.'

'I thought it was awful. I couldn't believe that an atheist would know his Bible. Or dress up as a vicar to deliver a sermon.'

'Brotherly love.'

'But he's not capable of any sort of love. He's a cad, and he's weak. I couldn't see why we should care about him or what happens to him.'

My impression was that we were really talking about Haley, not Edmund Alfredus. There was something strained in Max's tone. I thought I'd succeeded in making him jealous. I said, 'I thought he was extremely attractive. Clever, brilliant public speaker, sense of mischief, took interesting risks. Just no match for – what's her name? – Jean.'

'I couldn't believe in her at all. These destructive men-eating women are just fantasies of a certain kind of man.'

'What kind of man is that?'

'Oh I don't know. Masochistic. Guilty. Or self-hating. Perhaps you can tell me when you get back.'

He stood to indicate the meeting was over. I couldn't tell whether he was angry. I wondered whether in some perverse way he thought it was my fault he was getting married. Or perhaps he was angry with himself. Or my arranged marriage remark had offended him.

'Do you really think Haley's not right for us?'

153

'That's Nutting's department. What's odd is sending you down to Brighton. We don't usually get our own involved like this. The usual way would be to get the Foundation to send someone, do it all at one remove. Besides, I think the whole thing's, well, anyway, it's not my, um . . .'

He was leaning forward on his fingertips which were splayed against the desk and he seemed to be indicating the door behind me by faintly inclining his head. Throwing me out with minimal effort. But I didn't want the conversation to end.

'There's one other thing, Max. You're the only one I could say this to. I think I'm being followed.'

'Really? Quite an achievement at your level.'

I ignored this sneer. 'I'm not talking about Moscow Centre. I mean the Watchers. Someone's been in my room.'

Since my conversation with Shirley, I'd looked around carefully on the way home, but I'd seen nothing suspicious. But I didn't know what to look for. It wasn't part of our training. I had some vague notions derived from films and I'd doubled back on myself in the street, and I'd peered into hundreds of rush-hour faces. I'd tried getting on the Tube and straight off, and achieved nothing beyond a longer journey to Camden.

But I achieved my purpose now, for Max was sitting down and the conversation resumed. His face had gone hard, he looked older.

'How do you know?'

'Oh, you know, things out of place in my room. I suppose the Watchers can be rather clumsy.'

He looked at me steadily. I was already beginning to feel foolish.

'Serena, be careful. If you pretend to know more than you do, if you pretend to knowledge that hardly tallies with a few months in the Registry, you'll give the wrong impression. After the Cambridge Three and George Blake, people are still nervous and a bit demoralised. They jump to conclusions rather too quickly. So stop acting as though you know more than you do. You end up getting followed. In fact, I think that's your problem.'

'Is this a guess or something you know?'

'It's a friendly warning.'

'So I really am being followed.'

'I'm a relatively lowly figure here. I'd be the last to know. People have seen us around together . . .'

'Not any more, Max. Perhaps our friendship was harming your career prospects.'

It was shallow stuff. I couldn't quite admit to myself how upset I was by the news of his engagement. His self-control irritated me. I wanted to provoke and punish him and here it was, I had my wish, he was on his feet, fairly quivering.

'Are women really incapable of keeping their professional and private lives apart? I'm trying to help you, Serena. You're not listening. Let me put it another way. In this work the line between what people imagine and what's actually the case can get very blurred. In fact that line is a big grey space, big enough to get lost in. You imagine things – and you can make them come true. The ghosts become real. Am I making sense?'

I didn't think he was. I was on my feet with a clever retort ready, but he'd had enough of me. Before I could speak he said more quietly, 'Best to go now. Just do your own work. Keep things simple.'

I was intending to make a stormy exit. But I had to slide my chair under his desk and squeeze round it to get out, and when I was out in the corridor I couldn't slam the door behind me because it was warped in its frame.

11

This was a bureaucracy and delay followed as though by policy directive. My draft letter to Haley was submitted to Max, who made alterations to this as well as my second attempt, and, when at last a third was passed on to Peter Nutting and to Benjamin Trescott, I waited almost three weeks for their notes. They were incorporated, Max put in some final touches, and I posted the fifth and final version five weeks after my first. A month went by and we heard nothing. Enquiries were made on our behalf and eventually we learned that Haley was abroad for research. It was not until late September that we had his reply, scrawled at a slant on a lined sheet torn from a notepad. It looked deliberately insouciant. He wrote that he would be interested to know more. He was making ends meet by working as a postgraduate teacher, which meant he now had an office on the campus. Better to meet there, he said, because his flat was rather cramped.

I had a short final briefing with Max.

He said, 'What about that *Paris Review* story, the one about the shop-window dummy?'

'I thought it was interesting.'

'Serena! It was completely implausible. Anyone that deluded would be in the secure wing of a psychiatric institution.'

'How do you know he isn't?'

'Then Haley should have let the reader know.'

He told me as I was leaving his office that three Sweet Tooth writers had accepted the Freedom International stipend. I was not to let him or myself down by failing to nail down a fourth.

'I thought I had to play hard to get.'

'We've fallen behind everyone else. Peter's getting impatient. Even if he's no good, just sign him up.'

It was a pleasant break in routine to travel down to Brighton one unseasonably warm morning in mid-October, to cross the cavernous railway station and smell the salty air and hear the falling cries of herring gulls. I remembered the word from a summer Shakespeare production of *Othello* on the lawn at King's. A gull. Was I looking for a gull? Certainly not. I took the dilapidated three-carriage Lewes train and got out at the Falmer stop to walk the quarter mile to the red-brick building site called the University of Sussex, or, as it was known in the press for a while, Balliol-by-the-Sea. I was wearing a red mini-skirt and black jacket with high collar, black high heels and a white patent leather shoulder bag on a short strap. Ignoring the pain in my feet, I swanked along the paved approach to the main entrance through the student crowds, disdainful of the boys – I regarded them as boys – shaggily dressed out of army surplus stores, and even more so of the girls with their long plain centre-parted hair, no make-up and cheesecloth skirts. Some students were barefoot, in sympathy, I assumed, with peasants of the undeveloped world. The very word 'campus' seemed to me a frivolous import from the USA. As I self-consciously strode towards Sir Basil Spence's creation in a fold of the Sussex Downs, I felt dismissive of the idea of a new university. For the first time in my life I was proud of my Cambridge and Newnham connection. How could a serious university be *new*? And how could anyone resist me in my confection of red, white and black, intolerantly scissoring my way towards the porters' desk, where I intended to ask directions?

I entered what was probably an architectural reference to a quad. It was flanked by shallow water features, rectangular ponds lined with smooth river-bed stones. But the water had been drained off to make way for beer cans and sandwich wrappers. From the brick, stone and glass structure ahead of me came the throb and wail of rock music. I recognised the rasping, heaving flute of Jethro Tull. Through the plate-glass windows on the first floor I could see figures, players and spectators, hunched over banks of table football. The students' union, surely. The same everywhere, these places, reserved for the exclusive use of lunk-headed boys, mathematicians and chemists mostly. The girls and the aesthetes went elsewhere. As a portal to a university it made a poor impression. I quickened my pace, resenting the way my stride fell in with the pounding drums. It was like approaching a holiday camp.

The paved way passed under the students' union and here I turned through glass doors to a reception area. At least the porters in their uniforms behind a long counter were familiar to me – that special breed of men with their air of weary tolerance, and gruff certainty of being wiser than any student had ever been. With the music fading behind me, I followed their directions, crossed a wide open space, went under giant concrete rugby posts to enter Arts Block A and came out the other side to approach Arts Block B. Couldn't they name their buildings after artists or philosophers? Inside, I turned down a corridor, noting the items posted on the teachers' doors. A tacked-up card that said, 'The world is everything that is the case', a Black Panthers poster, something in German by Hegel, something in French by Merleau-Ponty. Show-offs. Right at the end of a second corridor was Haley's room. I hesitated outside it before knocking.

I was at the corridor's dead-end, standing by a tall, narrow window that gave onto a square of lawn. The light was such that I had a watery reflection of myself, so I took out a comb and quickly tidied my hair and straightened my collar. If I was slightly nervous it was because in the past weeks I had become intimate with my own private version of Haley, I had read his thoughts on sex and deceit, pride and failure. We were on terms already and I knew they were about to be reformed or destroyed. Whatever he was in reality would be a surprise and probably a disappointment. As soon as we shook hands our intimacy would go into reverse. I had re-read all the journalism on the way down to Brighton. Unlike the fiction it was sensible, sceptical, rather schoolmasterish in tone, as if he'd supposed he was writing for ideological fools. The article on the East German uprising of 1953 began 'Let no one think the Workers' State loves its workers. It hates them', and was scornful of the Brecht poem about the government dissolving the people and electing another. Brecht's first impulse, in Haley's account, was to 'toady' to the German State by giving public support to the brutal Soviet suppression of the strikes. Russian soldiers had fired directly into the crowds. Without knowing much about him, I'd always assumed that Brecht had sided with the angels. I didn't know if Haley was right, or how to reconcile his plain-speaking journalism with the crafty intimacy of the fiction, and I assumed that when we met I would know even less.

A feistier piece excoriated West German novelists as weak-minded cowards for ignoring in their fiction the Berlin Wall. Of course they loathed its existence, but they feared that saying so would seem to align them with American foreign policy. And yet it was a brilliant and necessary subject, uniting the geopolitical with personal tragedy. Surely, every British writer would have something to say about a London Wall. Would Norman Mailer ignore a wall that divided Washington? Would Philip Roth prefer not to notice if the houses of Newark were cut in two? Would John Updike's characters not seize the opportunity of a marital affair across a divided New England? This pampered, over-subsidised literary culture, protected from Soviet repression by the pax Americana, preferred to hate the hand that kept it free. West German writers pretended the Wall didn't exist and thereby lost all moral authority. The title of the essay, published in *Index on Censorship*, was 'La Trahison des Clercs'.

With a pearly pink painted nail I tapped lightly on the door and, at the sound of an indistinct murmur or groan, pushed it open. I was right to have prepared

161

myself for disappointment. It was a slight figure who rose from his desk, slightly stooped, though he made the effort to straighten his back as he stood. He was girlishly slender, with narrow wrists and his hand when I shook it seemed smaller and softer than mine. Skin very pale, eyes dark green, hair dark brown and long, and cut in a style that was almost a bob. In those first few seconds I wondered if I'd missed a transsexual element in the stories. But here he was, twin brother, smug vicar, smart and rising Labour MP, lonely million-aire in love with an inanimate object. He wore a collarless shirt made of flecked white flannel, tight jeans with a broad belt and scuffed leather boots. I was confused by him. The voice from such a delicate frame was deep, without regional accent, classless.

'Let me clear these things away so you can sit.'

He shifted some books from an armless soft chair. I thought, with a touch of annoyance, that he was letting me know that he had made no special preparations for my arrival.

'Was your journey down all right? Would you like some coffee?'

The journey was pleasant, I told him, and I didn't need coffee.

He sat down at his desk and swivelled his chair to face me, crossed an ankle over a knee and with a little smile opened out his palms in an interrogative manner. 'So, Miss Frome . . .'

'It rhymes with plume. But please call me Serena.'

He cocked his head to one side as he repeated my name. Then his eyes settled softly on mine and he waited. I noted the long eyelashes. I'd rehearsed this moment and it was

162

easy enough to lay it all out for him. Truthfully. The work of Freedom International, its wide remit, its extensive global reach, its open-mindedness and lack of ideology. He listened to me, head still cocked, and with a look of amused scepticism, his lips quivering slightly as though at any moment he was ready to join in or take over and make my words his own, or improve upon them. He wore the expression of a man listening to an extended joke, anticipating an explosive punchline with held-in delight that puffs and puckers his lips. As I named the writers and artists the Foundation had helped, I fantasised that he had already seen right through me and had no intention of letting me know. He was forcing me to make my pitch so he could observe a liar at close hand. Useful for a later fiction. Horrified, I pushed the idea away and forgot about it. I needed to concentrate. I moved on to talk about the source of the Foundation's wealth. Max thought Haley should be told just how rich Freedom International was. The money came from an endowment by the artistic widow of a Bulgarian immigrant to the USA who had made his money buying and exploiting patents in the twenties and thirties. In the years following his death, his wife bought up Impressionist paintings after the war from a ruined Europe at pre-war prices. In the last year of her life she had fallen for a culturally inclined politician who was setting up the Foundation. She left her and her husband's fortune to his project.

Everything I had said so far had been the case, easily verified. Now I took my first tentative step into mendacity. 'I'll be quite frank with you,' I said. 'I sometimes feel Freedom International doesn't have enough projects to throw its money at.'

'How flattering then,' Haley said. Perhaps he saw me blush because he added, 'I didn't mean to be rude.'

'You misunderstand me, Mr Haley . . .'

'Tom.'

'Tom. Sorry. I put that badly. What I meant was this. There are plenty of artists being imprisoned or oppressed by unsavoury governments. We do everything we can to help these people and get their work known. But, of course, being censored doesn't necessarily mean a writer or sculptor is any good. For example, we've found ourselves supporting a terrible playwright in Poland simply because his work is banned. And we'll go on supporting him. And we've bought up any amount of rubbish by an imprisoned Hungarian abstract impressionist. So the steering committee has decided to add another dimension to the portfolio. We want to encourage excellence wherever we can find it, oppressed or not. We're especially interested in young people at the beginning of their careers . . .'

'And how old are you, Serena?' Tom Haley leaned forward solicitously, as if asking about a serious illness.

I told him. He was letting me know he was not to be patronised. And it was true, in my nervousness I had taken on a distant, official tone. I needed to relax, be less pompous, I needed to call him Tom. I realised I wasn't much good at any of this. He asked me if I'd been at university. I told him, and said the name of my college.

'What was your subject?'

I hesitated, I tripped over my words. I hadn't expected to be asked, and suddenly mathematics sounded suspect and without knowing what I was doing I said, 'English.'

He smiled pleasantly, appearing pleased at finding common ground. 'I suppose you got a brilliant first?'

'A two one actually.' I didn't know what I was saying. A third sounded shameful, a first would have set me on dangerous ground. I had told two unnecessary lies. Bad form. For all I knew, a phone call to Newnham would establish there had been no Serena Frome doing English. I hadn't expected to be interrogated. Such basic preparatory work, and I'd failed to do it. Why hadn't Max thought of helping me towards a decent watertight personal story? I felt flustered and sweaty, I imagined myself jumping up without a word, snatching up my bag, fleeing from the room.

Tom was looking at me in that way he had, both kindly and ironic. 'My guess is that you were expecting a first. But listen, there's nothing wrong with a two one.'

'I was disappointed,' I said, recovering a little. 'There was this, um, general, um . . .'

'Weight of expectation?'

Our eyes met for a little more than two or three seconds, and then I looked away. Having read him, knowing too well one corner of his mind, I found it hard to look him in the eye for long. I let my gaze drop below his chin and noticed a fine silver chain around his neck.

'So you were saying, writers at the beginning of their careers.' He was self-consciously playing the part of the friendly don, coaxing a nervous applicant through her entrance interview. I knew I had to get back on top.

I said, 'Look, Mr Haley . . .'

'Tom.'

'I don't want to waste your time. We take advice from very good, very expert people. They've given a lot of thought to this. They like your journalism, and they love your stories. Really love them. The hope is . . .'

'And you. Have you read them?'

'Of course.'

'And what did you think?'

'I'm really just the messenger. It's not relevant what I think.'

'It's relevant to me. What did you make of them?'

The room appeared to darken. I looked past him, out of the window. There was a grass strip, and the corner of another building. I could see into a room like the one we were in, where a tutorial was in progress. A girl not much younger than me was reading aloud her essay. At her side was a boy in a bomber jacket, bearded chin resting in his hand, nodding sagely. The tutor had her back to me. I turned my gaze back into our room, wondering if I was not overdoing this significant pause. Our eyes met again and I forced myself to hold on. Such a strange dark green, such long childlike lashes, and thick black eyebrows. But there was hesitancy in his gaze, he was about to look away, and this time the power had passed to me.

I said very quietly, 'I think they're utterly brilliant.'

He flinched as though someone had poked him in the chest, in the heart, and he gave a little gasp, not quite a laugh. He went to speak but was stuck for words. He stared at me, waiting, wanting me to go on, tell him more about himself and his talent, but I held back. I thought my words would have more power for being undiluted. And I wasn't sure I could trust myself to say anything profound. Between us a certain formality had been peeled away to expose an embarrassing secret. I'd revealed his hunger for affirmation, praise, anything I might give. I guessed that nothing mattered more to him. His stories in the various reviews had probably gone unremarked, beyond a routine thanks and pat on the head from an editor. It was likely that no one, no stranger at least, had ever told him that his fiction was brilliant. Now he was hearing it and realising that he had always suspected it was so. I had delivered stupendous news. How could he have known if he was any good until someone confirmed it? And now he knew it was true and he was grateful.

As soon as he spoke, the moment was broken and the room resumed its normal tone. 'Did you have a favourite?'

It was such a stupid, sheepish excuse of a question that I warmed to him for his vulnerability. 'They're all remarkable,' I said. 'But the one about the twin brothers, "This Is Love", is the most ambitious. I thought it had the scale of a novel. A novel about belief and emotion. And what a wonderful character Jean is, so insecure and destructive and alluring. It's a magnificent piece of work. Did you ever think of expanding it into a novel, you know, filling it out a bit?'

He looked at me curiously. 'No, I didn't think of filling it out a bit.' The deadpan reiteration of my words alarmed me.

'I'm sorry, it was a stupid . . .'

'It's the length I wanted. About fifteen thousand words. But I'm glad you liked it.'

Sardonic and teasing, he smiled and I was forgiven, but my advantage had dimmed. I had never heard fiction quantified in this technical way. My ignorance felt like a weight on my tongue.

I said, 'And "Lovers", the man with the shop-window mannequin, was so strange and completely convincing, it swept everyone away.' It was now liberating to be telling outright lies. 'We have two professors and two well-known reviewers on our board. They see a lot of new writing. But you should have heard the excitement at the last meeting. Honestly, Tom, they couldn't stop talking about your stories. For the first time ever the vote was unanimous.'

The little smile had faded. His eyes had a glazed look, as though I was hypnotising him. This was going deep.

'Well,' he said, shaking his head to bring himself out of the trance. 'This is all very pleasing. What else can I say?' Then he added, 'Who are the two critics?'

'We have to respect their anonymity, I'm afraid.'

'I see.'

He turned away from me for a moment and seemed lost in some private thought. Then he said, 'So, what is it you're offering, and what do you want from me?'

'Can I answer that by asking you a question? What will you do when you've finished your doctorate?'

'I'm applying for various teaching jobs, including one here.'

'Full time?'

'Yes.'

'We'd like to make it possible for you to stay out of a job. In return you'd concentrate on your writing, including journalism if you want.'

He asked me how much money was on offer and I told him. He asked for how long and I said, 'Let's say two or three years.'

'And if I produce nothing?'

'We'd be disappointed and we'd move on. We won't be asking for our money back.'

He took this in and then said, 'And you'd want the rights in what I do?'

'No. And we don't ask you to show us your work. You don't even have to acknowledge us. The Foundation thinks you're a unique and extraordinary talent. If your fiction and journalism get written, published and read, then we'll be happy. When your career is launched and you can support yourself we'll fade out of your life. We'll have met the terms of our remit.'

He stood up and went round the far side of his desk and stood at the window with his back to me. He ran his hand through his hair and muttered something sibilant under his breath that may have been 'Ridiculous', or perhaps, 'Enough of this'. He was looking into the same room across the lawn. Now the bearded boy was reading his essay while his tutorial partner stared ahead of her without expression. Oddly, the tutor was speaking on the phone.

Tom returned to his chair and crossed his arms. His gaze was directed across my shoulder and his lips were pressed shut. I sensed he was about to make a serious objection.

I said, 'Think it over for a day or two, talk to a friend . . . Think it through.'

He said, 'The thing is . . .' and he trailed away. He looked down at his lap and he continued. 'It's this. Every day I think about this problem. I don't have anything bigger to think about. It keeps me awake at night. Always the same four steps. One, I want to write a novel. Two, I'm broke. Three, I've got to get a job. Four, the job will kill the writing. I can't see a way round it. There isn't one. Then a nice young woman knocks on my door and offers me a fat pension for nothing. It's too good to be true. I'm suspicious.'

'Tom, you make it sound simpler than it is. You're not passive in this affair. The first move was yours. You wrote these brilliant stories. In London people are beginning to talk about you. How else do you think we found you? You've made your own luck with talent and hard work.'

The ironic smile, the cocked head – progress.

He said, 'I like it when you say brilliant.'

'Good. Brilliant, brilliant, brilliant.' I reached into my bag on the floor and took out the Foundation's brochure. 'This is the work we do. You can come to the office in Upper Regent Street and talk to the people there. You'll like them.'

'You'll be there too?'

'My immediate employer is Word Unpenned. We work closely with Freedom International and are putting money their way. They help us find the artists. I travel a lot or work from home. But messages to the Foundation office will find me.'

He glanced at his watch and stood, so I did too. I was a dutiful young woman, determined to achieve what was expected of me. I wanted Haley to agree now, before lunch, to be kept by us. I would break the news by phone to Max in the afternoon and by tomorrow morning I hoped to have a routine note of congratulation from Peter Nutting, un-emphatic, unsigned, typed by someone else, but important to me.

'I'm not asking you to commit to anything now,' I said, hoping I didn't sound like I was pleading. 'You're not bound to anything at all. Just give me the say-so and I'll arrange a monthly payment. All I need is your bank details.'

The say-so? I'd never used that word in my life. He

blinked in assent, but not to the money so much as to my general drift. We were standing less than six feet apart. His waist was slender and through some disorder in his shirt I caught a glimpse below a button of skin and downy hair above his navel.

'Thanks,' he said. 'I'll think about it very carefully. I've got to be in London on Friday. I could look in at your office.'

'Well then,' I said and put out my hand. He took it, but it wasn't a handshake. He took my fingers in his palm and stroked them with his thumb, just one slow pass. Exactly that, a pass, and he was looking at me steadily. As I took my hand away, I let my own thumb brush along the length of his forefinger. I think we may have been about to move closer when there was a hearty, ridiculously loud knock on the door. He stepped back from me as he called, 'Come in.' The door swung open and there stood two girls, centre-parted blonde hair, fading suntans, sandals and painted toenails, bare arms, sweet expectant smiles, unbearably pretty. The books and papers under their arms didn't look at all plausible to me.

'Aha,' Tom said. 'Our *Faerie Queene* tutorial.'

I was edging round him towards the door. 'I haven't read that one,' I said.

He laughed, and the two girls joined in, as if I'd made a wonderful joke. They probably didn't believe me.

12

I was the only passenger in my carriage on the early afternoon train back to London. As we left the South Downs behind and sped across the Sussex Weald, I tried to work off my agitation by walking up and down the aisle. I sat for a couple of minutes, then I was back on my feet. I blamed myself for a lack of persistence. I should have waited out the hour until his teaching was over, forced him to have lunch with me, gone through it all again, got his consent. But that wasn't it really. I'd come away without his home address. Nor that. Something may or may not have started between us, but it was just a touch – almost nothing at all. I should have stayed and built on it, left with a little more, a bridge to our next meeting. One deep kiss on that mouth that wanted to do my talking for me. I was bothered by the memory of the skin between the shirt buttons, the pale hair in a whorl around the edges of the navel, and the light and slender childlike body. I took up one of his stories to re-read but my attention soon slipped. I thought of getting off at Haywards Heath and going back. Would I have been so troubled if he hadn't caressed my fingers? I thought I would. Might the touch of his thumb have been entirely accidental? Impossible. He meant it, he was telling me. *Stay.* But when the train stopped, I didn't move, I didn't trust myself. Look what happened, I thought, when I threw myself at Max.

Sebastian Morel is a teacher of French at a large comprehensive school near Tufnell Park, north London. He is married to Monica and they have two children, a girl and a boy aged seven and four, and they live in a rented terraced house near Finsbury Park. Sebastian's work is *tough, pointless and ill-paid*, the pupils are insolent and unruly. Sometimes he spends his entire day trying to keep order in class and handing out punishments he doesn't believe in. He marvels at how irrelevant knowledge of rudimentary French is to the lives of these kids. *He wanted to like them, but he was repelled by their ignorance and aggression and the way they jeered at and bullied any of their number who dared to show an interest in learning. In this way they kept themselves down.* Nearly all of them will leave school as soon as they can and get unskilled jobs or get pregnant or make do with unemployment benefit. He wants to help them. Sometimes he pities them, sometimes he struggles to suppress his contempt.

He is in his early thirties, *a wiry man of exceptional strength*. At university in Manchester, Sebastian was a keen mountaineer and led expeditions in Norway, Chile and Austria. But these days he no longer gets out onto the heights because his life is too constrained, there is never enough money or time and his spirits are low. *His climbing*

173

gear was stowed in canvas bags in a cupboard under the stairs, well behind the Hoover and mops and buckets. Money is always a problem. Monica trained as a primary school teacher. Now she stays at home to look after the children and the house. She does it well, she is a loving mother, the children are adorable, but she suffers from bouts of restlessness and frustration that mirror Sebastian's. Their rent is outrageous for such a small house in a dingy street and their marriage of nine years is dull, flattened by worries and hard work, marred by the occasional row – usually about money.

One dark late afternoon in December, three days before the end of term, he is mugged in the street. Monica has asked him to go to the bank at lunchtime to draw out seventy pounds from the joint account so that she can buy presents and Christmas treats. It is almost all they have by way of savings. He has turned into his own road, which is narrow and poorly lit, and is a hundred yards from his front door when he hears steps behind him and feels a tap on his shoulder. He turns and *standing before him was a kid of sixteen or so, West Indian, holding a kitchen knife, a big one with a serrated blade. For a few seconds the two stood close, less than three feet apart, staring at each other in silence.* What troubles Sebastian is the boy's agitation, the way the knife trembles in his hands, the terror in his face. Things could easily get out of control. In a quiet shaky voice the boy asks for his wallet. Sebastian raises his hand slowly to the inside pocket of his coat. He is about to give away his children's Christmas. He knows he is stronger than the kid and he calculates that as he holds out his wallet he could strike out, hit him hard on the nose and snatch the knife off him.

174

But it is more than the kid's agitation that restrains Sebastian. *There was a general view, strongly held in the staffroom, that crime, especially burglary and mugging, was caused by social injustice.* Robbers are poor, they've never had the right chances in life and can hardly be blamed for taking what isn't theirs. This is Sebastian's view too, though he's never given the matter much thought. In fact, it isn't even a view, it's a general atmosphere of tolerance that surrounds decent educated people. Those who complain about crime are likely to complain also about graffiti and litter in the streets and hold a whole set of distasteful views on immigration and the unions, tax, war and hanging. *It was important therefore, for the sake of one's self-respect, not to mind too much about being mugged.*

So he hands over his wallet and the thief runs away. Instead of going straight home Sebastian walks back towards the High Street and goes to the police station to report the incident. As he speaks to the desk sergeant, he feels a bit of a cad or a snitch, for the police are clearly agents of the system that forces people to steal. His discomfort increases in the face of the sergeant's grave concern, and the way he keeps asking about the knife, the length of the blade, and whether Sebastian was able to see anything of the handle. Of course, armed robbery is a very serious offence. That kid could go to jail for years. Even when the sergeant tells him that there was a fatal stabbing only the month before of an old lady who tried to hang on to her purse, Sebastian's unease is not dispelled. He shouldn't have mentioned the knife. As he walks back along the street, he regrets his automatic impulse to report the matter. He's becoming middle-aged and bourgeois. He should have taken responsibility for himself. He is no longer the sort of guy who puts his life on the line and climbs up sheer faces of granite, trusting his agility, strength and skill.

Because he is beginning to feel weakness and trembling in his legs he goes into a pub and with the loose change in his pocket is just about able to afford a large Scotch. He downs it in one, and then he goes home.

The mugging marks a decline in his marriage. Though Monica never says so, it is clear she doesn't believe him. It's the old story. He's come home stinking of drink, protesting that someone has run off with the holiday money. The Christmas is wretched. They have to borrow from her haughty brother. Her distrust kindles his resentment, they are distant with each other, they have to pretend to be jolly on Christmas Day for the sake of their children, and that seems to heighten the bleakness that comes down to trap them into silence. *The idea that she thought he was a liar was like a poison in his heart*. He works hard, he is loyal and faithful and keeps no secrets from her. How dare she doubt him! One evening when Naomi and Jake are in bed, he challenges her to tell him that she believes him about the mugging. She is immediately angry, and won't say whether she does or not. Instead, she changes the subject, a trick in argument, he thinks bitterly, she is supremely good at and one he should learn himself. She is sick of her life, she tells him, sick of being financially dependent on him, of being stuck at home all day while he is out advancing his career. Why have they never considered the possibility of him doing the housework and looking after the children while she resumes her career?

Even as she says all this he is thinking what an attractive prospect it is. He could turn his back on those awful kids, who never keep quiet or stay in their seats in his classes. He could stop pretending to care whether they ever spoke a word of French. And he likes being with his children. He would get them to their school and playgroup, then take a couple of hours for himself, perhaps fulfil an old ambition and get some writing done before picking up Jake and giving him lunch. Then an afternoon of child-care and light housework. Bliss. Let her be the wage slave. But they are having a row and he is in no mood to make conciliatory offers. He brings Monica back sharply to the mugging. He challenges her again to call him a liar, he tells her to go to the police station and read his statement. In reply, she leaves the room, slamming the door hard behind her.

A sour peace prevails, the holidays end and he goes back to work. It's as bad as ever at school. The kids are absorbing from the culture at large a cocky spirit of rebellion. *Hash, spirits and tobacco were playground currencies,* and teachers, including the headmaster, are confused, half believing that this atmosphere of insurrection is a token of the very freedom and creativity they are supposed to be imparting, and half aware that nothing is being taught or learned and the school is going to the dogs. The 'sixties', whatever they were, have entered this decade wearing a sinister new mask. *The same drugs that were said to have brought peace and light to middle-class students were now shrinking the prospects of the hard-edged urban poor.* Fifteen-year-olds come to Sebastian's classes stoned or drunk or both. Kids younger than them have taken LSD in the playground and have to be sent home. Ex-pupils sell drugs at the school gates, standing there openly with their wares alongside the mums and their pushchairs. The headmaster dithers, everyone dithers.

At the end of the day Sebastian is often hoarse from raising his voice in class. Walking home slowly is his one comfort, when he can be alone with his thoughts as he makes his way from one bleak setting to another. It's a relief that Monica is out at evening classes four times a week – yoga, German lessons, angelology. Otherwise, they step around each other at home, speaking only to manage the household. He sleeps in the spare room, explaining to the children that his snoring keeps Mummy awake. He is ready to give up his job so that she can go back to hers. But he can't forget that she thinks he's the sort of man who can drink away the children's Christmas. And then lie about it. Clearly, there is a far deeper problem. Their trust in each other has vanished and their marriage is in crisis. Swapping roles with her would be merely cosmetic. The thought of divorce fills him with horror. *What wrangling and stupidity would follow! How could they inflict such pain and sadness on Naomi and Jake?* It is his and Monica's responsibility to sort this matter out. But he does not know how to begin. Whenever he thinks of that boy and the kitchen knife in his hand, the old anger returns. Monica's refusal to believe him, to believe in him, has broken a vital bond and seems to him a monstrous betrayal.

And then there is the money: there is never enough money. In January their twelve-year-old car needs a new clutch. This in turn delays the repayment to Monica's brother – the debt is not settled until early March. It is a week later, while Sebastian is in the staff room at lunch-time, that he is approached by the school secretary. His wife is on the phone and needs to speak to him urgently. *He hurried to the office nauseous with dread. She had never phoned him at work before, and it could only be very bad news, perhaps something to do with Naomi or Jake.* So it's with some relief that he hears her tell him that there has been a break-in that morning at the house. After dropping off the children, she went to her doctor's appointment, then to the shops. When she got home the front door was ajar. The burglar had got in round the back garden, broken a window at the rear of the house, lifted a catch and climbed in, gathered up the stuff and gone out by the front. What stuff? *She listed it all tonelessly.* His precious 1930s Rolleiflex, bought years ago with the proceeds of a French prize he won at Manchester. Then, their transistor radio and his Leica binoculars, and her hairdryer. She pauses, and then she tells him, in that same flat voice, that all his climbing gear has been taken too.

At that point he feels the need to sit down. The secretary, who has been hovering, tactfully leaves the office and closes the door. *So much good stuff carefully accumulated over the years, and so much of sentimental value, including a rope he once used to save a friend's life during a descent in a storm in the Andes.* Even if the insurance covers it all, which Sebastian doubts, he knows he will never replace his mountaineering equipment. There was too much of it, there are too many other priorities. His youth has been stolen. *With his upright, good-hearted tolerance deserting him, he imagined his hands closing around the thief's windpipe.* Then he shakes his head to dismiss the fantasy. Monica is telling him that the police have already been round. There is blood on the broken windowpane. But it looks like the thief wore gloves, as there are no fingerprints. He tells her that there must have been two burglars at least, to lift all his gear out of the cupboard and carry it quickly from the house. *Yes, she agreed in her affectless voice that there must have been two.*

At home that evening he can't resist punishing himself by opening the cupboard under the stairs and gazing at the space where his equipment was. *He restored the buckets and mops and brushes to their upright position, then he went upstairs to look in his sock drawer, where he had kept his camera.* The thieves knew what to take, though the hairdryer matters less since there are two. This latest setback, this assault on their domestic privacy, does nothing to bring Sebastian and Monica closer. After a brief discussion they agree not to tell the children about the break-in and she goes off to her class. In the days that follow he feels so low he can barely bring himself to make the insurance claim. The full-colour handbook boasts of 'solid protection' but the small print in the schedule is miserly and punitive. Only a fraction of the camera's value is covered, and the climbing gear not at all because he failed to itemise it.

Their dreary co-existence resumed. A month after the burglary, the same school secretary seeks out Sebastian at break to tell him that there's a gentleman to see him in the school office. In fact he is waiting for Sebastian in the corridor, holding a raincoat over his arm. He introduces himself as Detective Inspector Barnes and he has a matter to discuss. Would Mr Morel care to drop by the police station after work?

A few hours later he is back at the front desk where he reported the mugging before Christmas. He is obliged to wait for half an hour before Barnes is free. The DI apologises as he shows him up three flights of concrete stairs and ushers him into a small darkened room. *There was a fold-down screen on a wall and a film projector in the centre of*

180

the room balanced on what looked like a bar stool. Barnes showed Sebastian a seat and began his account of a successful sting. A year ago the police rented a run-down shop in a side street and staffed it with a couple of plainclothes officers. The shop bought secondhand goods from the public, the idea being to film thieves as they came in with stolen goods. With a number of prosecutions now under way, the cover has been blown and the shop has closed. But there are one or two loose ends. He dims the lights.

A hidden camera is positioned behind the 'shop assist-ant' and gives a view of the door onto the street and, in the foreground, the counter. Sebastian has already guessed that he is about to see the young guy who mugged him come into the shop. With a successful identification, he'll be done for armed robbery, and that will be fine. But Sebastian's guess is wildly wrong. The person who comes in with a holdall and sets down on the counter a radio, a camera and a hairdryer is his wife. There she is, in the coat he bought her some birthdays ago. By chance she turns and looks towards the camera, as if she has seen Sebastian and is saying, Watch this! Soundlessly, she exchanges a few words with the assistant and together they go outside and come back moments later dragging three heavy canvas bags. The car must be parked right outside. The shop assistant peers inside each of the bags, then goes back behind the counter, glances over the items. There follows what must be a negotiation over prices. *Monica's face was lit by a bar of fluorescent light. She seemed animated, even elated in a nervous sort of way. She smiled a lot and at one point even laughed at a joke the plainclothes policeman made.* A price is agreed, banknotes are counted out, and Monica turns to leave. *At the door she stopped to*

181

make a parting remark, something more elaborate than a goodbye, and then she was gone and the screen went black.

The DI switches off the projector and turns up the lights. His manner is apologetic. They could have prosecuted, he says. Wasting police time, perverting the course of justice, that sort of thing. But clearly this is a delicate domestic matter and Sebastian will have to decide for himself what to do. The two men go down the stairs and out into the street. As he shakes Sebastian's hand the DI says he is terribly sorry, he can see that this is a difficult situation and he wishes him all the best with it. Then, before he goes back into the station, he adds that *it was the view of the police team working in the shop, who had recordings of what was said at the counter, that 'Mrs Morel probably needed help'.*

On the way home – has he ever walked more slowly? – he would have stopped in that same pub for another fortifying drink, but he does not have on him even the price of a half pint. Perhaps it's just as well. He needs a clear head and clean breath. It takes him an hour to walk the mile to his house.

She is cooking with the children when he comes in. *He lingers in the doorway of the kitchen watching his little family at work on a cake. It was terribly sad, the way Jake and Naomi's precious heads bobbed so eagerly at their mother's murmured instructions.* He goes upstairs and lies on the bed in the spare room, staring at the ceiling. He feels heavy and tired and wonders if he is suffering from shock. And yet, despite the awful truth he has learned that day, he is troubled now by something new and equally shocking. Shocking? Is that the right word?

When he was downstairs just now watching Monica and the children, there was a moment when she glanced

182

back over her shoulder at him. Their eyes met. He knows her well enough, he has seen that look many times before and has always welcomed it. It promises much. It is a tacit suggestion that when the moment is right, when the children are asleep, they should seize their chance and obliterate all thoughts of domestic duties. In the new circumstances, with what he knows now, he should be repelled. But he is excited by that glance because it came from a stranger, from a woman he knows nothing about beyond her obvious taste for destruction. *He had seen her in a silent movie and realised that he had never understood her.* He had got her all wrong. She was no longer his familiar. In the kitchen *he had seen her with fresh eyes and realised, as though for the first time, how beautiful she was. Beautiful and mad. Here was someone he had just met, at a party say, noticed her across a crowded room, the sort of woman who, with a single unambiguous look, offers a dangerous and thrilling invitation.*

He has been doggedly faithful throughout his marriage. His fidelity now seems like one more aspect of the general constriction and failure in his life. His marriage is over, there can be no going back, for how can he live with her now? How can he trust a woman who has stolen from him and lied? It's over. But here is the chance of an affair. An affair with madness. If she needs help, then this is what he can offer.

That evening he plays with the children, cleans the hamster's cage with them, gets them into their pyjamas, and reads to them three times over, once together, then to Jake on his own, then to Naomi. It is at times like these that his life makes sense. How soothing it is, the scent of clean bedlinen and minty toothpaste breath, and his children's eagerness to hear the adventures of imaginary beings, and how touching, to watch the children's eyes grow heavy as they struggle to hang on to the priceless last minutes of their day, and finally fail. All the while he is aware of Monica moving about downstairs, he hears the distinctive clunk of the oven door a few times and is aroused by the simple distracting logic: if there is to be food, if they are eating together, then there will be sex.

When he goes down, their tiny sitting room has been tidied, the usual junk has been cleared from the dining table and there is candlelight, Art Blakey on the hi-fi, a bottle of wine on the table and a roast chicken in an earthenware dish. *When he remembered the police film – his thoughts kept returning to it – he hated her. And when she came in from the kitchen in fresh skirt and blouse, bearing two wine glasses, he wanted her.* What is missing now is the love, or the guilty memory of love, or the need for it, and that is a liberation. She has become another woman, devious, deceitful, unkind, even cruel, and he is about to make love to her.

During the meal they avoid talk of the ill-feeling that has stifled their marriage for months. They don't even talk about the children as they so often do. Instead they talk about successful family holidays in the past, and holidays they will take with the children when Jake is a little older. It is all false, none of it will ever happen. *Then they talked politics, of strikes and the state of emergency and the sense of impending ruin in parliament, in cities, in the country's sense of itself – they talked of all the ruin but their own.* He watches her closely as she talks, and knows that every word is a lie. Doesn't she think it extraordinary, as he does, that after all this silence they are behaving as though nothing has happened? She is counting on sex to put everything right. He wants her all the more. And more again when she asks in passing about the insurance claim and expresses concern. *Amazing. What an actress. It was as if she was alone and he was watching her through a peep-hole.* He has no intention of confronting her. If he did, they would surely row, because she would deny everything. Or she would tell him that her financial dependence forced her to desperate measures. And he would have to point out that all their accounts are jointly held and that he has as little money as she does. But this way they will make love and he at least will know that it is for the very last time. *He would make love to a liar and a thief, to a woman he would never know. And she in turn would convince herself that* she *was making love to a liar and a thief. And doing so in the spirit of forgiveness.*

In my opinion Tom Haley spent too long over this farewell chicken dinner, and it seemed especially drawn out on a second reading. It wasn't necessary to mention the vegetables, or to tell us that the wine was a Burgundy. My train was approaching Clapham Junction as I turned the pages to locate the finale. I was tempted to skip it altogether. I made no claims to sophistication – I was a simple sort of reader, temperamentally bound to consider Sebastian as Tom's double, the bearer of his sexual prowess, the receptacle of his sexual anxieties. I became uneasy whenever one of his male characters became intimate with a woman, with *another* woman. But I was curious too, I had to watch. If Monica was daffy as well as deceitful (what was this angelology business?) then there was something obtuse and dark in Sebastian. His decision not to confront his wife about her deception may have been a cruel exercise of power for sexual ends, or a simple matter of cowardice, of an essentially English preference to avoid a scene. It didn't reflect well on Tom.

Over the years, uxorious repetition has streamlined the process and they are *swiftly naked and embracing on the bed*. They have been married long enough to be thorough experts on each other's needs, and the ending of long weeks of *froideur* and abstinence surely contribute a certain bonus, but it can't explain away the passion that overwhelms them now. *Their customary, companionable rhythms were violently discarded*. They are hungry, ferocious, extravagant and loud. At one point little Naomi in the next room *let out a cry in her sleep, a pure silvery rising wail in the dark that they mistook at first for a cat*. The couple freeze and wait for her to settle.

And then came the final lines of 'Pawnography', with the characters perched uneasily on ecstasy's summit. The desolation was to follow, off the page. The reader was spared the worst.

The sound was so icy and bleak that he imagined his daughter had seen in her dreams the unavoidable future, all the sorrow and confusion to come, and he felt himself shrink in horror. But the moment passed, and soon Sebastian and Monica sank again, or they rose, for there seemed to be no physical dimensions in the space they swam or tumbled through, only sensation, only pleasure so focused, so pointed it was a reminder of pain.

13

Max was taking a week's holiday in Taormina with his fiancée, so there could be no immediate debriefing when I returned to the office. I lived in a state of suspension. Friday came and there was no word from Tom Haley. I decided that if he'd visited the office in Upper Regent Street that day, he must have made a firm decision against seeing me. On Monday I picked up a letter from a PO Box service in Park Lane. A Freedom International secretary had typed a memo confirming that Mr Haley had come by on Friday in the late morning, stayed an hour, asked many questions and seemed impressed by the Foundation's work. I should have felt encouraged, and I suppose I was in a remote sort of way. But mostly I felt I'd been dumped. Haley's thumb action, I decided, was reflexive, the sort of move he tried on any woman he thought he had a chance with. I schemed sulkily, imagining that when he finally told me he would deign to accept the Foundation's money, I would wreck his chances by telling Max that he had turned us down and that we should look for someone else.

At work the one topic was the war in the Middle East. Even the most light-headed of the society girls among the secretaries was drawn into the daily drama. People were saying that with the Americans lining up behind Israel and the Soviets behind Egypt and Syria and the Palestinian cause, there was potential for the sort of proxy war that could bring us a step closer to a nuclear exchange. A new Cuban Missile Crisis! A wall map went up in our corridor with sticky plastic beads representing the opposing divisions and arrows to show their recent movements. The Israelis, reeling from the surprise attack on Yom Kippur, began to pull themselves together, the Egyptians and Syrians made some tactical errors, the United States airlifted weapons to their ally, Moscow issued warnings. All this should have excited me more than it did, daily life should have had a keener edge. Civilisation threatened by nuclear war, and I'm brooding about a stranger who caressed my palm with his thumb. Monstrous solipsism.

But I wasn't only thinking of Tom. I was also worrying about Shirley. Six weeks had passed since our parting at the Bees Make Honey gig. She had left her place, her desk at the Registry, at the end of a working week without saying goodbye to anyone. Three days later a new new-joiner was in her place. Some of the girls who had gloomily predicted Shirley's promotion were now saying that she was forced to leave because she was *not one of us*. I'd been too angry with my old friend to seek her out. At the time I was relieved that she crept away without a fuss. But as the weeks passed, the sense of betrayal faded. I began to think that in her place I would have done the same. Perhaps with greater willingness, given my hunger for approval. I suspected that she'd been wrong – I wasn't being followed. But I was missing her, her boisterous laugh, the heavy hand on my wrist when she wanted to confide, her carefree taste for rock and roll. By comparison, the rest of us at work were timid and buttoned up, even when we were gossiping or teasing each other.

My evenings now were empty. I came home from work, took my groceries from 'my' corner of the fridge, cooked my supper, passed the time with the solicitors if they happened to be around, then read in my room in my boxy little armchair until eleven, my bedtime. That October I was absorbed by the short stories of William Trevor. The constrained lives of his characters made me wonder how my own existence might appear in his hands. The young girl alone in her bedsit, washing her hair in the basin, daydreaming about a man from Brighton who didn't get in touch, about the best friend who had vanished from her life, about another man she had fallen for whom she must meet tomorrow to hear about his wedding plans. How grey and sad.

A week after my meeting with Haley I walked from Camden to the Holloway Road with all kinds of foolish hopes, and apologies at the ready. But Shirley had abandoned her room and had left no forwarding address. I didn't have her parents' address in Ilford and they wouldn't give it to me at work. I looked up Bedworld in the Yellow Pages and spoke to an unhelpful assistant. Mr Shilling could not come to the phone, his daughter didn't work there and might or might not be away. A letter addressed to her care of Bedworld might or might not reach her. I wrote a postcard, unnaturally cheery, pretending nothing had happened between us. I asked her to get in touch. I didn't expect a reply.

I was due to meet Max on his first day back at work. That morning I had a miserable time getting to the office. Everyone did. It was cold and the rain fell in that steady, pitiless way it has in a city, letting you know it could go on for a month. There was a bomb scare on the Victoria line. The Provisional IRA had phoned a newspaper and given a special code. So I walked the last mile to the office, past queues for buses, too long to be worth joining. Part of the fabric of my umbrella had come away from the spokes, which gave me the appearance of a Chaplinesque tramp. My court shoes had cracks in the leather that sucked in the damp. On the news-stands every front page carried the story of OPEC's 'oil price shock'. The West was being punished with a hefty rise for supporting Israel. Exports to the US were embargoed. The leaders of the mineworkers' union were holding a special meeting to discuss how best they could exploit the situation. We were doomed. The skies grew darker over the Conduit Street crowds shuffling along, hunched into their raincoats, trying to keep their umbrellas out of each other's faces. It was only October and barely four degrees above freezing – a taste of the long winter to come. I thought back gloomily to the talk I'd attended with Shirley, and how every vile prediction was coming true. I remembered those turned heads, those accusing looks, my black mark, and my old anger against her revived and my mood darkened further. Her friendship had been a pretence, I was a dupe, I belonged in another line of work. I wished I was still in my soft sagging bed with the pillow over my head.

I was already late but I checked the PO Box first before running round the corner to Leconfield House. I spent a quarter of an hour in the women's bathroom, trying to dry my hair on the roller towel and wiping the puddle stains from my tights. Max was a lost cause but I had my dignity to protect. I was ten minutes late when I squeezed into his triangular office, conscious of how cold and wet my feet were. I watched him across his desk as he arranged his files and made a show of being business-like. Did he look different after a week of making love in Taormina to Dr Ruth? He'd had a haircut before coming back to work and his ears had reverted to jug formation. There was no gleam of new confidence in his eyes, or dark patches beneath them. Beyond the new white shirt and a tie of a darker blue and a new dark suit, I saw no transformation. Was it just possible that they took separate rooms to save themselves for their wedding night? Not from what I knew of medical types and their long and rowdy apprentice-ships. Even if Max, in obedience to some improbable instruction from his mother, had made a half-hearted attempt to hang back, Dr Ruth would have eaten him alive. The body, in all its frailty, was her profession. Well, I still wanted Max, but I also wanted Tom Haley and that was protection of a sort, if I ignored the fact that he wasn't interested in me.

'So,' he said at last. He looked up from the Sweet Tooth file and waited.

'How was Taormina?'

'Do you know, it rained every day we were there.'

He was telling me they had stayed in bed all day. As if acknowledging the fact he added quickly, 'So we saw the inside of a lot of churches, museums, that kind of thing.'

'Sounds fun,' I said in a flat tone.

He glanced up sharply, ready to detect irony but, I think, saw none.

He said, 'Have we heard back from Haley?'

'Not yet. The meeting went well. Clearly needs the money. Can't quite believe his luck. Came up to town last week to check out the Foundation. I guess he's mulling it over.'

It was odd how, in putting it this way, I cheered myself up. Yes, I thought. I should try to be more sensible.

'What was he like?'

'Very welcoming actually.'

'No, I mean, what *is* he like?'

'No fool. Highly educated, very driven about his writing, obviously. Students adore him. Good-looking in an unusual sort of way.'

'I've seen his photograph,' Max said. It occurred to me that he might be regretting his mistake. He could have made love to me and *then* announced his engagement. I felt I had a duty to my self-respect to flirt with Max, make him sorry for passing me over.

'I was hoping for a postcard from you.'

'Sorry, Serena. I never write them – just not in the habit.'

'Were you happy?'

The directness of the question took him by surprise. I was gratified to see him flustered. 'Yes, yes we were in fact. Very happy. But there's . . .'

'But?'

'There's something else . . .'

'Yes?'

'We can talk about holidays and all that later. But before I tell you about it, still on Haley, give him another week, then write to him and say we need to hear from him straight away, or else the offer is withdrawn.'

'Fine.'

He closed the file. 'The thing is this. Remember Oleg Lyalin?'

'You mentioned him.'

'I shouldn't know any of this. And you certainly shouldn't. But it's gossip. It's going the rounds. I think you might as well know. He was a great coup for us. He wanted to come across in 'seventy-one but apparently we kept him in place here in London for a few extra months. Five was about to arrange his defection when he was picked up by Westminster police for drunk driving. We got to him before the Russians did – they would have certainly killed him. He came across to us with his secretary, his lover. He was a KGB officer connected to their sabotage department. Pretty low-level guy, something of a thug apparently, but priceless. He confirmed our worst nightmare, that there were dozens, scores of Soviet intelligence officers working here under diplomatic immunity. When we threw out the hundred and five – and by the way, Heath was a trouper on that, whatever they're saying about him now – it seemed to take Moscow Centre completely by surprise. We didn't even tell the Americans, and that caused a stink which hasn't quite settled down yet. But the important thing was that it showed that we no longer had a mole at any significant level. Nothing since George Blake. Huge relief all round.

'We'll probably go on talking to Lyalin until the end of his life. There are always loose ends, things in the past, old stories with a new angle, procedural stuff, structures, order of battle and so on. There was one particular minor mystery, a cryptonym no one could crack because the information was too vague. It was an Englishman codenamed Volt, active in the very late forties until the end of 'fifty, working for us, not Six. The interest was the hydrogen bomb. Not really our department. Nothing spectacular like Fuchs, nothing technical. Not even long-range planning or logistics. Lyalin saw the Volt material when he was still in Moscow. It didn't add up to much, but he knew the source was Five. He saw some speculative things, you know, "What if" papers, what the Americans call scenarios. What we call smart weekends in country houses. Hot air. What happens when the Chinese get the bomb, what price a pre-emptive strike, what's the optimum stockpile assuming no cost restraints and kindly pass the port.'

It was at this point I guessed what was coming. Or my body knew. My heart was going a little harder.

'Our people spent months on this, but we had too little on Volt to match the payroll or anyone's biography. Then last year someone came over to the Americans through Buenos Aires. I don't know what our friends learned. I do know they were slow passing it across, still huffy about the expulsions, I expect. Whatever they gave us, it was enough.'

He paused. 'You know where this is leading, don't you?'

I went to say 'Yes', but my tongue couldn't move itself in time. What came out was a grunt.

'So this is what's going round. Twenty-odd years ago Canning was passing documents to a contact. It lasted fifteen months. If there was more damaging stuff, we don't know about it. We don't know why it stopped. Perhaps it was disappointment all round.'

While I was in my well-sprung royal blue pram with silver spokes, still an only child, wheeled in bonneted splendour from the Rectory to the village shops, Tony was doing business with his contact, trying out a few phrases in Russian in that show-off way he had. I saw him in a bus-station greasy spoon, pulling from the inside pocket of a double-breasted suit a folded brown envelope. Perhaps an apologetic smile and shrug because the material was not first grade – he liked to be the best. But I couldn't quite see his face. In the past few months, whenever I summoned it, the image dissolved before the inner eye. Perhaps that was why I'd been less tormented. Or, other way round, my fading grief had begun to erase his features.

But not his voice. The inner ear is the more acute organ. I could play Tony's voice in my mind like turning on a radio. A way he had of resisting until the very end the rising pitch of a question, the hint of a 'w' sound for an 'r', and certain phrases of demurral – 'If you say so', 'I wouldn't put it like that', 'Well, up to a point' and 'Hang on' – and the college-claret plumminess, his way of being so sure that he would never think or say anything stupid or extreme. Only the considered, balanced view. Which was why it was easy to summon up his explanation over breakfast in the cottage, early summer sunshine pouring through the open door with its countless inexplicable rivets, across the flagstones, to illuminate the lime-white lath and plaster of the dining room's far wall, where the Churchill watercolour hung. And on the table between us, muddy coffee made in a special way, by 'the jug method' with a pinch of salt thrown in, and under-cooked toast like stale bread piled on a pale green plate with a spidery glaze and bitter thick-cut marmalade made by the house-keeper's sister.

I heard it plainly, Tony's justification, which, his tone would suggest, only a fool dared oppose. My dear girl. I hope you remember our first tutorial. These terrifying new weapons can only be restrained by a balance of power, by mutual fear, mutual respect. Even if it means yielding secrets to a tyranny it would be preferable to the lopsided dominion of American swagger. Kindly recall the voices from the American right after 1945 urging the nuclear extermination of the Soviet Union while it still had no means of retaliation. Who could ignore that insidious logic? If Japan had possessed such a weapon there would have been no horrors of Hiroshima. Only a balance of power can keep the peace. I did what I had to. The Cold War was upon us. The world had arranged itself into hostile camps. I wasn't alone in thinking the way I did. However grotesque its abuses, let the Soviet Union be similarly armed. Let small minds accuse me of unpatriotic betrayal, the rational man acts for global peace and the continuance of civilisation.

'Well,' Max said. 'Don't you have anything to say?'

His tone suggested that I was complicit or somehow responsible. I allowed a short silence to neutralise his question. I said, 'Did they confront him before he died?'

'I don't know. All I have is the gossip that trickles down from the fifth floor. They certainly had time – about six months.'

I was remembering the car that came with the two men in suits, and the walk I was obliged to take in the woods, and our sudden return to Cambridge. In those first few minutes after Max's revelation I didn't feel much at all. I understood the importance of it, I knew that there were emotions lying in wait for me, but I would have to be alone to confront them. For now I felt protected by an unreasonable hostility to Max, by my impulse to blame the messenger. He talked down Tom Haley at every opportunity and now he was demolishing my former lover, trying to strip the men out of my life. He could have kept the Canning story to himself. It was only a rumour and, even if it was true, there was no operational reason for me to be told. It was a rare case of prospective and retrospective jealousy running side by side. If he couldn't have me, then no one could, not even from the past.

I said, 'Tony wasn't a communist.'

'I expect he dabbled in the thirties like everyone else.'

'He was in the Labour Party. He hated the show trials and the purges. He always said he would have voted for king and country in that Oxford union debate.'

Max shrugged. 'I can see it's hard.'

But he couldn't, and nor could I just yet.

I went from Max's room straight to my desk, determined to numb myself with the tasks in hand. It was too soon to be thinking. Or rather, I didn't dare think. I was in shock and I set about my tasks like an automaton. I was working with a desk officer called Chas Mount, a genial sort, ex-army, a former computer salesman who was happy to give me proper responsibilities. I had at last graduated to Ireland. We had two agents in the Provisionals – there may have been more but I wasn't aware of them. And these two were not aware of each other. They were sleepers, expected to spend some years rising through the military hierarchy, but almost immediately we'd had a flood of information from one of the men relating to chains of arms supply. We needed to expand and rationalise the files by creating sub-groupings and opening new files on the suppliers and middlemen, with cross-references and a degree of duplicated material that would lead any misplaced enquiry to the right place. We knew nothing about our agents – to us they were only 'Helium' and 'Spade', but I often thought about them, the dangers they ran and how safe I was back here in the dingy office I so often complained about. They would be Irish Catholic certainly, meeting in tiny front parlours in Bogside or in function rooms in pubs, aware that one slip, one obvious inconsistency could cost a bullet in the back of the head. And the body dumped in the street so that everyone could see what happened to informers. They would have to live the part in order to be convincing. Already, to protect his cover, Spade had seriously injured two British soldiers in an ambush and been involved in the deaths of members of the RUC and the torture and murder of a police informant.

Spade, Helium, and now Volt. After a couple of hours trying to block out Tony, I went to the women's lavatory, locked myself in a cubicle and sat there a while, and attempted to take in the news. I wanted to cry, but my turmoil had dry elements of anger and disappointment. It was all so long ago and he was dead, but the act seemed to me as fresh as yesterday. I thought I knew his arguments, but I couldn't accept them. You let down friends and colleagues, I heard myself tell him at that same sunlit breakfast. It's a matter of dishonour, and when it gets out, which it's bound to, this will be the one act you'll be remembered for. Everything else you achieved will be irrelevant. Your reputation will rest only on this, because ultimately reality is social, it's among others that we have to live and their judgements matter. Even, or especially, when we're dead. Your entire existence now will be reduced in the minds of the living to something seedy and underhand. No one will doubt that you wanted to do more harm than you did, that you would have handed over complete blueprints if you could have got your hands on them. If you thought that your actions were so noble and rational, why not present them openly and argue your case in public and face the consequences? If Stalin could murder and starve twenty million of his own for the sake of the revolution, who's to say he couldn't sacrifice more for the same cause in a nuclear exchange? If a dictator values life so much less than an American President, where is your balance of power?

Arguing with a dead man in a lavatory is a claustrophobic experience. I came out of the cubicle, splashed my face with cold water and tidied myself up, then went back to work. By lunchtime I was desperate to get out of the building. The rain had stopped and the pavements gleamed cleanly in the surprising sunlight. But there was a biting wind and there was no possibility of wandering idly through the park. I went briskly along Curzon Street, full of irrational thoughts. I was angry with Max for bringing me the news, angry with Tony for failing to live, for abandoning me with the burden of his mistakes. And because he had steered me into my career – I now thought of it as more than a job – I felt myself to be contaminated by his disloyalty. He had added his name to an inglorious list – Nunn May, the Rosenbergs, Fuchs – but unlike them had given away nothing of significance. He was a footnote in the history of nuclear spying, and I was a footnote to his treachery. I'd been diminished. Clearly, Max thought so. Another reason to be angry with *him*. And I was angry with myself for being a fool about him, for thinking that this stuffy jug-eared idiot could ever have brought me happiness. What luck it was for me, to be inoculated by his ridiculous engagement.

I went through Berkeley Square, where we'd remembered the nightingale song, and turned right down Berkeley Street towards Piccadilly. By Green Park station I saw the headlines on the noon edition of the evening newspapers. Petrol rationing, energy crisis, Heath to address the nation. I didn't care. I walked towards Hyde Park Corner. I was too upset to be hungry for lunch. There was a curious burning sensation in the balls of my feet. I wanted to run or kick. I wanted a game of tennis with a ferocious opponent, one I could beat. I wanted to shout at someone – that was it, I wanted a full-on row with Tony and then to leave him before he had a chance to leave me. The wind blew harder, right into my face as I turned into Park Lane. Rain clouds were piling up over Marble Arch, getting ready to drench me again. I walked faster.

I was passing the PO Box office so I went in, partly to get out of the cold. I'd checked only hours before and I had no real expectation of a letter, but there it suddenly was, in my hand, postmarked Brighton and yesterday's date. I fumbled with it, I pulled the envelope apart like a child on Christmas Day. Let one thing be right today, I thought as I went to stand by the glass door to read. *Dear Serena*. And it *was* right. It was more than right. He apologised for taking his time. He liked meeting me, he had given careful thought to my offer. He was accepting the money and he was grateful, it was an amazing opportunity. And then there was a new paragraph. I brought the letter closer to my face. He'd used a fountain pen, crossed out a word, made a smudge. He wanted to impose a condition.

If you don't mind, I'd like us to keep in regular contact – for two reasons. The first is that I'd prefer this generous Foundation to have a human face, so the money that comes to me each month is not simply an impersonal, bureaucratic matter. Second, your appreciative remarks meant a lot to me, more than I can say in a note like this. I'd like to be able to show you my work from time to time. I promise I won't be looking for constant praise and encouragement. I'd like your honest criticism. Naturally, I'd want to feel free to ignore any notes of yours that don't seem right to me. But the main thing is that by having your occasional input I wouldn't be writing into a void, and that's important if I'm starting out on a novel. As far as hand-holding goes, it won't be much of an imposition. Just a cup of coffee now and then. I'm nervous about writing something longer, more so now that there's some expectation laid upon me. I want to be worthy of this investment you're making in me. I'd like the Foundation people who chose me to feel that they made a decision they can be proud of.

I'm coming to London on Saturday morning. I could meet you in the National Portrait Gallery at ten by Severn's painting of Keats. Don't worry, if I haven't heard from you and you're not there, I won't rush to any conclusions.

Best wishes, Tom Haley

14

By five o'clock that Saturday afternoon we were lovers. It didn't run smoothly, there was no explosion of relief and delight in the meeting of bodies and souls. It wasn't ecstatic, the way it was for Sebastian and Monica, the thieving wife. Not at first. It was self-conscious and awkward, it had a theatrical quality, as if we were aware of the expectations of an unseen audience. And the audience was real. As I opened the front door of number seventy and showed Tom in, my three solicitor housemates were grouped at the foot of the stairs, mugs of tea in hand, clearly wasting time before making their way back to their rooms and an afternoon of legal grind. I closed the door behind us with a loud slam. The women from the north stared at my new friend with undisguised interest as he stood there on the doormat. There was a fair amount of meaningful grinning and shuffling as I made my reluctant introductions. If we'd arrived five minutes later no one would have seen us. Too bad.

Rather than conduct Tom to my bedroom pursued by

their looks and nudges, I took him through to the kitchen and waited for them to disperse. But they lingered. While I made tea I could hear them murmuring in the hall. I wanted to ignore them and have a conversation of our own, but my mind was a blank. Sensitive to my discomfort Tom filled the silence by telling me about the Camden Town of Dickens's *Dombey and Son*, the line north from Euston station, the colossal cutting dug by Irish navvies that forced its way through the poorest neighbourhoods. He even had a line or two by heart and his words defined my own confusion. 'There were a hundred thousand shapes and substances of incompleteness, wildly mingled out of their places, upside down, burrowing in the earth, aspiring in the air, mouldering in the water, and unintelligible as any dream.'

At last my housemates went back to their desks, and after a few minutes we climbed the creaky stairs with our own mugs of tea. The silence behind each of their doors as we passed them on the way up seemed intensely alert. I was trying to remember whether my bed also creaked and how thick my bedroom walls were – hardly sensual thoughts. Once Tom was installed in my room, in my reading armchair while I sat on the bed, it seemed a better idea to go on talking.

At this at least we were already adept. We had passed an hour in the Portrait Gallery showing each other our favourites. Mine was Cassandra Austen's sketch of her sister, his, William Strang's Hardy. Looking at pictures with a stranger is an unobtrusive form of mutual exploration and mild seduction. It was an easy slide from aesthetics to biography – the subject's obviously, but also the painter's, at least, the scraps we knew. And Tom knew far more than I did. Basically, we gossiped. There was an element of showing off – this is what I like, this is the kind of person I am. It was no great commitment to say that Branwell Brontë's painting of his sisters was deeply unflattering, or that Hardy told people he was often mistaken for a detective. Somehow, between paintings, we joined arms. It wasn't clear whose initiative it was. I said, 'The hand-holding has begun,' and he laughed. It was probably then, as we linked fingers, that we assumed we would end up in my room.

He was easy company. He didn't have the compulsion of so many men on a date (this was now a date) to want to make you laugh at every turn, or point at things and sternly explain them, or constrain you with a string of polite questions. He was curious, he listened, he offered a story, he accepted one. He was relaxed in the to and fro of conversation. We were like tennis players warming up, rooted to our baselines, sending fast but easy balls down the centre of the court to our opponent's forehand, taking pride in our obliging accuracy. Yes, tennis was on my mind. I hadn't played in almost a year.

We went to the gallery cafe for a sandwich and it was here that everything could have fallen apart. The conversation had moved off paintings – my repertoire was tiny – and he had started to talk about poetry. This was unfortunate. I'd told him I had a good degree in English and now I couldn't remember when I last read a poem. No one I knew read poetry. Even at school I had managed to avoid it. We never 'did' poetry. Novels, of course, a couple of Shakespeare plays. I nodded encouragingly as he told me what he'd been re-reading. I knew what was coming and I was trying to think of a ready answer, with the consequence that I wasn't listening to him. If he asked, could I say Shakespeare? At that moment I couldn't name a single poem by him. Yes, there were Keats, Byron, Shelley, but what did they write that I was supposed to like? There were modern poets, of course I knew their names, but nervousness was whiting out my thoughts. I was in a snowstorm of mounting anxiety. Could I make the case that the short story was a kind of poem? Even if I came up with a poet, I would have to name a particular work. There it was. Not a poem in the world that I could name. Not at this moment. He had asked something, he was staring at me, waiting. *The boy stood on the burning deck.* Then he repeated his question.

'What do you think of him?'

'He's not really my kind of . . .' Then I stopped. I had only two options – to be revealed as a fraud or to own up. 'Look, I've got a confession to make. I was going to tell you at some point. It might as well be now. I lied to you. I didn't get an English degree.'

'You went straight from school to work?' He said this encouragingly and was looking at me in that way I remembered from our interview, both kindly and teasing.

'I've a degree in maths.'

'From Cambridge? Christ. Why conceal that?'

'I thought my opinion of your work would matter less to you. It was stupid, I know. I was pretending to be the person I once wanted to be.'

'And who was that?'

So I told him the whole story of my speed-reading fiction compulsion, of my mother turning me away from studying English, my academic misery at Cambridge, and of how I continued reading, and still did. How I hoped he would forgive me. And how I really loved his work.

'Listen, a maths degree is far more demanding. You've got the rest of your life to read poetry. We can start with the poet I was just talking about.'

'I've forgotten his name already.'

'Edward Thomas. And the poem – a sweet, old-fashioned thing. Hardly the stuff of poetic revolutions. But it's lovely, one of the best-known, best-loved poems in the language. It's marvellous you don't know it. You've got so much ahead of you!'

We had already paid for our lunch. He stood abruptly and took my arm and propelled me out of the building, up the Charing Cross Road. What could have been a disaster was drawing us closer, even though it now meant that my date was telling me things in the traditional manner. We stood in a corner of a basement of a second-hand bookshop in St Martin's Court, with an old hardback *Collected Thomas* opened by Tom for me at the right page.

Obediently, I read it, and looked up. 'Very nice.'

'You can't have read it in three seconds. Take it slowly.'

There wasn't much to take. Four verses of four short lines. A train makes an unscheduled stop at an obscure station, no one gets on or off, someone coughs, a bird sings, it's hot, there are flowers and trees, hay drying in the fields and lots of other birds. And that was it.

I closed the book and said, 'Beautiful.'

His head was cocked and he was smiling patiently. 'You don't get it.'

'Of course I do.'

'Then tell it to me.'

'What do you mean?'

'Say it back to me, everything in it that you can remember.'

So I told him all I knew, almost line by line, and even remembered the haycocks, cloudlets, willows and meadow-sweet, as well as Oxfordshire and Gloucestershire. He seemed impressed and he was looking at me oddly, as if he was making a discovery.

He said, 'There's nothing wrong with your memory. Now try to remember the feelings.'

We were the only customers downstairs in the shop and there were no windows and only two dim bulbs, without shades. There was a pleasant dusty soporific smell, as though the books had stolen most of the air.

I said, 'I'm sure there isn't a single mention of a feeling.'

'What's the first word of the poem?'

'Yes.'

'Good.'

'It goes, "Yes, I remember Adlestrop."'

He came closer. 'The memory of a name and nothing else, the stillness, the beauty, the arbitrariness of the stop, birdsong spread out across two counties, the sense of pure existence, of being suspended in space and time, a time before a cataclysmic war.'

I angled my head and his lips brushed mine. I said very quietly, 'The poem doesn't mention a war.'

He took the book from my hands as we kissed, and I remembered that when Neil Carder kissed the mannequin for the very first time, her lips *were hard and cool from a lifetime of trusting no one.*

I made my lips go soft.

Later we doubled back on ourselves, crossed Trafalgar Square, towards St James's Park. Here, as we strolled past staggering toddlers with fistfuls of bread for the mallards, we talked about our sisters. His, Laura, once a great beauty, was seven years older than Tom, had studied for the bar, had had a brilliant future, then by degrees, with this or that difficult case and difficult husband, became an alcoholic and lost everything. Her descent was complicated by some near-successful attempts at recovery, heroic comebacks in the courtroom, until drink pulled her back down again. There were various dramas that used up the last of the family's patience. And finally, a car accident in which the youngest of her children, a five-year-old girl, lost a foot. There were three children by two fathers. Laura had fallen through every safety net the modern liberal State could devise. Now she was living in a hostel in Bristol, but the management was ready to throw her out. The children were looked after by their fathers and stepmothers. There was a younger sister, Joan, married to a Church of England vicar, who also looked out for them, and two or three times a year Tom took his two nieces and nephew on holiday.

His parents were also marvellous with their grandchildren. But Mr and Mrs Haley had lived through twenty years of shock, false hopes, embarrassments and night-time emergencies. They dreaded her next phone call and lived in a condition of constant sadness and self-blame. However much they loved Laura, however they kept alive on the mantelpiece the essence of what she had been in the silver-framed photos of her tenth birthday and degree ceremony and first wedding, even they could not deny she had become a terrible person, terrible to look at, to listen to, terrible to smell. Terrible to remember the calm intelligence, then hear her wheedling self-pity and lies and sodden promises. The family had tried everything in the way of coaxing, then gentle confrontation, then outright blaming, and clinics and therapies and hopeful new drugs. The Haleys had spent almost all they had in tears and time and money, and there was really nothing to do now but concentrate their affection and resources on the children and wait for their mother to be permanently hospitalised, and die.

In the race to such ruin as Laura's, my sister Lucy could hardly compete. She had dropped out of her medical degree and was back living near our parents, even as she discovered in herself, through therapy, a bitter reserve of anger against my mother for arranging the abortion. In every town there's a cadre who refuse or fail, sometimes quite happily, to move on to the next stage, the next place. Lucy found a snug community of old school friends who had returned too soon from forays on the hippie trail, or to art college or universities, and were settling down to a marginal life in their pleasant home town. Despite the crises and states of emergency, these were good years for staying out of a job. Without asking too many impertinent questions, the State paid the rent and granted a weekly pension to artists, out-of-work actors, musicians, mystics, therapists and a network of citizens for whom smoking cannabis and talking about it was an engrossing profession, even a vocation. The weekly handout was fiercely defended as a hard-won right, though everyone, even Lucy, knew in their hearts that it had not been devised to keep the middle classes in such playful leisure.

Now that I was a taxpayer with a meagre income, my scepticism about my sister ran deep. She was clever, brilliant at biology and chemistry at school, and she was kind, she had the human touch. I wanted her to be a doctor. I wanted her to want what she used to want. She lived rent-free with another woman, a circus-skills instructor, in a Victorian terraced cottage renovated by the local council. She signed on, smoked dope, and for three hours a week on Saturday mornings sold rainbow-coloured candles from a stall in the city-centre market. On my last visit home she had talked of the neurotic, competitive 'straight' world she had left behind. When I suggested that this was the world that supported her work-free existence she laughed and said, 'Serena, you're so right wing!'

While I was filling in the background and telling Tom this story I was fully aware that he was about to become a State pensioner too, on a grander scale, from the Secret Vote, that portion of government expenditure that parliament may never scrutinise. But T.H. Haley was going to work hard and produce great novels, not rainbow candles or tie-dye T-shirts. As we made our three or four turns about the park, I did feel queasy about withholding information from him, but it helped to remember that he'd visited our cut-out, the Foundation, and had approved of it. No one was going to tell him what to write or think or tell him how he should live. I had helped bring freedom to a genuine artist. Perhaps the great patrons of the Renaissance felt the way I did. Generous, above immediate earthly concerns. If that seems a grand claim, remember that I was feeling a little drunk and lit up by the afterglow of our long kiss in the bookshop basement. We both were. Talking about our less fortunate sisters was our unintentional way of marking our own happiness, of keeping our feet on the ground. Otherwise we might have floated off above Horse Guards Parade, away over Whitehall and across the river, especially after we stopped under an oak, still hoarding its load of rusty dry leaves, and he pressed me against its trunk and we kissed again.

This time I put my arms round him and felt beneath the tightness of his belted jeans the sinewy slenderness of his waist and, below, the hard muscle of his buttocks. I felt weak and sick, my throat was parched and I wondered if I was getting flu. I wanted to lie down with him and stare into his face. We decided to go to my place, but we couldn't face public transport and we couldn't afford a taxi. So we walked. Tom carried my books, the Edward Thomas and his other gift, the *Oxford Book of English Verse*. Past Buckingham Palace to Hyde Park Corner, along Park Lane, past my work street – which I failed to point out – then a long trudge up the Edgware Road, passing the new Arab restaurants, eventually turning right onto St John's Wood Road, past Lord's cricket ground, along the top of Regent's Park and into Camden Town. There are far quicker ways, but we didn't notice or care. We knew what we were walking towards. Mostly, not thinking about it made the walking easier.

In the usual way of young lovers, we talked about our families, placing ourselves for each other in the scheme of things, counting up our comparative luck. At one point Tom said he wondered how I found it possible to live without poetry.

I said, 'Well, you can show me how to be unable to live without poetry.' Even as I said this I was reminding myself that this could be a one-off and that I should be prepared.

I knew the outline of his family's story from the profile Max had given me. Tom's luck had been not too bad at all, give or take a Laura and an agoraphobic mother. We shared the protected prosperous lives of post-war children. His father was an architect working in the town planning department of Kent County Council and about to retire. Like me, Tom was the product of a good grammar school. Sevenoaks. He chose Sussex over Oxford and Cambridge because he liked the look of the courses ('themes not surveys'), and had arrived at a stage of life when it was interesting to upset expectations. I couldn't quite believe him when he insisted that he had no regrets. His mother was a peripatetic piano teacher until her growing fear of stepping outdoors confined her to lessons at home. A glimpse of sky, of a corner of a cloud was enough to bring her to the edge of a panic attack. No one knew what brought the agoraphobia on. Laura's drinking came later. Tom's sister Joan, before her marriage to the vicar, had been a dress designer – the source of the shop-window dummy as well as the Rev. Alfredus, I thought, but did not say.

His MA in international relations had been about justice at the Nuremberg Trials, and his PhD was on *The Faerie Queene*. He adored Spenser's poetry, though he wasn't sure I was ready for it just yet. We were walking along Prince Albert Road, within earshot of London Zoo. He had finished his thesis over the summer, had it specially bound in hard covers with gold embossed title. It contained acknowledgements, abstract, footnotes, bibliography, index and four hundred pages of minute examination. Now it was a relief to contemplate the relative freedom of fiction. I talked about my own background and then for the length of Parkway and the top of the Camden Road, we fell into a companionable silence, odd between near strangers.

I was wondering about my sagging bed and whether it would support us. But I didn't really care. Let it go through the floor onto Tricia's desk, I would be in it with Tom when it went down. I was in a strange state of mind. Intense desire mixed with sorrow, and a muted sense of triumph. The sorrow was prompted by walking past my workplace, which had stirred up thoughts of Tony. All week I'd been haunted by his death again, but in different terms. Was he alone, full of blustering self-justifying thoughts right to the end? Did he know what Lyalin had told his interrogators? Perhaps someone from the fifth floor had gone out to Kumlinge to forgive him in exchange for all he knew. Or someone from the other side had arrived unannounced to pin on the lapel of his old windcheater the Order of Lenin. I tried to spare him my sarcasm, but generally I failed. I felt doubly betrayed. He could have told me about the two men who came in the chauffeured black car, he could have told me he was ill. I would have helped him, I would have done anything he asked. I would have lived with him on a Baltic island.

My small triumph was Tom. I'd received what I'd been hoping for, a typed one-line note from Peter Nutting upstairs thanking me for 'the fourth man'. His little joke. I had delivered the fourth writer to Sweet Tooth. I snatched a glance at him. So lean, loping along by my side, hands deep in his jeans, his gaze turned to one side, away from me, perhaps pursuing an idea. I already felt proud of him, and just a little proud of myself. If he didn't want to, he would never have to think of Edmund Spenser again. The Sweet Tooth Faerie Queene had delivered Tom from academic struggle.

So here we were, indoors at last, in my twelve-feet-by-twelve bedsit, Tom in my junk-shop chair, and I perched on the edge of the bed. It was better to go on talking for a while. My housemates would hear the drone of our voices and soon lose interest. And there were many subjects for us because scattered about the room, piled on the floor and on the chest of drawers were two hundred and fifty prompts in the form of paperback novels. Now at last he could see that I was a reader and not just an empty-headed girl who cared nothing for poetry. To relax, to ease ourselves towards the bed I was sitting on, we talked books in a light and careless way, hardly bothering to make a case when we disagreed, which was at every turn. He had no time for my kind of women – his hand moved past the Byatt and the Drabbles, past Monica Dickens and Elizabeth Bowen, those novels I had inhabited so happily. He found and praised Muriel Spark's *The Driver's Seat*. I said I found it too schematic and preferred *The Prime of Miss Jean Brodie*. He nodded, but not in agreement, it seemed, more like a therapist who now understood my problem. Without leaving the chair he stretched forward and picked up John Fowles's *The Magus* and said he admired parts of that, as well as all of *The Collector* and *The French Lieutenant's Woman*. I said I didn't like tricks, I liked life as I knew it recreated on the page. He said it wasn't possible to recreate life on the page without tricks. He stood and went over to the dresser and picked up a B.S. Johnson, *Albert Angelo*, the one with holes cut in the pages. He admired this too, he said. I said I detested it. He was amazed to see a copy of Alan Burns's *Celebrations* – by far the best experimentalist in the country was the verdict. I said I hadn't yet made a start. He saw I had a

214

handful of books published by John Calder. Best list around. I went over to where he stood. I said I hadn't managed to read further than twenty pages in a single one. And so terribly printed! And how about J.G. Ballard – he saw I had three of his titles. Couldn't face them, I said, too apocalyptic. He loved everything Ballard did. He was a bold and brilliant spirit. We laughed. Tom promised to read me a Kingsley Amis poem, 'A Bookshop Idyll', about men and women's divergent tastes. It went a bit soppy at the end, he said, but it was funny and true. I said I'd probably hate it, except for the end. He kissed me, and that was the end of the literary discussion. We went towards the bed.

It was awkward. We'd been talking for hours, pretending that we weren't thinking constantly of this moment. We were like pen friends who exchange chatty then intimate letters in each other's language, then meet for the first time and realise they must begin again. His style was new to me. I was sitting on the edge of the bed once more. After a single kiss, and without further caresses, he leaned over me and set about undressing me, and doing it efficiently, routinely, as though he were getting a child ready for bed. If he'd been humming to himself it wouldn't have surprised me. In different circumstances, if we'd been closer, that might have been an attractive tender moment of role-playing. But this was done in silence. I didn't know what it meant and I was uneasy. When he stretched across my shoulders to unfasten my bra, I could have touched him, I was about to, then I didn't. Supporting my head, he gently pushed me back on the bed and took off my knickers. None of this had any appeal for me at all. It was getting too tense. I had to intervene.

215

I sprang up and said, 'Your turn.' Obediently, he sat where I had been. I stood in front of him, so that my breasts were close to his face, and unbuttoned his shirt. I could see that he was hard. 'Bedtime for big boys.' When he took my nipple into his mouth I thought we were going to be all right. I'd almost forgotten the sensation, hot and electric and piercing, spreading up round the base of my throat and right down to my perineum. But when we pulled back the covers and lay down, I saw that he was now soft and thought I must have done something wrong. I was also surprised by a glimpse of his pubic hair – so scant it was almost non-existent, and what was there was straight and silky, like head hair. We kissed again – he was good at that – but when I took his cock in my hand it was still soft. I pushed his head down towards my breasts since that had worked before. A fresh partner. It was like learning a new card game. But he went down past my breasts, lowered his head and brought me off with his tongue beautifully. I came in less than a glorious minute with a little shout I disguised as a strangled cough for the benefit of the lawyers downstairs. When I came to my senses I was relieved to see how aroused he was. My pleasure had loosened his own. And so I drew him towards me and it began.

It was not a great experience for either of us, but we made it through, we saved face. The limitation for me was partly, as I've said, my awareness of the other three, who seemed to have no love lives of their own and who would be straining to hear a human sound above the creak of bed springs. And it was partly that Tom was so silent. He said nothing endearing or affectionate or appreciative. Even his breathing didn't change. I couldn't banish the thought that he was quietly recording our lovemaking for future use, that he was making mental notes, creating and adjusting phrases to his liking, looking out for the detail that rose above the ordinary. I thought again of the story of the false vicar, and Jean of the 'monstrous' clitoris, the size of a little boy's penis. What did Tom think of mine while he was down there measuring its length with his tongue? Too average to be worth remembering? When Edmund and Jean are reunited in the flat in Chalk Farm and make love, she reaches her orgasm and makes a series of *high-pitched bleats, as pure and evenly spaced as the BBC's time signal*. What then of my politely muted sounds? Such questions bred other, unhealthy thoughts. Neil Carder delights in his mannequin's 'stillness', he thrills to the possibility that she was contemptuous of him and was ignoring him. Was this what Tom wanted, total passivity in a woman, an inwardness that *rolled back upon itself to become its opposite, a force that overwhelmed and consumed him*? Should I lie completely still and let my lips part as I fixed my gaze on the ceiling? I didn't really think so, and I didn't enjoy these speculations.

I added to my torments by fantasising about him reaching for a notebook and pencil from his jacket as soon as we were finished. Of course I would throw him out! But these self-harming thoughts were merely bad dreams. He lay on his back, I lay on his arm. It wasn't cold but we drew the sheet and blanket over us. We dozed lightly for some minutes. I woke when the front door slammed downstairs and I heard the receding voices of my house-mates in the street. We were alone in the house. Without being able to see, I sensed Tom coming fully awake. He was silent for a while and then he proposed taking me

217

out to a good restaurant. His Foundation money hadn't arrived, but he was sure it would come soon. I silently confirmed this. Max had signed off on the payment two days before.

We went to the White Tower at the south end of Charlotte Street and ate kleftiko with roast potatoes and drank three bottles of retsina. We could take it. How exotic, to be dining at the expense of the Secret Vote and not be able to say. I felt so grown up. Tom told me that during the war this famous restaurant had served spam *à la grecque*. We joked that soon those days would be back. He filled me in on the literary associations of the place while I smiled loopily, not quite listening because, again, some sort of music was playing in my mind, this time a symphony, a majestic slow movement on the grand scale of Mahler. This very room, Tom was saying, was where Ezra Pound and Wyndham Lewis founded their vorticist *Blast* magazine. The names meant nothing to me. We walked back from Fitzrovia to Camden Town, arm in arm and drunk, talking nonsense. When we woke the next morning in my room the new card game was easy. In fact, it was a delight.

15

L ate October brought the annual rite of putting back
the clocks, tightening the lid of darkness over our
afternoons, lowering the nation's mood further. November
began with another cold snap and it rained most days.
Everyone was speaking of 'the crisis'. Government presses
were printing petrol rationing coupons. There had been
nothing like this since the last war. The general sense was
that we were heading for something nasty but hard to
foresee, impossible to avoid. There was a suspicion that
the 'social fabric' was about to unravel, though no one
really knew what this would entail. But I was happy and
busy, I had a lover at last, and I was trying not to brood
about Tony. My anger at him gave way to, or at least
blended with, guilt for condemning him so harshly. It was
wrong to lose sight of that distant idyll, our Edwardian
summer in Suffolk. Now I was with Tom, I felt protected,
I could afford to think nostalgically rather than tragically
of our time together. Tony may have betrayed his country
but he'd given me my start in life.

I revived my newspaper habit. It was the opinion pages that drew me, the complaints and laments, known in the trade, so I'd learned, as why-oh-why pieces. As in, why-oh-why did university intellectuals cheer on the carnage wrought by the Provisional IRA and romanticise the Angry Brigade and the Red Army Faction? Our empire and our victory in the Second World War haunted and accused us, but why-oh-why must we stagnate among the ruins of our former greatness? Crime rates were soaring, everyday courtesies declining, the streets filthy, our economy and morale broken, our living standards below those of communist East Germany, and we stood divided, truculent and irrelevant. Insurrectionary trouble-makers were dismantling our democratic traditions, popular television was hysterically silly, colour TV sets cost too much and everyone agreed there was no hope, the country was finished, our moment in history had passed. Why-oh-why?

I also followed the woeful daily narrative. By the middle of the month oil imports were right down, the Coal Board had offered the miners 16.5 per cent but, seizing the opportunity granted by OPEC, they were holding out for 35 per cent and were starting their overtime ban. Children were sent home because there was no heating in their schools, street lights were turned off to save energy, there was wild talk of everyone working a three-day week because of electricity shortages. The government announced the fifth state of emergency. Some said pay off the miners, some said down with bullies and blackmailers. I followed all this, I discovered I had a taste for economics. I knew the figures and I knew my way round the crisis. But I didn't care. I was absorbed by Spade and Helium, I was trying to forget Volt and my heart belonged to Sweet Tooth, my private portion of it. This meant travelling ex officio at the weekends to Brighton, where Tom had a two-room flat at the top of a thin white house near the station. Clifton Street resembled a row of iced Christmas cakes, the air was clean, we had privacy, the bed was of modern pine, the mattress silent and firm. Within weeks I came to think of this place as home.

The bedroom was just a little larger than the bed. There wasn't enough space to open the wardrobe door by more than nine inches or so. You had to reach inside and feel for your clothes. I sometimes woke in the early morning to the sound of Tom's typewriter through the wall. The room he worked in also served as kitchen and sitting room and felt more spacious. It had been opened up to the rafters by the ambitious builder who was Tom's landlord. That uneven tapping of the keys and the cawing of gulls – I woke to these sounds and, keeping my eyes closed, I'd luxuriate in the transformation in my existence. How lonely I'd been in Camden, especially after Shirley had left. What a pleasure it was, to arrive at seven on a Friday at the end of an arduous week and walk the few hundred yards up the hill under streetlight, smelling the sea and feeling that Brighton was as remote from London as Nice or Naples, knowing that Tom would have a bottle of white wine in the miniature fridge and wine glasses ready on the kitchen table. Our weekends were simple. We made love, we read, we walked on the seafront and sometimes on the Downs, and we ate in restaurants – usually in the Lanes. And Tom wrote.

He worked on an Olivetti portable on a green baize card table pushed into a corner. He would get up in the night or at dawn and work through until nine or so, when he would come back to bed, make love to me, then sleep until midday while I went out for a coffee and a croissant near the Open Market. Croissants were a novelty in England then and they made my corner of Brighton seem all the more exotic. I would read the paper cover to cover, minus the sport, then shop for our fry-up brunch.

Tom's Foundation money was coming through – how else could we afford to eat at Wheeler's and fill the fridge with Chablis? During that November and December he was doing the last of his teaching and working on two stories. He'd met in London a poet and editor, Ian Hamilton, who was starting up a literary magazine, the *New Review*, and wanted Tom to submit fiction for one of the early issues. He had read all of Tom's published stuff and had told him over drinks in Soho that it was 'quite good' or 'not bad' – high praise from this quarter, apparently.

In the self-congratulatory way of new lovers, we had developed by now a number of smug routines, catch phrases and fetishes, and our Saturday evening pattern was well established. We often made love in the early evening – our 'main meal of the day'. The early morning 'cuddle' did not really count. In a mood of elation and post-coital clarity, we'd dress for an evening out and before leaving the flat we'd sink most of a bottle of Chablis. We would drink nothing else at home though neither of us knew a thing about wine. Chablis was a joke choice because, apparently, James Bond liked it. Tom would play music on his new hi-fi, usually bebop, to me no more than an arrhythmic stream of random notes, but it sounded sophisticated and glamorously urban. Then we would step out into the icy sea breeze and saunter down the hill to the Lanes, usually to Wheeler's fish restaurant. Tom had semi-drunkenly over-tipped the waiters there often enough, so we were popular and were shown with some flourish to 'our' table, well positioned to one side for us to observe and mock the other diners. I suppose we were unbearable. We made a thing of telling the waiters to bring us as a starter 'the usual' – two glasses of champagne and a dozen oysters. I'm not sure we really liked them, but we liked the idea of them, the oval arrangement of bar-nacled ancient life among the parsley and halved lemons and, glinting opulently in the candlelight, the bed of ice, the silver dish, the polished cruet of chilli sauce.

When we weren't talking about ourselves, we had all of politics – the domestic crisis, the Middle East, Vietnam. Logically, we should have been more ambivalent about a war to contain communism, but we took the orthodox view of our generation. The struggle was murderously cruel and clearly a failure. We also followed that soap opera of over-reaching power and folly, Watergate, though Tom, like most men I knew, was so well up on the cast, the dates, every historical turn in the narrative and minor constitutional implication that he found me a useless companion in outrage. We should also have had all of literature. He showed me the poems he loved, and there was no problem with that – I loved them too. But he couldn't interest me in the novels of John Hawkes, Barry Hannah or William Gaddis, and he failed with my hero-ines, Margaret Drabble, Fay Weldon and, my latest flame, Jennifer Johnston. I thought his lot were too dry, he thought mine were wet, though he was prepared to give Elizabeth Bowen the benefit of the doubt. During that time, we managed to agree on only one short novel, which he had in a bound proof, William Kotzwinkle's *Swimmer in the*

Secret Sea. He thought it was beautifully formed, I thought it was wise and sad.

Since he didn't like talking about his work before it was finished, I felt it was reasonable and dutiful to take a peek when he was out one Saturday afternoon researching in the library. I kept the door open so I could hear him coming up the stairs. One story, completed in a first draft by the end of November, was narrated by a talking ape prone to anxious reflections about his lover, a writer struggling with her second novel. She has been praised for her first. Is she capable of another just as good? She is beginning to doubt it. The indignant ape hovers at her back, hurt by the way she neglects him for her labours. Only on the last page did I discover that the story I was reading was actually the one the woman was writing. The ape doesn't exist, it's a spectre, the creature of her fretful imagination. *No.* And no again. Not that. Beyond the strained and ludicrous matter of cross-species sex, I instinctively distrusted this kind of fictional trick. I wanted to feel the ground beneath my feet. There was, in my view, an unwritten contract with the reader that the writer must honour. No single element of an imagined world or any of its characters should be allowed to dissolve on authorial whim. The invented had to be as solid and as self-consistent as the actual. This was a contract founded on mutual trust.

If the first was disappointing, the second piece amazed me before I started reading. It was over a hundred and forty pages long, with last week's date written in longhand below the last sentence. The first draft of a short novel, and he'd kept it a secret from me. I was about to start reading when I was startled by the door to the outside landing slamming shut, pushed by a draught through the leaky windows. I got up and propped the door open with a coil of oily rope that Tom had once used to haul single-handedly the wardrobe up the stairs. Then I turned on the light that hung from the rafters and settled down to my guilty speed-reading.

From the Somerset Levels described a journey a man makes with his nine-year-old daughter across a ruined landscape of burned-out villages and small towns, where rats, cholera and bubonic plague are constant dangers, where the water is polluted and neighbours fight to the death for an ancient can of juice, where the locals consider themselves lucky to be invited to a celebration dinner at which a dog and a couple of scrawny cats will be roasted over a bonfire. The desolation is even greater when father and daughter reach London. Among the decaying skyscrapers and rusting vehicles and uninhabitable terraced streets where rats and feral dogs teem, warlords and their thugs, faces done up in streaks of primary colours, terrorise the impoverished citizenry. Electricity is a distant memory. All that functions, though barely, is government itself. A ministerial tower block rises over a vast plain of cracked and weedy concrete. On their way to stand in line outside a government office, father and daughter cross the plain at dawn, passing over *vegetables, rotten and trodden down, cardboard boxes flattened into beds, the remains of fires and the carcasses of roasted pigeons, rusted tin, vomit, worn tyres, chemical green puddles, human and animal excrement. An old dream of horizontal lines converging on the thrusting steel and glass perpendicular was now beyond recall.*

This plaza, where much of the central section of the novel takes place, is a giant microcosm of a sad new world.

In the middle is a disused fountain, the air above it is *grey with flies. Men and boys came there daily to squat on the wide concrete rim and defecate.* These figures *perch like featherless birds.* Later in the day the place teems like an ant colony, the air is thick with smoke, the noise is deafening, people spread their pathetic goods on coloured blankets, the father haggles for an ancient used bar of soap, though fresh water will be hard to find. Everything for sale on the plain was made long ago, by processes no longer understood. Later, the man (annoyingly, we are never told his name) meets up with an old friend who is lucky enough to have a room. She's a collector. On the table there is a telephone, *its wire severed at four inches and, beyond that, propped against the wall, a cathode ray tube. The television's wooden casing, the glass screen and control buttons had long ago been ripped away and now bunches of bright wires coiled against the dull metal.* She cares for such objects because, she tells him, they're *the products of human inventiveness and design. And not caring for objects is one step away from not caring for people.* But he thinks her curating impulses are pointless. *Without a telephone system, telephones are worthless junk.*

Industrial civilisation and all its systems and culture are fading from recall. Man is tracking back through time to a brutal past where constant competition for scarce resources allows little kindness or invention. The old days will not be back. *Everything has changed so much that I can hardly believe it was us who were there*, the woman tells him of the past they once shared. *This was where we were always heading*, one shoeless philosophical character says to the father. It's made clear elsewhere that civilisation's collapse began with the injustices, conflicts and contradictions of the twentieth century.

The reader doesn't find out where the man and the little girl are headed until the final pages. They have been searching for his wife, the girl's mother. There are no systems of communication or bureaucracy to help them. The only photograph they have is of her as a child. They rely on word of mouth, and after many false trails, they are bound to fail, especially when they begin to succumb to bubonic plague. Father and daughter die in one another's arms in the rank cellar of the ruined headquarters of a once-famous bank.

It had taken me an hour and a quarter to read to the end. I replaced the pages by the typewriter, taking care to spread them as untidily as I'd found them, shifted the rope and closed the door. I sat at the kitchen table trying to think through my confusion. I could easily rehearse the objections of Peter Nutting and colleagues. Here were the doomed dystopia we did not want, the modish apocalypse that indicted and rejected all we had ever devised or built or loved, that relished in the entire project collapsing into the dirt. Here were the luxury and privilege of the well-fed man scoffing at all hopes of progress for the rest. T.H. Haley owed nothing to a world that nurtured him kindly, liberally educated him for free, sent him to no wars, brought him to manhood without scary rituals or famine or fear of vengeful gods, embraced him with a handsome pension in his twenties and placed no limits on his freedom of expression. This was an easy nihilism that never doubted that all we had made was rotten, never thought to pose alternatives, never derived hope from friendship, love, free markets, industry, technology, trade and all the arts and sciences.

His story (I made my phantom Nutting go on to say)

inherited from Samuel Beckett a dispensation in which the human condition was a man lying alone at the end of things, bound only to himself, without hope, sucking on a pebble. A man who knows nothing of the difficulties of public administration in a democracy, of delivering good governance to millions of demanding, entitled, free-thinking individuals, who cares nothing for how far we have come in a mere five hundred years from a cruel, impoverished past.

On the other hand . . . what was good about it? It would annoy them all, especially Max, and for that alone it was glorious. It would annoy him even as it confirmed his view that taking on a novelist was a mistake. Paradoxi-cally, it would strengthen Sweet Tooth by showing how free this writer was of his paymasters. *From the Somerset Levels* was the incarnation of the ghost that was haunting every headline, a peep over the edge of the abyss, the dramatised worst case – London become Herat, Delhi, São Paulo. But what did I really think about it? It had depressed me, it was so dark, so entirely without hope. He should have spared the child at least, given the reader a little faith in the future. I suspected my phantom Nutting might be right – there was something modish in this pessimism, it was merely an aesthetic, a literary mask or attitude. It wasn't really Tom, or it was only the smallest part of him, and therefore it was insincere. I didn't like it at all. And T.H. Haley would be seen as my choice and I'd be held responsible. Another black mark.

I stared across the room at his typewriter and the empty coffee cup beside it, and I considered. Might the man I was having an affair with prove incapable of fulfilling the moment of his earliest promise, like the woman with the ape at her back? If his best work was already behind him, I would have made an embarrassing error of judgement. That would be the accusation, but the truth was he'd been handed to me on a plate, in a file. I'd fallen for the stories and then the man. It was an arranged marriage, a marriage made on the fifth floor, and it was too late, I was the bride who couldn't run away. However disappointed I was, I would stick by him, or with him, and not only out of self-interest. For of *course* I still believed in him. A couple of weak stories were not going to dislodge my conviction that he was an original voice, a brilliant mind – and my wonderful lover. He was my project, my case, my mission. His art, my work and our affair were one. If he failed, I failed. Simple then – we would flourish together.

It was almost six o'clock. Tom was still out, the pages of his novel were convincingly spread around the typewriter and the pleasures of the evening lay ahead of us. I ran a heavily scented bath. The bathroom was five feet by four (we had measured it) and featured a space-saving hipbath in which you lowered yourself into the water and sat or crouched on a ledge in the manner of Michelangelo's *Il Penseroso*. And so I crouched and stewed and thought some more. One benign possibility was that this editor, Hamilton, if he was as sharp as Tom made out, was likely to turn both pieces down and give good reasons. In which case I should say nothing and wait. Which was the whole idea, to set him free with money, stay out of the way and hope for the best. And yet . . . and yet, I believed myself to be a good reader. I was convinced he was making a mistake, this monochrome pessimism didn't serve his talent, didn't permit him the witty reversals of, say, the false-vicar story or the ambiguities of a man making passionate love to a wife he knows to be a crook. I thought Tom liked me enough to listen. Then again, my instructions were clear. I should fight my interfering impulses.

Twenty minutes later I was drying myself by the bath, nothing resolved, thoughts still turning, when I heard footsteps on the stairs. He tapped on the door and came into my steamy boudoir and we embraced without speaking. I felt the cold street air in the folds of his coat. Perfect timing. I was naked, fragrant and ready. He led me to the bedroom, everything was fine, all troublesome questions fell away. An hour or so later we were dressed for the evening, drinking our Chablis and listening to 'My Funny Valentine' by Chet Baker, a man who sang like a woman. If there was bebop in his trumpet solo it was mild and tender. I thought I could even begin to like jazz. We chinked glasses and kissed, then Tom turned away from me and went with his wine to stand by the card table, looking down for some minutes at his work. He lifted one page after the other, searched the pile for a certain passage, found it and picked up a pencil to make a mark. He was frowning as he turned the carriage with slow meaningful clicks of the mechanism to read the sheet in the typewriter. When he looked up at me I was nervous.

He said, 'I've got something to tell you.'

'Something good?'

'I'll tell you at dinner.'

He came over to me and we kissed again. He had yet to put on his jacket and he was wearing one of the three shirts he'd had made in Jermyn Street. They were identical, of fine white Egyptian cotton, cut generously around the shoulders and arms to give him a vaguely piratical look. He'd told me that all men should have a 'library' of white shirts. I wasn't sure about the styling, but I liked the feel of him beneath the cotton, and I liked the way he was adapting to the money. The hi-fi, the restaurants, the Globe-trotter suitcases, an electric typewriter on the way – he was shrugging off the student life, doing it with style, without guilt. In those months before Christmas he also had his teaching money. He was flush, and good to be around. He bought me presents – a silk jacket, perfume, a soft leather briefcase for work, the poetry of Sylvia Plath, novels by Ford Madox Ford, all in hardback. He also paid for my return railfare, which was well over a pound. At the week-ends I forgot my scrimping London life, my pitiable food hoard in one corner of the fridge, and counting out the change in the mornings for my Tube fare and lunch.

We finished the bottle and fairly rolled down Queen's Road, past the Clock Tower and into the Lanes, pausing only for Tom to give directions to an Indian couple carrying a baby with a harelip. The narrow streets had a forlorn out-of-season air, salty-damp and deserted, the cobbles treacherously slick. In a good-humoured, teasing way, Tom was interrogating me about my 'other' writers supported by the Foundation. We'd been through this a few times and it was almost a routine. He was indulging sexual as well as writerly jealousy or competitiveness.

'Just tell me this. Are they mostly young?'

'Mostly immortal.'

'Come on. You can tell me. Are they famous oldsters? Anthony Burgess? John Braine? Any women?'

'What use are women to me?'

'Do they get more money than I do? You can tell me that.'

'Everyone gets at least twice what you get.'

'Serena!'

'OK. Everyone gets the same.'

'As me.'

'As you.'

'Am I the only one unpublished?'

'That's all I'm saying.'

'Have you fucked any of them?'

'Quite a few.'

'And you're still working through the list?'

'You know I am.'

He laughed and pulled me into the doorway of a jeweller's shop to kiss me. He was one of those men who are occasionally turned on by the idea of his lover making love to another man. In certain moods it aroused him, the daydream of being a cuckold, even though the reality would have sickened or wounded or enraged him. Clearly, the origin of Carder's fantasy about his mannequin. I didn't understand it at all but I had learned how to play along. Sometimes, when we made love, he would prompt me in whispers and I would oblige by telling him about the man I was seeing and what I did for him. Tom preferred him to be a writer, and the less probable, the more status-laden, the greater his exquisite agony. Saul Bellow, Norman Mailer, pipe-smoking Günter Grass, I went with the best. Or his best. Even at the time, I realised that a deliberate and shared fantasy was usefully diluting my own necessary untruths. It wasn't easy talking about the work I did for the Foundation with a man I was so close to. My appeal to confidentiality was one way out, this vaguely humorous erotic dream was another. But neither was enough. This was the little dark stain on my happiness.

Of course we knew very well the reason for our warm welcome at Wheeler's, for the nodding enquiries after Miss Serena's week, Mr Tom's health, our appetites, for the snappish drawing out of chairs, and napkins laid across our laps, but it also made us so very happy, and almost convinced us that we really were admired and respected, and far more so than the rest of the dull and ageing crowd. Back then, apart from a few pop stars, the young had not yet got their hands on the money. So the diners' frowns that stalked us to our table also heightened our pleasure. We were so special. If only they'd known they were paying for our meal with their taxes. If only Tom could know. Within a minute, while others who were there before us had nothing, we had our champagne, and soon after that the silver dish and its cargo of ice, and shells containing the glistening cowpats of briny viscera that we dared not cease pretending to like. The trick was to knock them back without tasting them. We knocked back the champagne too and called for a top-up. As on previous occasions we reminded ourselves to order a bottle next time. We could save so much money.

In the restaurant's moist warmth Tom had removed his jacket. He reached across the table to put his hand on mine. Candlelight deepened the green of his eyes, and touched his pallor with a faint, healthy tint of brownish-pink. Head as always slightly tipped to one side, lips as usual parted and tensed, not to speak so much as to antici-pate my words or speak them with me. Just then, already tipsy, I thought I'd never seen a man more beautiful. I forgave him his tailored pirate's shirt. Love doesn't grow at a steady rate, but advances in surges, bolts, wild leaps, and this was one of those. The first had been in the White

233

Tower. This was far more powerful. Like Sebastian Morel in 'Pawnography', I was tumbling through dimensionless space, even as I sat smiling demurely in a Brighton fish restaurant. But always, at the furthest edges of thought, was that tiny stain. I generally tried to ignore it, and I was so excited I often succeeded. Then, like a woman who slips over the edge of a cliff and makes a lunge for a tuft of grass that will never hold her weight, so I remembered yet again that Tom did not know who I was and what I really did and that I should tell him now. *Last chance! Go on, tell him now.* But it was too late. The truth was too weighty, it would destroy us. He would hate me forever. I was over the cliff edge and could never get back. I could remind myself of the benefits I had brought into his life, the artistic freedom that came with me, but the fact was that if I was to go on seeing him, I would have to keep telling him these off-white lies.

His hand moved up towards my wrist and tightened. The waiter arrived to refill our glasses.

Tom said, 'So this is just the moment to tell you.' He raised his glass, obediently I raised mine. 'You know I've been writing this stuff for Ian Hamilton. It turned out there was one piece that kept growing and I realised I was drifting into the short novel that I've been thinking about for a year. I was so excited and I wanted to tell you, I wanted to show it to you. But I didn't dare, in case it didn't work. I finished a draft last week, photocopied some of it and sent it to this publisher everyone's been telling me about. Tom Mischler. No, Maschler. His letter came this morning. I didn't expect such a quick reply. I didn't open it until this afternoon when I was out of the house. Serena, he wants it! Urgently. He wants a final draft by Christmas.'

My arm was aching from holding out my glass. I said, 'Tom, this is fantastic news. Congratulations! To you!'

We drank deeply. He said, 'It's sort of dark. Set in the near future, everything's collapsed. A bit like Ballard. But I think you'll like it.'

'How does it end? Do things get better?'

He smiled at me indulgently. 'Of course not.'

'How marvellous.'

The menu came and we ordered Dover sole and a red rather than a white wine, a hearty rioja, to demonstrate that we were free spirits. Tom talked more about his novel, and about his new editor, publisher of Heller, Roth, Marquez. I was wondering how I'd break the news to Max. An anti-capitalist dystopia. While other Sweet Tooth writers handed in their non-fiction versions of *Animal Farm*. But at least my man was a creative force who went his own way. And so would I, once I'd been sacked.

Preposterous. This was a time for celebration, for there was nothing I could do about Tom's story, which we were now referring to as 'the novella'. So we drank and ate and talked and raised our glasses to this or that good outcome. Towards the end of the evening, when there were only half a dozen diners left and our waiters were yawning and hovering, Tom said in a tone of mock reproach, 'I'm always telling you about poems and novels, but you never tell me anything about maths. It's time you did.'

'I wasn't much good,' I said. 'I've put it all behind me.'

'Not good enough. I want you to tell me something . . . something interesting, no, counter-intuitive, paradoxical. You owe me a good maths story.'

Nothing in maths had ever seemed counter-intuitive to me. Either I understood it, or I didn't, and from

Cambridge onwards, it was mostly the latter. But I liked a challenge. I said, 'Give me a few minutes.' So Tom talked about his new electric typewriter and how fast he would be able to work. Then I remembered.

'This was going the rounds among Cambridge mathematicians when I was there. I don't think anyone's written on it yet. It's about probability and it's in the form of a question. It comes from an American game show called *Let's Make a Deal*. The host a few years ago was a man called Monty Hall. Let's suppose you're on Monty's show as a contestant. Facing you are three closed boxes, one, two and three, and inside one of the boxes, you don't know which, is a wonderful prize – let's say a . . .'

'Beautiful girl gives you a fat pension.'

'Exactly. Monty knows which box your pension is in and you don't. You make a choice. Let's say you choose box one, but we don't open it yet. Then Monty, who knows where the pension is, opens a box he knows to be empty. Let's say it's box three. So you know your fat pension for life is either in box one, the one you chose, or it's in box two. Now Monty offers you the chance of changing to box two or staying where you are. Where is your pension more likely to be? Should you move or stay where you are?'

Our waiter brought the bill on a silver plate. Tom reached for his wallet, then changed his mind. For all the wine and champagne he sounded clear-headed. We both did. We wanted to show each other we could hold our drink.

'It's obvious. With box one I had a one in three chance to start with. When box three is opened my chances narrow to one in two. And the same has to be true for box two. Equal chances that my fat pension is in either box. It makes no difference whether I move or not. Serena, you're looking unbearably beautiful.'

'Thank you. You'd be in good company with that choice. But you'd be wrong. If you go for the other box you double your chances of never needing to take a job again.'

'Nonsense.'

I watched him take out his wallet to settle the bill. It was almost thirty pounds. He slapped down a twenty-pound tip, and the looseness of the gesture revealed how drunk he was. This was more than my weekly wage. He was trapped by precedent.

I said, 'Your chance of choosing the box with your pension remains one in three. The sum of probabilities has to add up to one. So the chances of it being in one of the other two boxes has to be two in three. Box three is open and empty, so it's two in three that it's in box two.'

He was looking at me pityingly, as though I were an evangelical member of some extreme religious sect. 'Monty has given me more information by opening the box. My chances were one in three. Now they're one in two.'

'That would only be true if you had just come in the room after he opened the box and *then* you were asked to choose between the other two boxes. Then you'd be looking at odds of one in two.'

'Serena. I'm surprised you can't see what's there.'

I was beginning to feel a distinctive and unusual kind of pleasure, a sense of being set free. In a portion of mental space, perhaps quite a large portion, I was actually cleverer than Tom. How strange that seemed. What was so very simple for me, for him was apparently beyond comprehension.

'Look at it this way,' I said. 'Moving from box one to

box two is only a bad idea if you'd made the right choice at the start and your pension is in box one. And the chances of that are one in three. So, one-third of the time it's a bad idea to move, which means that two-thirds of the time it's a good idea.'

He was frowning, struggling. He had glimpsed for a moment the truth, and then he blinked and it was gone.

'I know I'm right,' he said. 'I'm just not explaining it well. This Monty has chosen at random the box to put my pension in. There are only two boxes it can be in, so there has to be an equal chance it's one or the other.' He was about to get up and slumped back in his chair. 'Thinking about it is making me dizzy.'

'There's another way of approaching it,' I said. 'Suppose we have a million boxes. Same rules. Let's say you choose box seven hundred thousand. Monty comes along the line opening box after box, all empty. All the time he's avoiding opening the box that has your prize. He stops when the only closed boxes left are yours and, say, number ninety-five. What are the chances now?'

'Equal,' he said in a muffled voice. 'Fifty–fifty each box.'

I tried not to sound like I was speaking to a child. 'Tom, it's a million to one against it being in your box, and almost certain that it's in the other.'

He had that same look of fleeting insight, then it was gone. 'Well, no, I don't think that's right, I mean I . . . Actually, I think I'm going to be sick.'

He lurched to his feet and hurried past the waiters without saying goodbye. When I caught up with him outside he was leaning by a car, staring at his shoes. The cold air had revived him and he hadn't been sick after all. Arm in arm we headed for home.

When I thought he had recovered sufficiently I said, 'If it helps, we could test this empirically using playing cards. We could get . . .'

'Serena, darling, no more. If I think about this again I really will throw up.'

'You wanted something counter-intuitive.'

'Yes. Sorry. I won't ask you again. Let's stick with pro-intuitive.'

So we talked of other things and as soon as we got back to the flat we went to bed and slept deeply. But early on Sunday morning Tom, in a state of excitement, shook me awake from confused dreams.

'I get it! Serena, I understand how it works. Everything you were saying, it's so simple. It just popped into place, like, you know, that drawing of a what's-it cube.'

'Necker.'

'And I can *do* something with it.'

'Yes, why not . . .'

I fell asleep to the rattle of his typewriter keys next door and didn't wake for another three hours. We barely referred to Monty Hall during the rest of that Sunday. I made a roast lunch while he worked. It may have been the lowering effect of a hangover, but I was more than usually sad at the prospect of returning to St Augustine's Road and my lonely room, of turning on my single-bar electric fire, of washing my hair in the sink and ironing a blouse for work.

In sombre afternoon light Tom walked me to the station. I was almost tearful as we embraced on the platform, but I didn't make a big scene, and I don't think he noticed.

16

Three days later his story arrived in the post. Attached to the first page was a postcard of the West Pier and on the reverse was, 'Have I got this right?'

I read 'Probable Adultery' in the icy kitchen over a mug of tea before I left for work. Terry Mole is a London architect whose childless marriage is being steadily destroyed by the serial affairs of his wife Sally. She has no job and, with no children to attend to and a housekeeper to do the chores, she's able *to dedicate herself to constant and reckless infidelity*. She also applies herself each day to smoking pot and prefers a large whisky or two before lunch. Meanwhile, Terry puts in a seventy-hour week designing cheap high-rise council flats which will probably be pulled down within fifteen years. Sally has assignations with men she barely knows. *Her lies and excuses were insultingly transparent but he could never disprove them. He didn't have the time.* But one day a number of on-site meetings are cancelled and the architect decides to spend his free hours following his wife. *He was eaten away by sadness and jealousy and needed to see her with a man in order to feed his desolation and strengthen his resolve to leave her.* She's told him she's going to spend the day with her aunt in St Albans. Instead, she heads for Victoria station and Terry follows.

She boards a train for Brighton, and so does he, two carriages back. He tracks her through the town, across the Steine and into the back streets of Kemp Town until she comes to a small hotel in Upper Rock Gardens. From the pavement he sees her in the lobby with a man, fortunately a rather puny fellow, Terry thinks. He sees the couple take a key from the receptionist and begin to climb the narrow stairs. Terry enters the hotel and, unnoticed or ignored by the receptionist, also goes up the stairs. He can hear their footsteps above him. He hangs back as they reach the fourth floor. He hears a door being opened, then closed. He arrives on the landing. Facing him there are only three rooms, 401, 402 and 403. His plan is to wait until the couple are in bed, then he'll kick their door down, shame his wife and give that little fellow a hard smack to the head.

But he doesn't know which room they're in.

He stands quietly on the landing, hoping to hear a sound. *He craved to hear it, a moan, a yelp, a bedspring, anything would do. But there was nothing.* The minutes pass and he has to make a choice. He decides on 401 because it's the nearest. All the doors look flimsy enough and he knows a good flying kick will do the job. He's stepping back to make his run when the door of 403 opens and out step an Indian couple with their baby, who has a harelip. They smile shyly as they go past him and then they descend the stairs.

When they've gone Terry hesitates. Here the story

becomes tense as it rises towards its climax. As an architect and an amateur mathematician he has a good grasp of numbers. He makes a hurried reckoning. There was always a one-in-three chance his wife is in 401. Which means that until just now there was a two-in-three chance she's either in 402 or 403. And now that 403 is shown to be empty, there must be a two-in-three chance she's in 402. *Only a fool would stay with his first choice, for the steely laws of probability are inflexibly true.* He makes his run, he leaps, the door of 402 smashes open and there are the couple, naked in bed, just getting going. He gives the man *a beefy slap round the chops, threw his wife a look of cold contempt*, then leaves for London, where he'll institute divorce proceedings and start a new life.

All that Wednesday I sorted and filed documents relating to one Joe Cahill of the Provisionals, his connection with Colonel Qaddafi and an arms shipment from Libya, tracked by Six and intercepted by the Irish navy off the coast of Waterford at the end of March. Cahill was on board and didn't know a thing until he felt the barrel of a gun in the back of his neck. As far as I could tell from paper-clipped addenda, our lot had been out of the loop and were irritated. 'This mistake', read one furious minute, 'must not be made again.' Interesting enough, up to a point. But I knew which location – the good ship *Claudia* or the inside of my lover's mind – interested me more. More than that, I was worried, fretful. Whenever I had a break, my thoughts returned to the doors on the fourth floor of a Brighton hotel.

It was a good story. Even if it wasn't one of his best, he was back on form, the right kind of form. But when I read it that morning, I knew at a stroke that it was flawed, built on specious assumptions, unworkable parallels, hopeless mathematics. He hadn't understood me or the problem at all. His excitement, his Necker-cube moment, had carried him away. Thinking about his boyish exultation and how I had drifted back to sleep and failed to discuss his idea when I woke made me feel ashamed. He had been thrilled by the prospect of carrying over into his fiction the paradox of weighted choice. His ambition was magnificent – to dramatise and give ethical dimension to a line of mathematics. His message on the postcard was clear. He depended on me in his heroic attempt to bridge the chasm between art and logic, and I had let him charge off in the wrong direction. His story couldn't stand, it made no sense, and it touched me that he thought it could. But how could I tell him that his story was worthless when I was, in part, responsible for it?

For the simple truth, self-evident to me, to him quite opaque, was that the Indian couple emerging from 403 could not possibly tip the odds in favour of 402. They could never replace the part that Monty Hall has in the TV game. Their emergence is random, while Monty's choices are constrained, determined by the contestant. Monty cannot be replaced by a random selector. If Terry had chosen 403, the couple and their baby couldn't magically transfer themselves to another room so they could emerge through a different door. After their appearance Terry's wife is just as likely to be in Room 402 as 401. He might as well kick down the door of his first choice.

Then, as I went along the corridor to get a mid-morning tea from the trolley, I suddenly understood the source of Tom's mistake. It was me! I stopped and would have put

243

a hand over my mouth, but there was a man coming towards me carrying a cup and saucer. I saw him clearly, but I was too preoccupied, too shocked by my insight to take him in properly. A handsome man with protruding ears, now slowing down, blocking my way. Max, of course, my boss, my one-time confidant. Did I owe him another de-briefing?

'Serena. Are you all right?'

'Yes. Sorry. Head in the clouds, you know . . .'

He was staring at me in an intense way and his bony shoulders looked awkwardly hunched inside his over-sized tweed jacket. His cup clinked in its saucer until he steadied it with his free hand.

He said, 'I think we really ought to talk.'

'Tell me when and I'll come to your office.'

'I mean, not here. A drink after work, or a meal, or something.'

I was edging around him. 'That would be nice.'

'Friday?'

'I can't do Friday.'

'Monday then.'

'Yes, OK.'

When I was well clear of him, I half turned and gave him a little wave with my fingers, walked on and instantly forgot him. For I'd remembered clearly what I'd said in the restaurant last weekend. I'd told Tom that Monty chooses an empty box *at random*. And of course, two-thirds of the time that couldn't be true. In the game, Monty can only open an unchosen empty box. In two out of three occasions the contestant is bound to choose just that – an empty box. In which case there's only one box that Monty can go for. Only when the contestant guesses right and chooses the box with the prize, the pension, does Monty have two empty boxes to choose from randomly. Of course, I knew all this, but I hadn't explained it well. This was a shipwreck of a short story and it was my fault. It was from me that Tom had got the idea that fate could play the part of a game-show host.

With my burden of guilt doubled, I realised that I could not simply tell Tom that his story didn't work. The obligation was on me to come up with a solution. Instead of going out of the building, as I usually did at lunchtime, I stayed by my typewriter and took Tom's story from my handbag. As I threaded in a fresh sheet of paper I felt a stirring of pleasure, and then, as I started to type, even excitement. I had an idea, I knew how Tom could rewrite the end of the story, and let Terry kick down the door that doubles his chances of finding his wife in bed with another man. First of all, I got rid of the Indian couple and their harelipped baby. Charming as they were, they could play no part in this drama. Then, as Terry takes a few paces back, the better to run at the door of Room 401, he overhears two chambermaids talking on the landing below. Their voices drift up to him clearly. One of them says, 'I'll just pop upstairs and do one of them two empty rooms.' And the other says, 'Watch out, that couple are in their usual.' They laugh knowingly.

Terry hears the maid coming up the stairs. He's a decent amateur mathematician and realises he has a fantastic opportunity. He needs to think quickly. If he goes and stands close to any of the doors, and 401 will do, he will force the maid to go into one of the other two rooms. She knows where the couple are. She'll think he's either a new guest about to enter his room, or a friend of the couple, waiting outside their door. Whatever room she chooses, Terry will transfer to the other and double his chances. And that's exactly what happens. The maid, who has inherited the harelip, glances at Terry, gives him a nod, and goes into 403. Terry makes his decisive switch, runs and leaps at 402 and there they are, Sally and her man, *in flagrante*.

While I was in full flow I thought I'd suggest to Tom that he tidy up some other loose ends. Why doesn't Terry break down all the doors, especially now that he knows two are empty? Because the couple will hear him and he wants to preserve the element of surprise. Why not wait to see if the maid will clean a second room, at which point he'll know for certain where his wife is? Because it's established early on that he has an important site meeting at the end of the day and he has to get back to London.

I'd been typing for forty minutes and had three pages of notes to send. I scribbled a covering letter explaining in the simplest terms why the Indian couple would not do, found a blank envelope without an HMSO insignia, located a stamp at the bottom of my handbag and just had time to get to the letterbox on Park Lane and back before starting work again. How dull it was after Tom's story, to go through the *Claudia*'s illegal manifest, five tons of explosives, arms and ammunition, a relatively disappointing haul. One memo suggested that Qaddafi didn't trust the Provisionals, another reiterated that 'Six has overstepped the mark'. I couldn't care less.

That night in Camden I went to bed happier than I'd been all week. On the floor was my little suitcase, ready to be packed tomorrow night for my Friday-evening journey to Brighton. Just two days of work to get through. By the time I saw Tom he would have read my letter. I'd tell him again how good his story was, I'd explain the probability once more, and make a better job. We'd be together with our routines and rituals.

Finally, the calculations of probability were mere technical details. The strength of the story was elsewhere. As I lay in the dark, waiting for sleep, I thought I was beginning to grasp something about invention. As a reader, a speed-reader, I took it for granted, it was a process I never troubled myself with. You pulled a book from the shelf and there was an invented, peopled world, as obvious as the one you lived in. But now, like Tom in the restaurant grappling with Monty Hall, I thought I had the measure of the artifice, or I almost had it. Almost like cooking, I thought sleepily. Instead of heat transforming the ingredients, there's pure invention, the spark, the hidden element. What resulted was more than the sum of the parts. I tried to list them: Tom had donated my grasp of probability to Terry, as well as consigning to him his own secret arousal at the idea of being a cuckold. But not before turning it into something more acceptable – jealous anger. Something of the mess of Tom's sister's life had found its way into Sally's. Then, the familiar train journey, the streets of Brighton, those impossibly tiny hotels. The Indian couple and their baby with the harelip were enlisted to fill a role in Room 403. Their pleasantness and vulnerability contrasted with the rutting couple in the room next door. Tom had taken control of a subject ('only a fool would stay with his first choice'!) which he barely understood, and tried to make it his own. If he incorporated my suggestions, then it

247

would surely be his own. By a sleight of hand he made Terry far better at maths than his creator. At one level it was obvious enough how these separate parts were tipped in and deployed. The mystery was in how they were blended into something cohesive and plausible, how the ingredients were cooked into something so delicious. As my thought scattered and I drifted towards the borders of oblivion, I thought I almost understood how it was done.

Some time later, when I heard the doorbell, it featured in my dream as the culmination of an elaborate sequence of coincidences. But as the dream evaporated I heard the bell again. I didn't move because I was hoping one of the others would go down. They were nearer the front door, after all. On the third ring I turned on the light and looked at my alarm clock. Ten to midnight. I'd been asleep for an hour. The bell rang again, more insistently. I put on my dressing gown and slippers and went down the stairs, too sleepy to question why I should be hurrying. My guess was that one of the other girls had forgotten her key. It had happened before. In the hallway I felt the chill of the lino penetrate the soles of my slippers. I put on the security chain before opening the door. Peering through a three-inch gap I could make out a man on the step but I couldn't see his face. He was wearing a gangsterish fedora and a belted raincoat on whose shoulders raindrops glistened from the street light behind him. Alarmed, I pushed the door shut. I heard a familiar voice say quietly, 'I'm sorry to disturb you. I need to talk to Serena Frome.'

I lifted the chain and opened the door. 'Max. What are you doing?'

He'd been drinking. He swayed a little and his tightly controlled features were slack. When he spoke I smelled whisky.

He said, 'You know why I'm here.'

'No, I don't.'

'I have to talk to you.'

'Tomorrow, Max, please.'

'It's urgent.'

I was fully awake now and knew that if I sent him away I wouldn't sleep, so I let him in and took him into the kitchen. I lit a couple of rings on the gas stove. It was the only source of heat. He sat down at the table and took off his hat. There was mud on his trousers below the knee. I guessed he'd walked across town. He had a faintly deranged look, loose about the mouth, and under his eyes the skin was blue-ish black. I thought about making him a hot drink and decided not to. I felt some resentment that he was pulling rank on me, entitled to wake me because I was the junior. I sat down opposite him and watched while he carefully brushed the rain off his hat with the back of his hand. He seemed anxious not to appear drunk. I felt shivery and tense, and not just from the cold. I suspected Max had come to tell me more bad news about Tony. But what could be worse than being a dead traitor?

'I can't believe you don't know why I'm here,' he said.

I shook my head. He smiled at what he took to be a forgivable little lie.

'When we met in the corridor today I knew you were thinking exactly the same thing as me.'

'Did you?'

'Come on, Serena. We both knew it.'

He was looking at me earnestly, pleading, and at that

point I thought I knew what was coming, and something inside me sagged with weariness at the prospect of hearing it, denying it, sorting it all out. And having to accommodate it somehow into the future.

Despite that I said, 'I don't understand.'

'I've had to break off my engagement.'

'Had to?'

'You made your own feelings clear when I told you about it.'

'So?'

'Your disappointment was obvious. I was sorry about it, but I had to ignore it. I couldn't let feelings get in the way of work.'

'I don't want that either, Max.'

'But each time we meet I know we're both thinking about what might have been.'

'Look . . .'

'As for all the, you know . . .'

He took up his hat again and examined it closely.

'. . . wedding preparations. Our two families have been busy with it all. But I couldn't stop thinking about you . . . I thought I was going mad. When I saw you this morning, it hit us both. You looked like you were going to pass out. I'm sure I looked the same. Serena, this pretence . . . this madness of saying nothing. I spoke to Ruth this evening and told her the truth. She's very upset. But this has been coming towards us, you and me, it's inevitable. We can't go on ignoring it!'

I couldn't bear to look at him. I was irritated by the way he conflated his own shifting needs with an impersonal destiny. I want it, therefore . . . it's in the stars! What was it with men, that they found elementary logic so difficult? I looked along the line of my shoulder towards the hissing gas rings. The kitchen was warming up at last and I loosened my dressing gown at the neck. I pushed my dishevelled hair clear of my face to help me think clearly. He was waiting for me to make the correct confession, to align my desires with his, to confirm him in his solipsism and join him in it. But perhaps I was being too hard on him. This was a simple misunderstanding. At least, that was how I intended to treat it.

'It's true your engagement came out of nowhere. You'd never mentioned Ruth before and I did get a bit upset. But I got over it, Max. I was hoping for a wedding invitation.'

'That's all over. We can start again.'

'No, we can't.'

He looked up sharply. 'What do you mean by that?'

'I mean we can't start again.'

'Why not?'

I shrugged.

'You've met someone.'

'Yes.'

The effect was frightening. He stood up quickly, tipping over the kitchen chair behind him. I thought the din it made as it smacked against the floor was bound to wake the others. He stood in front of me unsteadily, looking ghastly, greenish in the yellow light of a single bare bulb, lips glistening. I was waiting to hear for the second time in a week a man tell me he was about to be sick.

However, he stood his ground, or swayed on it, and said, 'But you've been giving the impression that . . . that you wanted, well, to be with me.'

251

'Have I?'

'Every time you came to my office. You flirted with me.'

There was some truth in this. I thought for a moment and said, 'But not since I started seeing Tom.'

'Tom? Not Haley, I hope?'

I nodded.

'Oh God. So you meant it. You idiot!' He picked up the chair and sat heavily. 'Is this to punish me?'

'I like him.'

'So unprofessional.'

'Oh, come on. We all know what goes on.'

Actually, I didn't. All I knew was the gossip, which may have been fantasy, about desk officers taking up with female agents. What with the intimacy and stress and all, why wouldn't they?

'He'll find out who you are. Bound to happen.'

'No, it won't.'

He was hunkered down with his head propped on his hands. He blew noisily through his cheeks. It was hard to tell just how drunk he was.

'Why didn't you tell me?'

'I thought we didn't want feelings getting in the way of work.'

'Serena! This is Sweet Tooth. Haley's ours. And so are you.'

I was beginning to wonder if I was in the wrong, and it was for that reason that I went on the attack. 'You encouraged me to get close to you, Max. And all the while you were getting ready to announce your engagement. Why should I put up with you telling me who I can see?'

He wasn't listening. He groaned and pushed the heel

of his hand into his forehead. 'Oh God,' he murmured to himself. 'What have I done?'

I waited. My guilt was an amorphous black shape in the mind, growing larger, threatening to suck me in. I had flirted with him, teased him, caused him to dump his fiancée, ruined his life. It would take an effort to resist.

He said abruptly, 'Have you got a drink here?'

'No.' Wedged behind the toaster was a miniature of sherry. It would make him sick, and I wanted him to go.

'Tell me one thing. What happened in the corridor this morning?'

'I don't know. Nothing.'

'You were playing games, weren't you, Serena. That's what you really like.'

It wasn't worth responding to. I just stared at him. There was a thread of saliva attached to the skin at the corner of his mouth. He caught the direction of my gaze and wiped it with the back of his hand.

'You're going to wreck Sweet Tooth with this.'

'Don't pretend that's your objection. You hate the whole thing anyway.'

To my surprise he said, 'Bloody right I do.' It was the kind of rough frankness that a drink brings on and now he wanted to inflict some damage. 'The women in your section, Belinda, Anne, Hilary, Wendy and the rest. Ever ask them what kind of degrees they got?'

'No.'

'Pity. Firsts, starred firsts, double firsts, you name it. Classics, History, English.'

'Clever them.'

'Even your friend Shirley got one.'

'Even?'

'Ever wonder why they let you in with a third. In *maths*?'

He waited but I didn't reply.

'Canning recruited you. So they thought, better to have you on the inside, see if you had someone to report to. You never know. They followed you for a bit, took a look at your room. Usual stuff. They gave you Sweet Tooth because it's low level and harmless. Put you in there with Chas Mount because he's a dud. But you were a disappointment, Serena. No one was running you. Just an ordinary girl, averagely stupid, glad to have a job. Canning must have been doing you a favour. My theory is he was making amends.'

I said, 'I think he loved me.'

'Well, there you are then. He just wanted to make you happy.'

'Has anyone ever loved you, Max?'

'You little bitch.'

The insult made things easier. It was time for him to go. The kitchen was tolerable now but the warmth off the gas rings felt clammy. I stood up, drew my dressing gown firmly around me and turned them off.

'So why leave your fiancée for me?'

But we hadn't quite reached the end, for his mood was taking another turn. He was crying. Or at least tearful. His lips were stretched tight in a hideous smile.

'Oh God,' he cried out in a squeezed high-pitched voice, 'I'm sorry, I'm sorry. That's the last thing you are. You never heard it, I never said it. Serena, I'm sorry.'

'It's fine,' I said. 'It's forgotten. But I think you should leave.'

He stood and groped in his trouser pocket for a hand-kerchief. When he was done blowing on it he was still crying. 'I've messed everything up. I'm a fucking fool.'

I led him back along the hall to the front door and opened it.

We had a final exchange on the steps. He said, 'Promise me one thing, Serena.'

He was trying to take my hands. I felt sorry for him but I stepped back. It wasn't the moment to be holding hands.

'Promise me you'll think about this. Please. Just this. If I can change my mind, so can you.'

'I'm awfully tired, Max.'

He seemed to be getting a hold of himself. He took a deep breath. 'Listen. It's possible that you're making a very serious mistake with Tom Haley.'

'Walk that way and you'll pick up a cab on the Camden Road.'

He was standing on a lower step, looking up at me, imploring and accusing me as I closed the door. I hesitated behind it, and then, even though I heard his retreating steps, I fixed the security chain before going back to bed.

17

One Brighton weekend in December, Tom asked me to read *From the Somerset Levels*. I took it into the bedroom and went through it carefully. I noted various minor alterations but, by the time I'd finished, my opinion was unchanged. I dreaded the conversation he was waiting to have because I knew I wouldn't be able to pretend. That afternoon we went for a walk on the Downs. I spoke of the novel's indifference to the fate of the father and little girl, of the assured depravity of its minor characters, the desolation of the crushed urban masses, the raw squalor of rural poverty, the air of general hopelessness, the cruel and joyless narrative, the depressing effect on the reader.

Tom's eyes shone. I couldn't have said anything kinder. 'Exactly!' he kept saying. 'That's it. That's right. You've got it!'

I'd picked up a few typos and repetitions for which he was disproportionately grateful. Over the following week or so he completed another draft of light revisions – and he was done. He asked me if I would go with him when he delivered it to his editor and I told him it would be an honour. He came up to London on the morning of Christmas Eve, the beginning of my three-day break. We met at Tottenham Court Road Tube station and walked together to Bedford Square. He gave me the package to carry to bring him luck. One hundred and thirty-six pages, he told me proudly, of double-spaced typing on old-fashioned foolscap. As we walked along I kept thinking of the little girl in the final scene, dying in agony on the wet floor of a burned-out cellar. If I was really to do my duty I should have posted the whole thing in its envelope down the nearest drain. But I was excited for him and held the grim chronicle securely against my chest as I would my – our – baby.

I'd wanted to spend Christmas with Tom holed up in the Brighton flat, but I'd received a summons home and was due to take the train up that afternoon. I hadn't been back in many months. My mother was firm on the phone and even the Bishop had taken a view. I wasn't enough of a rebel to refuse, though I felt ashamed when I explained myself to Tom. In my early twenties the last threads of childhood still bound me. He, however, a free adult in his late twenties, was sympathetic to my parents' view. Of course they needed to see me, of course I should go. It was my grown-up duty to spend Christmas with them. He himself would be with his family in Sevenoaks on the twenty-fifth, and he was determined to get his sister Laura out of the Bristol hostel and unite her with her children around the festive table, and try to keep her off the drink.

So I hauled his package towards Bloomsbury, conscious that we only had a few hours together, and then we'd be apart for over a week, for I'd be going straight back to work on the twenty-seventh. As we walked he told me his latest news. He had just heard back from Ian Hamilton at the *New Review*. Tom had recast the climax of 'Probable Adultery' as I'd suggested in my notes and submitted it along with his talking-ape story. Hamilton had written to say that 'Probable Adultery' was not for him, he had no patience for the ins and outs of the 'logic stuff' and he doubted that 'anyone but a Senior Wrangler would'. On the other hand, he thought the garrulous monkey was 'not bad'. Tom wasn't sure if that was an acceptance. He was going to meet Hamilton in the New Year and find out.

We were shown into Tom Maschler's grand office or library on the first floor of a Georgian mansion overlooking the square. When the publisher came in, almost at a run, I was the one who handed over the novel. He tossed it on the desk behind him, kissed me wetly on both cheeks and pumped Tom's hand, congratulated him, guided him towards a chair and began to interrogate him, barely waiting for an answer to one question before starting the next. What was he living on, when were we getting married, had he read Russell Hoban, did he realise that the elusive Pynchon had sat in that same chair the day before, did he know Martin, son of Kingsley, would we like to meet Madhur Jaffrey? Maschler reminded me of an Italian tennis coach who once came to our school and in an afternoon of impatient jovial instruction rebuilt my backhand. The publisher was lean and brown, hungry for information, and pleasantly agitated, as though perpetually suspended on the edge of a joke, or a revolutionary new idea that might come to him through a chance remark.

I was grateful to be ignored and wandered up to the

far end of the room and stood looking at the wintry trees in Bedford Square. I heard Tom, my Tom, say that he lived by his teaching, that he hadn't yet read *One Hundred Years of Solitude* or Jonathan Miller's book on McLuhan but intended to, and that no, he had no clear idea of his next novel. He skipped the question about marriage, agreed that Roth was a genius and *Portnoy's Complaint* a masterpiece, and that the English translations of Neruda's sonnets were exceptional. Tom, like me, knew no Spanish and was in no position to judge. Neither of us had read Roth's novel at that point. His answers were guarded, even pedestrian, and I sympathised – we were the innocent country cousins, overwhelmed by the range and speed of Maschler's references, and it seemed only right after ten minutes that we should be dismissed. We were too dull. He came with us to the top of the stairs. As he said goodbye he said he might have taken us to lunch at his favourite Greek place in Charlotte Street, but he didn't believe in lunch. We found ourselves back on the pavement, a little dazed, and as we walked on spent a good while discussing whether the meeting had 'gone well'. Tom thought on balance it had, and I agreed, though I actually thought it hadn't.

But it didn't matter, the novel, the terrible novel, was delivered, we were about to part, it was Christmas, and we ought to be celebrating. We wandered south, into Trafalgar Square, passing on the way the National Portrait Gallery and, like a couple of thirty years' standing, we reminisced about our first meeting there – did we both think it was going to be a one-night affair, could we have guessed what would follow? Then we doubled back and went to Sheekey's and managed to get in without a booking. I was wary of drinking. I had to go home and pack, get to Liverpool Street for a five o'clock train, and prepare to throw off my role as secret agent of the State and become a dutiful daughter, the one who was sleekly rising through the ranks of the Department of Health and Social Security.

But well ahead of the Dover sole, an ice bucket arrived followed by a bottle of champagne, and down it went, and before the next one came Tom reached across the table for my hand and told me he had a secret to confess and though he didn't want to trouble me with it just before we separated, he wouldn't sleep unless he told me. It was this. He didn't have an idea, not even a scrap of an idea, for another novel and he doubted that he ever would. *From the Somerset Levels* – we referred to it as *The Levels* – was a fluke, he had blundered into it by accident when he thought he was writing a short story about something else. And the other day, walking past Brighton Pavilion, an inconsequential line of Spenser had come to mind – *Put in porphyry and marble do appear* – Spenser in Rome, reflecting on its past. But perhaps it needn't only be Rome. Tom found himself beginning to map out an article about poetry's relation to the city, the city through the centuries. Academic writing was supposed to be behind him, there had been times when his thesis had driven him to despair. But nostalgia was creeping in – nostalgia for the quiet integrity of scholarship, its exacting protocols, and above all, for the loveliness of Spenser's verse. He knew it so well, the warmth beneath its formality – this was a world he could inhabit. The idea for the article was original and bold, it was exciting, it crossed the boundaries of disparate disciplines. Geology, town planning, archaeology. There was an editor of a specialist journal who would be delighted to have something from him. Two days before, Tom had found himself wondering about a teaching job he had heard was going at Bristol university. The MA in international relations had been a diversion. Perhaps fiction was too. His future lay in teaching and academic research. How fraudulent he had felt at Bedford Square just now, how constrained during the conversation. It was a real possibility that he would never write another novel again, or even a story. How could he admit such a thing to Maschler, the most respected publisher of fiction in town?

Or to me. I disengaged my hand. This was my first free Monday in months but I was back at work for the Sweet Tooth cause. I told Tom it was a well-known fact that writers felt emptied out at the end of their labours. As if I knew a thing about it, I told him that there was nothing incompatible about writing the occasional scholarly essay and writing novels. I cast about for an example of a celebrated writer who did just that, but couldn't think of one. The second bottle arrived and I embarked on a celebration of Tom's work. It was the unusual psychological slant of his stories, their strange intimacy in combination with his worldly essays on the East German uprising and the Great Train Robbery, it was that *breadth* of interest that marked him out, and was the reason why the Foundation was so proud to have an association with him, why the name of T.H. Haley was conjured in literary circles, and why two of its most important figures, Hamilton and Maschler, wanted him to write for them.

Tom was watching me throughout this performance

with his little smile – it sometimes infuriated me – of tolerant scepticism.

'You told me you couldn't write *and* teach. Would you be happy on an assistant lecturer's salary? Eight hundred pounds a year? That's assuming you get a job.'

'Don't think I haven't thought of that.'

'The other night you told me you might write an article for *Index on Censorship* about the Romanian security service. What's it called?'

'The DSS. But it's really about poetry.'

'I thought it was about torture.'

'Incidentally.'

'You said it might even become a short story.'

He brightened a little. 'It might. I'm meeting my poet friend Traian again next week. I can't do anything without his say-so.'

I said, 'No reason why you shouldn't write the Spenser essay too. You have all this freedom and that's what the Foundation wants for you. You can do anything you like.'

After that he seemed to lose interest and wanted to change the subject. So we talked about the things that everybody was talking about – the government's energy-conserving three-day week, due to start on New Year's Eve, yesterday's doubling of the price of oil, the several explosions round town in pubs and shops, 'Christmas presents' from the Provisional IRA. We discussed why people seemed strangely happy conserving energy, doing things by candlelight, as though adversity had restored purpose to existence. At least, it was easy enough to think so as we finished the second bottle.

It was almost four when we said our goodbyes outside Leicester Square Tube station. We embraced and kissed, caressed by a warming breeze wafting up the subway steps. Then he set off on a mind-clearing walk to Victoria station while I headed to Camden to pack my clothes and meagre Christmas presents, blearily aware there was no chance of making my train and that I would be late for Christmas Eve dinner, an occasion to which my mother gave selfless days of preparation. She wouldn't be pleased.

I took the six thirty, got in just before nine, and walked from the station, crossing the river then following by a clear half-moon the semi-rural path along it, past dark boats tethered to the bank, inhaling air icy and pure, blown in across East Anglia from Siberia. The taste of it reminded me of my adolescence, its boredom and longing, and all our little rebellions tamed or undone by the desire to please certain teachers with dazzling essays. Oh, the elated disappointment of an A minus, as keen as a cold wind from the north! The path curved below the rugger pitches of the boys' school, and the spire, my father's spire, creamily lit, rose up across the expanse. I cut away from the river to cross the pitches, passed the changing rooms that used to smell to me of all that was sourly fascinating about boys, and got into the cathedral close by an old oak door that never used to be locked. It pleased me that it was unlocked now, still squeaked on its hinge. It took me by surprise, this walk across an ancient past. Four or five years – nothing at all. But no one over thirty could understand this peculiarly weighted and condensed time, from late teens to early twenties, a stretch of life that needed a name, from school leaver to salaried professional, with a university and affairs and death and choices in between. I had forgotten how recent my childhood was, how long and inescapable it once seemed. How grown-up and how unchanged I was.

I don't know why my heart beat harder as I went towards the house. As I came closer I slowed. I'd forgotten just how immense it was and it amazed me now that I could ever have taken this pale-red brick Queen Anne palace for granted. I advanced between the bare forms of cut-back rose shrubs and box hedging rising from beds framed by massive slabs of York paving. I rang, or pulled, the bell and to my astonishment the door opened almost immediately and there was the Bishop, with a grey jacket on over his purple clerical shirt and dog collar. He would be conducting a midnight service later. He must have been crossing the hall when I rang, for answering the door was something that would never occur to him. He was a big man, with a vague and kindly face, and a boyish though entirely white forelock that he was always brushing aside. People used to say that he resembled a benign tabby cat. As he processed in stately manner through his fifties, his gut had swelled, which seemed to suit his slow self-absorbed air. My sister and I used to mock him behind his back and sometimes were even bitter, not because we disliked him – far from it – but because we could never get his attention, or never for long. To him our lives were distant foolish things. He didn't know that sometimes Lucy and I fought over him in our teens. We longed to have him for ourselves, if only for ten minutes in his study, and we each suspected the other was the more favoured. Her tangle with drugs, pregnancy and the law had permitted her many such privileged minutes. When I'd heard about them on the phone, despite all my concern for her, I felt a twinge of the old jealousy. When would it be my turn?

It was now.

'Serena!' He said my name with a kindly, falling tone, with just a hint of mock surprise, and put his arms about me. I dropped my bag at my feet and let myself be enfolded, and as I pressed my face into his shirt and caught the familiar scent of Imperial Leather soap, and of church – of lavender wax – I started to cry. I don't know why, it just came from nowhere and I turned to water. I don't cry easily and I was as surprised as he was. But there was nothing I could do about it. This was the copious hopeless sort of crying you might hear from a tired child. I think it was his voice, the way he said my name, that set me off.

Instantly, I felt his body tense, even though he continued to hold me. He murmured, 'Shall I fetch your mother?'

I thought I knew what he was thinking – that now it was the turn of his older daughter to be pregnant or lost to some other modern disaster, and that whatever womanly mess was now soaking his freshly ironed purple shirt was better managed by a woman. He needed to hand the matter over and continue to his study to look over his Christmas Day sermon before dinner.

But I didn't want him to let go of me. I clung to him. If only I could have thought of a crime, I would have begged him to summon down the magic cathedral powers to forgive me.

I said, 'No, no. It's all right, Daddy. It's just, I'm so happy to be back, to be . . . here.'

I felt him relax. But it wasn't true. It wasn't happiness at all. I couldn't have said precisely what it was. It had something to do with my walk from the station, and with coming away from my London life. Relief perhaps, but with a harsher element, something like remorse, or even despair. Later I persuaded myself that drinking at lunch-time had softened me up.

This moment on the doorstep could not have lasted more than thirty seconds. I got a grip of myself, picked up my bag and stepped inside, apologised to the Bishop, who was still regarding me warily. Then he patted my shoulder and resumed his route across the hall to his study and I went into the cloakroom – easily the size of my Camden bedsit – to douse my red and swollen eyes with cold water. I didn't want an interrogation by my mother. As I went to find her I was aware of all that used to suffocate me and now seemed comforting – the smell of roasting meat, the carpeted warmth, the gleam of oak, mahogany, silver and glass, and my mother's spare, tasteful arrangements in vases of bare hazel and dogwood branches, minimally sprayed with silver paint to denote a light frost. When Lucy was fifteen and trying, like me, to be a sophisticated adult she came in one Christmas evening and gestured at the branches and exclaimed, 'How positively Protestant!'

She earned herself the sourest look I ever saw the Bishop give. He rarely stooped to reprimands but this time he said coldly, 'You'll rephrase that, young lady, or go to your room.'

Listening to Lucy intone contritely something like, 'Mummy, the decorations are truly wonderful,' gave me the giggles and I decided that I had better be the one who left the room. 'Positively Protestant' became an insurrectionary catchphrase for us two, but always muttered well out of the Bishop's hearing.

There were five of us at dinner. Lucy had come across

town with her long-haired Irish boyfriend, six-foot-six Luke, who worked for the city council as a parks gardener and was an active member of the recently formed Troops Out movement. As soon as I knew this I made a quick decision not to be drawn into argument. It was easy enough because he was pleasant and funny, despite a phoney American drawl, and later, after dinner, we found common ground in a discussion, almost an outraged celebration, of loyalist atrocities, of which I knew almost as many as he did. At one point during the meal the Bishop, who had no interest in politics, leaned across and enquired mildly whether Luke would be expecting a massacre of the Catholic minority if he had his way and the army was to withdraw. Luke replied that he thought the British army had never done much for the Catholics in the north, who would be able to take care of themselves.

'Ah,' my father replied, pretending to be reassured. 'A bloodbath all round then.'

Luke was confused. He didn't know if he was being mocked. In fact he wasn't. The Bishop was merely being polite and now was moving the conversation on. The reason he wouldn't be drawn into political or even theological debate was because he was indifferent to other people's opinions and felt no urge to engage with or oppose them.

It turned out to have suited my mother's schedule to serve up a roast dinner at ten o'clock and she was pleased to have me home. She still took pride in my job and the independent existence she had always wanted for me. I had boned up once more on my supposed department in order to be able to answer her questions. A good while back I'd discovered that nearly all the girls at work had told their parents exactly who they worked for, on the understanding that they wouldn't press for details. In my case my cover story had been elaborate and well researched and I had told too many unnecessary white lies. It was too late to go back. If my mother had known the truth, she would have told Lucy, who might never speak to me again. And I wouldn't have wanted Luke to know what I did. So I bored myself for a few minutes while I described departmental views on reforming the social-security system, wishing that my mother would find it as dull as the Bishop and Lucy did and would stop prompting me with bright new questions.

It was one of the blessings of our family life, and perhaps of Anglicanism in general, that we were never expected to go to church to hear or see our father officiate. It was of no interest to him whether we were there or not. I hadn't been since I was seventeen. I don't think Lucy had been since she was twelve. Because this was his busy time of year, he stood abruptly just before dessert and wished us all a happy Christmas and excused himself. From where I sat, it looked like my tears had left no stain on the ecclesiastical shirt. Five minutes later we heard the familiar swish of his cassock as he passed the dining room on his way to the front door. I had grown up with the ordinariness of his daily business, but now, returning home after an absence, from my London preoccupations, it seemed exotic to have a father who dabbled routinely in the supernatural, who went out to work in a beautiful stone temple late at night, house keys in his pocket, to thank or praise or beseech a god on our behalf.

My mother went upstairs to a small spare bedroom known as the wrapping room to see to the last of her presents while Lucy, Luke and I cleared away and washed the dishes. Lucy tuned the kitchen radio to John Peel's show and we toiled away to the kind of progressive rock I hadn't heard since Cambridge. It no longer moved me. Where once it had been the call sign of a freemasonry of the liberated young and promised a new world, now it had shrunk into mere songs, mostly about lost love, sometimes about the open road. These were striving musicians like any others, keen for advancement in a crowded scene. Peel's informed ramblings between the tracks suggested as much. Even a couple of pub rock songs failed to stir me. It must be, I thought as I scrubbed at my mother's baking dishes, that I was getting old. Twenty-three next birthday. Then my sister asked if I wanted to go for a stroll round the close with her and Luke. They wanted to smoke and the Bishop wouldn't tolerate it in the house, at least, not from family – an eccentric position in those days, and an oppressive one, we thought.

The moon was higher now and the touch of frost on the grass was light, even more tasteful than our mother's efforts with the spray can. The cathedral, lit from the inside, looked isolated and displaced, like a stranded ocean liner. From a distance we heard a ponderous organ introducing 'Hark! The herald angels sing' and then the congregation gamely belting it out. It sounded like a good crowd, and I was glad for my father's sake. But grown-ups singing in ragged unironic unison about *angels* . . . I experienced a sudden lurch in my heart, as though I'd looked over a cliff edge into emptiness. I believed in nothing much – not carols, not even rock music. We strolled three abreast along the narrow road that ran past the other fine houses in the close. Some were solicitors' offices, one or two were cosmetic dentists. It was a worldly place, the cathedral precinct, and the Church imposed high rents.

It turned out that it wasn't only tobacco my companions were wanting. Luke produced from his coat a joint the size and shape of a small Christmas cracker, which he lit as we walked along. He went in for a good deal of solemn ritual, inserting the thing between his knuckles and cupping his hands in order to suck between his thumbs with loud hissing intakes of air, and showy retention of breath and smoke while continuing to talk, making himself sound like a ventriloquist's dummy – a fuss and nonsense I'd completely forgotten about. How provincial it seemed. The sixties were over! But when Luke presented his cracker to me – in a rather menacing way, I thought – I took a couple of polite puffs in order not to come across like Lucy's uptight older sister. Which was exactly what I was.

I was uneasy on two counts. I was still in the aftermath of my moment at the front door. Was it overwork rather than a hangover? I knew that my father would never refer to the matter again, never ask me what was up. I should have felt resentful, but I was relieved. I wouldn't have known what to tell him anyway. And secondly, I had on a coat I hadn't worn in a while, and as we began our walk around the close I felt in the pocket a piece of paper. I ran a finger along its edge and knew exactly what it was. I'd forgotten about it, the scrap I'd picked up in the safe house. It reminded me of much else that was messily unfinished, a scattering of mental litter – Tony's disgrace, Shirley's disappearance, the possibility that I was only taken on because Tony was exposed, the Watchers going through my room and, messiest of all, the row with Max. We'd avoided each other since his visit to my place. I hadn't been to see him with my Sweet Tooth report. Whenever I thought of him I felt guilt, immediately displaced by indignant reflection. He dumped me for his fiancée, then, too late, his fiancée for me. He was looking out for himself. Where was my share of blame? But next time I thought of him I had the same guilty turn, and had to explain it away to myself all over again.

All this, streaming behind one piece of paper like the tail of a misshapen kite. We walked round to the cathedral's west end and stood in the deep shadow of the high stone portal that led through to the town while my sister and her boyfriend passed the joint between them. I strained to hear my father's voice above Luke's transatlantic drone, but there was silence from the cathedral. They were praying, surely. In the other pan of the scales of my fortunes, apart from the minor fact of my promotion, was Tom. I wanted to tell Lucy about him, I would have loved a sisterly session. We occasionally managed one, but set between us now was Luke's giant form and he was doing that inexcusable thing that men who liked cannabis tended to do, which was to go on about it – some famous stuff from a special village in Thailand, the terrifying near-bust one night, the view across a certain holy lake at sunset under the influence, a hilarious misunderstanding in a bus station and other stultifying anecdotes. What was wrong with our generation? Our parents had the war to be boring about. We had this.

After a while we girls fell completely silent while Luke, in elated urgent terms, plunged deeper into the misapprehension that he was interesting, that we were enthralled. And almost immediately I had a contrary insight. I saw it clearly. Of course. Lucy and Luke were waiting for me to leave so they could be alone. That's what I would have wanted, if it had been Tom and me. Luke was deliberately and systematically boring me to drive me away. It was insensitive of me not to have noticed. Poor fellow, he was having to overreach himself and it was not a good performance, hopelessly overdone. No one in real life could be as boring as this. But in his round-about way he was only trying to be kind.

So I stretched and yawned noisily in the shadows and cut across him to say irrelevantly, 'You're dead right, I should go,' and I walked off, and within seconds felt better, easily able to ignore Lucy calling after me. Freed from Luke's anecdotes, I went quickly, retracing the route we had come by, and then I cut across the grass, feeling the frost crunch pleasantly underfoot, until I was right by the cloisters, well out of the half-moon's light, and found in the near darkness a stone protrusion to sit on and turned up the collar of my coat.

I could hear a voice from inside, faintly intoning, but I couldn't tell if it was the Bishop. He had a large team working for him on occasions like this. In difficult moments it's sometimes a good idea to ask yourself what it is you most want to be doing and consider how it can be achieved. If it can't, move on to the second best thing. I wanted to be with Tom, in bed with him, across a table from him, holding his hand in the street. Failing that, I wanted to think about him. So that is what I did for half an hour on Christmas Eve, I worshipped him, I thought about our times together, his strong yet childlike body, our growing fondness, his work, and how I might help. I pushed away any consideration of the secret I was keeping from him. Instead, I thought about the freedom I'd brought into his life, how I'd helped him with 'Probable Adultery' and would help with much more. All so rich. I decided to write down these thoughts in a letter to him, a lyrical, passionate letter. I'd tell him how I came apart at my own front door and wept on my father's chest.

It wasn't a good idea to be sitting motionless on stone in sub-zero temperatures. I was beginning to shiver. Then I heard my sister calling me again from somewhere in the close. She sounded concerned, and that was when I began to come to my senses and realise that my behaviour must have seemed unfriendly. It had been influenced by a puff on the Christmas cracker. How unlikely it now seemed, for Luke to have been wilfully dull in order to secure a few moments alone with Lucy. It was difficult to understand one's own errors of judgement when the entity, the mind, that was attempting the understanding was befuddled. Now I was thinking clearly. I stepped out onto the moonlit grass and saw my sister and her boyfriend on the path a hundred yards away, and I hurried towards them, keen to apologise.

18

At Leconfield House the thermostats were turned down to 60°F, two degrees lower than other government departments, in order to set a good example. We worked in our overcoats and finger gloves, and some of the better-off girls wore knitted woolly hats with pompoms from their skiing holidays. We were issued with squares of felt to put under our feet against the cold coming up through the floor. The best way to warm your hands was to keep typing. Now that the train drivers were on an overtime ban in support of the miners, it was reckoned that power stations could run out of coal by the end of January, just as the nation ran out of money. In Uganda Idi Amin was arranging a whip-round and offering a lorryload of vegetables to the stricken former colonial masters, if only the RAF would care to come and collect it.

There was a letter from Tom waiting for me when I got back to Camden from my parents. He was going to borrow his father's car to drive Laura back to Bristol. It wasn't going to be easy. She was telling the family that she wanted to take the children with her. There had been shouting scenes around the Christmas turkey. But the hostel only took adults and Laura, as usual, was in no shape to care for her kids.

His plan was to come to London so that we could see in the New Year together. But on the 30th he sent a telegram from Bristol. He couldn't leave Laura yet. He'd have to stay and try to settle her in. So I saw in 1974 with my three housemates at a party in Mornington Crescent. I was the only one in the teeming squalid flat who wasn't a solicitor. I was at some kind of trestle table pouring tepid white wine into a used paper cup when someone actually pinched my bottom, really hard. I whirled round and was furious, possibly with the wrong person. I came away early and was home in bed by one, lying on my back in the freezing dark, feeling sorry for myself. Before I fell asleep I remembered Tom telling me how superb the support people were at Laura's hostel. If so, how strange it was that he needed to stay in Bristol for two whole days. But it didn't seem important and I slept deeply, barely troubled by my legal friends coming in drunk at four.

The year turned and the three-day week began, but we were officially defined as a vital service and worked the full five. On 2 January, I was called to a meeting in Harry Tapp's office on the second floor. There was no advance warning, no indication of the subject. It was ten o'clock when I got there, and Benjamin Trescott was on the door, checking names off a list. I was surprised to find more than twenty people in the room, among them two from my intake, all of us too junior to presume to take one of the moulded plastic chairs set out in a constricted horse-shoe around Tapp's desk. Peter Nutting came in, scanned the room and went out again. Harry Tapp got up from his desk and followed him out. I assumed therefore that this was a Sweet Tooth affair. Everyone was smoking, murmuring, waiting. I squeezed into an eighteen-inch gap between a filing cabinet and the safe. It didn't bother me, as it once would have, to have no one to talk to. I smiled across at Hilary and Belinda. They shrugged and rolled their eyes to show me that they thought it was all a great wheeze. They obviously had Sweet Tooth writers of their own, academics or hacks who couldn't resist the Foundation's shilling. But surely, no one with the lustre of T.H. Haley.

Ten minutes passed and the plastic chairs filled up. Max came in and took one in a middle row. I was behind him, so he didn't see me at first. Then he turned and glanced round the room, looking for me, I was certain. Our eyes met only briefly and he turned to face forwards again and took out a pen. My sight line wasn't good but I thought his hand was shaking. There were a couple of figures I recognised from the fifth floor. But no Director General – Sweet Tooth was nowhere near important enough. Then Tapp and Nutting came back in with a short muscular man in horn-rim glasses, with closely cropped grey hair and a well-cut blue suit and silk tie of darker blue polka dots. Tapp went to his desk while the other two stood before us patiently, waiting for the room to settle.

Nutting said, 'Pierre's based in London and has kindly agreed to say a few words about the way his work may have some bearing on our own.'

From the brevity of this introduction and Pierre's accent, we assumed he was CIA. He was certainly no Frenchman. His voice was a see-saw tenor, pleasantly tentative. He gave the impression that if any utterance of his were to be disproved, he would change his view in line with the facts. Behind the owlish near-apologetic manner, I began to realise, was limitless confidence. He was my first encounter with an American of the patrician class, a man from an established Vermont family, as I learned later, and the author of a book on the Spartan Hegemony and another on Agesilaus the Second and the beheading of Tissaphernes in Persia.

I warmed to Pierre. He began by saying that he was going to tell us something about 'the softest, sweetest part of the Cold War, the only truly interesting part, the war of ideas'. He wanted to give us three verbal snapshots. For the first, he asked us to think of pre-war Manhattan, and quoted the opening lines of a famous Auden poem that Tony had read to me once, and I knew that Tom loved. It wasn't famous to me and it hadn't meant much up until this point, but hearing an Englishman's lines quoted back to us by an American was touching. *I sit in one of the dives/ On Fifty-second Street/ Uncertain and afraid* . . . and that was Pierre in 1940, nineteen years old, visiting an uncle in midtown, bored by the prospect of college, getting drunk in a bar. Except he wasn't quite so uncertain as Auden. He longed for his country to join the war in Europe and assign him a role. He wanted to be a soldier.

Then Pierre evoked for us the year 1949, when mainland Europe and Japan and China were in ruins or enfeebled, Britain was impoverished by a long heroic war, Soviet Russia was counting its dead in the many millions – and America, its economy fattened and enlivened by the fight, was waking to the awesome nature of its new responsibilities as prime guardian of human liberty on the planet.

Even as he said this he spread his hands and appeared to regret it or apologise. It could have been otherwise.

The third snapshot was also of 1949. Here is Pierre, the Moroccan and Tunisian campaigns, Normandy and the Battle of Hurtgen Forest and the liberation of Dachau behind him, and he's an associate professor of Greek at Brown university, walking towards the entrance of the Waldorf Astoria hotel on Park Avenue, passing a crowd of assorted demonstrators, American patriots, Catholic nuns and right-wing nutters.

'Inside,' Pierre said dramatically, holding up an open hand, 'I witnessed a contest that would change my life.'

It was a gathering with the unexceptional title of Cultural and Scientific Conference for World Peace, nominally organised by an American professional council but in fact an initiative of the Soviet Cominform. The thousand delegates from all over the world were those whose faith in the communist ideal had not yet been shattered, or not completely shattered, by show trials, the Nazi–Soviet Pact, repression, purges, torture, murder and labour camps. The great Russian composer, Dmitri Shostakovich, was there against his will, under orders from Stalin. Among the delegates from the American side were Arthur Miller, Leonard Bernstein and Clifford Odets. These and other luminaries were critical or distrustful of an American government that was asking its citizens to treat a former invaluable ally as a dangerous enemy. Many believed that the Marxist analysis still held, however messy events were turning out to be. And those events were much distorted by an American press owned by greedy corporate interests. If Soviet policy seemed surly or aggressive, if it leaned a little on its internal critics, it was in a defensive spirit, for it had faced Western hostility and sabotage from its inception.

In short, Pierre told us, the whole event was a propaganda coup for the Kremlin. It had prepared in capitalism's capital a world stage for itself on which it would appear as the voice of peace and reason, if not freedom, and it had scores of eminent Americans on its side.

'But!' Pierre raised an arm and pointed upwards with a rigid forefinger, trapping us all for several seconds in his theatrical pause. Then he told us that way up on the tenth floor of the hotel, in a suite of luxury rooms, was a volunteer army of subversion, a band of intellectuals gathered together by an academic philosopher called Sidney Hook, a group of mostly non-communist leftists, the democratic ex-communist or ex-Trotskyist left, determined to challenge the conference and, crucially, not to permit criticism of the Soviet Union to be the monopoly of the lunatic right. Bowed over typewriters, mimeograph machines and recently installed multiple phone lines, they had worked through the night, sustained by generous room-service snacks and booze. They intended to disrupt proceedings downstairs by asking awkward questions in the sessions, particularly about artistic freedom, and by issuing a stream of press releases. They too could claim heavyweight support, even more impressive than the other side's. Mary McCarthy, Robert Lowell, Elizabeth Hardwick, and international support at a distance from T.S. Eliot, Igor Stravinsky and Bertrand Russell, among many others.

The counter conference campaign was a success because it seized the media narrative and became the headline. All the right questions were insinuated into the conference sessions. Shostakovich was asked if he agreed with a

279

Pravda denunciation of Stravinsky, Hindemith and Schoenberg as 'decadent bourgeois formalists'. The great Russian composer got slowly to his feet and mumbled his agreement with the article and was shown to be miserably trapped between his conscience and his fear of displeasing his KGB handlers, and of what Stalin would do to him when he got home.

Between the sessions, in the upstairs suite, Pierre, with a telephone and a typewriter of his own in a corner near a bathroom, met the contacts who would transform his life, eventually prompting him to leave his teaching job and devote his life to the CIA and the war of ideas. For of course, the Agency was paying the bills of the conference opposition and it was learning in the process how effectively this war could be waged at one remove by writers, artists, intellectuals, many of them on the left, who had their own powerful ideas drawn from bitter experience of the seduction and false promises of communism. What they needed, even if they did not know it, was what the CIA could provide – organisation, structure and, above all, funding. This was important when operations moved to London, Paris and Berlin. 'What helped us back in the early fifties was that no one in Europe had a cent.'

And so, in Pierre's description, he became a different kind of soldier, drawn again into many new campaigns in liberated but threatened Europe. He was for a while an assistant to Michael Josselson, and later a friend of Melvin Lasky's until a rift opened up between them. Pierre was involved in the Congress for Cultural Freedom, wrote articles in German for the prestigious periodical, *Der Monat*, which was CIA funded, and did back-room work with the setting up of *Encounter*. He learned the delicate art of stroking the egos of intellectual prima donnas, helped organise tours by an American ballet company, and orchestras, modern art shows and more than a dozen conferences that occupied what he called the 'hazardous terrain where politics and literature meet'. He said he was surprised by the fuss and naivety that followed on from *Ramparts* magazine's 1967 exposure of the CIA funding of *Encounter*. Wasn't the case against totalitarianism a rational and decent one for governments to adopt? Here in Britain no one was ever troubled by the Foreign Office paying for the BBC World Service, which was highly regarded. And so was *Encounter* still, despite the hullaballoo and pretended surprise and nose-holding. And mentioning the FO reminded him to commend the work of IRD. He particularly admired what it had done in promoting Orwell's work and he liked its arm's-length funding of publishing lists like Ampersand and Bellman Books.

After almost twenty-three years on the job, what conclusions would he draw? He would make two points. The first was the most important. The Cold War was not over, whatever people said, and therefore the cause of cultural freedom remained vital and would always be noble. Although there weren't many left who held a torch for the Soviet Union, there were still the vast frozen intellectual hinterlands where people lazily adopted neutralist positions – the Soviet Union was no worse than the United States. Such people needed to be confronted. As for the second point, he quoted a remark by his old CIA friend turned broadcaster, Tom Braden, to the effect that the United States was the only country on the planet that didn't understand that some things work better when they're small.

This earned an appreciative murmur in the crowded room from our cash-strapped Service.

'Our own projects have gotten too big, too numerous, too diverse and ambitious and over-funded. We've lost discretion, and our message lost its freshness along the way. We're everywhere and we've become the heavy hand, and we've created resentment. I know you have your own new thing going here. I wish it luck, but seriously, gentlemen, keep it small.'

Pierre, if that was his name, was not taking questions and as soon as he finished he nodded curtly to the applause and let himself be guided by Peter Nutting towards the door.

As the room emptied, with the less senior automatically holding back, I was dreading the moment when Max turned and caught my eye and came over to tell me we needed to meet. For office reasons, of course. But when I saw his back and large ears among the crowd edging out of the door, I felt a mix of bewilderment and familiar guilt. I had hurt him so badly he couldn't bear to speak to me. The idea horrified me. As usual, I tried to summon up protective indignation. He was the one who had told me once that women couldn't keep their personal lives out of their work. Was it my fault that he now preferred me to his fiancée? I pleaded my own case all the way down the concrete stairs – I took them to avoid having to talk to colleagues in the lift – and my case intruded all day around my desk. Did I make a fuss, was I pleading and tearful when Max turned away from me? No. So why shouldn't I be with Tom? Didn't I deserve my happiness?

*　　*　　*

It was a joy two days later to be on the Friday-evening train to Brighton, after a separation of almost two weeks. Tom came to the station to meet me. We saw each other as the train slowed, and he ran alongside my carriage, mouthing something I didn't understand. Nothing in my life had been so sweetly exhilarating as stepping off that train into his embrace. His grip was so tight it knocked the air out of me.

He said into my ear, 'I'm just beginning to realise how special you are.'

I told him in a whisper that I'd longed for this moment. When we pulled apart he took my bag.

I said, 'You look different.'

'I am different!' He almost shouted it, and he laughed wildly. 'I've got this amazing idea.'

'Can you tell me?'

'It's so weird, Serena.'

'Then tell me.'

'Let's go home. Eleven days. Too long!'

So we went to Clifton Street, where the Chablis was waiting in a silver ice bucket which Tom had bought in Asprey's. It was strange to have ice cubes in January. The wine would have been colder left in the fridge, but who cared? We drank it as we undressed each other. Of course, separation had stoked us, the Chablis fired us up as usual, but neither were sufficient to explain the hour that followed. We were the strangers who knew exactly what to do. Tom had an air of yearning tenderness about him that dissolved me. It was almost like sorrow. It brought out in me such a powerful feeling of protectiveness that I found myself wondering as we lay together on the bed and he kissed my breasts whether I would ask him one

283

day if I should come off the pill. But it wasn't a baby I wanted, it was him. When I felt and squeezed the small tight roundness of his buttocks and drew him towards me, I thought of him as a child I would possess and cherish and never let out of my sight. It was a feeling I had long ago with Jeremy in Cambridge, but that time I was deceived. Now the sensation of enclosing and possessing him was almost like pain, as though all the best feelings I'd ever had were gathered to an unbearable sharp point.

This was not one of those loud sweaty sessions that follow a separation. A passing voyeur with a view through the bedroom curtains would have peeped at an unadventurous couple in missionary pose, barely making a sound. Our rapture held its breath. We hardly moved for fear of letting go. This particular feeling, that he was now entirely mine and always would be, whether he wanted it or not, was weightless, empty, I could disown it at any point. I felt fearless. He was kissing me lightly and murmuring my name over and over. Perhaps this was the time to tell him, when he couldn't get away. *Tell him now*, I kept thinking. *Tell him what you do.*

But when we came out of our dream, when the rest of the world poured back in on us, and we heard the traffic outside and the sound of a train pulling into Brighton station, and we started thinking about our plans for the rest of the evening, I realised how close I'd been to self-destruction.

We didn't go to a restaurant that night. Lately the weather had turned mild, to the government's probable relief and the miners' irritation. Tom was restless and wanted to walk along the seafront. So we went down West Street and set off along the broad deserted promenade in the direction of Hove, cutting inland to stop in a pub, and at another point to buy fish and chips. Even down by the sea there was no wind. The street lamps were dimmed to save energy, but they still smeared a bilious orange on the thick low cloud. I couldn't quite say what was different about Tom. He was affectionate enough, gripping my hand to make a point or putting an arm round me and drawing me closer to him. We walked fast and he talked quickly. We swapped Christmases. He described the scene, the terrible parting between his sister and her children, and how she tried to drag her little girl with the prosthetic foot into the car with her. And how Laura wept all the way to Bristol and said terrible things about the family, especially their parents. I recounted the moment when the Bishop embraced me and I cried. Tom made me go through the scene in detail. He wanted to know more about my feelings and how it had been, walking from the station. Was it like being a child again, did I suddenly realise just how much I missed home? How long did it take me to recover and why didn't I go and talk to my father about it later? I told him I cried because I cried, and I didn't know why.

We stopped and he kissed me and said I was a hopeless case. When I told him about my night walk around the cathedral close with Lucy and Luke, Tom was disapproving. He wanted me to promise never to smoke cannabis again. This puritan streak surprised me, and though it would have been an easy promise to keep, I simply shrugged. I thought he had no business demanding pledges from me.

I asked him about his new idea but he was evasive. Instead he gave me the news from Bedford Square.

Maschler loved *From the Somerset Levels* and was planning to bring it out by the end of March, a speed record in the publishing world and only possible because the editor was such a force. The idea was to meet the deadline for the Jane Austen Prize for Fiction, easily as prestigious as the newfangled Booker. The chances of making it onto the shortlist were remote but it appeared that Maschler was telling everyone about his new author, and the fact that the book was being raced into print specially for the judging panel had already been mentioned in newspapers. This was how you got a book talked about. I wondered what Pierre would have to say about the Service funding the author of an anti-capitalist novella. Keep it small. I said nothing and squeezed Tom's arm.

We sat on a municipal bench, facing out to sea like an old couple. There was supposed to be a waning half-moon, but it had no chance against the heavy lid of tangerine cloud. Tom's arm was round my shoulder, the English Channel was oily calm and silent, and for the first time in days I felt peaceful too as I shrank against my lover. He said he'd been invited to give a reading in Cambridge at an event for new young writers. He'd be sharing a stage with Kingsley Amis's son Martin, who would also be reading from his first novel, which, like Tom's, would be published this year – and by Maschler too.

'What I want to do,' Tom said, 'I'll only do with your permission.' The day after the reading he would travel on by train from Cambridge to my home town in order to talk to my sister. 'I'm thinking of a character who lives on the margins, scrapes by, but quite successfully, believes in Tarot cards and astrology and that sort of thing, likes drugs, though not to excess, believes a fair number of conspiracy theories. You know, thinks the moon landings were in a studio. And at the same time in other spheres she's perfectly sensible, a good mother to her little boy, goes on anti-Vietnam war marches, a reliable friend and so on.'

'It doesn't quite sound like Lucy,' I said, and immediately felt ungenerous and wanted to make amends. 'But she's very kind really and she'll like talking to you. One condition. You're not to talk about me.'

'Done.'

'I'll write and tell her you're a good friend who's broke and needs a bed for the night.'

We walked on. Tom had never given a public reading before and he was apprehensive. He was going to read from the very end of his book, the part he was most proud of, the grisly death scene of father and daughter in one another's arms. I said it would be a shame to give away the plot.

'Old-fashioned thinking.'

'Remember, I'm a middle-brow.'

'The end is already there in the beginning. Serena, there is no plot. It's a meditation.'

He was also wondering about protocol. Who should go first, Amis or Haley? How did one decide?

'Amis should. Top of the bill goes last,' I said loyally.

'Oh God. If I wake in the night and think about this reading, I can't sleep.'

'How about alphabetically?'

'No, I mean, standing up in front of a crowd, reading stuff people are perfectly capable of reading for themselves. I don't know what it's for. It's giving me night sweats.'

We went down onto the beach so that Tom could hurl

stones into the sea. He was strangely energetic. I sensed again his agitation or suppressed excitement. I sat leaning back against a bank of shingle while he kicked the pebbles over, looking for the right weight and shape. He took little runs at the water's edge and his throw went far out into the light mist, where the soundless splash was a faint patch of white. After ten minutes he came and sat beside me, breathless and sweaty, with a taste of salt in his kisses. The kisses began to get more serious and we were close to forgetting where we were.

He squeezed my face between his palms and said, 'Listen, whatever happens, you need to know how much I like being with you.'

I was worried. This was the corny sort of thing a cinema hero says to his girl before he goes off to die somewhere.

I said, 'Whatever happens?'

He was kissing my face, pushing me back against the uncomfortable stones. 'I mean, I'll never change my mind. You're very very special.'

I let myself be reassured. We were fifty yards across the beach from the railed pavement above and it looked like we were about to make love. I wanted it as much as he did.

I said, 'Not here.'

But he had a plan. He lay on his back and unzipped his fly while I kicked off my shoes, peeled off my tights and knickers and stuffed them into my coat pocket. I sat on him with my skirt and coat spilling around us, and each time I swayed slightly he groaned. We thought we looked innocent enough to any passer-by on the Hove promenade.

'Keep still a moment,' he said quickly, 'or it'll all be over.'

He looked so beautiful, with his head thrown back and his hair spilling over the stones. We stared into each other's eyes. We heard the traffic on the seafront road and only occasionally a wavelet tinkling on the shore.

A little later he said in a distant toneless voice, 'Serena, we can't let this stop. There's no way round it, I have to tell you. It's simple. I love you.'

I tried to say it back to him, but my throat was too constricted and I could only gasp. His words finished us, right there together, with our cries of joy lost to the sound of passing cars. This was the sentence we'd avoided saying. It was too momentous, it marked the line we were wary of crossing, the transition from an enjoyable affair to something weighty and unknown, almost like a burden. It didn't feel that way now. I brought his face near mine, kissed him and repeated his words. It was easy. Then I turned away from him and knelt on the shingle to rearrange my dress. As I did so, I knew that before this love began to take its course, I would have to tell him about myself. And then the love would end. So I couldn't tell him. But I had to.

Afterwards we lay with our arms linked, giggling like children in the dark at our secret, at the mischief we had got away with. We laughed at the enormity of the words we had spoken. Everyone else was bound by the rules, and we were free. We'd make love all over the world, our love would be everywhere. We sat up and shared a cigarette. Then we both began to shiver from the cold, and so we headed for home.

19

In February a depression settled over my section of the Service. Small talk was banished, or it banished itself. Wearing dressing gowns or cardigans as well as over-coats, we worked through tea breaks and lunches, as if to atone for our failures. The desk officer, Chas Mount, generally a cheerful, unflappable sort, hurled a file against the wall and another girl and I spent an hour on our knees putting the papers back in order. Our group counted the failure of our men in the field, Spade and Helium, as our own. Perhaps they had been too emphatically briefed on preserving their cover, or they simply knew nothing. Either way, as Mount kept saying in different ways, there was no point in such dangerous and expensive arrangements if we were to have a spectacular atrocity like this on our doorstep. It was not our place to tell him what he already knew, that we were dealing with cells that knew nothing of each other's existence, that according to a *Times* leader, we confronted the 'best organised, most ruthless terrorist outfit in the world'. And even in those days the competition was intense. At other times Mount muttered the ritual curses against the Met and the Royal Ulster Constabulary that among Service people were as common as the Lord's Prayer. Too many clodhopping coppers with no idea of intelligence gathering or analysis was the drift, though the language was generally stronger.

Our own doorstep in this case was a stretch of the M62 motorway between Huddersfield and Leeds. I heard someone in the office say that if it hadn't been for the train drivers' strike the servicemen and their families would not have been travelling on a late-night coach. But trade unionists had killed no one. The twenty-five-pound bomb was in the luggage storage at the rear of the bus and it instantly eradicated an entire family sleeping on the back seats, a serviceman, his wife and their two children aged five and two, scattering their body parts across two hundred yards of road, according to one of the cuttings that Mount insisted on pinning on a noticeboard. He had two children of his own, just a little older, and that was one reason why our section was obliged to take this matter personally. But it still wasn't clear that the Service was primarily responsible for preventing PIRA terrorism on the mainland. We flattered ourselves by thinking that if it had been, none of this would have happened.

A few days later, the Prime Minister, exasperated, bloated by an undiagnosed thyroid condition, plainly exhausted, addressed the nation on TV to explain that he was calling a snap election. Edward Heath needed a fresh mandate and told us that the question facing us all was – who governs Britain? Was it our elected representatives, or a small handful of extremists in the National Union of

Mineworkers? The country knew the real question was would it be Heath again or Wilson again? A Prime Minister crushed by events, or the Leader of the Opposition, who, according to rumours that even we girls heard, was showing signs of mental illness? An 'unpopularity contest', one wag wrote in an opinion column. The three-day week was well into its second month. It was too cold, too dark, we were too gloomy to think clearly about democratic accountability.

My immediate concern was that I couldn't go to Brighton that weekend because Tom was in Cambridge, and then travelling on to see my sister. He didn't want me to come to hear him read. It would 'destroy' him to know that I was in the audience. I had a letter from him the following Monday. I lingered over the salutation – *My darling one.* He said he was glad I hadn't been there. The event had been a disaster. Martin Amis was pleasant, and perfectly indifferent on the question of the running order. So Tom took top billing and let Martin go first as the warm-up act. A mistake. Amis read from his novel called *The Rachel Papers.* It was obscene, cruel and very funny – so funny that he had to pause now and then to let the audience recover. When he was done and Tom came out on stage to take his turn, the applause kept on and on, and Tom had to turn back into the darkness of the wings. People were still groaning and wiping their eyes as he finally made it to the lectern to introduce 'my three thousand words of buboes, pus and death'. During his reading some of the audience left, even before father and daughter had slipped into unconsciousness. People probably needed to catch last trains, but Tom found his confidence undermined, his voice became thin, he

292

stumbled over simple words, missed out a line and had to go back. He felt the whole room resenting him for undoing the merriment. The audience applauded at the end because they were glad the torment was over. Afterwards in the bar, he congratulated Amis, who did not return the compliment. Instead he bought Tom a triple Scotch.

There was also good news. He'd had a productive January. His article on persecuted Romanian poets had been accepted by *Index on Censorship*, and he'd finished a first draft of his monograph on Spenser and town planning. The story I helped with, 'Probable Adultery', turned down by the *New Review*, had been accepted by *Bananas* magazine and, of course, there was the new novel, the secret he would not share.

Three days into the general election campaign I received a summons from Max. It was not possible for us to go on avoiding each other. Peter Nutting wanted a progress report on all the Sweet Tooth cases. Max had no choice but to see me. We'd barely spoken since his late-night visit. We had passed in the corridor, muttered our 'good morning's, taken care to sit far apart in the canteen. I'd thought a lot about the things he'd said. He'd probably spoken the truth that night. It was likely the Service had let me in with a poor degree because I was Tony's candidate, likely they followed me for a while before losing interest. By sending me, harmless me, Tony may have wanted, as a farewell gesture, to show his old employers that he was harmless too. Or, as I liked to think, he loved me, and thought of me as his gift to the Service, his way of making amends.

I'd been hoping that Max would go back to his fiancée

and that we could continue as before. And that's how it seemed for the first quarter of an hour, as I got in behind the desk and gave an account of the Haley novella, the Romanian poets, *New Review*, *Bananas* and the Spenser essay.

'He's being talked about,' I said in conclusion. 'He's the coming man.'

Max scowled. 'I would have thought it would be all over between you by now.'

I said nothing.

'I've heard he gets about. Something of a swordsman.'

'Max,' I said quietly. 'Let's stick to business.'

'Tell me more about his novel.'

So I told him about the excitement in the publishing house, newspaper comment on the rush to meet the Austen Prize deadline, the rumour that David Hockney would design the cover.

'You still haven't told me what it's about.'

I wanted praise from upstairs as much as he did. But even more I wanted to get at Max for insulting Tom. 'It's the saddest thing I've ever read. Post-nuclear, civilisation regressed to savagery, father and daughter travel from the West Country to London looking for the girl's mother, they don't find her, catch bubonic plague and die. It's really beautiful.'

He was looking at me closely. 'As I remember it, this is just the kind of thing Nutting can't bear. Oh, and by the way. He and Tapp have got something for you. Have they been in touch?'

'No, they haven't. But, Max, we agreed we couldn't interfere with our writers.'

'Well, why are you so pleased?'

'He's a wonderful writer. It's very exciting.'

I was close to adding that we were in love. But Tom and I were secretive. In the spirit of the times, we'd made no plans to present ourselves to each other's parents. We'd made a declaration under the sky on the shingle somewhere between Brighton and Hove and it remained simple and pure.

What became clear in this short meeting with Max was that something had tilted, or shifted. That night before Christmas he'd forfeited some power along with dignity and I sensed he was aware of that, and he knew that I knew. I couldn't quite restrain the cockiness in my tone, he couldn't quite stop himself from sounding abject one moment and over-emphatic the next. I wanted to ask him about his intended, the medical woman he'd rejected for me. Had she taken him back or moved on? Either way, it was a humiliation and I knew enough, even in my elated state, not to ask.

There was a silence. Max had given up on the dark suits – I'd noticed this from across the canteen a few days before – and reverted to bristling Harris tweed and, a sickly new development, a knitted tie of mustard yellow against a check Viyella shirt. My guess was that no one, no woman, was guiding his taste. He was staring at his hands spread out palms down on the desk. He took a deep breath that whistled audibly through his nostrils.

'I now know this. We have ten projects, including Haley. Respected journalists and academics. I don't know the names, but I've an idea of the books they're taking time off to write. One is about how UK and US plant biology is making the Green Revolution across the rice-growing countries of the Third World, another is a biography of Tom

Paine, then there's going to be an account, first ever, of a detention camp in East Berlin, Special Camp Number Three, used by the Soviets in the years after the war to murder social democrats and children as well as Nazis, and now enlarged by the East German authorities to detain and psychologically torture dissidents or anyone they fancy. There'll be a book about the political disasters of post-colonial Africa, a new translation of the poetry of Akhmatova, and a survey of European utopias of the seventeenth century. We'll have a monograph on Trotsky at the head of the Red Army, and a couple more I don't remember.'

At last he looked up from his hands and his eyes were pale and hard.

'So, how the fuck is your T.H. Haley and his little fantasy world gone to shit adding to the sum of what we know or care about?'

I'd never heard him swear, and I flinched, as though he'd thrown something in my face. I'd never liked *From the Somerset Levels* but I liked it now. Usually I would have waited to be dismissed. I got to my feet and pushed the chair under the desk and began to edge out of the room. I would have left with a smart parting line but my mind was a blank. I was almost through the door when I glanced back at him sitting upright at his desk in the apex of his tiny room and saw on his face a look of pain or sorrow, a strange grimace, like a mask, and I heard him say in a low voice, 'Serena, please don't go.'

I could sense it welling up, another terrible scene. I had to get out. I went quickly down the corridor and when he called after me, I increased my pace, fleeing not only the mess of his emotions but my own unreasonable guilt. Before I reached my desk downstairs by way of the creaking lift I reminded myself that I belonged, I was loved and nothing Max said could touch me now and I owed him nothing.

Within minutes I was usefully immersed in the atmosphere of gloom and self-blame in Chas Mount's office, cross-checking dates and facts on a pessimistic memo the desk officer was sending up the chain of command. 'Notes on recent failures'. I hardly thought about Max for the rest of that day.

Which was as well, because it was Friday afternoon and Tom and I were meeting in a Soho pub at lunchtime the next day. He was coming up to see Ian Hamilton in the Pillars of Hercules in Greek Street. The magazine was due to be launched in April with mostly taxpayers' money – the Arts Council rather than the Secret Vote. Already there'd been some grumbling in the press about the proposed price of 75p for 'something we've already paid for', as one newspaper put it. The editor wanted some minor changes to the talking-ape story, which at last had a title – 'Her Second Novel'. Tom thought he might be interested in the Spenser essay or offer him some reviewing. There was to be no payment for articles, but Tom was convinced that this was going to be the most prestigious publication to appear in. The arrangement was that I would turn up an hour after him and then we'd have what was described to me as a 'chip-orientated pub lunch'.

On Saturday morning I tidied my room, went to the launderette, ironed clothes for the following week and washed and dried my hair. I was impatient to see Tom and left the house early and was walking up the stairs at Leicester Square Tube station almost an hour ahead of time. I thought I'd browse among the second-hand books on the Charing Cross Road. But I was too restless. I stood in front of shelves, taking nothing in, then I moved on to another shop and did the same. I went into Foyles with the vague idea of finding a present for Tom among the new paperbacks, but I couldn't focus. I was desperate to see him. I cut through Manette Street, which goes along the north of Foyles and passes under a building, with the bar of the Pillars of Hercules on its left. This brief tunnel, probably the remains of an old coaching courtyard, emerges into Greek Street. Right on the corner is a window with heavy wooden glazing bars. Through it I glimpsed Tom from an oblique angle, sitting right by the window, distorted by the old glass, leaning forward to talk to someone out of my view. I could have gone and tapped on a pane. But, of course, I didn't want to distract him from his important meeting. It was foolish to arrive so early. I should have wandered off for a while. At the very least, I should have gone in by the main door on Greek Street. Then he would have seen me and I would have witnessed nothing. But I turned back and went into the pub by a side entrance in the covered passageway.

I passed through the peppermint scent emanating from the gents' lavatory and pushed open another door. There was a man standing alone at the near end of the bar with a cigarette in one hand and a Scotch in the other. He turned to look at me and I knew instantly that it was Ian Hamilton. I'd seen his picture in the hostile diary pieces. But wasn't he supposed to be with Tom? Hamilton was watching me with a neutral, almost friendly look, and a lopsided smile that didn't part his lips. Just as Tom had described, he had the strong-jawed look of an old-fashioned movie star, the villain with a heart of gold in a black-and-white romance. He seemed to be waiting for me to approach. I looked through the blue-ish smoky light towards the raised corner seat by the window. Tom was sitting with a woman whose back was to me. She looked familiar. He was holding her hand across the table and his head was inclined, nearly touching hers as he listened. Impossible. I stared hard, trying to resolve the scene into sense, into something innocent. But there it was, Max's silly improbable cliché, *swordsman*. It had got under my skin like a burrowing parasite and released its neurotoxins into my bloodstream. It had altered my behaviour and brought me here early to see for myself.

Hamilton came over and stood by me, following the line of my gaze.

'She's a writer too. Commercial stuff. But not bad in fact. Nor is he. She's just lost her father.'

He said it lightly, knowing full well that I wouldn't believe him. It was tribal, one man covering for another.

I said, 'They seem to be old friends.'

'What'll you have?'

When I said I'd have a glass of lemonade he appeared to wince. He went to the bar and I stepped back behind one of the half-screens that were a feature of the pub, allowing drinkers to stand in privacy to talk. I was tempted to slip out of the side door, stay out of Tom's reach all weekend, let him sweat while I nursed my turmoil. Could it really be so crude, Tom's bit on the side? I peeped round the screen and the tableau of betrayal was unchanged, she still spoke, he still gripped her hand and listened tenderly as he dipped his head towards hers. It was so monstrous it was almost funny. I couldn't feel anything yet, no anger or panic or sorrow, and I didn't even feel numb. Horrible clarity was all I could claim.

Ian Hamilton brought me my drink, a very large glass of straw-yellow white wine. Exactly what I needed.

'Get this down you.'

He was watching me with wry concern as I drank, and then he asked me what I did. I explained that I worked for an arts foundation. Instantly, his eyelids looked heavy with boredom. But he heard me out and then he had an idea.

'You need to put money into a new magazine. I suppose that's why you're here, to bring me the cash.'

I said we only did individual artists.

'This way I'll be letting you back fifty individual artists.'

I said, 'Perhaps I could look at your business plan.'

'*Business* plan?'

It was just a phrase I'd heard and I guessed correctly that it would close down the conversation.

Hamilton nodded in Tom's direction. 'Here's your man.'

I stepped out from the shelter of the screen. Over in the corner Tom was already on his feet and the woman was reaching for her coat from the seat beside her. She stood too and turned. She was three stone lighter, hair straightened and almost touching her shoulders, her tight black jeans were tucked into calf-length boots, her face was longer and thinner, beautiful in fact, but instantly recognisable. Shirley Shilling, my old friend. The moment I saw her, she saw me. In the brief second that our eyes met, she began to raise a hand in greeting then let it drop hopelessly to her side, as if to acknowledge that there was too much to explain and she was in no mood for it. She went quickly out of the front entrance. Tom was coming towards me, smiling loopily and I, like an idiot, forced a smile back, aware that Hamilton at my side, now lighting another cigarette, was watching us. There was something in his manner that imposed restraint. He was cool, so we would have to be too. I was obliged to pretend that I didn't care.

So the three of us stood at the bar for a long time drinking. The men talked books and gossiped about writers, particularly the poet Robert Lowell, a friend of Hamilton and possibly going mad; and football, on which Tom was weak, but adept at making good use of the two or three things he knew. It didn't occur to anyone to sit down. Tom ordered pork pies with a round of drinks but Hamilton didn't touch his, and later used his plate and then the pie itself as an ashtray. I assumed that Tom, like me, dreaded leaving the conversation, for then we would have to have a row. After my second glass I chipped in occasionally, but mostly I pretended to listen while I thought about Shirley. So much change! She had made it as a writer, so no real coincidence in her meeting Tom in the Pillars of Hercules – he had told me it was already established as the *New Review*'s office extension, anteroom and canteen, and in preparation for the launch dozens of writers came through. She had shed her decency along with the fat. She'd shown no surprise at finding me here, so she must have known my connection to Tom. When the time came for me to be angry she'd get more than her share. I'd give her hell.

But I felt nothing now. The pub closed and we followed Hamilton through the afternoon gloom to Muriel's, a tiny dark drinking club where men of a certain age with jowly ruined faces were perched on stools at the bar, pronouncing loudly on international affairs.

As we came in one said loudly, 'China? Fuck off. China!'

We made a huddle on three velvet armchairs in a corner. Tom and Ian had reached that point in a drinking session when the conversation patrols endlessly the tiny perimeters of a minor detail. They were talking about Larkin, about some lines at the end of 'The Whitsun Weddings', one of the poems Tom had made me read. They were disagreeing, though without much passion, about an 'arrow shower/Sent out of sight, somewhere becoming rain'. Hamilton thought the lines were perfectly clear. The train journey was over, the just-married couples were released to go their ways, into London, into their separate fates. Tom less laconically said the lines were dark, touched with foreboding, the elements were negative – a sense of falling, wet, lost, somewhere. He used the word 'liquescence' and Hamilton said drily, 'Liquescence, eh?' Then they went around again, finding clever ways to make the same points, though I sensed that the older man may have merely been sounding Tom out for his judgement or agility in argument. I don't think Hamilton cared either way.

I wasn't listening all the time. The men ignored me and I was beginning to feel a bit of a writer's moll as well as a fool. I made a mental list of my possessions in the Brighton flat – I might not be going there again. A hair-dryer, underwear, a couple of summer frocks and a swimsuit, nothing I'd seriously miss. I was persuading myself that leaving Tom would lift from me the burden of honesty. I could go with my secret intact. We were drinking brandy with coffee at this point. I didn't mind parting from Tom. I'd forget him quickly and find someone else, someone better. It was all just fine, I could take care of myself, I'd spend my time well, dedicate myself to work, read Olivia Manning's Balkan trilogy, which I had lined up by my bed, use the Bishop's twenty-pound note to take a week's holiday in spring and be an interesting single woman in a small Mediterranean hotel.

We stopped drinking at six and went down into the street and walked in freezing rain towards Soho Square. Hamilton was due to give a reading at the Poetry Society in Earls Court that evening. He shook Tom's hand, embraced me, and then we watched him hurry away, nothing in his gait to suggest the kind of afternoon he'd had. And then Tom and I were alone, not sure which direction to walk in. Now it begins, I thought, and at that moment, revived by the cold rain in my face, and understanding the true measure of my loss and Tom's treachery, I was overcome with sudden desolation and couldn't move. A great black weight was on me and my feet were heavy and numb. I stood looking across the square towards Oxford Street. Some chanting Hare Krishna types, shaven-head dupes with tambourines, were filing back into their headquarters. Dodging their god's rain. I detested every last one of them.

'Serena, darling, what's the matter?'

He stood unsteadily before me, pissed, but no less good an actor for that, his face puckered with theatrical concern.

I could see us clearly, as though from a window two flights up, with the view distorted by black-edged rain-drops. A couple of Soho drunks about to have a row on the filthy slick pavement. I would have preferred to walk away, for the outcome was obvious. But I still couldn't move.

Instead, I started off the scene, and spoke through a weary sigh. 'You're having an affair with my friend.'

I sounded so plaintive and childish, and stupid too, as though an affair with a stranger would have been just fine. He was looking at me in amazement, and a fine show of being baffled. I could have hit him.

'What are you . . . ?' Then, a clumsy imitation of a man struck by a brilliant idea.

'Shirley Shilling! Oh God, Serena. Do you really think that? I should have explained. I met her at the Cambridge reading. She was with Martin Amis. I didn't know until today that you once worked in the same office somewhere. Then you and I started talking with Ian and I forgot all about it. Her father's just died and she's devastated. She would have come over but she was too upset . . .'

He put his hand on my shoulder but I shook him off. I didn't like to be pitied. And I thought I saw traces of amusement around his mouth.

I said, 'It was obvious, Tom. How dare you!'

'She's written a soppy romantic novel. But I like her. That's all there is to it. Her dad owned a furniture store and she was close to him, she worked for him. I felt truly sorry for her. Honestly, darling.'

At first I was simply confused, suspended between believing and hating him. Then, as I began to doubt myself, I felt a delicious sulky obstinacy, a perverse refusal to let go of the obliterating idea that he had made love to Shirley.

'I can't bear it, my poor darling, you've been suffering all afternoon. That's why you were so quiet. And of course!

You must have seen me holding her hand. Oh my sweet-heart, I'm so sorry. I love you, only you, and I'm so sorry . . .'

I kept a closed face as he went on protesting, and comforting me. Believing him didn't make me less angry with him. I was angry that he was making me feel foolish, that he might be secretly laughing at me, that he would work this up into a funny story. I was determined to make him try all the harder to win me back. I was coming to the point where I knew very well I was only pretending to doubt him. Perhaps that was better than appearing such a dolt, and besides, I didn't know how to get out of it, how to change my entrenched position and look plausible. So I remained silent, but when he took my hand, I didn't refuse him, and when he drew me towards him I complied reluctantly and let him kiss the top of my head.

'You're drenched, you're shivering,' he murmured in my ear. 'We need to get you indoors.'

I nodded, signalling the end of my truculence, the end of my disbelief. Even though the Pillars of Hercules was only a hundred yards away along Greek Street, I knew that indoors meant my room.

He pulled me closer towards him. 'Listen,' he said. 'We said it on the beach. We love each other. It's meant to be simple.'

I nodded again. All I could think of now was how cold I was, and how drunk. I heard a taxi's engine behind us and felt him turn and stretch to wave it down. When we were installed and heading north, Tom turned on the heater. It produced a roar and a trickle of cool air. On the screen that divided us from the cabbie was an adver-tisement for a taxi like this one, and as the lettering was drifting upwards and sideways, I worried that I would be sick. At my place I was relieved to find that my housemates were out. Tom ran a bath for me. The scalding water sent up clouds of steam that condensed on the icy walls and ran down to puddle on the floral lino. We got in the bath together, topped and tailed, and massaged each other's feet and sang old Beatles songs. He got out long before me, dried himself and went off to find more towels. He was drunk too, but he was tender as he helped me out of the bath, and dried me like a child, and led me to the bed. He went downstairs and came back with mugs of tea and got in beside me. Then he took very special care of me.

Months, and then years later, after all that happened, whenever I woke in the night and needed comfort, I'd summon that early winter evening when I lay in his arms and he kissed my face, and told me over and over again how silly I'd been, how sorry he was, and how he loved me.

20

At the end of February, not long before election day, the Austen Prize judges announced their shortlist and on it, tucked among the familiar giants – Burgess, Murdoch, Farrell, Spark and Drabble – was a complete unknown, one T.H. Haley. But no one took much notice. The press release was badly timed because that day everyone was talking about Enoch Powell's attack on the Prime Minister, his own party leader. Poor fat Ted! People had stopped worrying about the miners and 'Who governs?' and had started worrying about 20 per cent inflation and economic collapse and whether we should listen to Powell, vote Labour and get out of Europe. This was not a good moment to ask the country to contemplate contemporary fiction. Because the three-day week had successfully prevented blackouts, the whole affair was now regarded as a fraud. Coal stocks were not so low after all, industrial production was not much affected and there was a general impression that we'd been frightened for nothing, or for political purposes, and that none of it should have happened.

And so, against all the predictions, Edward Heath, his piano, sheet music and seascapes were moved out of Downing Street and Harold and Mary Wilson were installed for a second spell. On a TV at work I saw the new Prime Minister standing outside Number Ten in early March looking stooped and frail, almost as weary as Heath. Everyone was weary, and at Leconfield House they were depressed as well as weary because the country had chosen the wrong man.

I'd voted for Wilson a second time, for that wily survivor of the left, and I should have been more cheerful than most but I was exhausted from insomnia. I couldn't stop thinking about the shortlist. Of course, I wanted Tom to win, I wanted it more than he did. But I'd heard from Peter Nutting that he and others had read *From the Somerset Levels* in a proof copy and considered it 'flimsy and pathetic' as well as 'fashionably negative and boring' – Nutting told me this when he stopped me one lunchtime in Curzon Street. He strode on, striking the pavement with his rolled umbrella, leaving me to understand that if my choice was suspect, then so was I.

Gradually, press interest in the Austen Prize picked up and attention fixed on the only new name on the list. No first-time novelist had ever won the Austen. The shortest novel to be honoured in its one-hundred-year history was twice the length of *The Levels*. A lot of coverage seemed to suggest there was something unmanly or dishonest about a short novel. Tom was profiled in the *Sunday Times*, photographed in front of the Palace Pier looking nakedly happy and vulnerable. A couple of articles mentioned that he had a grant from the Foundation. We were reminded of how Tom's book was rushed into print to make the

Prize deadline. Journalists had not yet read his novel because Tom Maschler was tactically holding back review copies. An unusually benign diary piece in the *Daily Telegraph* said that it was generally agreed Tom Haley was handsome and girls went 'wobbly' when he smiled, at which I felt a vertiginous moment of jealousy and possession. What girls? Tom now had a phone in the flat and I was able to speak to him from an odorous phone box on the Camden Road.

'There are no girls,' he said cheerfully. 'They must be in the newspaper office, wobbling in front of my photograph.'

He was amazed to be on the list, but Maschler had phoned to say that he would have been furious if Tom had been left off. 'It's too obvious,' he'd apparently said. 'You're a genius and it's a masterpiece. They wouldn't dare ignore it.'

But the newly discovered writer was able to remain detached from the Austen fuss, even though he was bemused by the press. *The Levels* was already behind him, it was a 'five-finger exercise'. I warned him not to say so to any journalist while the judges were still making up their minds. He said he didn't care, he had a novel to write and it was growing at a pace that only obsession and a new electric typewriter could deliver. His output was all I knew of the book. Three or four thousand words most days, sometimes six, and once, in an afternoon and all-night frenzy, ten. The numbers meant little to me, though I took my cue from the croaky excitement down the phone.

'Ten thousand words, Serena. Do that every day for a month and I'd have an *Anna Karenina*!'

Even I knew that he wouldn't. I felt protective of him and worried that when they came, the reviews would turn against him and he'd be surprised at his own disappointment. For now his only anxiety was that a trip he'd just taken to Scotland for research had interrupted his concentration.

'You need a rest,' I said from the Camden Road. 'Let me come at the weekend.'

'OK. But I'll have to go on writing.'

'Tom, please tell me just a little bit about it.'

'You'll see it before anyone else, I promise.'

The day after the shortlist was announced I received, in place of the usual summons, a visit from Max. He went first to stand by Chas Mount's desk for a chat. As it happened we were frantic that morning. Mount had written the first draft of an internal report, a retrospective in which the RUC and the army also had a hand. The issue was what Mount bitterly referred to as 'the running sore', by which he meant internment without trial. Back in 1971 scores of the wrong people had been rounded up because the RUC Special Branch suspect lists were out of date and useless. And no killers from the loyalist side had been arrested, no members of the Ulster Volunteer Force. The detainees were kept in inadequate accommodation without being properly separated. And all due process, all legality abandoned – a propaganda gift to our enemies. Chas Mount had served in Aden and had always been sceptical of the interrogation techniques the army and RUC were using during internment – black hoods, isolation, restricted diet, white noise, hours of standing. He was keen to demonstrate that the Service's hands were relatively clean. We girls in the office took it on trust that they were. The whole sorry affair was heading towards the European Court of Human Rights. The RUC, at least as he explained it, wanted to drag us down with them, and the army was on their side. They weren't pleased at all by his version of events. Someone on our side higher up than Mount had sent his draft report back and told him to rewrite it to keep all factions happy. It was after all 'only' an internal report and would soon be filed and forgotten.

So he was calling for more files, and we were in and out of the Registry, and busy typing up inserts. Max chose a bad time to hover by Chas Mount and try to engage him in small talk. In strict security terms, with these dossiers open he shouldn't have stepped into our office at all. But Chas was too polite and good-natured to say so. Still, his responses were brief, and soon Max came over to me. In his hand was a small brown envelope which he placed ostentatiously on my desk and said in a voice loud enough for everyone to hear, 'Take a look as soon as you have a moment.' Then he left.

For a good while, perhaps as long as an hour, I decided that I didn't have a moment. What I dreaded most was a heartfelt declaration on office stationery. What I eventually read was a properly typed memo headed 'Restricted' and 'Sweet Tooth' and 'From MG to SF' and a circulation list that included the initials of Nutting, Tapp and two others I didn't recognise. The note, obviously written by Max for the record, began 'Dear Miss Frome'. It advised me of what I had 'likely already considered'. One of the Sweet Tooth subjects was receiving publicity and might well receive yet more. 'Staff are expected to avoid being photographed or written about in the press. You may well

311

consider it to be in the line of duty to attend the Austen Prize reception, but you are best advised to avoid it.'

Very sensible, however much I resented it. I had in fact planned to be there with Tom. Win or lose, he needed me. But why this circulated letter rather than a word in my ear? Was it too painful for Max to talk to me alone? I rather suspected some form of bureaucratic trap was being set for me. The question then was whether I should defy Max or stay away. Doing the latter seemed safer since it was procedurally correct, but I felt cross about it and on the way home that evening I felt indignant, and angry with Max and his schemes – whatever they were. I was annoyed too at having to invent for Tom a good explanation for my absence. Illness in the family, a bout of flu for myself, an emergency at work? I decided on a morbidly mouldy snack – rapid onset, total incapacity, quick recovery – and this deceit naturally brought me back to the old problem. There had never been a right moment to tell him. Perhaps if I'd turned him down for Sweet Tooth and then had the affair, or started the affair and left the Service, or told him on first meeting . . . but no, none of it made sense. I couldn't have known at the beginning where we were heading, and as soon as I did know, it became too precious to threaten. I could tell him and resign, or resign then tell him, but I would still risk losing him. All I could think of was never telling him. Could I live with myself? Well, I already was.

Unlike its boisterous infant cousin, the Booker, the Austen didn't go in for banquets, or for having the great and good on its judging panel. As Tom described it to me, there was going to be a sober drinks reception at the Dorchester, with a short speech by an eminent literary figure. The judges were mostly literary types, academics, critics, with an occasional philosopher or historian drafted in. The Prize money had once been considerable – in 1875 two thousand pounds took you a long way. Now it was no match for the Booker. The Austen was valued for prestige alone. There had been talk of televising the Dorchester proceedings, but the elderly trustees were said to be wary and, according to Tom, the Booker was more likely to make it onto television one day.

The reception was at six the following evening. At five I sent a telegram from the Mayfair post office to Tom, care of the Dorchester. *Am sick. Bad sandwich. Thoughts with you. Come to Camden after. Love you. S.* I slouched back to the office, loathing myself and the situation I was in. Once I would have asked myself what Tony would have done. No use now. It was easy enough to pass off my black mood as illness and Mount let me leave early. I arrived home at six, just when I should have been passing through the Dorchester entrance on Tom's arm. Towards eight I thought I should play my part in case he turned up early. It was easy enough to persuade myself that I was unwell. In pyjamas and dressing gown, I lay on my bed in a haze of sulkiness and self-pity, then I read for a while, then I dozed off for an hour or two and didn't hear the doorbell.

One of the girls must have let Tom in because when I opened my eyes he was standing by my bed, holding up by a corner his cheque and in the other hand a finished copy of his novel. He was grinning like a fool. Forgetting my poisonous sandwich, I leapt up to embrace him, we whooped and hollered and made such a din that Tricia tapped on the door and asked if we needed help. We reassured her, then we made love (he seemed so hungry for it), and straight afterwards took a taxi to the White Tower.

We hadn't been back there since our first date, so that was an anniversary of a sort. I'd insisted on bringing with me *From the Somerset Levels* and we passed it back and forth across the table, flipped through its one hundred and forty-one pages to admire the typeface, rejoiced in the author photograph and the cover, which showed in grainy black and white a ruined city that may have been Berlin or Dresden in 1945. Suppressing thoughts about the security implications, I exclaimed over the dedication, 'To Serena', got up from my seat to kiss him, and listened to his account of the evening, of William Golding's droll speech and an incomprehensible one by the chairman of the judges, a professor from Cardiff. When his name was announced, Tom in his nervousness had tripped on the edge of a carpet as he went forward and hurt his wrist on the back of a chair. Tenderly, I kissed that wrist. After the Prize ceremony he gave four short interviews, but no one had read his book, it didn't matter what he said and the experience made him feel fraudulent. I asked for two glasses of champagne and we toasted the only first-time novelist to take the Austen Prize. It was such a wonderful occasion that we didn't even bother to get drunk. I remembered to eat carefully, like the invalid I was supposed to be.

Tom Maschler had planned publication with the precision of a moon landing. Or as if the Austen was in his gift. The shortlist, the profiles, the announcement helped build the impatient expectation, which was fulfilled towards the end of the week when the book appeared in the shops just as the first notices appeared. Our weekend plan was simple. Tom would carry on writing, I would read his press on the train down. I travelled to Brighton on Friday evening with seven reviews on my lap. The world mostly approved of my lover. In the *Telegraph*: 'The only thread of hope is that which binds father to daughter (a love as tenderly achieved as anything in modern fiction) but the reader knows soon enough that this bleak master-piece cannot tolerate the thread uncut. The heart-piercing finale is almost more than one can bear.' In the *TLS*: 'A strange glow, an eerie subterranean light, suffuses Mr Haley's prose and the hallucinogenic effect on the reader's inner eye is such as to transform a catastrophic end-time world into a realm of harsh and irresistible beauty.' In the *Listener*: 'His prose gives no quarter. He has the drained, level stare of the psychopath and his characters, morally decent, physically lovely, must share their fates with the worst in a godless world.' In *The Times*: 'When Mr Haley sets on his dogs to tear out the viscera of a starving beggar, we know we are being tossed into the crucible of a modern aesthetic and challenged to object, or at least to blink. In the hands of most writers the scene would be a careless dabbling in suffering, and unforgivable, but Haley's spirit is both tough and transcendent. From the very first para-graph you are in his hands, you know he knows what he is doing, and you can trust him. This small book bears the promise and burden of genius.'

We had already passed through Haywards Heath. I took the book, *my* book, from my bag and read random pages and, of course, began to see them through different eyes. Such was the power of this assured consensus that *The*

Levels did look different, more confident of its terms, its destination, and rhythmically hypnotic. And so knowing. It read like a majestic poem as precise and suspended as 'Adlestrop'. Above the train's iambic racket (and who taught me *that* word?) I could hear Tom intone his own lines. What did I know, a humble operative who had once, only two or three years ago, made the case for Jacqueline Susann against Jane Austen? But could I trust a consensus? I picked up the *New Statesman*. It's 'back half', as explained to me by Tom, was important in the literary world. As the contents list announced, the arts editor herself presented a verdict in the lead review: 'Admittedly, there are moments of poise, a clinical descriptive power capable of generating occasional surges of disgust at humankind, but overall the impression is of something forced, a touch formulaic, emotionally manipulative and altogether slight. He deludes himself (but not the reader) that he is saying something profound about our common plight. What is lacking is scale, ambition and naked intelligence. However, he may do something yet.' Then a tiny item in the *Evening Standard*'s Londoner's Diary: 'One of the worst decisions ever taken by a committee . . . this year's Austen judges, perhaps with a collective eye to a role in the Treasury, decided to devalue the currency of their prize. They opted for an adolescent dystopia, a pimply celebration of disorder and beastliness, thankfully not much longer than a short story.'

Tom had said he didn't want to see the reviews, so in the flat that evening I read out the choicest parts of the good ones and summarised the negative articles in the blandest terms. He was pleased by the praise, of course, but it was obvious that he had moved on. He was glancing at one of his typed pages even as I was reading out the passage that included the word 'masterpiece'. He was typing again as soon as I'd finished, and he wanted to go on working through the evening. I went out for fish and chips and he ate his at the typewriter, straight off the page of yesterday's *Evening Argus*, which contained one of his best notices.

I read and we barely spoke a word until I went to bed. I was still awake an hour later when he got in beside me, and again, he made love to me in this new, hungry way of his, as if he'd lived without sex for a year. He made far more noise than I ever did. I teased him by calling this his pig-in-a-trough mode.

The next morning I woke to the muted sound of his new typewriter. I kissed the top of his head as I passed him on the way out to the Saturday market. I did the shopping there, collected up the newspapers and took them to my usual coffee shop. A table by the window, a cappuccino, an almond croissant. Perfect. And here was a brilliant review in the *Financial Times*. 'Reading T.H. Haley is like being driven too fast round tight corners. But be assured, this sleek vehicle never leaves the road.' I looked forward to reading that to him. Next on the heap was the *Guardian*, with Tom's name and a photograph of him at the Dorchester on the front page. Good. A whole article about him. I turned to it, saw the headline – and froze. 'Austen Prize-winning Author Funded by MI5'.

I was almost sick right there. My first stupid thought was that perhaps he would never see it. A 'reliable source' had confirmed to the paper that the Freedom International Foundation, perhaps unknowingly, 'had received funds from another body that was partly financed by an organisation indirectly funded by the Security Service'. I scanned the piece at the speed of panic. No mention of Sweet Tooth or of other writers. There was an accurate summary of monthly payments, of how Tom had given up his post-grad teaching post on receiving the first, and then, less harmfully, a mention of the Congress for Cultural Freedom and its connection to the CIA. The old *Encounter* story was warmed up, then, back to the scoop. It was noted that T.H. Haley had written

passionate anti-communist articles on the East German Uprising, on the silence of West German writers about the Berlin Wall and, most recently, on the State persecution of Romanian poets. This is perhaps just the sort of kindred spirit our intelligence services would like to see flourish on these shores, a right-wing author who is eloquently sceptical of the general left-leaning tendencies of his colleagues. But with this level of secret meddling in culture, questions are bound to be raised about openness and artistic freedom in our Cold War environment. No one yet doubts the integrity of the Austen Prize judges, but the trustees might be wondering just what kind of winner their learned committee has chosen, and whether champagne corks flew in certain secret London offices when Haley's name was announced.

I read the piece again and sat immobilised for twenty minutes while my untouched coffee cooled. Now it seemed obvious. It was bound to happen: if I wouldn't tell him, someone else would. My punishment for cowardice. How loathsome and ridiculous I'd appear now, forced into the open, trying to sound honest, trying to explain myself. I didn't tell you dearest because I love you. I was frightened of losing you. Oh yes, a perfect arrangement. My silence, his disgrace. I thought of going straight to the station to get the next London train, fading from his life. Yes, let him face the storm alone. More cowardice. But he wouldn't want me near him anyway. And so it went round, even though I knew there was no escape, I would have to confront him, I would have to go to the flat and show him the article.

I gathered up the chicken, vegetables and newspapers, paid for my uneaten breakfast, and walked slowly up the hill to his street. I heard him typing as I came up the stairs. Well, that was about to stop. I let myself in and waited for him to look up.

He was aware of me and faintly smiled in greeting and was about to continue when I said, 'You'd better look at this. It isn't a review.'

The *Guardian* was folded at the page. He took it and turned his back on me to read it. I was numbly wondering, when it came to it, whether I should pack, or just leave. I had a small suitcase under the bed. I would need to remember my hairdryer. But there might not be time. He might simply throw me out.

At last he looked at me and said neutrally, 'It's terrible.'

'Yes.'

'What am I supposed to say?'

'Tom, I don't . . .'

'I mean, these money trails. Listen to this. Foundation blah blah, "had received funds from another body that was partly financed by an organisation indirectly funded by the Security Service".'

'I'm sorry, Tom.'

'Partly? Indirectly? Three organisations back? How are we meant to know about that?'

'I don't know.' I heard the 'we' but I didn't really take it in.

He said, 'I went to their office, I've seen all their stuff. It's completely above board. '

'Of course it is.'

'I suppose I should have asked to audit the books. Like a fucking accountant!'

He was indignant now. 'I just don't understand it. If the government wants to put over certain views, why do it in secret?'

'Exactly.'

'They've got friendly journalists, Arts Council, scholarships, BBC, information departments, royal institutions. I don't know what the fuck they've got. They run a whole education system! Why use MI5?'

'It's insane, Tom.'

'It's madness. This is how these secret bureaucracies perpetuate themselves. Some squirt of an underling dreams up a scheme to please his masters. But no one knows what it's for, what the point is. No one even asks. It's right out of Kafka.'

He stood up suddenly and came over to me.

'Listen. Serena. No one has ever told me what to write. Speaking up for a Romanian poet in jail doesn't make me right wing. Calling the Berlin Wall a pile of shit doesn't make me a dupe of MI5. Nor does calling West German writers cowards for ignoring it.'

'Of course it doesn't.'

'But that's what they're implying. Fucking kindred spirit! That's what everyone's going to think.'

Was it really that simple, that he loved me so much, felt so loved by me, that he couldn't begin to suspect me? Was *he* that simple? I watched as he began to pace up and down the small attic room. The floor creaked noisily, the lamp suspended from the rafters stirred a little. This surely would be the time, when we were halfway there, to tell him the truth. But I knew I couldn't deny myself this reprieve.

He was in a frenzy of indignation again. Why him? It was unfair. It was vindictive. Just when his career had made a decent start.

Then he stopped and said, 'On Monday I'll go to the bank and tell them to refuse any more payments.'

'Good idea.'

'I can live on the Prize money for a while.'

'Yes.'

'But Serena . . .' He came over to me again and took my hands in his. We looked into each other's eyes, then we kissed.

'Serena, what am I going to do?'

My voice, when I found it, was flatly inexpressive. 'I think you're going to have to put out a statement. Write something and phone it through to the Press Association.'

'I need you to help me draft it.'

'Of course. You need to say that you knew nothing, you're outraged and you're stopping the money.'

'You're brilliant. I love you.'

He put away the loose pages of his new book in a

drawer and locked it. Then I sat at the typewriter and put in a clean sheet and we worked on a draft. It took me some minutes to adjust to the sensitive keys of an electric machine. When it was done I read it back to him and he said, 'You can also put, "I wish to make it clear that at no point have I ever had any communication from or contact with any member of MI5."'

I felt my knees go weak. 'You don't need that. It's clear from what you've already said. It sounds like you're protesting too much.'

'I'm not sure you're right. Isn't it good to make it clear?'

'It is clear, Tom. Honestly. You don't need it.'

Our eyes met again. His were red-rimmed from exhaustion. Otherwise, I saw nothing but trust.

'All right then,' he said. 'Forget it.'

I handed him the page and went next door to lie on the bed while he got the PA's number from the operator and phoned his statement through. To my amazement, I heard him dictate the sentence, or a version of it, that we had just agreed to drop.

'And let me make this clear. I have never in my life had contact with any member of MI5.'

I sat up, and was about to call out to him, but there was nothing to be done and I sank back into the pillows. I felt weary of thinking about the same thing all the time. *Tell him. Get it over with. No! Don't you* dare. Events were moving out of my control and I had no idea what I should be doing. I heard him put the phone down and go to his desk. Within minutes he was typing again. How extraordinary, how wonderful, to have such power of concentration, to be able to push on now into an imagined world. I continued to lie there on the unmade bed, devoid of

322

motive, oppressed by the certainty that the week ahead would be disastrous. I would be in deep trouble at work, even if the *Guardian* story wasn't followed up. But it was bound to be. It could only get worse. I should have listened to Max. It was possible that the journalist who wrote the piece knew no more than he had written. But if there was more, and I was exposed, then . . . then I should tell Tom before the newspapers did. *That* again. I didn't move. I couldn't.

After forty minutes the typewriter stopped. Five minutes later I heard the boards creak, and Tom came in wearing his jacket and sat by me and kissed me. He was restless, he said. He hadn't been out of the flat for three days. Would I walk to the seafront with him, and would I let him buy me lunch in Wheeler's? It was balm, instant forgetfulness. We were out of the house in the time it took me to put on my coat, and walking arm in arm down the hill towards the English Channel as if it was just another carefree weekend. As long as I could lose myself in the present with him, I felt protected. I was helped by Tom's lively mood. He seemed to think that his statement to the press had solved the problem. On the front we walked east, with a fretful frothy grey-green sea on our right whipped up by a fresh north wind. We went past Kemp Town, and then through a knot of demonstrators with placards protesting against plans to build a marina. We agreed we didn't care either way. When we came back past the same place twenty minutes later the demonstration had dispersed.

That was when Tom said, 'I think we're being followed.'

If I felt a brief dip of horror in my stomach it was because I thought he was implying he knew everything and was mocking me. But he was serious. I looked back. The cold blowy day had deterred promenaders. There was only one figure in sight, perhaps two hundred yards away or even more.

'That one?'

'He's got a leather coat. I'm sure I saw him when we left the flat.'

So we stopped and waited for this man to catch up with us, but within a minute he was crossing the road and turning up a side street away from the seafront. And at that point we became more concerned about getting to the restaurant before they stopped serving lunch, so we hurried back towards the Lanes and our table, and our 'usual', then Chablis with our grilled skate wings and, finally, a pot of sickly syllabub.

As we were leaving Wheeler's Tom said, 'There he is,' and pointed, but I saw nothing but an empty street corner. He broke away and jogged over to it, and it was clear from the way he stood there with his hands on his hips that he could see no one.

This time our priority, even more urgent, was to get back to the flat and make love. He was more frenetic, or ecstatic, than ever, so much so that I didn't dare tease him about it. I wouldn't have wanted to anyway. I could feel the chill of the coming week. Tomorrow I would take the afternoon train home, wash my hair, prepare my clothes, and on Monday I would have to account for myself at work to my superiors, face the morning newspapers and, sooner or later, face Tom. I didn't know which one of us was doomed, or more doomed, if that made any sense. Which of us would be disgraced? Please let it just be me, not both of us, I thought as I watched Tom leave the bed, pick up his clothes from a chair and go naked across the room to the bathroom. He didn't know what was coming and he deserved none of it. Just bad luck, to have met me. With this thought I fell asleep, as so often before to the sound of his typing. Oblivion seemed the only reasonable option. I slept deeply, without dreams. At some point in the early evening he came back quietly into the bedroom, slipped in beside me and made love to me again. He was amazing.

21

Back at St Augustine's Road on Sunday I had another sleepless night. I was too agitated to read. Through the branches of the chestnut tree and a gap in the curtains, a street lamp threw a crooked stick of light across the ceiling, and I lay on my back, staring at it. For all the mess I was in, I didn't know how I could have done things differently. If I hadn't joined MI5, I wouldn't have met Tom. If I'd told him who I worked for at our very first meeting – and why would I tell a stranger that? – he would've shown me the door. At every point along the way, as I grew fonder of him, then loved him, it became harder, riskier to tell him the truth even as it became more important to do so. I was trapped and I always had been. I fantasised at length of how it might be, to have enough money and single-mindedness to leave suddenly without explaining myself, go somewhere simple and clean, far from here, like the island of Kumlinge in the Baltic. I saw myself in watery sunlight, divested of all obligations and connections, walking without luggage along a narrow road by a sandy bay, with sea thrift and gorse and a solitary pine, a road that rose to a promontory and a plain white country church in whose tiny cemetery was a fresh stone, and a jam jar of harebells left by the housekeeper. I would sit on the grass by the mound of his grave and think about Tony, remember how we were fond lovers one whole summer, and I'd forgive him for betraying his country. It was a passing moment of stupidity, hatched from good intentions and it caused no real harm. I could forgive him because everything could be resolved in Kumlinge, where the air and light were pure. Was my life ever better and simpler than those weekends in a woodsman's cottage near Bury St Edmunds, where an older man adored me, cooked for me, guided me?

Even now, at four thirty, right across the country, bundled newspapers bearing Tom's picture were being hurled from trains and vans onto platforms and pavements. All would carry his Press Association denial. Then he would be at the mercy of Tuesday's press. I turned on the light, put on my dressing gown and sat in my chair. T.H. Haley, lackey of the security state, his integrity blown before he'd even got started, and I was the one, no, it was us, Serena Frome and her employers, who brought him down. Who could trust what a man wrote on Romanian censorship when his words were paid for out of the Secret Vote? Our Sweet Tooth darling spoiled. There were another nine writers, perhaps more important, more useful, and not in the frame. I could hear the fifth floor saying it – *the project will survive*. I thought of what Ian Hamilton would say. My feverish insomnia was making my fantasies active on my retina. I saw in the dark a ghostly smile and shrug as he turned away. *Well, we'll have to find someone else.*

Too bad. The kid was bright. Perhaps I was exaggerating. Spender survived the *Encounter* scandal, and so did *Encounter* itself. But Spender had not been as vulnerable. Tom would be taken for a liar.

I slept for an hour before the alarm rang. I washed and dressed in a fog, too exhausted to think about the day ahead. I could feel it though, a numbing dread. The house was damp as well as cold this time in the morning, but the kitchen was cheerful. Bridget had a big exam at nine, and Tricia and Pauline were sending her off with a fried breakfast. One of the girls passed me a mug of tea and I sat to one side, warming my hands on it, listening to the banter and wishing that I too was about to qualify as a conveyancing solicitor. When Pauline asked me why I looked so glum I answered honestly that I'd had a sleepless night. For that I received a pat on the shoulder and a fried egg and bacon sandwich. Such kindness almost made me tearful. I volunteered to do the washing-up while the others got ready, and it was comforting, the domestic order of hot water, froth and steaming clean wet plates.

I was the last to leave the house. As I approached the front door, I saw among the junk mail scattered across the lino a postcard for me. The picture showed a beach in Antigua and a woman with a basket of flowers balanced on her head. It was from Jeremy Mott.

Hello, Serena. Escaping the long Edinburgh winter. What a joy to get out of my overcoat at last. Nice mystery rendezvous the other week and much talk of you! Come up and see me some time. xxx Jeremy.

Rendezvous? I was in no mood for puzzles. I put the card in my bag and left the house. I was feeling a little better once I was walking quickly towards Camden Tube station. I was trying to be brave and fatalistic. It was a local storm, a funding story, there was nothing I could do anyway. I could lose my lover and my job, but no one was actually going to die.

I'd already decided to look through the press in Camden because I didn't want to be seen with a pile by somebody from work. So I stood in the icy gale that swept through the twin-entrance booking hall, trying to manage the flapping sheets of several newspapers. Tom's story was not on any front page, but it was inside all the broadsheets, the *Daily Mail* and the *Express*, with different photographs. All versions were repetitions of the original piece, with the addition of parts of his Press Association statement. All carried his insistence that he knew no one from MI5. Not good, but it could have been worse. Without fresh information the story might die. So twenty minutes later there was something like a spring in my step as I walked down Curzon Street. Five minutes later, when I reached the office, my pulse hardly varied as I picked up an internal mail envelope from my desk. It was as I'd expected, a summons to a meeting in Tapp's office at 9 a.m. I hung up my coat and took the lift up.

They were waiting for me – Tapp, Nutting, the greyish, shrunken-looking gentleman from the fifth floor and Max. I had the impression I was walking in on a silence. They were drinking coffee, but no one offered to pour me one as Tapp indicated with an open hand the only unoccupied chair. On a low table before us was a pile of press cuttings. By it was a copy of Tom's novel. Tapp picked it up, turned a page and read, 'To Serena'. He tossed the book onto the press cuttings.

'Well then, Miss Frome. Why are we in all the newspapers?'

'It didn't come from me.'

Some soft, incredulous throat-clearing filled a brief pause before Tapp said unemphatically, 'Really.' And then, 'You're . . . seeing this man?'

He made the verb sound obscene. I nodded, and when I looked round I met Max's stare. He was not avoiding me this time and I forced myself to return his look, and only glanced away when Tapp spoke again.

'Since when?'

'October.'

'You see him in London?'

'Mostly Brighton. At weekends. Look, he doesn't know anything. He doesn't suspect me.'

'Really.' It was said in the same flat tone.

'And even if he did, he'd hardly want to tell the press about it.'

They were watching me, waiting for me to say more. I was beginning to feel as stupid as I knew they thought I was.

Tapp said, 'You realise you're in serious trouble?'

It was a proper question. I nodded.

'Tell me why you think you are.'

'Because you think I can't keep my mouth shut.'

Tapp said, 'Shall we say we have reservations about your professionalism.'

Peter Nutting opened a folder on his lap. 'You wrote a report for Max, recommending we take him on.'

'Yes.'

'You were already Haley's lover when you wrote that.'

'Certainly not.'

'But you fancied him.'

'No. That came later.'

Nutting turned his head to show me his profile while he thought of some other way to make me look self-serving. At last he said, 'We took this man into Sweet Tooth on your say-so.'

As I remembered it they presented Haley to me and sent me away with a dossier. I said, 'Before I ever met Haley, Max told me to go down to Brighton to sign him up. I think we were behind schedule.' I could also have said that it was Tapp and Nutting who caused the delay. Then I added after a pause, 'But I certainly would have chosen him if it had been left to me.'

Max stirred. 'It's true in fact. I thought he was good enough on paper and clearly I was wrong. We needed to get a move on with a novelist. But my impression was she had her sights on him from the start.'

It was annoying, the way he spoke about me in the third person. But I'd just done the same to him.

'Not so,' I said. 'I loved his stories and when I met him they made it easier to like the man.'

Nutting said, 'It doesn't sound like there's much disagreement.'

I tried not to sound like I was pleading. 'He's a brilliant writer. I don't see why we can't be proud of backing him. Even in public.'

'Obviously, we're cutting him loose,' Tapp said. 'No choice. The whole list could be in trouble. As for that novel, the Cornish whatever—'

'Utter drivel,' Peter Nutting said, shaking his head in

wonder. 'Civilisation brought down by the internal contra-dictions of capitalism. Bloody marvellous.'

'I have to say I hated it.' Max said this with the eager-ness of the classroom sneak. 'I can't believe it won that prize.'

'He's writing another one,' I said. 'It sounds very promising.'

'No thanks,' Tapp said. 'He's out.'

The shrunken fellow stood suddenly and with a sigh of impatience went towards the door. 'I don't want to see any more newspaper stories. I'm meeting the editor of the *Guardian* this evening. You can take care of the rest. And I want to see a report on my desk by lunchtime.'

As soon as he was gone, Nutting said, 'That means you, Max. Make sure we're copied in. You'd better get started. Harry, we'll divide the editors in the usual way.'

'D notice?'

'Too late and we'll look stupid. Now . . .'

His *now* meant me, but first we waited for Max to leave the room. He made a point of meeting my eye as he turned right round at the last moment to step backwards through the doorway. In his blank expression I read some sort of victory, but I may have been wrong.

We listened to his footsteps recede along the corridor then Nutting said, 'The gossip is, and perhaps you can set the record straight, that you were the cause of his engagement falling apart, and that generally, being a nice-looking girl, you may be rather more trouble than you're worth.'

I could think of nothing to say. Tapp, who had been chain-smoking through the meeting, lit another. He said, 'We yielded to a lot of pressure and fashionable arguments to bring women on. The results are more or less as we predicted.'

By now I was assuming they intended to sack me and that I had nothing to lose. I said, 'Why did you take me on?'

'I keep asking myself that,' Tapp said pleasantly.

'Was it because of Tony Canning?'

'Ah yes. Poor old Tony. We had him in a safe house for a couple of days before he went off to his island. We knew we wouldn't be seeing him again and we wanted to be sure there were no loose ends. Sad business. There was a heatwave. He spent most of the time having nosebleeds. We decided he was harmless.'

Nutting added, 'Just for interest, we pressed him on motivation. He gave us a lot of guff about balance of power, but we already knew from our Buenos Aires source. He was blackmailed. 1950, just three months into his first marriage. Moscow Centre put someone irresistible in his path.'

'He liked them young,' Tapp said. 'Speaking of which, he wanted us to give you this.'

He held up an opened envelope. 'We'd have given it to you months ago but the technical boys in the basement thought there might just be some embedded code.'

I tried to appear impassive as I took the envelope from him and pushed it into my handbag. But I'd seen the handwriting and I was shaking.

Tapp noted this and added, 'Max tells us that you've been worked up about a small piece of paper. That was probably me. I jotted down the name of his island. Tony mentioned that the sea-trout fishing round there is exceptional.'

333

There was a pause while this irrelevant fact dissipated.

Then Nutting resumed. 'But you're right. We took you on just in case we were wrong about him. Kept an eye on you. As it turned out, the danger you posed was of the more banal sort.'

'So you're getting rid of me.'

Nutting looked at Tapp, who passed across his cigarette case. When Nutting was smoking he said, 'No, actually. You're on probation. If you can keep out of trouble, keep us out of trouble, you might just scrape through. You're to go down to Brighton tomorrow and tell Haley he's off the payroll. You'll keep your Foundation cover, of course. How you do it is your own business. For all we care you can tell him the truth about his atrocious novel. And you'll also break off relations with him. Again, do it however you like. You're to disappear into the woodwork as far as he's concerned. If he comes looking for you, you're to turn him away firmly. Tell him you've found someone else. It's over. Is that understood?'

They waited. Again, I had that feeling I sometimes used to have when the Bishop called me into his study for a talk about my teenage progress. The feeling of being naughty and small.

I nodded.

'Let me hear you.'

'I understand what you want me to do.'

'Yes. And?'

'I'll do it.'

'Again. Louder.'

'Yes, I'll do it.'

Nutting remained seated while Tapp stood and with a yellowish hand politely indicated the door.

I walked down one flight of stairs and went along the corridor to a landing where there was a view down Curzon Street. I looked over my shoulder before I took the envelope from my bag. The single sheet of paper was grubby from much handling.

September 28th, 1972

My dear girl,

I learned today that you were accepted last week. Congratulations. I'm thrilled for you. The work will give you much fulfilment and pleasure and I know you'll be good at it.

Nutting has promised to put this note in your hands, but knowing how these things work, I suspect that some time will pass before they do. By then, you will have heard the worst. You'll know why I had to go, why I had to be alone, and why I had to do everything in my power to push you away. I've done nothing so vile in my life as drive off, leaving you in that lay-by. But if I'd told you the truth, I would never have been able to dissuade you from following me to Kumlinge. You're a spirited girl. You wouldn't have taken no for an answer. How I would have hated it, you watching me slide down. You would have been sucked into such a pit of sorrow. This illness is relentless. You're too young for it. I'm not being a noble and selfless martyr. I'm dead certain I can do this better alone.

I'm writing this to you from a house in London where I've been staying for a couple of nights seeing some old friends. It's midnight. Tomorrow I set off. I want to leave you not in sorrow but in gratitude for the joy you brought into my life at a time when I knew there was no way back. It was weak and selfish of me to get involved with you – ruthless even. I hope you'll forgive me. I like to think you found some happiness too, and perhaps even a career. Good luck in all you do in life. Please preserve a little corner in your memories for those summer weeks, those glorious picnics in the woods, when you delivered such kindness and love to a dying man's heart.

Thank you, thank you, my darling.

Tony

I stayed in the corridor pretending to look out of the window, and I cried for a little while. Fortunately, no one came by. I washed my face in the ladies' room, then I went downstairs and tried to lose myself in work. Our part of the Irish section was in a state of muted turmoil. As soon as I came in Chas Mount set me to collating and typing up three overlapping memos he had written that morning. They were to be made into one. The issue was that Helium had gone missing. There was an unconfirmed rumour that he'd been uncovered and shot, but as of late last night we knew this not to be true. A report from one of the officers on the ground in Belfast described Helium coming to an arranged meeting, but staying only for two minutes, long enough to say to his controller that he was getting out, going away, that he was sick of both sides. Before our man could apply pressure or offer enticements, Helium walked out. Chas was certain he knew the reason why. His memos were versions of a strong protest to the fifth floor.

When an undercover agent was considered to be no longer useful, he might find he was brutally abandoned.

Instead of looking after him as promised, fitting him out with a fresh identity and a new location for him and his family and giving him money, it sometimes suited the security services to have the man killed by the enemy. Or at least, to make it look like that. Safer, neater, cheaper and, above all, more secure. At least, this was the rumour going about and matters weren't helped by the case of the undercover man, Kenneth Lennon, who'd made a statement to the National Council for Civil Liberties. He was caught between Special Branch, his employer, and the Provisionals, whom he'd reported back on. He had learned, he said, that Special Branch was finished with him and had tipped off the other side, which was pursuing him in England. If the Provisionals didn't get him, Special Branch would do the job. He told the NCCL he didn't have long to live. Two days later he was found dead in a ditch in Surrey, shot three times in the head.

'It breaks my heart,' Chas said when I handed him the draft to read. 'These chaps risk everything, we cut them loose, word gets round. Then we wonder why we can't sign up anyone else.'

At lunchtime I went out to a phone box on Park Lane and called Tom. I wanted to let him know to expect me the next day. There was no reply, but at the time it didn't bother me much. We'd arranged to speak in the evening at seven to discuss the press stories. I could tell him then. I didn't feel like eating and I didn't want to go back indoors, so I went for a melancholy stroll through Hyde Park. It was March but it still felt wintry, with no sign yet of the daffodils. The bare architecture of the trees looked stark against a white sky. I thought of the times I used to come here with Max and how I'd made him kiss me, right by that tree. Perhaps Nutting was right and I was more trouble than I was worth. I stopped in a doorway, took Tony's letter out and read it once more, tried to think about it but started to cry again. Then I went back to work.

I spent all afternoon on a further draft of Mount's memo. He'd decided over lunch to tone down his attack. He must have known the fifth floor would not be pleased by criticism from below and could be vengeful. The new draft contained phrases like 'from a certain perspective', and 'it could be argued that . . . though granted, the system has served us well'. The final version excluded any reference to Helium – or to any deaths of undercover agents – and simply made the case for treating them well, giving them good aliases when their time was up in order to make it easier to recruit. It wasn't until almost six that I left, taking the rickety lift down, calling goodnight to the taciturn men on the door, who had finally come round to not scowling at me as I passed by their station.

I needed to get hold of Tom, I needed to read Tony's letter again. It was impossible to think, I was in such turmoil. I stepped out of Leconfield House and was about to head off towards Green Park Tube when I saw a figure across the street, standing in the doorway of a nightclub, in turned-up coat collar and broad-brimmed hat. I knew exactly who it was. I waited by the kerb to let the traffic pass, then I called across the road, 'Shirley, are you waiting for me?'

She hurried over. 'I've been here half an hour. What have you been doing in there? No, no, you don't have to tell me.'

She kissed me on each cheek – her new bohemian style. Her hat was in soft brown felt and her overcoat was tightly belted around her freshly narrowed waist. Her face was long, daintily freckled and fine-boned, with delicate hollows beneath her cheekbones. It was such a transformation. Looking at her now reminded me of my bout of jealousy, and though Tom had persuaded me of his innocence, I couldn't help being wary.

She took my arm and steered me along the street. 'At least they're open now. C'mon. I've got so many things to say to you.'

We turned off Curzon Street down an alley where there was a small pub whose intimate interior of velvet and brass she would once have dismissed as 'poncey'.

When we were installed behind our half pints she said, 'First thing is an apology. I couldn't talk to you that time in the Pillars. I had to get out of there. I was no good in groups.'

'I'm so sorry about your dad.'

I saw the tiniest of ripples in her throat as she held down the emotion released by my sympathy.

'It's been terrible for the family. It's really knocked us back.'

'What happened?'

'He stepped out into the road, looked the wrong way for some reason and got hit by a motorbike. Right outside the shop. The only good thing they could tell us was he died straight away, didn't know a thing about it.'

I commiserated, and she talked for a while of how her mother had become catatonic, of how the close family had nearly broken up over funeral arrangements, of the absence of a will and what should happen to the shop. Her footballer brother wanted to sell the business to a mate of his. But now the shop, run by Shirley, was open again, her mother was out of bed and talking. Shirley went to the bar for another round and when she came back her tone was brisk. That subject was closed.

'I saw the stuff about Tom Haley. What a fuck-up. I guessed it had something to do with you.'

I didn't even nod.

'I wish I'd been in on that one. I could've told them what a bad idea it was.'

I shrugged and drank my beer, vaguely hiding behind the glass, I suppose, until I could think of something to say.

'It's all right. I'm not going to probe. I just wanted to say this, put a little idea in your head, and you don't have to answer me now. You'll think I'm running ahead of myself, but the way I read that story this morning, you stand a good chance of being kicked out. If I'm wrong, bloody marvellous. And if I'm right, and you're stuck for something, come and work for me. Or *with* me. Get to know sunny Ilford. We could have fun. I can pay you more than twice what you're getting now. Learn all there is to know about beds. These aren't great times to be in business, but people are always going to need somewhere to kip.'

I put my hand on hers. 'That's very kind, Shirley. If I need it, I'll think about it carefully.'

'It's not charity. If you'd learn how the business works, I could spend more time writing. Listen. My novel was in an auction. They paid a bloody fortune. And now someone's bought the film rights. Julie Christie wants to be in it.'

'Shirley! Congratulations! What's it called?'

'*The Ducking Stool.*'

340

Ah yes. A witch, innocent if she drowned, guilty if she survived, then sentenced to death by burning. A metaphor for some young girl's life. I told her I'd be her ideal reader. We talked about her book, and then her next, an eighteenth-century love affair between an English aristocrat and an actress from the slums who breaks his heart.

Then Shirley said, 'So you're actually seeing Tom. Amazing. Lucky girl! I mean, he's lucky too. I'm just pulp fiction, but he's one of the best. I'm glad he got the Prize, but I'm not sure about that funny little novel, and it's rough what he's going through now. But Serena, I don't think anyone believes he knew where his grant money came from.'

'I'm glad you think that,' I said. I'd been keeping an eye on the clock mounted above the bar, behind Shirley's head. My arrangement with Tom was for seven. I had five minutes to get clear and find a quiet phone box, but I lacked the energy to do it gracefully. Talk of beds had revived my exhaustion.

'I've got to be going,' I muttered into my beer.

'First you've got to hear my theory of how this got into the press.'

I stood and reached for my coat. 'Tell me later.'

'And don't you want to know why they threw me out? I thought you'd be full of questions.' She stood close to me, blocking my way out from behind the table.

'Not now, Shirley. I've got to get to a phone.'

'Perhaps one day you'll tell me why they put the Watchers on you. I wasn't going to start informing on my friend. I was really ashamed of myself for going along with it. But that's not why they sacked me. There's a way they have of letting you know. And don't call me paranoid.

Wrong school, wrong university, wrong accent, wrong attitude. In other words general incompetence.'

She pulled me towards her and embraced me and kissed me on the cheeks again. Then she pushed a business card into my hand.

'I'll keep the beds warm for you. And you think about it. Be the manager, start a chain, build an empire! But off you go, darling. Turn left out of here and there's a phone box at the end. Give him my best.'

I was five minutes late getting to the phone. There was no reply. I replaced the receiver, counted to thirty and tried again. I phoned him from Green Park Tube station and again from Camden. At home I sat on my bed, still in my coat, and read Tony's letter again. If I hadn't been worrying about Tom, I might have seen the beginnings of some relief there. The slight easing of an old sorrow. I waited for the minutes to pass until it seemed right to go out to the box on the Camden Road. I made the journey four times that evening. The last was at eleven forty-five, when I asked the operator to check if there was a fault on the line. When I was back at St Augustine's Road and ready for bed, I came close to getting dressed and going out one last time. Instead, I lay in the dark and summoned all the harmless explanations I could think of in the hope of distracting myself from the ones I didn't dare frame. I considered going to Brighton right away. Wasn't there such a thing as a milk train? Did they really exist and didn't they come into London in the early hours rather than out of it? Then I kept my thoughts off the worst possibilities by dreaming up a Poisson distribution. The more often he didn't answer the phone, the less likely it was he would answer the next time. But surely the human factor made a nonsense of that, for he was bound to come home at some point – which was when my weariness from the night before overcame me and I knew nothing until my alarm rang at six forty-five.

I got all the way to Camden Tube the next morning before I realised that I'd left home without my key to Tom's flat. So I tried him again from the station, letting the phone ring for over a minute in case he was asleep, then gloomily walked back to St Augustine's Road. At least I wasn't carrying luggage. But what was the point of my mission to Brighton if he wasn't there? I knew I had no choice. I had to see for myself. If he wasn't there, the search for him would begin in his flat. I found the key in a handbag and set out again.

Half an hour later I was crossing the concourse of Victoria station against the flow of commuters pouring off the suburban trains from the south. I happened to glance to my right, just as the crowd parted, and I saw something quite absurd. I had a momentary glimpse of my own face, then the gap closed and the vision was gone. I swung to my right, pushed through the crush, got clear and ran the last few yards into the open shop front of Smith's newsagents. There I was, on the rack. It was the *Daily Express*. I was arm in arm with Tom, our heads lovingly inclined, walking towards the camera, with Wheeler's restaurant out of focus behind us. Above the photograph, the ugly block capitals shouted out, HALEY'S SEXY SPY. I grabbed a copy, folded it double and queued to buy it. I didn't want to be seen next to a picture of myself, so I took the newspaper to a public lavatory, locked myself in a cubicle and sat there long enough to miss my train. On the inside pages were two more photographs. One showed Tom and me coming out of his house, our 'love nest', and another was of us kissing on the seafront.

Despite the breathless tone of excitement and outrage, there was hardly a word of the article that didn't have an element of truth. I was described as an 'undercover agent', working for MI5, Cambridge educated, a 'specialist' in mathematics, based in London, given the task of liaising with Tom Haley to facilitate a generous stipend. The money trail was vaguely but properly described, with references to the Freedom International Foundation as well as Word Unpenned. Tom's statement that he had never had any connection with a member of the intelligence services was highlighted in bold. A spokesman for the Home Secretary, Roy Jenkins, told the newspaper that the matter was of 'grave concern' and that the relevant officials had been called to a meeting later today. Speaking for the Opposition, Edward Heath himself said that, if true, the story showed that the government had 'already lost its way'. But most significant of all, Tom had told a reporter that he had 'nothing to say on the matter'.

That would have been yesterday. Then he must have gone into hiding. How else to explain his silence? I came out of the cubicle, binned the paper and just made the next train. All my journeys to Brighton lately had been on Friday evenings, in the dark. Not since that first time, when I travelled to the university in my best outfit to interview Tom, had I crossed the Sussex Weald in full daylight. Staring at it now, at the charm of its hedgerows and bare trees just thickening in early spring, I experienced again the vague longing and frustration that came with the idea that I was living the wrong sort of life. I hadn't chosen it for myself. It was all down to chance. If I hadn't met Jeremy, and therefore Tony, I wouldn't be in this mess, travelling at speed towards some kind of disaster I didn't dare contemplate. My single consolation was Tony's farewell. For all its sorrow, the affair was put to rest and I had at last my token. Those summer weeks were not my private fantasy, they were shared. It had meant as much to him as to me. More, in his dying days. I had evidence of what had passed between us, I had given some comfort.

It had never been my intention to obey Nutting and Tapp's order to break off with Tom. The privilege of ending the affair belonged to Tom. Today's headlines meant my time with the Service was over. I didn't even need to be disobedient. The headlines also meant that Tom had no choice but to be shot of me. I almost hoped that I wouldn't find him in the flat, that I'd be spared the final confrontation. But then I'd be in agony, it would be intolerable. And so I went round my problem and my scrap of consolation and I was in a daze until the train stopped with a jolt in the lattice steel cavern of the Brighton terminus.

As I climbed the hill behind the station I thought the cawing and keening of the herring gulls had an emphatic falling note, a far stronger terminal cadence than usual, like the predictable final notes of a hymn. The air, with its taste of salt and traffic fumes and fried food, made me feel nostalgic for the carefree weekends. It was unlikely that I would ever come back. I slowed as I turned into Clifton Street, expecting to see journalists outside the building where Tom lived. But the pavements were empty. I let myself in and began to climb the stairs to the attic flat. I passed the sound of pop music and the smell of cooked breakfast on the second floor. I hesitated on his landing, gave the door a hearty innocent knock to scatter the demons, waited, then I fumbled with the key, turned it first the wrong way, cursed in a whisper, and shoved the door wide open.

The first thing I saw were his shoes, his scuffed brown brogues, toes pointing slightly inwards, a leaf stuck to the side of a heel, laces trailing. They were under the kitchen table. Otherwise, the room was unusually neat. All the pans and crockery had been put away, the books were in tidy piles. I went towards the bathroom, heard the familiar creak of the boards, like an old song from another time. My small inventory of cinema suicide scenes included a corpse collapsed considerately over the bath with a bloodied towel around its neck. Fortunately, the door was open and I didn't have to go in to see that he wasn't there. That left the bedroom.

The door was shut. Again, stupidly, I knocked and waited because I thought I heard the sound of a voice. Then I heard it again. It was from the street below, or from a radio in one of the flats downstairs. I also heard the thud of my own pulse. I turned the handle and pushed the door open, but remained where I was, too frightened to go in. I could see the bed, all of it, and it was made, and the Indian print bedspread was smoothly in place. It was usually in a tangle on the floor. The room was too small for there to be anywhere else to hide.

Feeling sick and thirsty, I turned back into the kitchen for a glass of water. It was only as I came away from the sink that I saw what was on the kitchen table. The shoes must have distracted me. There was a parcel done up with brown paper and string, and, lying on top of it, a white envelope with my name on it in his writing. I drank the water first, then I sat down at the table, opened the envelope and began to read my second letter in as many days.

22

Dear Serena,

You may be reading this on the train back to London, but my guess is that you're sitting at the kitchen table. If so, my apologies for the state of the place. When I started clearing out the junk and scrubbing the floors I convinced myself I was doing it for you – as of last week your name is on the rent book and the flat may be of use. But now that I've finished, I look around and wonder if you'll find it sterile, or at least unfamiliar, stripped clean of our life here together, all the good times wiped away. Won't you miss the cardboard boxes filled with the Chablis empties and those piles of newspapers we read in bed together? I suppose I was cleaning up for myself. I'm bringing this episode to an end, and there's always a degree of oblivion in tidiness. Consider it a form of insulation. Also, I had to clear the decks before I could write this letter, and perhaps (do I dare say this to you?) with all this scrubbing I was erasing you, you as you were.

I apologise too for not answering the phone. I've been

avoiding journalists, and I've been avoiding you because it didn't seem the right time for us to be talking. I think by now I know you well enough and I'm confident that you'll be here tomorrow. Your clothes are all in one place, at the bottom of the wardrobe. I won't tell you my state of mind as I folded your things away, but I did linger over the job, as one might over an old photo album. I remembered you in so many guises. I found at the bottom of the wardrobe, screwed up in a ball, the black suede jacket you wore in Wheeler's the night you tried to explain the Monty Hall problem to me. Before I folded it, I did up all the buttons with a sense of locking something down, or locking it away. I still don't understand probability. Similarly, under the bed, the short pleated orange skirt you wore to our rendezvous at the National Portrait Gallery, the skirt that helped kick the whole thing off, as far as I was concerned. I've never folded a skirt before. This one wasn't easy.

Typing 'folded' reminds me that at any point before I've finished you could put this letter back into its envelope, in sorrow or anger or guilt. Please don't. This is not an extended accusation, and I promise you it will end well, at least in certain respects. Stay with me. I've left the heating on in order to tempt you to remain here. If you become weary, the bed is yours, the sheets are clean, all traces of our former selves lost to the launderette opposite the station. It was a service wash, and the kind lady there agreed for an extra pound to do the ironing. Ironed sheets, the uncelebrated privilege of childhood. But they remind me too of the blank page. The blank page writ large and sensual. And that page was certainly large in my thoughts before Christmas, when I was convinced that I would never write fiction again. I told you about my writing block after we went to deliver *The Levels* to Tom Maschler. You were sweetly (and ineffectually) encouraging, though I know now that you had good professional reasons. I spent most of December staring at that blank page. I thought I was falling in love, but I couldn't summon a useful thought. And then something extraordinary happened. Someone came to see me.

It happened after Christmas, when I'd taken my sister back to her hostel in Bristol. I was feeling emptied out after all the emotional scenes with Laura and I wasn't looking forward to the dull drive back to Sevenoaks. I suppose I was a little more passive than I am usually. When a stranger approached me as I was getting into the car, my defences were down. I didn't automatically assume he was a beggar or a con artist. He knew my name and he told me he had something important to tell me about you. Since he seemed harmless and I was curious, I let him buy me a coffee. You'll have guessed by now that this was Max Greatorex. He must have tailed me all the way from Kent, and perhaps before that, from Brighton. I never asked. I own up to lying to you about my movements. I didn't stay down in Bristol to spend time with Laura. I listened to your colleague for a couple of hours that afternoon, and I stayed in a hotel for two nights.

So we sat in this dim evil-smelling relic of the fifties, tiled like a public lavatory, drinking the worst coffee I've ever tasted. I'm sure Greatorex told me only a fraction of the story. First, he told me who you and he worked for. When I asked for proof he produced various internal documents, some of which referred to you, others were notes in your handwriting on headed paper, and two included

photographs of you. He said he'd taken these papers from
his office at great risk to himself. Then he laid out the
Sweet Tooth operation for me, though he didn't tell me
the names of other writers. Having a novelist in the scheme
was, he said, a whimsical afterthought. He told me he was
passionate about literature, knew and liked my stories and
articles and that his own principled opposition to the
project hardened when he heard that I was on the list. He
said he was concerned that if it ever came out that I was
funded by an intelligence agency, I would never outlive
the disgrace. I couldn't know it at the time, but he was
being less than honest about his motives.

Then he talked about you. Because you were beautiful
as well as clever – actually, the word was cunning – you
were considered ideal for the job of getting down to
Brighton and signing me up. It wasn't his style to use a
vulgar locution like honeytrap but that was what I was
hearing. I got angry and had a shoot-the-messenger
moment and almost popped him one on the nose. But I
have to hand it to him – he took care not to appear to
relish what he was telling me. His tone was sorrowful. He
gently let me know that he would far rather be enjoying
his short holiday break than discussing my squalid affairs.
He was risking his prospects, his job, even his freedom
in this breach of security. But he cared for openness and
literature and decency. So he said.

He described your cover, the Foundation, the precise
sums and all the rest – in part, I suppose, as corroboration
for his story. And by this time I had no doubts. I was so
worked up, so hot and agitated that I had to go outside.
I walked up and down the street for a few minutes. I was
beyond anger. This was a new dark place of hatred – for

351

you, for myself, for Greatorex, for the Bristol Blitz and the grisly cheap horrors the post-war developers had heaped upon the bomb sites. I wondered if there was a single day when you hadn't told me an outright or implicit lie. That was when I leaned into a doorway of a boarded-up shop and tried and failed to throw up. To get the taste of you out of my gut. Then I went back inside Kwik-Snax for more.

I felt calmer when I sat down and was able to take in my informant. Even though he was the same age as me, he had an assured, patrician manner, the touch of the smooth civil servant about him. He may have been talking down to me. I didn't care. He had an extra-terrestrial look, the way his ears were mounted on mounds of flesh or bone. Since he's a scrawny fellow, with a thin neck and a shirt collar a size too big for him, I was surprised to learn that you were once in love with him, to the point of obsession, to the point at which his fiancée walked out on him. I wouldn't have thought he was your type at all. I asked him if bitterness was his motive for talking to me. He denied it. The marriage would have been a disaster, and in a way he was grateful to you.

We went over the Sweet Tooth stuff again. He told me that it wasn't at all unusual for intelligence agencies to promote culture and cultivate the right kind of intellectuals. The Russians did it, so why wouldn't we? This was the soft Cold War. I said to him what I said to you on Saturday. Why not give the money openly, through some other government department? Why use a secret operation? Greatorex sighed and looked at me, shaking his head in pity. He said I had to understand, any institution, any organisation eventually becomes a dominion, self-contained, competitive, driven by its own logic and bent on survival and on extending its territory. It was as inexorable and blind as a chemical process. MI6 had gained control over a secret section of the Foreign Office and MI5 wanted its own project. Both wanted to impress the Americans, the CIA – which over the years had paid for more culture in Europe than anyone would ever realise.

He walked with me back to the car and by this time it was raining hard. We didn't waste much time in parting. Before he shook my hand he gave me his home phone number. He said he was sorry to be the bearer of such news. Betrayal was an ugly matter and no one should have to deal with it. He hoped I would find a way through. When he was gone I sat in the car with the ignition key drooping from my hand. The rain was coming down like it was the end of the world. After what I'd heard I couldn't face the drive or my parents or coming back to Clifton Street. I wasn't going to see the New Year in with you. I couldn't imagine doing anything but watch the rain clean the filthy street. After an hour I drove to a post office and sent you a telegram, then I found a hotel, a decent one. I thought I might as well use up the last of my suspect money on luxury. In a mood of self-pity, I ordered up to my room a bottle of Scotch. An inch of that with an equal amount of water was enough to persuade me that I didn't want to get drunk, not at five in the afternoon. I didn't want to be sober either. I didn't want anything, even oblivion.

But beyond existence and oblivion there's no third place to be. So I lay on this silky bed and thought about you, and replayed the scenes that would make me feel worse. Our earnest and inept first fuck, our brilliant second, all the poetry, fish, ice buckets, stories, politics, the Friday-evening reunions, playfulness, shared baths, shared sleep, all the kissing and stroking and touching tongues – how accomplished you were at appearing to be no more than you seemed to be, no more than yourself. Bitterly, sardonically, I wished meteoric promotion on you. Then I wished for more. I should tell you that in that hour, if your lovely pale throat had appeared upturned on my lap and a knife had been pushed into my hand, I would have done the job without thinking. It is the cause, it is the cause, my soul. Unlike me, Othello didn't want to shed blood. He was a softie.

Don't walk away now, Serena. Keep reading. This moment doesn't last. I hated you all right, and loathed myself for being the dupe, the conceited dupe who easily convinced himself that a cash fountain was his due, as was the beautiful woman on his arm as we promenaded on the Brighton seafront. As was the Austen Prize, which I took without much surprise as my rightful possession.

Yes, I sprawled on my four-poster king-sized bed, on a silk counterpane with medieval hunting motifs, and I pursued all the pain and insult that memory could flush from the thickets. Those long dinners in Wheeler's, the raised glasses chinked, literature, childhood, probability – all of it congealed into a single fleshy carcass, turning over slowly like a good spit-roast. I was thinking back before Christmas. Weren't we permitting into our conversation the first hints of a future together? But what future could we have had when you hadn't told me who you were? Where did you think it would end up? Surely you didn't intend to keep this secret from me for the rest of your life. The Scotch I drank at eight that night tasted better than the Scotch at five. I had a third without water, and phoned down for a bottle of Bordeaux and a ham sandwich. In the forty minutes that it took for room service to arrive, I continued with the Scotch. But I didn't get roaring drunk, didn't trash the room or make animal noises or raise curses against you. Instead, I wrote you a savage letter on hotel stationery, found a stamp, addressed the envelope and put it in my coat pocket. I drank one glass of wine, ordered up a second sandwich, had no more coherent thoughts and was meekly asleep by ten.

I woke some hours later into total darkness – the curtains in that room were thick – and entered one of those moments of untroubled but total amnesia. I could feel a comfortable bed around me, but who and where I was lay beyond my grasp. It lasted only a few seconds, this episode of pure existence, the mental equivalent of the blank page. Inevitably, the narrative seeped back, with the near details arriving first – the room, the hotel, the city, Greatorex, you; next, the larger facts of my life – my name, my general circumstances. It was then, as I sat up and groped for the bedside light switch, that I saw the whole Sweet Tooth affair in utterly different terms. This brief, cleansing amnesia had delivered me into common sense. This wasn't, or wasn't only, a calamitous betrayal and personal disaster. I'd been too busy being insulted by it to see it for what it was – an opportunity, a gift. I was a novelist without a novel, and now luck had tossed my way a tasty bone, the bare outline of a useful story. There was a spy in my bed, her head was on my pillow, her lips were pressed to my ear. She concealed her real purpose, and crucially, she didn't know that I knew. And I wouldn't tell her. So I wouldn't confront you, there'd be no accusations or terminal row and parting of ways, not yet. Instead, silence, discretion, patient watching, and writing. Events would decide the plot. The characters were ready-made. I would invent nothing, only record. I'd watch you at work. I too could be a spy.

I was sitting upright in bed, mouth open, staring across the room, like a man watching his father's ghost step through the wall. I'd seen the novel I was going to write. I had also seen the dangers. I would go on receiving the money in the full knowledge of its source. Greatorex knew that I knew. That made me vulnerable, and gave him power over me. Was this novel conceived in the spirit of revenge? Well, no, but you did set me free. You didn't ask me if I wanted to be part of Sweet Tooth, I wouldn't ask you if you wanted to be in my story. Ian Hamilton once told me of a writer friend who'd put intimate details of his marriage into a novel. His wife was outraged to read their sex lives and pillow talk minutely reproduced. She divorced him and he regretted it forever, not least because she was very rich. No such problem here. I could do as I pleased. But I couldn't sit here for long with my mouth agape. I dressed hurriedly, found my notebook and filled it in two hours. I merely had to tell the story as I saw it, from the moment you came to my office at the university, to my rendezvous with Greatorex – and beyond.

The next morning, buzzing with purpose, I went out before breakfast and bought three exercise books from a friendly newsagent. Bristol, I decided, was a decent place after all. Back in my room I ordered coffee and set to work, making notes, setting out the sequences, trying out a paragraph or two for taste. I wrote almost half of an opening chapter. By mid-afternoon I was feeling uneasy. Two hours later, after a read-through, I threw down my pen with a shout and stood up suddenly, knocking over the chair behind me. Fuck! It was dull, it was dead. I'd covered forty pages, as easily as counting. No resistance or difficulty or spring, no surprises, nothing rich or strange. No hum, no torque. Instead, everything I saw and heard and said and did was lined up like beans in a row. It wasn't mere clumsy surface ineptitude. Buried deep in the concept was a flaw, and even that word sounded too good for what it was trying to name. It simply wasn't interesting.

I was spoiling a precious gift and I was disgusted. I took a walk through the city in the early evening darkness, and wondered whether I should post that letter to you after all. The problem, I decided, was me. Without thinking, I was presenting myself in the guise of the typical hero of an English comic novel – inept and almost clever, passive, earnest, over-explained, urgently unfunny. *There I was, minding my own business, thinking about sixteenth-century poetry, when, would you believe it, this beautiful girl walks into my office and offers me a pension.* What was I protecting with this veneer of farce? All the heartache, I supposed, that I hadn't yet touched on.

I walked to the Clifton Suspension Bridge, where, it was said, you could sometimes spot a prospective suicide casing the joint, calculating the fall. I crossed and stopped halfway to stare down into the blackness of the gorge. I was thinking again about the second time we ever made love. In your room, the morning after the White Tower. Remember? I lay back on the pillows – what luxury – and you swayed above me. A dance of bliss. As I read it then, your face as you looked down showed nothing but pleasure and the beginnings of real affection. Now I knew

357

what you knew, what you had to conceal, I tried to imagine being you, being in two places at once, loving and . . . *reporting back*. How could I get in there and report back too? And that was it. I saw it. So simple. This story wasn't for me to tell. It was for you. Your job was to report back to me. I had to get out of my skin and into yours. I needed to be translated, to be a transvestite, to shoehorn myself into your skirts and high heels, into your knickers, and carry your white glossy handbag on its shoulder strap. On my shoulder. Then start talking, as you. Did I know you well enough? Clearly not. Was I a good enough ventriloquist? Only one way to find out. I had to begin. I took from a pocket my letter to you and tore it up, and let the bits drift down into the darkness of the Avon Gorge. Then I hurried back across the bridge, eventually waved down a taxi and spent that New Year's Eve and part of the next day in my hotel room filling another exercise book, trying your voice. Then I checked out late and drove the car home to my anxious parents.

Do you remember our first meeting after Christmas? It must have been January 3rd or 4th, another of our Friday evenings. You must have noticed how I made a point of coming to meet your train. Perhaps it crossed your mind that it was unusual. I'm a hopeless actor and I was worried that it would be impossible to behave naturally in your company, that you'd see through me. You'd know that I knew. Easier to greet you on a crowded platform than in the silence of the flat. But when your train came in and I saw the carriage containing you slide by, with you reaching so prettily above your seat for your bag, and seconds later, when we went into that powerful embrace, I felt such desire for you that I didn't need to fake a thing. We kissed and I knew it was going to be easy. I could want you and watch you. The two weren't mutually exclusive. In fact, they fed each other. When we made love an hour later, you were so sweetly and inventively possessive, even as you carried on with your usual pretence – I put this at its simplest: it thrilled me. I almost passed out. So it began, what you kindly termed my 'pig-in-a-trough mode'. And it multiplied my pleasures, to know that I could retreat to the typewriter to describe the moment, from your point of view. Your duplicitous point of view, which would have to include your understanding, your version, of me, lover and Sweet Tooth item. My task was to reconstruct myself through the prism of your consciousness. If I gave myself a good press, it was because of those nice things you said about me. With this recursive refinement, my mission was even more interesting than yours. Your masters did not require you to investigate how you yourself appeared through my eyes. I was learning to do what you do, then better it with one extra fold in the fabric of deception. And how well I took to it.

Then, a few hours later, Brighton beach – strictly, Hove, which doesn't chime romantically, despite the half-rhyme with love. For only the second time in our affair I was on my back, now with damp shingle cooling my coccyx. A passing policeman on the promenade would have done us for public indecency. How could we have explained to him those parallel worlds that we spun around us? In one orbit, our mutual deceit, a novelty in my case, habitual in yours, possibly addictive, probably fatal. In the other, our affection bursting through ecstasy to love. We reached the glorious summit at last and traded our 'I love you's even as we each reserved our secrets. I saw how we could do it, live with these sealed compartments side by side, never letting the dank stench of one invade the sweetness of the other. If I mention again how exquisite our lovemaking became after my rendezvous with Greatorex, I know you'll be thinking of 'Pawnography'. (How I regret now that punning title.) The foolish husband lusting after the wife who stole his stuff, his pleasure sharpened by his secret knowledge of her deceit. All right, she was a rehearsal for you before I knew of your existence. And I don't deny the common root is me. But I have in mind my other story, the one about the vicar's brother who ends up loving the woman who'll destroy him. You always liked that one. Or how about the writer driven to her second novel by the spectre of her apish lover? Or the fool who believes his lover is real when in fact he's dreamed her up and she's only a counterfeit, a copy, a fake?

But don't leave the kitchen. Stay with me. Let me exorcise this bitterness. And let's talk about research. By the time you came to Brighton that Friday, I'd had a second meeting with Max Greatorex, at his place in Egham, Surrey. Even at the time, I was surprised how open he was, filling me in on the Sweet Tooth meetings, your various encounters in the park and in his office, his late-night visit to St Augustine's Road and, generally, the workplace. As I learned more, I wondered if he was longing, in a self-destructive way, to become the Fourth Man, or if he was in sexual competition with your Tony Canning. Max assured me that Sweet Tooth was so low level that it hardly mattered. I also got the impression that he'd already decided to leave the Security Service and go into something else. Now I know from Shirley Shilling that his purpose in meeting me in Bristol was to break up our affair. He was indiscreet because all he cared about was destroying you. When I asked to see him again, he thought I was driven by angry obsession, which he was happy to feed. Later, he was surprised to discover that I was still seeing you. He was furious when he heard you intended to come to the Austen event at the Dorchester. So he called his press contacts and threw us to the dogs. In all, I've met him three times this year. He gave me so much, he was so helpful. It's a pity I detest him. He told me Canning's story, how he was interviewed one last time in a safe house before he went off to the Baltic to die, how he had a nosebleed, which ruined a mattress and nourished some lurid fantasies of yours. Greatorex was much entertained by all that.

At our last meeting he gave me an address for your old friend Shirley Shilling. I'd read about her in the papers, how a clever agent had lined up five publishers to bid for her first novel, how they were queuing up for the movie rights in LA. She was on Martin Amis's arm when we were reading together in Cambridge. I liked her, and she adores you. She told me about your pub-rock crawls around London. After I said I knew about your work she told me about your time together as cleaning ladies, and how she was asked to snoop on you. She also mentioned your old friend Jeremy, so while I was in Cambridge I went to his college and got a forwarding address for him in Edinburgh. I also visited Mrs Canning. I told her that I'd been a student of her husband. She was polite enough, but I didn't learn much. You'll be pleased to hear that she knows nothing about you. Shirley had offered to drive me to the Canning cottage in Suffolk. (She drives like a maniac.) We peered into the garden and went for a stroll in the woods. By the time we left I felt I had enough to reconstruct the scene of your secret affair, your apprenticeship in secrecy.

From Cambridge, remember, I went on to see your sister and her boyfriend Luke. As you know, I dislike getting stoned. It's such a mental constriction. That prickly, electric self-consciousness just doesn't suit me and nor does a joyless chemical appetite for sweet things. But it was the only way Lucy and I could really get along and talk. The three of us sat in low light on cushions on the floor of their flat, incense smouldering from homemade clay pots, a sitar raga leaking onto our heads from unseen speakers. We drank purifying tea. She's in awe of you, poor girl, desperate for her big sister's good opinion, which I think she rarely gets. At one point she said forlornly that it wasn't fair that you were cleverer *and* prettier. I got what I had come for – your childhood and teenage years, though I might have forgotten most of it in a haze of hash. I do remember that we ate cauliflower cheese and brown rice for supper.

I stayed the night in order to go on Sunday to the cathedral to hear your father. I was curious, because you'd described to me in a letter how you collapsed into his arms on your front doorstep. And there he was, in distant splendour, saying nothing at all on that particular day. Underlings, grand enough in their own right, undeterred by the feeble turn-out, conducted the service with all the brio of unshaken faith. One fellow with a nasal voice preached the sermon, a sure-footed exegesis of the Good Samaritan parable. I shook your father's hand on my way out. He looked at me with interest and asked in a friendly way if I'd be coming back. How could I tell him the truth?

362

I wrote to Jeremy to present myself as your good friend who was passing through Edinburgh. I told him that you'd suggested I get in touch. I knew you wouldn't mind a lie, and I also knew I was taking a chance. If he mentioned me to you my cover would be blown. This time, I had to get drunk to make real progress. How else would I have got the story of how you came to write for *?Quis??* It was you who told me about his elusive orgasm, his peculiar pubic bone and the folded towel. Jeremy and I had the sixteenth century, its history and literature, in common too, and I was able to bring him up to date on Tony Canning as traitor, and then your affair, which shocked him. And so our evening sped along beautifully and I thought it was money well spent when I picked up the bill at the Old Waverley Hotel.

But why trouble you with details of my research? First, to let you know I took this matter seriously. Second, to be clear, that above all it was you who were my principal source. There was, of course, everything that I saw for myself. And then the small cast among whom I wandered in January. That leaves an island of experience, an important fraction of the whole, that was you alone, you with your thoughts, and sometimes you invisible to yourself. On this terrain, I've been obliged to extrapolate or invent.

Here's an example. Neither of us will forget our first meeting in my office. From where I sat, when you stepped through the door and I took in your old-fashioned peaches-and-cream look, and your summer-blue eyes, I thought it was just possible that my life was about to change. I've imagined you minutes before that moment, making your way from Falmer station, approaching the Sussex campus filled with the snobbish distaste you've expressed to me since for the idea of a new university. Sleek and fair, you strode through the crowds of long-haired bare-foot kids. Your scorn was barely fading from your face by the time you introduced yourself and started telling me your untruths. You've complained to me about your time at Cambridge, you've told me it was intellectually stultifying, but you defend your place to the hilt and look down on mine. Well, for what it's worth, think again. Don't be fooled by loud music. I reckon my place was more ambitious, more serious, more enjoyable than yours. I speak as a product, an explorer, of Asa Briggs's new map of learning. The tutorials were demanding. Two essays a week for three years, no let-up. All the usual literary studies, but on top compulsory historiography for all newcomers, and then for me, by choice, cosmology, fine art, international relations, Virgil, Dante, Darwin, Ortega y Gasset . . . Sussex would never have allowed you to stagnate the way you did, would never have permitted you to do nothing else but mathematics. Why am I bothering you with this? I can hear you say to yourself, He's jealous, he's chippy about his plate-glass learning emporium, about not having been at my place with the snooker-table lawns and honey limestone. But you're wrong. I only wanted to remind you why I painted a curl on your lips as you passed under the sound of Jethro Tull, a sneer I wasn't there to see. It was an informed guess, an extrapolation.

So much for research. I had my material, the wafer of gold, and the motivation to hammer it out. I went at it in a frenzy, more than a hundred thousand words in just over three months. The Austen Prize, for all the excitement and recognition, seemed like a monstrous distraction. I set myself a target of fifteen hundred words a day, seven days

364

a week. Sometimes, when my invention ran out, it was near impossible, and at others it was a breeze because I was able to transcribe our conversation minutes after we'd had it. Sometimes events wrote whole sections for me.

A recent example was last Saturday, when you came back to the flat from shopping to show me the *Guardian* story. I knew then that Greatorex had upped his game and things were going to move fast. I had a ringside seat for the deception, yours and mine. I could see you thought you were about to be exposed and accused. I pretended to love you too much to suspect you – it was easy to do that. When you suggested making a statement to the Press Association, I knew it was pointless, but why not? The story was writing itself. Besides, it was time to renounce the Foundation's money. It touched me when you tried to dissuade me from claiming to know no one from the intelligence service. You knew how vulnerable I was, how vulnerable you'd rendered me, and you were in agonies as you tried to protect me. So why did I make the claim anyway? More story! I couldn't resist it. And I wanted to seem like an innocent in your hearing. I knew I was about to do myself a lot of harm. But I didn't care, I was reckless and obsessed, I wanted to see what happened. I thought, correctly as it turned out, that this was the endgame. When you went to lie on the bed to brood on your dilemma, I set about describing you reading the newspapers in your cafe near the market, and then, while it was still fresh, our entire exchange. After our Wheeler's lunch we made love. You fell asleep and I worked on, typing and revising the recent hours. When I came into the bedroom in the early evening to wake you and make love to you again, you whispered as you took my cock in your hand and brought me into you, 'You're amazing.' I hope you won't mind. I've included that.

Face it, Serena, the sun is setting on this decaying affair, and the moon and stars are too. This afternoon – your yesterday, I expect – the doorbell rang. I went down to find standing on the pavement a woman from the *Daily Express*. She was pleasant and frank as she told me what was going to be in the next day's paper, how I would be presented as a mendacious, greedy fraud. She even read me passages she'd written. She also described the photographs and asked politely if I'd care to give her a quote. I had nothing to say. As soon as she'd gone I took notes. I won't be in a position to buy a copy of the *Express* tomorrow but it won't matter because this afternoon I'll incorporate what she told me, and have you read the story on the train. Yes, it's over. The reporter told me her paper already had quotes from Edward Heath and Roy Jenkins. I'm headed for public ignominy. We all are. I'll be accused, and rightly, of lying in my statement to the Press Association, of taking money from an inappropriate source, of selling my independence of thought. Your employers foolishly meddled where they don't belong and they've embarrassed their political masters. It can't be long before the list of other Sweet Tooth beneficiaries comes out. There'll be derision and blushes and a sacking or two. As for you, you have no chance of surviving tomorrow's press. You appear stunning in the photographs, I was told. But you'll be looking for a job.

Soon I'm going to ask you to make an important decision, but before I do, let me tell you my favourite spy story. MI5 had a hand in it, as well as Six. 1943. The struggle was starker and more consequential than it is now. In April that year the decomposing body of an officer of the Royal Marines washed up on the coast of Andalucia. Attached to the dead man's wrist by a chain was a brief-case containing documents referring to plans for the invasion of southern Europe through Greece and Sardinia. The local authorities contacted the British attaché, who at first seemed to take little interest in the corpse or its luggage. Then he appeared to change his mind and worked frantically to get both returned. Too late. The Spanish were neutral in the war, but generally more favourable to the Nazi cause. The German intelligence community was on to the matter, the documents in the briefcase found their way to Berlin. German High Command studied the contents of the briefcase, learned of the Allies' intentions and altered their defences accordingly. But as you probably know from *The Man Who Never Was*, the body and the plans were fake, a plant devised by British intelligence. The officer was actually a Welsh tramp, retrieved from a morgue and, with thorough attention to detail, dressed up in a fictional identity, complete with love letters and tickets to a London show. The Allied invasion of southern Europe came through the more obvious route, Sicily, which was poorly defended. At least some of Hitler's divisions were guarding the wrong portals.

Operation Mincemeat was one of scores of wartime deception exercises, but my theory is that what produced its particular brilliance and success was the manner of its inception. The original idea came from a novel published in 1937 called *The Milliner's Hat Mystery*. The young naval commander who spotted the episode would one day be a famous novelist himself. He was Ian Fleming, and he included the idea along with other ruses in a memo which appeared before a secret committee chaired by an Oxford don who wrote detective novels. Providing an identity, a background and a plausible life to a cadaver was done with novelistic flair. The naval attaché who orchestrated the reception of the drowned officer in Spain was also a novelist. Who says that poetry makes nothing happen? Mincemeat succeeded because invention, the imagination, drove the intelligence. By miserable comparison, Sweet Tooth, that precursor of decay, reversed the process and failed because intelligence tried to interfere with invention. Our moment was thirty years ago. In our decline we live in the shadow of giants. You and your colleagues must have known the project was rotten, and doomed from the start, but your motives were bureaucratic, you kept going because the order came down from on high. Your Peter Nutting should have listened to the chairman of the Arts Council, Angus Wilson, another novelist with connections to wartime intelligence.

I told you that it wasn't anger that set me writing the pages in the parcel in front of you. But there was always an element of tit for tat. We both reported back. You lied to me, I spied on you. It was delicious, and I thought you had it coming. I really believed that I could wrap the matter up between the covers of a book and write you out of my system and say goodbye. But I reckoned without the logic of the process. I had to go to Cambridge to get your terrible degree, make love in a Suffolk cottage to a kind old toad, live in your Camden bedsit, suffer a bereavement, wash your hair and iron your skirts for work and suffer the morning Tube journey, experience your urge for independence as well as the bonds that held you to your parents and made you cry against your father's chest. I had to taste your loneliness, inhabit your insecurity, your longing for praise from superiors, your unsisterliness, your minor impulses of snobbery, ignorance and vanity, your minimal social conscience, moments of self-pity, and orthodoxy in most matters. And do all this without ignoring your cleverness, beauty and tenderness, your love of sex and fun, your wry humour and sweet protective instincts. Living inside you, I saw myself clearly: my material greed and status hunger, my single-mindedness bordering on autism. Then my ludicrous vanity, sexual, sartorial, above all aesthetic – why else make you linger interminably over my stories, why else italicize my favourite phrases?

To recreate you on the page I had to become you and understand you (this is what novels demand), and in doing that, well, the inevitable happened. When I poured myself into your skin I should have guessed at the consequences. I still love you. No, that's not it. I love you more.

You may think we're too mired in deceit, that we've told each other enough lies to outlast a lifetime, that our deception and humiliation have doubled the reasons for going our separate ways. I prefer to think they've cancelled out and that we're too entwined in mutual surveillance to let each other go. I'm in the business now of watching over you. Wouldn't you like to do the same for me? What I'm working my way towards is a declaration of love and a marriage proposal. Didn't you once confide to me your old-fashioned view that this was how a novel should end, with a 'Marry me'? With your permission I'd like to publish one day this book on the kitchen table. It's hardly an apologia, more an indictment of us both, which would surely bind us further. But there are obstacles. We wouldn't want you or Shirley or even Mr Greatorex to languish

369

behind bars at Her Majesty's leisure, so we'll have to wait until well into the twenty-first century to be clear of the Official Secrets Act. A few decades is time enough for you to correct my presumptions on your solitude, to tell me about the rest of your secret work and what really happened between you and Max, and time to insert those paddings of the backward glance: in those days, back then, these were the years of . . . Or how about, 'Now that the mirror tells a different story, I can say it and get it out of the way. I really was *pretty*.' Too cruel? No need to worry, I'll add nothing without your say-so. We won't be rushing into print.

I'm sure I won't always be an object of public contempt, but it may take a while. At least the world and I are now in agreement – I need an independent source of income. There's a job coming up at University College London. They want a Spenser specialist and I'm told I have a decent chance. I'm feeling a little more confident that teaching needn't prevent me writing. And Shirley told me she may have something for you in London, if you're interested.

Tonight I'll be on a plane to Paris to stay with an old school friend who says he can give me a room for a few days. When things have quietened down, when I've faded from the headlines, I'll come straight back. If your answer is a fatal no, well, I've made no carbon, this is the only copy and you can throw it to the flames. If you still love me and your answer is yes, then our collaboration begins and this letter, with your consent, will be Sweet Tooth's final chapter.

Dearest Serena, it's up to you.

Acknowledgements

I owe particular thanks to Frances Stonor Saunders for her book, *Who Paid the Piper? The CIA and the Cultural Cold War*; and also to Paul Lashmar and Oliver James's *Britain's Secret Propaganda War: 1948–1977*, and to Hugh Wilford's *The CIA, the British Left and the Cold War: Calling the Tune?* The following were also extremely helpful: *Writing Dangerously: Mary McCarthy and her World* by Carol Brightman; *The Theory & Practice of Communism* by R.N. Carew Hunt; *Operation Mincemeat* by Ben MacIntyre; *Reluctant Judas* by Geoffrey Robertson; *Open Secret: The Autobiography of the Former Director-General of MI5* by Stella Rimington; *The Defence of the Realm: The Authorized History of MI5* by Christopher Andrew; *Spooks: The Unofficial History of MI5* by Thomas Hennessey and Claire Thomas; *Spy Catcher: The Candid Autobiography of a Senior Intelligence Officer* by Peter Wright; *State of Emergency: The Way We Were: Britain, 1970–1974* by Dominic Sandbrook; *When the Lights Went Out: Britain in the Seventies* by Andy Beckett; *Crisis? What Crisis? Britain in the*

1970s by Alwyn W. Turner; *Strange Days Indeed* by Francis Wheen.

I am grateful to Tim Garton Ash for his thoughtful comments; to David Cornwell for irresistible reminiscences; to Graeme Mitchison and Karl Friston for stripping out the Monty Hall problem; to Alex Bowler, and, as always, to Annalena McAfee.

penguin.co.uk/vintage